Europe

This edition published 2025
by Living Book Press
Copyright © Living Book Press, 2025

ISBN: 978-1-76153-812-4 (hardcover)
        978-1-76153-796-7 (softcover)

First published in 1913.

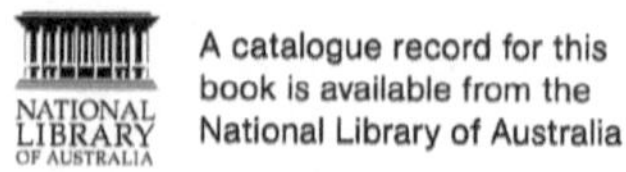

A catalogue record for this book is available from the National Library of Australia

Europe

by

NELLIE BURNHAM ALLEN

UNLOADING SUPPLIES DURING THE WORLD WAR FOR
OUR BOYS "OVER THERE"

Contents

PREFACE

We are told that geography is a description of the Earth as the home of man. If we accept this definition, then it is not the Earth but man in his relation to it that should be the central point of our teaching.

Children are primarily interested in life. Maps and the names of rivers, mountains, and cities convey little significance unless they represent the actual life of the places they symbolize. The teacher should aim to help pupils form clear mental pictures of the life and conditions underlying all map symbols.

The aim of this volume is to depict graphically, yet simply, the life of Europe; to help children envision the lofty mountains, fertile valleys, clustering villages, broad plains, crowded cities, busy seaports, vineyards, shipyards, olive orchards, flax fields, castles, palaces, and toiling peasants, along with the changes wrought by the World War in their lives and countries. These things define Europe as it is today. Both the text and illustrations are designed to show the people and their work, for it is through the life of the people that one learns the character of a nation. What the people of the world are doing determines what the world is today. The life of the United States depends, in great measure, on the life — and especially the industrial life — of other nations with whom, in the future, our relations will be closer than in the past. For this reason, our future voters, who are currently enrolled in our schools, should become as intimately acquainted as possible with our commercial neighbors across the water. This is the practical, twentieth-century geography.

Locational geography should not be neglected. The maps provided are intended to be used alongside the text, so that pupils may identify the location of a place while becoming familiar with its life. The lists at the end of each chapter will be found helpful for location drills and for reinforcing the most important facts. Many places from other continents beyond Europe are included in these lists, broadening pupils' knowledge to encompass the whole world.

We are indebted to the Corticelli Silk Mills, Florence, Massachusetts, for permission to use their splendid, lifelike, copyrighted photographs of silkworms. Many teachers will be glad to know that specimen cocoons and other aids for object-lesson teaching can be obtained from the Corticelli Mills at a slight expense.

NELLIE B. ALLEN

ACKNOWLEDGMENTS

Thanks are due to the following individuals and business firms for their valuable assistance through suggestions, criticisms, photographs, and other material: American Manufacturing Co., cordage and twines, New York City; Anger Baking Co., manufacturers of macaroni, New York City; Armstrong Cork Co., Pittsburgh, Pennsylvania; B. E. Baker, Corona Kid Co., Boston, Massachusetts; Oscar Baner, Staudt and Co., importers, Berlin and New York; Dr. Alfred Cann, principal of Municipal Day Training School for Teachers, Manchester, England; Cheney Bros., manufacturers of silk, South Manchester, Connecticut; Antoine Chiris Co., Essential Oils, Grasse, Cannes, and Paris, France, London, and New York City; Adolph Cohen, editor of *Scandinavia* (the oldest Swedish newspaper in New England); Cornforth and Marx, silk manufacturers, Fitchburg, Massachusetts; Bruno Court, parfumeur, distillateur, Grasse, France; William Cramp and Sons, Ship and Engine Building Co., Philadelphia, Pennsylvania; Cunard Steamship Co., New York City; William B. Dennis, brokers in canned goods, Portland, Maine; John H. Duncan, salt manufacturing, Ithaca, New York; Eelswick Ordnance Co., Newcastle upon Tyne, England; Fore River Shipbuilding Co., Quincy, Massachusetts; Hanson and Orth, hemp brokers, New York City and London; D. O. Haynes, editor of *Pharmaceutical Era*, New York City; H. J. Heinze and Co., Pittsburgh, Pennsylvania; Hope Foundry, manufacturers of jute machinery, Leeds, England; International Harvester Co., Chicago, Illinois; International Salt Co., Ithaca, New York; Professor Alois von Isakovics, proprietor of Synfleur Scientific Laboratories, Monticello, New York; Kentucky Agricultural Experiment Station, Lexington, Kentucky; William Kenyon and Sons, rope manufacturers, Dukinfield, England; J. W. Lovatt, secretary of Silk Association of America, New York City; Ludlow Manufacturing Associates, jute and hemp, Boston, Massachusetts; Manchester Ship Canal Co., Manchester, England, and New York City; Roger and Gallet, perfumers, Paris and New York

City; Henry Scholtz, Lisbon, Portugal; G. R. Schroeder, Italian Chamber of Commerce, New York City.

A. Stowell and Co., jewelers, Boston, Massachusetts; *Sunset Magazine*, San Francisco, California; Lee J. Vance, editor of *American Wine Press*, and secretary of American Wine Growers' Association; White Star Steamship Co., New York City; York St. Flax Spinning Co., Belfast, Ireland; officials of the Public Library, Boston, Massachusetts; officials of the Public Library, Fitchburg, Massachusetts; departments of government, Washington, D.C.; American and European consuls; Chamber of Commerce, Boston, Massachusetts; Board of Trade, Paterson, New Jersey; Board of Trade and Transportation, New York City; W. L. Manson, *Glasgow Herald*, Glasgow, Scotland; Robert McBratney, secretary of Linen Trade Association; Mitsui and Co., raw silk importers, New York City; Will S. Munroe, author of *Turkey and the Turk, In Viking Land*, etc.; H. C. Newcomb, olive importer, Philadelphia, Pennsylvania; Hartvig Nissen, director of physical training, Brookline, Massachusetts; North German Lloyd Steamship Co., New York City; Nozawaya and Co., raw silk importers, New York City; S. S. Pierce Co., wholesale and retail grocers, Boston, Massachusetts; Plymouth Cordage Co., Plymouth, Massachusetts; C. L. Preston, Corona Kid Co., Riga, Russia; Jerome C. Read, president of Silk Association of America, New York City.

EUROPE
SCALE OF MILES
0   100   200   300   400   500
ARCTIC
LOFOTE
IS.
ARCTIC CIRCLE
Reikjavik
ICELAND
Mt. Hekla
FAROE IS.
Trondhjem
SHETLAND IS.
Bergen
Christiania
HEBRIDES
ORKNEY IS.
Skagerrack
Kattegat
Gothe
SCOTLAND
NORTH
DENMARK
Glasgow
Copenhagen
BRITISH
Belfast
Edinburgh
BAL
ISLES
Dublin
Irish
Manchester
SEA
IRELAND
Sea
Liverpool
NETHER
Hamburg
Oder
IRISH FREE
Birmingham
ENGLAND
The Hague
LANDS
Berlin
STATE
WALES
Amsterdam
OCEAN
C. Clear
Antwerp
Leipzig
Land's End
London
Brussels
Cologne
Frankfort
Dresd
English Channel
Str. of Dover
BEL.
Pra
Havre
Rhine
CZEC
Seine R.
SLOV
BAY OF
Paris
GER
Munich
Loire R.
Berne
Zurich
AUSTRIA
Cape Finisterre
BISCAY
FRANCE
SWITZERLAND
The Alps
Trieste
Bordeaux
FR.E
Lyon
OF FIU
Oporto
Cantabrian Mts.
Rhone R.
Mt. Blanc
Milan
Douro R.
Pyrenees
Po R.
Venice
Genoa
ADRIATIC
Lisbon
Madrid
Marseille
PORTUGAL
SPAIN
CORSICA
Cape St. Vincent
Tagus R.
Valencia
Barcelona
Rome
Guadalquivir R.
SARDINIA
Naples
Str. of Gibraltar
Malaga
BALEARIC
Mt. Vesuvius
MADEIRA
Gibraltar
IS.
Palermo
IS.
MEDITER
FEZ
ALGIERS
SICILY Mt. Etna
TUNIS
MALTA Mt.
MOROCCO
(Br.)
RA
MOROCCO
ALGERIA
TRIPOLI
A
F
R
I
C
A
LIB
ATLANTIC
NORTH SEA
OCEAN
Longitude   10   West   from   Greenwich   0   Longitude   East   10

OCEAN
POLAND
FINLAND
Tundras
Pechora R.
Ob R.
Ural Mts.
Tobolsk
White Sea
Archangel
Dwina R.
Perm
R.
Lake Onega
Lake Ladoga
Finland
Petrograd
Valdai Hills
Volga R.
Kazan
Kama R.
Orenburg
ESTHONIA
Nizhni Novgorod
Moscow
R U S S I A
LATVIA
Düna R.
LITHUANIA
Saratov
Warsaw
Aral Sea
Kiev
U K R A I N E
Dnieper R.
Volga R.
Astrakhan
Dniester
Don R.
CASPIAN SEA
Pruth R.
Odessa
ROUMANIA
Belgrade
Sea of Azov
CRIMEA
Mt. Elbruz
Caucasus Mts.
Baku
Bucharest
Sebastopol
Danube R.
BULGARIA
B L A C K   S E A
Trebizond
Tiflis
TRANS-CAUCASIA
Adrianople
TURKEY
Bosporus
Mt. Ararat
Teheran
Constantinople
GREECE
Dardanelles
A N A T O L I A
P E R S I A
Smyrna
MESOPOTAMIA
Tigris R.
Athens
AEGEAN SEA
Euphrates R.
Bagdad
CRETE
S E A
CYPRUS
SYRIA
PHOENICIA
Jerusalem
Alexandria
A R A B I A
PERSIAN GULF
CAIRO
SUEZ CANAL
Nile R.
E G Y P T

CHAPTER I

INTRODUCTION

Across the Atlantic Ocean, three thousand miles from the United States, lies the continent of Europe, which we are to study. In many respects, it is very different from North America, and one of the best ways to become better acquainted with it is to observe some of the differences and compare them with our own continent and country.

Because of the industrious nature of its people and the advantages Mother Nature has so liberally bestowed upon it, Europe holds significant importance in manufacturing and commerce. Its significance is not due to its size; in fact, Europe is the smallest continent, except for Australia. It is less than half the size of North America, with an area comparable to that of the United States and Mexico combined. Imagine these two countries divided among more than twenty nations, each differing in government, laws, language, and customs, and you will have an idea of the conditions in Europe.

The people of these various countries frequently interact with neighboring nations that speak different languages and follow different customs. Nowhere else in the world do people learn foreign languages as readily as the Europeans. It is not unusual for the educated classes to speak five or six languages, while even the working classes can often converse in one or two additional languages besides their native tongue.

The situation of Europe favors a high level of civilization. Contrast this with the position of North America. We are surrounded by vast oceans — three thousand miles from Europe on one side, nearly twice that distance from Asia on the other. The length of our continent from north to south places our closest neighbor, South America, a significant distance from our northern ports.

In contrast, Europe is part of the world's largest landmass, where all the oldest civilizations developed. Long before America was discovered, overland journeys to China and India were already made. Only the inland Mediterranean Sea lay between southern Europe and the civilization of Egypt. At the eastern end of this sea stretched Phoenicia, the land of the earliest sailors, and just beyond was the home of the ancient Babylonians and Persians, who lived in luxury ages before anyone knew of a land beyond the western sea, or dared to venture far upon its waters. Europe was surrounded by civilization, and its small size, navigable rivers, and deeply indented coastline stimulated communication with the countries around.

Europe lies farther north than the United States, yet it seems as if Nature has made numerous efforts to moderate the long, cold winters typical of such latitudes, which pose a challenge to commerce and many types of manufactures.

Throughout the temperate zone, westerly winds prevail. If you were to keep a record of the direction of the wind every day for several years, you would find that, in summing up your results, for the greater part of the time, it blows from some quarter of the west. These westerly winds blow across the Atlantic Ocean toward Europe. The ocean has a much more even temperature than the land; it is warmer in winter and cooler in summer. People like to spend their summers near the water because it is cooler there. In the winter, the low temperatures that we hear of in the northern interior states of our country are seldom heard of in the shore states in the same latitude. The winds that blow over the Atlantic Ocean toward Europe carry this even temperature to the western shores of that continent. Thus, the winters of western Europe are much less cold than they would be if the direction of the wind were reversed, and the summers are not nearly so hot.

Doubtless, you have read of that warm ocean current, the Gulf Stream, and traced its course from the Gulf of Mexico out across the Atlantic Ocean in a northeasterly direction.

The warm air from over this current makes the westerly winds even warmer than they would otherwise be, and their effect on European countries is very marked. England, in the latitude of southern Labrador with its short summers and long, cold winters, seldom sees snow. Norway, as far north as Greenland, has no icebound ports on its western coast. As the winds blow farther and farther over the land, they lose their modifying effects, and in the eastern half of the continent, we find greater extremes of heat and cold. The Neva River and the canal that leads from Petrograd to Kronstadt are frozen for many weeks in the winter, while the port of Bergen on the west coast of Norway is never closed by ice. In Russia, in the same latitude as that of southern England, where the grass remains green through the winter, many of the French army, during their invasion of the country, perished with cold in a temperature of several degrees below zero. The summers of Russia are correspondingly hot, and the thermometer often registers more than one hundred degrees.

The ocean winds also have another beneficial effect upon Europe in the abundant rainfall they bring. The winds that blow from the Pacific Ocean upon the western coast of the United States do not affect either the temperature or the rainfall of the country far from the coast. This is because the lofty Sierra Nevada Mountains extend from north to south across their path and cause most of the moisture to fall on their western slopes. In Europe, there is no great north-south mountain system such as is found in North America. On the contrary, the principal highland extends from east to west through the central part of the continent. Thus, it presents no barrier to the moisture-laden winds, which deposit their life-giving load very liberally throughout western and central Europe and more sparingly through the portions of the continent farther east.

Though the easterly and westerly direction of the chief highland does not greatly affect the rainfall of Europe, it does have a remarkable effect in another way. The warm winds from the Mediterranean Sea cannot easily climb this barrier and spread northward but are confined to the southern portion of the continent and distribute their heat throughout those

FIG. 1. ST. BERNARD PASS

countries. Similarly, the great mountain barrier shuts out the cold arctic winds that sweep down over the northern plains. Thus, southern Europe, though much farther north than our Southern States, has a more tropical climate. Naples is in about the same latitude as Pittsburgh, Pennsylvania, but its climate is very different. In the vicinity of Naples, oranges, lemons, and olives are raised, and mulberry trees are cultivated for silkworms; none of these products can be raised successfully in Pennsylvania. Many of the houses of Naples are built with no provision for heating; the people of Pennsylvania would be very uncomfortable in winter if it were not for their stoves and furnaces.

Besides its influence on the climate, the surface of Europe affects the life of the countries in other important ways. It furnishes one of the chief reasons why the people are divided into so many different nations. The British Isles are entirely separated from the rest of the continent by water. The Spanish peninsula is nearly surrounded by arms of the ocean, its only land boundary being the lofty Pyrenees Mountains, which form a high wall between it and France. Except in the desolate, frozen north, the Scandinavian peninsula is cut off from the rest of the continent by water, while the Kiolen Mountains, the backbone of the peninsula, separate Norway from Sweden. Switzerland nestles by itself in the mountains, and Italy is separated from

FIG. 2. THE ITALIAN VILLAGE OF ISELLE AT THE END OF THE SIMPLON TUNNEL

its northern neighbors and the rest of Europe by the snowy ranges of the Alps.

To the people of olden times, the high mountains were a more impassable barrier than the water, and so, living by itself, each nation developed its own language and customs. Today, mountains are not impassable barriers to communication. Roads over them and tunnels under them bring the people on both sides into close touch with each other.

The longest tunnel in the world, the Simplon, is one of several that extend under the Alps and connect central and southern Europe. For some years, the oldest tunnel, the Mont Cenis, eight miles long, furnished a direct route for traffic between England, France, and Italy. Later, the St. Gotthard Tunnel, nine miles in length, provided an easy means of communication between Central Europe and the Mediterranean countries. The Arlberg, six and one-half miles long, came next. Now, the Simplon Tunnel, twelve miles in length, extending between the Swiss town of Brieg and the small Italian village of Iselle, furnishes a more direct route than the others. The construction of the tunnel was a great undertaking, but it was built more rapidly and at a lower cost per mile than any then existing. One writer describes the building of "this great wormhole under the Alps" in the following words: "Two million charges of dynamite, sixteen million dollars, four thousand Italian laborers, six years of work, and a dozen or so heads of the best engineering brains in Europe."

A hundred years ago, Napoleon dragged his army on foot over the Simplon Pass, more than seven thousand feet high, by means of a road that he built with great hardship, suffering, and loss of life. Today, through this great hole in the earth, made at a cost of one and one-third million dollars per mile, we can ride in comfortable cars from one side of the Alps to the other in as many minutes as it took hours for Napoleon's soldiers.

The building of this tunnel was a grand victory of railroad engineering. The temperature at times ran up to more than one hundred thirty degrees, and the workmen had to be supplied from overhead pipes with fresh air cooled by water from the Rhone glacier. Beds of soft rock that caved in as fast as they were dug out hindered the workers, and through this formation, for nearly a year, the tunnel advanced only about six yards a month. At one place, an underground lake of boiling water

FIG. 3. TAKING CARE OF THE BABY IN YUGOSLAVIA

was accidentally tapped, and the men had to flee for their lives before a stream that rushed into the tunnel at the rate of eight thousand gallons a minute. But the work went on in spite of all these obstacles, and on February 24, 1905, the two borings from the Swiss and Italian ends exactly met more than a mile below the summit of the pass, and the gigantic task was accomplished.

The natural advantages that Europe possesses, however, far outweigh the disadvantages of mountain barriers and separated peoples, for these have been largely overcome by the ingenuity of man. The coastlines of Europe have greatly helped in the development of the continent. They are so long and so deeply indented that if you were to follow all their windings for their entire length, you would travel a distance more than twice as great as the circumference of the earth at the equator. This is more — proportionately — than is found on any other continent, and this fact has had a tremendous effect on the development of Europe. The inland seas, gulfs, and bays extend far into the interior, so that all the countries, with the exception of some parts of Russia, have easy communication with the ocean.

Perhaps none of the physical features of a continent affects the welfare of the people, their occupations, and particularly their commerce more than the rivers. Europe is as fortunate in this respect as in her other natural features, for she has many rivers, and most of them are navigable. The interior of the continent is thus opened, and communication with the coast and with other continents is made easy. Contrast this condition with that of Africa. There, all the important rivers except the Nile break through mountain ranges near the coast, and the rapids and falls thus formed have made it impossible to explore the interior by means of rivers. This one obstacle delayed the opening of the Dark Continent for many years.

Most of the European rivers are short compared to those of North America, with only one exceeding two thousand miles in length, while in our continent, more than half a dozen surpass that. In Europe, only four rivers are longer than one thousand miles, while North America has nearly three times that number.

There are many more canals in Europe than in North Amer-

FIG. 4. A SCENE IN HOLLAND

ica, and they furnish thousands of miles of additional water
communication. Some countries have a complete network of
canals, which bring all portions of the territory into close touch
with the rivers and seaports. Holland, Belgium, France, England,
and Russia are foremost among the countries having fine canal
systems, while the other nations have developed theirs to a lesser
extent. It is said that one can go anywhere in Holland by canal
if one only takes enough time, and it is possible to go across
the immense area of Russia from north to south and from east
to west entirely by water.

Much of the benefit derived from the rivers of Europe is due
to the surface of the continent. The eastward and westward trend

of the mountains sends many important rivers flowing down the long slopes across the great plain of Europe to northern waters, while swifter streams make their way down the short, steep southern slopes to the Mediterranean Sea. The headwaters of some of these rivers, such as the Rhine, the Rhone, and the Danube, come very near to each other. These three important streams are connected by canals, and the same is true of other northward and southward flowing rivers. Thus, communication between northern countries and seas with southern Europe and the Mediterranean is made easy.

It is in the great plain of Russia that the longest rivers are found. Some of these Russian rivers, however, are of little use because they are frozen for much of the year. Most of them rise in the Valdai Hills, the only elevation in the interior of Russia, with the other mountains being on its borders. You will become better acquainted with many of the rivers of Europe when visiting the different countries, so we will not attempt further descriptions of them here.

The people of Europe, no less than the continent itself, are in many ways different from those of North America. Although most Europeans are of the white race and are the ancestors of the people on this side of the Atlantic, among them we find great differences in conditions of life, customs, ideals, and government.

The governments of the nations of the world are divided into monarchies and republics. A monarchy is ruled by a person called a king, queen, emperor, or empress, or some other title. Such rulers usually inherit their position by right of birth, while in a republic the ruler is elected by the people. Monarchies have been of two kinds. An absolute monarchy is so called because the ruler has unlimited, or absolute, power and could do as he pleased with his subjects. If the ruler was kind and intelligent, his people might fare well; if he was cruel and tyrannical, their sufferings could be horrible. There are no absolute monarchies today in Europe or, indeed, in any other continent of the world.

In a limited monarchy, the ruler's power is so limited by a parliament or some similar body that he may have no more

FIG. 5. A LITTLE TARTAR BOY
Courtesy of Mr. B. E. Baker, Boston

authority than the president of the United States.

Before the World War, there were only three republics in Europe — France, little Switzerland, and Portugal. All the other countries were monarchies. In most of these European monarchies, the people had less voice in the government and fewer rights and privileges than they would have in a republic. One of the great results of the war was to give more freedom to the people and to prevent their oppression by tyrannical governments. Out of the terrible sufferings caused by four years of war, several new nations have been born, of which you will read in later chapters. Can you tell whether these nations are monarchies or republics?

No other war ever changed the maps of the world as much as the great conflict of 1914–1918 did. Not only the map of Europe, but those of Asia and Africa are different from what they were before the peace treaty was signed. To find out how great these changes are, you must study both the old and new maps. Learn what countries have disappeared from the map of Europe, what ones have grown smaller, what ones have become larger, and from which ones the new nations have been made.

Peasant life in Europe is very different in many respects from that of the poorer people in our country. The peasants in many regions do not dress like the people of higher rank but have their own typical costumes. Their food, too, is quite different from that of the upper classes. They do not have cheaper foods of the same kind — cheaper cuts of meat, similar puddings and pastries — but instead eat their own simple

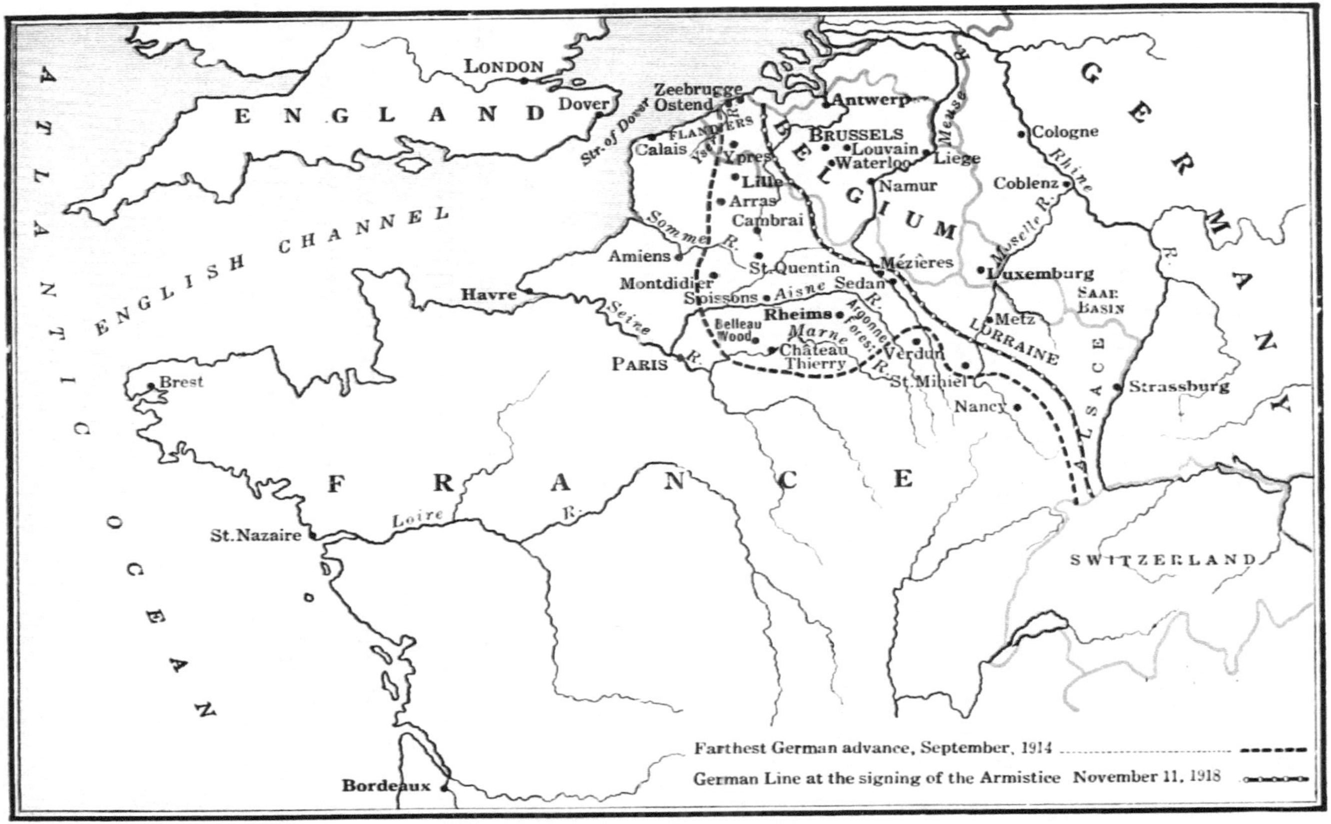

THE WESTERN FRONT IN THE WORLD WAR

meals of coarse, nourishing bread, soup, fish, and vegetables. Meat is seldom seen on their tables, but they make wholesome foods out of materials that many of our more wasteful housekeepers would consider of no use.

In our country, anyone, even the poorest or most ignorant, can, by hard work, education, and persistence, rise from the lowest place in a factory to that of manager or from office boy to the position of president of a great corporation. In the past, such upward mobility has been almost unknown in European countries. In most cases, a peasant has followed the same occupation that his father and grandfather before him followed and lived and dressed in the same way. Often this life was comfortable and happy; often it was not. But it was the way of his class, and he followed it without a thought of there being anything else to do. With better government, more education, and greater rights and privileges, there will be more opportunities for the common people of Europe, like boys and girls in the United States, to make what they will out of their lives and to occupy those positions for which they are willing, by hard work and right living, to fit themselves.

We have spoken of the peasants more than the higher classes because, industrially, they are more important. They form the greater part of the population in Europe and carry on most of the work. Their occupations are, for the most part, much the same as in our country. They till the soil, raise livestock, and engage in fishing, mining, and manufacturing. As in the United States, agriculture is the most important of all these pursuits and occupies the majority of people in most European countries.

You are eager to visit this land from which the settlers of our country came. So, with this introduction to the continent across the water, we will board our steamer, which waits beside the pier in New York harbor.

TOPICS FOR STUDY

I

1. Importance of Europe.
2. Size.
3. Situation of Europe.
4. Climate and rainfall.
5. Surface.
6. Tunnels.
7. Drainage and canals.
8. Governments.
9. Map changes.
10. Peasant customs.

II

1. Name the continents in order of size.
2. What countries fought in the World War on the side of the Allies and the Central Powers?
3. Find the area and population of Belgium, Russia, England, Germany, and the United States. Find the average number of people per square mile in each country. How does the United States compare in population density with European countries? How does population density affect the industries of a country?
4. List the advantages and disadvantages of the position of the United States and Europe.
5. Research some interesting facts about Phoenicia, Babylon, and ancient Persia in an encyclopedia or history book.
6. Sketch a map showing the eastern coast of North America and the western coast of Europe. Trace the course of the Gulf Stream.
7. List the states crossed by the Sierra Nevada Mountains. What surface division of the United States lies east of these mountains? Describe its climate and the reason for the lack of rainfall.
8. Name the countries in Europe through which the chief highland passes. Identify the countries north and south of it. List the ranges of this highland and other European ranges.
9. Name the states in the U.S. that are in the same latitude as Greece and Italy.
10. Identify the waters that cut off the British Isles from the continent and the waters surrounding the Spanish and Scandinavian peninsulas. Name the mountains that form the backbone of the Scandinavian Peninsula.

11. Write the names of European countries in one column and indicate whether they are monarchies or republics in another. Mark new countries formed after the war with a cross.

12. Sketch a map of Switzerland and surrounding countries, marking the locations of four great Alpine tunnels.

13. Identify the river in Europe over two thousand miles long and those over one thousand miles. Sketch a map and trace their courses, noting the countries they pass through.

14. Name the rivers in North America over two thousand miles long and those over one thousand. Sketch a map and locate them.

15. Identify the rivers in Russia least useful and most useful for commerce and navigation.

16. List some differences between Europe and North America.

III

Be able to spell and pronounce the following names. Locate each place and note what was said about it in the chapter, adding any additional information if possible:

Africa	Phoenecia	Kronstadt
Asia	Portugal	Naples
Australia	Russia	New York
Belgium		Petrograd
China	Scandinavian	Pittsburgh
Egypt	Peninsula	
England	South America	Alps Mountains
France	Spain	Kiolen
Greenland	Sweden	Mountains
Holland	Switzerland	
India	United States	Pyrenees
Italy		Mountains
Labrador	Babylon	Sierra Nevada
Mexico	Bergen	Mountains
Norway	Brieg	Simplon Pass
Persia	Iselle	Valdai Hills

Danube River
Gulf of Mexico
Gulf Stream
Mediterranean
    Sea
Neva River

Nile River
Rhine River
Rhone River

Arlberg Tunnel

Mont Cenis
    Tunnel
St. Gotthard
    Tunnel
Simplon Tunnel

CHAPTER II

SHIPS AND SHIPBUILDING

At the pier in New York City, we find the ocean liner on which we have engaged passage for Europe. A crowd has gathered on the wharf to say good-bye to friends who are going, for business or pleasure, across the wide ocean. As the great ship moves slowly away from the wharf, her rails are lined with people, all anxious for another parting word with the friends left behind.

The vessel is so large, and there are so many decks, that we do not at first realize how many people there are on board. It is really a floating town, for the ship accommodates between two and three thousand passengers, besides her crew of eight hundred.

If this floating town were on land instead of on water, the steel contained in it would be sufficient to supply the framework of houses for all the passengers and crew. Her steel plates would surround the town for a distance of eight or ten miles with a wall four or five feet high. The coal with which the vessel is supplied would furnish fuel for the inhabitants for several months. Her electric plant would light the streets and the houses, and her engines would drive enough machinery to employ all the people. Her funnels would be large enough for a tunnel or subway in which a double line of trolley cars could run. The grocery and provision stores of the town could be well-stocked with the thousands of pounds of meat, vegetables, eggs, flour, butter, and other food necessities stored away on the great liner.

These immense ships are the express trains of the ocean. They cross at high speed and follow schedules as regular as those of railroad trains. The great cargo steamers, carrying much freight and many passengers, might be likened to combination

© Underwood & Underwood
FIG. 6. "THE GREAT SHIP MOVES SLOWLY AWAY FROM THE WHARF"

freight and passenger trains. These also follow regular schedules. Besides these, there are the tramp steamers, in which the greater part of the world's merchandise is carried. These are like freight cars, which are seen at one time on the tracks of one railroad and at another time on those of some other road. You have doubtless seen at the railroad station long trains made up of cars from a dozen different railroads whose tracks lie many hundreds of miles away.

Such a tramp steamer may have been built in a British shipyard and may have been on the ocean for many years without re-entering the port from which it started. Could we have accompanied it on its wanderings, we would have entered many a foreign harbor. It might have originally started from Liverpool with a cargo of cotton goods, tools, and machinery bound for

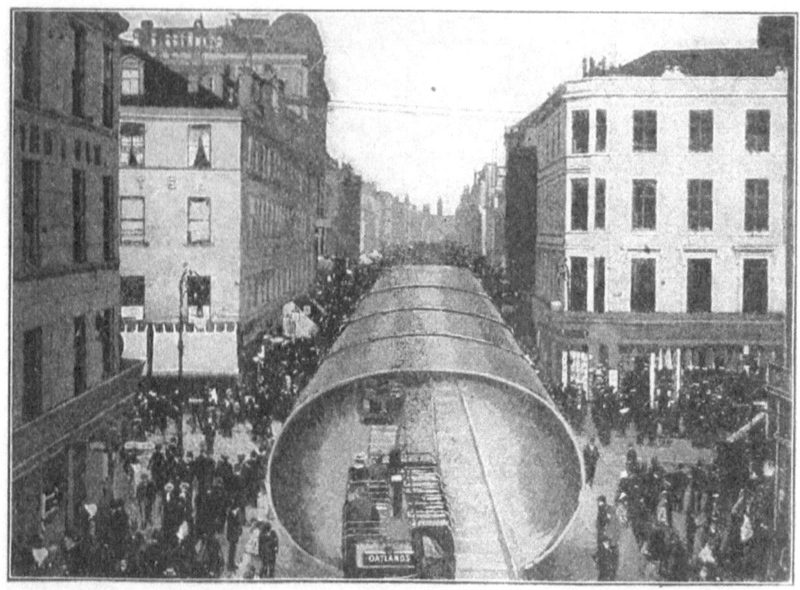

FIG. 7. HER FUNNELS WOULD BE LARGE ENOUGH FOR A SUBWAY
(Courtesy of the Cunard Steamship Company)

Hong Kong. There, it took on a cargo of rice, tea, and silk, and cleared for San Francisco. It went without cargo from that city to Seattle, and there loaded with lumber for Japan. At Yokohama, it took on tea, raw silk, camphor, and fine hand-wrought articles in metal and lacquerware and started for Marseille, in France. In that port, it picked up a cargo of wine, silk, olives, and perfumery for New York, and there loaded with machinery for Chile, where a cargo of nitrates was obtained and carried to San Francisco.

Think of the many, many tramp steamers which make their way from country to country, from island to island, and from far-away, almost unknown harbors to the great seaports of the world; of the powerful battleships, cruisers, torpedo boats, and colliers which every nation possesses in her navy; of the hundreds and thousands of schooners, from the small fishing craft to the large seven-masted vessels capable of carrying heavy cargoes. Yet besides all these, there are coast and river steamers, yachts, ferryboats, oil-tank ships, barges, and tugs,

BRITISH ISLES
SCALE OF MILES
0 25 50 75 100 125
SHETLAND IS.
ORKNEY IS
HEBRIDES OR WESTERN IS.
NORTH SEA
Moray Firth
Aberdeen
SCOTLAND
Highlands
Dundee
Ben Nevis
L. Katrine
Tay R.
L. Lomond
Firth of Lorne
Firth of Clyde
Leith
Firth of Forth
Glasgow
EDINBURGH
Clyde R.
R. Tweed
Lowlands
Cheviot Hills
North Channel
R. Tyne
Newcastle
Wear R.
Pennine Mts.
NORTHERN IRELAND
BELFAST
Solway Firth
LAKE DISTRICT
R. Tees
IRELAND
I. OF MAN
YORKSHIRE
IRISH FREE STATE
DUBLIN
Liffey
IRISH SEA
Leeds
Hull
Aire R.
Liverpool
Bradford
Humber R.
Mersey R.
Manchester
Grimsby
Eastham
Sheffield
Chester
Don R.
KILKENNY
Derby
Trent R.
LIMERICK
Nottingham
TIPPERARY
Birmingham
Leicester
Yarmouth
Lakes of Killarney
Lee R.
ENGLAND
Stratford-on-Avon
Cambridge
Cork
Queenstown
Severn R.
Oxford
St. Georges Chan.
WALES
LONDON
Pembroke
Thames R.
Chatham
Dover
Bristol Channel
Bristol
Southampton
Portsmouth
Dover Strait
Cowes
Calais
Devonport
Dartmouth
Lands End
Falmouth
ENGLISH CHANNEL
ATLANTIC OCEAN
FRANCE

to say nothing of the smaller pleasure boats which ply on rivers and lakes all over the world.

Where are they built? Where are the shipyards of the world that supply these ocean carriers, which are as necessary to the world's commerce and intercourse as are the trains, the electric cars, and the motor vans that run on land?

The United States is one of the greatest shipbuilding nations on earth. Another place where many ships are built is the British Isles. Before the World War, nearly as many vessels were built annually in the waters of the British Isles as were put together

©Underwood & Underwood

FIG. 8. "THE GREAT SHIPYARDS ARE ONE OF THE SIGHTS WHICH WE HAVE COME ACROSS THE OCEAN TO SEE"

in all other shipyards of the world. Because of her water boundaries, her great commerce, and her dependence on other lands for raw materials and for food and clothing, the shipyards of the British Isles surpass all others in Europe.

In most of the harbors and at the mouths of the principal rivers of the British Isles, one can hear the clang of hammers and the noise of machinery, and can see the skeletons of vessels growing into form and beauty. There are shipyards of more or less importance along the entire length of the eastern coast, on the Tay, Forth, Tyne, Wear, Tees, Humber, and Thames rivers, from Aberdeen in the north to the English Channel on the south. On the Channel, there are shipyards at Cowes, Southampton, Dartmouth, Falmouth, Portsmouth, Devonport, Chatham, and Pembroke. At the last four places are the royal dockyards, which do little actual building but a great deal of overhauling, repairing, and refitting of the ships of the navy. Following the western coast, we find shipyards on Bristol Channel, on the Mersey and Solway rivers, across the Irish Sea in Belfast, and, last but by no means least, on the Clyde River in Scotland.

In these various yards, all kinds of seagoing craft are built. One yard may make a specialty of one kind and another yard of another, while some yards build a variety. Grim, powerful war vessels; swift, elegant yachts; fishing craft of all kinds; big ocean liners; tramps; barges; tugs; lighters; colliers; torpedo and submarine boats — these and many others are constructed every year in the yards of this great shipbuilding nation. The northeastern coast near the Tyne River, the northwestern region in the Clyde Basin, and the Belfast district are the three most important regions, and the only three which build vessels of over ten thousand tons. With few exceptions, the ocean-mail service of the world is carried on by vessels built in one or another of these three places.

Some of the largest ocean liners are constructed at Belfast, Ireland. The giants of the White Star Line — the ill-fated *Titanic* and her sister ship, the *Olympic* — were built in the yards of Belfast, on the Lagan River. The *Olympic* is eight hundred eighty-two feet long. Compare this length with that of your

FIG. 9. BOILERS OF THE *OLYMPIC* (Courtesy of the White Star Steamship Company)

schoolhouse and find out how many buildings placed end to end would equal in length this immense liner.

The most famous of all shipbuilding districts, where the greatest number and the largest variety of craft are constructed, is on the Clyde River in Scotland. This is a small river to be so famous, less than one hundred miles from source to mouth, not one-third as long as the little New England river, the Connecticut. It is formed in the hills of Scotland by small streams that come trickling down the heather-covered slopes. Over a series of falls and rapids, the little river leaps and sings in its plunge into the valley below. Here, in the green, fertile meadows filled with apple orchards famous for generations, the Clyde, now richer by many small tributaries, flows gently on toward the place where its chief work for mankind begins. At one place, it is separated from the Tweed River by only seven miles. Geologists tell us that ages ago, it probably bent to the east and joined the Tweed. Had it not been for the slight change of level wrought by the great force of nature, which sent the little river on its course to the west, there would have been no port of Glasgow, no shipyards on the Clyde, and no ocean liners and mighty warships built on its banks.

As we come down the river toward Glasgow, the smoke from a thousand chimneys shuts out the blue sky, and we know we are approaching the coal and iron region of Scotland. These mineral deposits extend across the country in a northeasterly direction from the Clyde Basin to the Firth of Forth. It is due to these deposits, to the surface of the country, and to the rivers that this part of Scotland has become an important industrial and commercial center.

The northern part of Scotland consists largely of highlands, bare and rugged, made beautiful by the blue, misty light that always hangs over them and by the lakes, or "lochs," as the Scottish people call them, that nestle in every glen.

Near the southern boundary are other highlands, lower and not so beautiful, of which one range, the Cheviot Hills, forms a partial boundary between Scotland and England. Between the two highlands are the lowlands of Scotland, which, though they comprise only one-sixth of the area of the country, have made possible her industrial life. Here are the rich deposits of coal and iron, the fertile farms, the great manufacturing cities, and it is in this region that more than half of the people of Scotland live.

The wonderful lake region and the beautiful wooded country known as the Trossachs, which are visited annually by thousands of tourists, together with some of the more famous mountains, skirt the southern edge of the highlands. A trip from Glasgow to Edinburgh takes one through this lovely region which Sir Walter Scott has so vividly described in "The Lady of the Lake."

No one can pass by or sail on Loch Katrine without appreciating better its beauty and the beauty of the lines in which Scott describes it:

> "And thus an airy point he won,
> Where, gleaming with the setting sun,
> One burnished sheet of living gold,
> Loch Katrine lay beneath him rolled."

The lake, once queen of poetry, has now become the servant of industry, for the city of Glasgow has taken it to serve as a water supply and has built an aqueduct more than forty miles long to bring the pure mountain water to the city.

Of all the Scottish lakes, Loch Lomond is the most beautiful. It is long and winding, dotted with green islands where deer feed in the dim shade of the trees. Its shores are adorned with beautiful country residences, half-hidden in green foliage. To the north rises the bold outline of Ben Lomond, softened by the gray mists that hang low on the slopes purple with heather.

The wide mouth of the Forth River, with its busy port of

© Keystone View Co.

FIG. 10. "OF ALL THE SCOTTISH LAKES LOCH LOMOND IS THE MOST BEAUTIFUL"

Leith and the city of Edinburgh nearby, connects the lowlands of Scotland with the North Sea and the continent of Europe. The deep inlet of the Clyde River is the passageway westward to the ocean and the world beyond. Situated on the Clyde, just where it narrows too much for navigation, lies Glasgow, with great stores of mineral wealth to the east and the waters of river, sea, and ocean opening toward the west. No wonder that the city has spent millions of dollars in deepening and improving the Clyde, for on this small river most of her commerce depends. Originally, it was but a shallow stream. Today, except at low tide, the largest ocean steamers can ascend to the city.

Glasgow, with its broad, straight streets and massive gray stone buildings, is a typical Scotch city. It impresses one as being grave and dignified, like the true Scotchman. Like him, too, it is reserved. One cannot become thoroughly acquainted with it or learn all its secrets in a day or a week. In order to realize its greatness, one must have intimate knowledge of this city, which, in commerce and trade, ranks first in Scotland and second in the British Isles.

Its manufactures are also very important. As you may imagine, some of these are connected with iron and steel and many with the shipbuilding industry. The textile manufactures also rank high. There is much spinning and weaving, as well as bleaching, dyeing, and calico printing.

At the busy quay of the city, we can take a small steamer for the part of the river known in Glasgow as "Doon the Water." This is where the Clyde widens into the sea and becomes a maze of

FIG. 11. THE *MACRETANIA*, AND THE CAPITOL AT WASHINGTON
(Courtesy of the Cunard Steamship Company)

peninsulas, sea lochs, and islands. This part of the river, with its green, winding shores, is very beautiful. Long inlets extending toward the hills are fringed with pleasant villages and towns or decorated with villas and beautiful country houses set deep in the wooded slopes. Many people from Glasgow have their summer homes here, and thousands of pleasure seekers crowd the steamers on every summer holiday and weekend.

Between this lovely river mouth and the city of Glasgow lies the busiest part of the Clyde River; indeed, it is the busiest and most crowded district of river industry to be found anywhere in Europe. On either bank, loom the skeletons of great ships in all stages of completion. The factories, engines, shops, gas tanks, warehouses, and giant cranes rise in a confused mass. Engines toot, steamers whistle, foundries roar, bells clang, and tugs shriek. All around are forests of masts, funnels, and chimneys. This is the birthplace of ocean liners and racing yachts, of tugs and tramps, of fishing dories and seven-masted schooners, of revenue cutters and river steamers, of excursion boats and grim war vessels.

In the Clyde district, there are hundreds of thousands of workmen representing many trades — architects, draftsmen, carpenters and joiners, masons, calkers, steamfitters, engineers, molders, ironworkers, electricians, platers, riveters, painters, pattern makers, plumbers, blacksmiths, and many others.

Here, too, is some of the most wonderful machinery ever invented. See that giant crane lifting a smokestack large enough for a double row of electric cars to stand inside it without touching each other or the sides of the stack. The great load rises high in the air, hovers a moment like a huge bird poised on the wing, and then descends slowly into the precise spot made for it in the partially constructed vessel. Another crane grasps a huge engine in its jaws, raises it, and lowers it into place as easily as a boy picks up a stone.

More than one thousand horses would be needed to draw the millions of rivets used in an ocean liner. The smaller rivets are fixed by hand, and the noise of the hammering is deafening. The larger ones are fastened by power. A machine picks up a

FIG. 12. "WHAT A TREMENDOUS TASK IS THE BUILDING OF A BIG SHIP!"
(Courtesy of the Cunard Steamship Company)

red-hot rivet weighing perhaps a couple of pounds and places it into the proper hole. Then, the monster jaws close on either side of the plate. When they open again, the crushed, rounded head of the rivet is seen securely binding together the heavy steel sheets.

What a tremendous task is the building of a big ship! When the order is given, the vessel must first be born in the mind of the master. No ship, no building, no machine is ever made until it exists in the human mind. Then comes the making of the plans, the transferring of the mental dream from brain to paper. This work may take weeks or even months, for the planning of a great ship is no light task.

There must be no guesswork in its construction. The builder must know the exact size of each part, which will give the greatest strength and speed yet occupy the least room. He cannot build as he would but must work within certain limits. If he increases the size of the engines so that the ship may achieve greater speed, there may not be enough room left for coal to run them, for passengers, and for freight. If the vessel is too wide, it will not achieve speed; if too deep, it will not float in the great harbors of the world. Certain proportions of breadth, length, depth, and weight must be carefully kept throughout the work.

The dream of the master mind must be worked out in accurate, definite plans, down to the smallest detail, before any work on the actual construction of the ship begins. Every item of space and dimension must be carefully decided upon. Every part of the huge hull must be adjusted and balanced so that it will ride the waters evenly and plow its long furrow in the ocean with the least resistance.

The making of the plans may take a score of draftsmen several months. When they are finally completed, the lines to show the exact size and shape of the vessel are laid down on the great floor of what is known as the molding loft. Soon, carloads of plates and beams begin to arrive from shops and foundries and are stored in the yard near the slip where the vessel is to be built. Some of the plates on an ocean liner are more than thirty feet long and weigh two or three tons each. To press them into the desired shape, they are fed into a gigantic steel roller in much the same way that clothes are fed into a wringer. A machine that cuts the hard steel as easily as a child snips a piece of cloth trims the edges of the plates.

In the meantime, the keel has been laid, and the great ribs — the framework that gives the vessel its shape — have been positioned. The making of the ribs is an interesting process. They come from the foundry in straight beams, which must be heated and bent into the ship's side curves. The heating is done in immense furnaces long enough to hold the longest rib of a great ship. On the iron floor full of holes, the workmen have outlined the rib's curve by fitting strong iron pins into the holes. At the right moment, the furnace door is opened, and a man, in the blinding glare and intense heat, fastens a strong cable to the white-hot metal. Other workmen bend their muscles to the work and, with strong cables, drag the hot steel timber from the furnace to its place on the floor. The men hammer and pound, drive in new pegs, and remove others until the huge steel beam lies dull and cold in the graceful curves of the ship's rib.

After the skeleton frame of the decks and the beams to support them have been laid, the outside sheathing of steel plates is put on. The drawings from which these plates are made must be very accurate, as the plates are finished in the shops, even to the rivet holes, which must fit exactly in place when the great steel sheets are fastened upon the ship's side.

In the building of an ocean liner, a thousand men may work on the huge frame simultaneously. Yet, so large is the ship and so varied are the occupations that no one interferes with another's work.

When the ship is nearly completed, the launching takes place. It is a wonderful sight to see the massive vessel glide slowly down from her slip into the water, and many costly preparations must be made to ensure the journey of a few seconds is successful.

From this description of giant steamships and the labor and

FIG. 13. THE GREAT BATTLESHIP *NORTH DAKOTA*, AFTER ITS LAUNCHING
(Courtesy of the Fore River Shipbuilding Company)

material necessary to build one, you can imagine that their cost must be very high. The *Olympic* cost about ten million dollars, while the *Lusitania* and the *Mauretania* each cost between seven and eight million dollars. Yet, significant as the expense of building an ocean liner is, it is not the only consideration in its construction. No building erected on land has the safety of its occupants more carefully safeguarded than that of a big ship's passengers and crew.

Most liners today are fitted with two bottoms several feet apart, so that if hidden rocks damage the outer one, the inner one keeps the vessel watertight. All large, modern ships are divided into compartments by huge steel doors, which can be closed at a minute's warning. If several of these compartments are damaged and fill with water, the others, being watertight, are amply sufficient to keep the vessel afloat. On the captain's bridge, right at his hand, are devices to enable him, without a second's delay, to stop the vessel, to give the fire alarm, to close the bulkheads between the compartments, and to give other signals to ensure the safety of the vessel and the protection of the passengers.

Perhaps the greatest safety device of modern times is that of wireless telegraphy. Is it not wonderful that a ship far out in mid-ocean, with no other craft within sight or hearing, can summon to her aid in case of danger a score of vessels?

Before the World War, Germany had greatly developed her shipbuilding industry. She saw in England her strongest European rival, and she knew that, in order to win the position of world supremacy of which she dreamed, her power on the ocean must be tremendously increased. Some of the largest ships afloat were built in Germany. Along her coasts on the North and Baltic seas, there are many large shipyards. In those at Stettin, some of her largest ocean liners were built. Here also were constructed more than half of the Chinese navy, and many war vessels for Russia, Greece, Japan, and other countries. At Kiel, the city at the eastern end of the famous Kiel Canal, many of the finest warships of the German navy were built and repaired. You remember that, during the World War, these splendidly equipped vessels were penned up near the German coast by "the watchdogs of the British navy." At the end of the war, they were surrendered to the Allied Nations.

When the United States entered the war, one of our greatest problems was to get our fighting men, their arms, munitions, food, and other supplies to the other side of the Atlantic. We could not call on England to furnish all the necessary ships. She was already straining her resources to the utmost to get vessels enough to guard her coast and her possessions in other parts of the world, to pen up the German navy, to protect the food and other supply ships on the open ocean from the dreaded U-boats, and to carry her soldiers to France, where the heaviest fighting took place. The war finally reached such a critical stage that it was absolutely necessary for our soldiers to get to Europe at the earliest possible moment. As we did not have ships enough to take them across, England hampered her own plans in order to furnish some vessels to transport our troops and supplies. We furnished some others, but the need for more and more men to drive back the German army still continued. Then, under the direction of our government, there began such a boom in shipbuilding in the United States as was never before known in the history of the world. The shores of the Pacific in the Northwest and along the coast of California were alive with workers, and the skeleton frames of hundreds of vessels grew swiftly into sturdy ocean carriers. The shores of the Gulf of Mexico, the Great Lakes, and the Atlantic Ocean were not less busy. In Delaware and Chesapeake bays, at New York City, along the coasts of New England, and at nearly every bay and harbor on our eastern border, the great Liberty fleet grew like magic. In the last year of the war, hundreds of vessels a month were built and launched, joining the procession which moved in ever-increasing numbers across the Atlantic to the shores of France.

Around Philadelphia, the industry grew to unbelievable proportions. The Delaware River and Bay furnished special facilities for the building and launching of vessels, and great steel-producing centers were not far away. In this district, more than one hundred thousand workers were "doing their bit" to furnish ships to carry needed supplies to our boys "over there."

The most wonderful of all the shipyards in this district was the plant at Hog Island. A few months before the call came for ships, this island was only wasteland. Soon after, there grew here the greatest shipbuilding plant in the world. There were acres of ships and miles of railroads; there were more than fifty ways on which that number of vessels could be built at once, and here at one time, thirty-five thousand men were working.

In this great shipbuilding period when all the shipyards of the world were working at record-breaking speed, wonderful things were accomplished. A hundred vessels have been launched in our country in a single day. Ships have been built and launched in three weeks. Concrete ships have become more than an experiment. It was thought a wonderful invention when steel ships replaced those of wood, but a ship of solid stone seems even more wonderful. During the war, vessels of concrete were built in several countries. First, a steel skeleton was made, which was packed around and filled in with concrete strengthened by steel rods. Concrete ships were heavier and more difficult to launch than those of steel, and bad weather delayed their construction. They had advantages, however, which offset these defects. They were cheaper and more quickly built than steel ships. Less skilled labor was required, and in some localities, the material was easier to obtain.

No one can predict what giant ships may in the future sail on the oceans. The large shipyards of the United States and the British Isles are able today to build vessels so immense that no harbor in the world can accommodate them and give the necessary traffic to make them financially successful. Vessels which, twenty years ago, were considered models of perfection are as different from the ocean greyhounds of today as the first small, jolting horse cars are unlike the large, comfortable electrics. The hold of a modern ocean liner would easily accommodate one of the earlier steamships, and room would still be left for other freight.

There are many stages between the first birch-bark canoe

FIG. 14. COMPARE THE HEIGHT OF THE RUDDER OF THE *OLYMPIC* WITH THE HEIGHT
OF THE MAN (Courtesy of the White Star Steamship Company)

of some primitive race and the floating palace of today, and the
birch canoe was, in itself, a great advance over former methods
of water conveyance.

We do not know when man first learned of the buoyancy
of water and of the art of swimming. Ages may have elapsed
before his descendants dragged the fallen tree to the river and,
striding the log, propelled this first boat through the water by
using their hands as paddles. His ingenuity taught him to make
the dugout, and then the birch canoe and coracle. Later, the
use of sails saved him from laboring with his hands. Improve-

ments have kept pace with the ages, and since the introduction of steam, they have come thick and fast. What the future may bring forth, no one knows. Whether our ships sail through the air or on the water, they are sure to be larger and swifter than anything we possess at the present time.

TOPICS FOR STUDY

I.

1. Description of a large ocean steamer.
2. Cargo steamers.
3. Tramp steamers.
4. Log of a tramp steamer.
5. Variety of ocean craft.
6. Shipbuilding in the British Isles.
7. Location and number of British shipyards.
8. The Clyde River.
9. Scotland: Highlands, lowlands, Glasgow.
10. Shipyards on the Clyde.
11. Building an ocean liner.
12. German shipyards.
13. Shipbuilding in the United States.
14. The growth and future of shipbuilding.

II.

1. Write the log of a tramp steamer, including stops at six different ports. Give the cargo taken on at each one and its destination. On an outline map of the world, trace the voyage of the steamer. Trace also, with a dotted line, the route followed by the tramp steamer mentioned in the text.
2. Write a list of the different kinds of vessels of which you have heard.
3. What is included in the terms "Great Britain," "British Isles," "British Commonwealth of Nations"?
4. Write a list of the rivers of England and Scotland spoken of in the chapter. Make a map of Great Britain and on it show the

rivers in your list. Indicate also the cities in which shipbuilding is carried on.

5. Write a list of the different kinds of workmen employed in building an ocean liner.

6. Make a map of the United States and locate some of our great shipyards.

7. Make a map of Scotland. Show the surrounding waters, the highlands, lowlands, the coal and iron deposits, the cities mentioned, and the lakes.

III.

Be able to spell and pronounce the following names. Locate each place and tell what was said about it in this and in the previous chapter. Add other facts if possible:

British Isles
California
Chile
China
England
France
Germany
Greece
Ireland
Japan
New England
Russia
Scotland
United States

Aberdeen
Belfast
Chatham
Cowes
Dartmouth
Devonport
Edinburgh
Falmouth
Glasgow

Hong Kong
Kiel
Leith
Liverpool
Marseille
New York
Pembroke
Philadelphia
Portsmouth
San Francisco
Seattle
Southampton
Stettin
Yokohama

Ben Lomond
Cheviot Hills
Hog Island
Scottish Highlands
Scottish Lowlands
Trossachs

Baltic Sea
Bristol Channel
Chesapeake Bay

Clyde River
Columbia River
Connecticut River
Delaware Bay
Delaware River
English Channel
Forth River
Great Lakes
Gulf of Mexico
Humber River
Irish Sea
Kiel Canal
Lagan River
Loch Katrine
Loch Lomond
Mersey River
North Sea
Solway River
Tay River
Tees River
Thames River
Tweed River
Tyne River
Wear River

CHAPTER III

IRELAND AND THE LINEN INDUSTRY

The southern part of Ireland is known as the Irish Free State. This, with the Government of Northern Ireland, makes up the country of Ireland. We will land at Cobh. This city was formerly called Queenstown, but the name has been changed to Cobh. The city is beautifully situated on Great Island, in the harbor of Cork. The bay is about six miles wide at its mouth but narrows rapidly inland to where the city rises from the water in green hills terraced by zigzag streets.

Every summit and island is strongly fortified, for Cobh, guarding as it does the western coast of England, is an all-important military and naval station of the British Isles. On the green slopes are many fine estates overlooking the harbor, and a splendid cathedral towers from the summit of a hill. A large marine hospital for British sailors is also situated on the heights, while just beyond are the long, low barracks, from which come the rattle of a drum and the shrill sound of a bugle calling the soldiers to the daily drill.

From the heights, we can look down over the beautiful harbor with its encircling hills and green islands, out to the broad entrance, where its blue waters meet the wide expanse of the ocean. A great steamer is sailing majestically out into the dim blue beyond, and as we watch it grow smaller and smaller in the distance, until it is only a tiny speck on the horizon, we think of the mothers and fathers, the wives and sisters, and sweethearts, who have watched the ships sail out from this "port of tears," bearing away the strongest and finest of Ire-

© Underwood & Underwood

FIG. 15. "THINK OF THE MOTHERS AND FATHERS WHO HAVE WATCHED THE SHIPS SAIL OUT FROM THIS 'PORT OF TEARS'"

land's sons and daughters to seek their fortunes in the New World. Since the great potato famine, which occurred near the middle of the nineteenth century, nearly one-half of the entire population of Ireland has emigrated to America. There are but few families in the southern part of the country which have not lost a father, a brother, a sister, or some other relative through the port of Cobh. Conditions in Ireland are much better than in former years. Her people are intensely patriotic, and future years will see fewer of her young men and women emigrating to other countries.

We can go from Cobh to Cork, a distance of less than a dozen miles, by train or by boat up the river Lee. As the river is walled in nearly the entire distance and is lined on either side with docks, factories, and storehouses, we shall find the trip by rail more pleasant. From the car windows, we get flying glimpses of the country around, and we begin to understand why Ireland is known as the Emerald Isle, for surely no fields or meadows in any part of the world can be greener. There are no high mountains to shut out the moist, westerly winds which blow in from the Atlantic Ocean, and as a consequence, rains are very frequent. Everyone travels with a raincoat and umbrella, and no one minds very much the frequent showers, because, as the cheery natives tell us, it's such a gentle rain.

We realize, after a walk through the streets of Cork, a city

© Underwood & Underwood

FIG. 16. WE WALK DOWN ST. PATRICK'S STREET

considerably smaller than Portland, Oregon, that we are really in the land of St. Patrick, for we cross St. Patrick's bridge, climb the hill named in his honor, walk down the street called by his name, and rest awhile in St. Patrick's Square.

We should know that we are in the land of the Blarney Stone by the kindly greeting, "May Heaven bless your sweet face," given to us by an old woman who, with her small cart filled with butter, eggs, and gooseberries, is on her way to market. In her stout shoes and short skirt, with her black shawl over her head, she has driven in from the country in a queer-looking, low-backed donkey cart. We see similar carts piled high with blocks of dried turf, called peat, which the natives use for fuel. The blocks are shaped somewhat like bricks and make a slow, hot fire.

In Cork, we engage an Irish jaunting car, such as you see in the picture (Fig. 17), for a ride to Blarney Castle. We sit back to back, with our feet on boards over the wheels, and enjoy the ride, while our driver entertains us with stories, half legend and half history, of old days in Cork and of sieges of the castle.

The object of our trip is not to kiss the Blarney Stone, which is built into one of the walls of the castle, and thus acquire the "golden tongue," which is said to be given to those who accomplish the feat, but to enjoy the view from the top of the tower. It is certainly worth the climb. Spread out at our feet are the greenest of green meadows, dotted with white daisies and red poppies. Fat, contented-looking cattle and sheep are feed-

©Keystone View Co.

FIG. 17. "IN CORK WE ENGAGE AN IRISH JAUNTING CAR"

ing all around. White roads, hedged in with old stone walls, some of them covered with beautiful fuchsias, wind in and out over the hills and through the valleys. We catch a glimpse of an old ruined castle and see here and there a fine estate of the gentry, set in a grove of grand old trees and enclosed by high stone walls.

Most of the buildings in sight, however, are low cottages with thatched roofs, which look very picturesque in the distance. A nearer view soon robs them of much of their charm, for they are poor little shanties at best, built of stone or mud, with the leaves not more than five or six feet from the ground. Small windows, with only a few panes each, are on either side of the door, and the interior of the cottage seems rather damp and gloomy. There are several skillets and other cooking dishes hanging on the walls around, and a smoldering fire of peat, sending out a not unpleasant odor into the room, glows in the fireplace. You will read further on in this chapter a description of the cutting and preparing of peat, which is the common fuel of Ireland.

Near the house, we see small patches of potatoes and vegetables and perhaps a small field of wheat or corn, but most of the land is given over to pasturage for the cattle. Since the emigration of so many of the young men from this part of Ireland, fewer farm products are grown, and hay and cattle, which require a smaller number of hands, are raised instead. All over central and southern Ireland, stock raising is the chief industry. We understand now the reason for the great stores of butter and bacon and the large number of cattle, which we saw being loaded at Cork onto steamers bound for England and the Continent.

© Underwood & Underwood

FIG. 18. IT IS IN SUCH A HOME AS THIS THAT SOME OF THE POORER PEOPLE OF IRELAND LIVE

Twice as many cattle are imported into Great Britain from Ireland as come from all the rest of the world put together.

It would require a train of cars nearly ten miles long to carry the butter which is sent every year out of the harbor of Cork. As for the eggs, it would take you several years, counting as rapidly as possible and stopping neither to eat nor to sleep, to count the millions of dozens that are exported from Cork in one year. If we were to load into wagons the cans of condensed milk which are shipped from the harbor in the same time, estimating a ton to a horse, we would need more than seven thousand horses to draw the loads to the wharves.

The government has been of great help in developing the dairy industry throughout Ireland. Efforts have been made to teach the people better methods of farming, and in many places, dairies and creameries have been established where the farmers can find a steady sale for their milk at fair prices.

The flax fields, which we are to visit, lie in the northern part of the country, and reluctantly we leave the tower and return to Cork, where we take a train for Dublin, one hundred sixty miles away. Our route lies through a rolling country similar to that which we saw from the top of Blarney Castle. There are the same green pastures and fat cattle, the same little thatched cottages, and the same kindly old people who greet us with a cheerier smile and a more hearty "God bless you" because we come from the country where so many friends, neighbors, and relatives have gone.

Emigration has drawn most heavily from the counties through which we are passing — the names of which you have heard many times — Cork, Limerick, Tipperary, Kilkenny, and others. They are the most fertile parts of Ireland, yet many of the villages and towns have lost, through the departure of so many of their inhabitants for America, more than one-half of their population. Where once grew great crops of wheat, oats, barley, potatoes, turnips, and other vegetables, we now see hayfields and pastures where many cattle and sheep are feeding.

Every cabin has its garden patch, and in all of them, potatoes are the chief crop. In parts of the country, especially in the south and west, these vegetables form the chief food of the people. Ireland is not quite as large as the state of Maine, yet several times as many potatoes are raised in the Emerald Isle as in our Pine Tree State. To store them all, you would need a cellar so huge that it would be several times as deep as your schoolhouse is high. It would, in fact, have to be more than five hundred feet long and of the same width and depth.

Our journey to Dublin takes us through the peat bogs, or, as someone has called them, "the gold mines of Ireland." These low, green meadows are made of accumulations of a peculiar kind of moss, which has grown and decayed for centuries, until the layers are several feet thick.

Over there to our right are some men and boys cutting peat. Many hundreds of people earn their living by preparing the blocks for fuel and selling them. Let us see how the work is done. We make our way through the coarse grass and the tall rushes toward the long, black mounds of peat, beside the trenches where the cutters are at work. The men are standing in the black mud and water halfway up to their knees, and their two garments, which we shall have to dignify by the names of shirt and trousers, are the color of the mud. Using a long, narrow spade, they cut the peat into blocks about the size of a brick or larger and throw them out of the ditch onto the bank.

Another workman piles these onto a curiously made wheel-

FIG. 19. "THEY CUT THE PEAT INTO BLOCKS ABOUT THE SIZE OF A
BRICK OR LARGER, AND THROW THEM OUT OF THE DITCH"

barrow, while a third wheels the load away toward the black pile, where the women stack the blocks to dry. Here they remain for several weeks, until dry enough to be sold or carted away for use. Nearly all the people in Ireland burn peat for fuel, and it is hard to say what would become of the poorer classes if the supply should fail, for there is no coal and but little wood in the country. There is no immediate danger of exhausting the supply, however, as one-sixth of the island, an area larger than the whole state of Connecticut, is covered with bogs from which, though immense quantities are cut each year, Ireland can be supplied with fuel for centuries.

We will delay our trip to the flax fields for a short stay in Dublin, the capital of the Irish Free State and the second city in importance. It is about the size of New Orleans and is situated near Dublin Bay. We will take a tram, as the electric cars in Europe are usually called, for a tour through the city. Instead of taking the seats inside the car, we choose those on the top as being the best for sightseeing. Most of the finer residences are surrounded by high stone walls, behind which the people enjoy in privacy their beautiful parks and gardens, and the higher seats give us a chance to peep over the walls.

Several handsome bridges span the Liffey River, on which Dublin is situated, and broad, green-banked canals connect the city with the interior of the country. On these waterways, queer, flat boats bring to Dublin many cattle and great quantities of dairy products, potatoes, and grain, to be shipped to England and to other countries. Since Dublin is the capital city of Ireland, it contains many fine buildings, including courthouses, hospitals, asylums, libraries, cathedrals, colleges, and the Custom House. We pass many of these on our trip, and on our return, we go through the business and industrial portions of the city, where we see many breweries and distilleries. The making of ale, beer, whisky, and other liquors is one of the most important indus-

© Underwood & Underwood

FIG. 20. "ON THE GREEN MEADOWS ARE YARDS AND YARDS OF LINEN BLEACHING IN THE SUN AND RAIN"

tries in Dublin, and these products are exported in immense quantities across the globe.

As we travel from Dublin northward, the appearance of the country changes significantly. The farms become larger, and the fields of flax, grain, potatoes, and other vegetables are well-cultivated and carefully tended. The houses are also larger and more comfortable; they feature wooden floors, stoves, beds, and other conveniences not found in the cottages farther south. From the train, we can see the smokestacks of factories in the busy towns, and on the green meadows, there are yards and yards of linen bleaching in the sun and rain. We pass field after field of growing flax and realize that, at last, we are in the midst of the famous Irish linen region. On one of the farms, we see some men pulling flax. They knock the dirt from the roots by striking the plant against their foot and lay the straw in neat bundles. Farther along, we see meadows covered with straw spread out, seemingly spoiling, as it appears to us, in the dampness. What a peculiar plant flax is! It is pulled up by the roots instead of being cut, and it is laid out in the dew and rain instead of being kept dry, as most crops are.

The part of the plant that is used for manufacturing is the soft inner fiber, which lies beneath the outer bark or covering. We find, by taking one of the stalks and attempting to break it, that the fiber is seldom more than two or three inches long. Before it can be used, it must be separated from the woody part of the stem. To help in this process, the stalk is rotted, or "retted," as it is usually called, by putting it into running water, or into natural or artificial pools of still water, or by spreading it out on damp meadows. You would not like this part of the work, I am sure, for the smell from the decaying wood is very unpleasant. The fields where we saw the straw lying on the ground are better examined from a distance. We now understand, however, that the flax was not being spoiled by the dampness, as we initially thought, but was, in fact, being prepared for use.

After retting, the decayed, woody matter is separated from the soft, silky fiber. The bundles of straw are removed from the water or from the meadows where they have been lying

© Underwood & Underwood

FIG. 21. ARRIVING AT THE FACTORY,
THE TANGLED FIBERS ARE HACKLED

and are thoroughly dried. Afterward, the stalks are run through machines consisting of fluted rollers, which break up and loosen the brittle pieces of woody matter. They are then scraped using flat wooden paddles. When this process, known as scutching, was done by hand, the farmer would hold the straw in one hand and strike it with a glancing blow using the paddle held in the other hand. Today, however, scutching is done not by hand but by machinery. A wheel carrying several blades revolves so rapidly that these paddles strike the fiber nearly two thousand times per minute. This quickly breaks the woody matter up into fine bits, which, along with the dust, are removed by currents of air. The silky, gray fibers are then sorted, tied up in small bundles, and packed into bales, each weighing about two hundred pounds.

Arriving at the factory, the tangled, uneven fibers are combed or "hackled" until they lie straight and smooth, and the shorter ones, called "tow," from which only cheap goods can be made, are combed out and discarded.

The fibers are then spun into yarn or thread and are subsequently woven into cloth or fashioned into fine lace. The spinning and weaving processes are similar to those used for cotton or wool, except that the flax thread is usually kept moist during the process. For this reason, the damp climate of Ireland plays a crucial role in making the manufacture of linen so successful in that country.

As we approach the Belfast district, everything becomes as different from southern Ireland as a bustling manufacturing city is from a peaceful country village. However, the sunshine and the rain — or "the smiles and tears of Ireland," as someone has called them — remain the same, and the tears come just as frequently in the north of Ireland as they do in the south. In one particular year, Belfast recorded two hundred thirty-two days of rain out of the three hundred sixty-five. The linen industry would not be as important as it is if the air were less moist, so the people have good reason to be glad rather than to grieve over the frequent rains.

Belfast, often referred to as the "Chicago of Ireland," is the largest linen-manufacturing center in the world. It is nearly as large as Cincinnati and, with its bustle and activity, resembles the great manufacturing cities of the United States. The city has a more Scottish than Irish character, as many of its inhabitants are descendants of early settlers from Scotland.

The coal fields of Scotland, located across the North Channel, are largely responsible for the city's manufacturing development. Coal can be brought to Belfast by water more cheaply than it can be carried by rail for a shorter distance to inland cities in Great Britain. These and other large centers in England and on the Continent provide good markets for the manufactured products of Belfast.

The city is beautifully situated near the mouth of the Lagan River. The green hills that encircle it are thickly studded with villas and country houses belonging to wealthy merchants. The streets are wide and well-paved, and there are fine drives, parks, and gardens. However, we are less interested in the beauty of the city than in its industries, which are truly remarkable. Belfast is home to some of the largest shipyards in the world, where thousands of people find employment. The city also has extensive rope and twine works, for which many thousands of tons of fiber are imported annually. The great foundries and machine shops in Belfast produce spinning and weaving machines that are used in the linen industry all over the world. Additionally, Belfast is one of the world's most notable cities for the production of bottled waters, ginger ale, soda water, and other refreshing beverages.

Besides these industries, Belfast is also home to many others, including bleacheries, dyehouses, flour mills, oil mills, sawmills, calico printing and chemical works, breweries, distilleries, tobacco factories, and other large manufacturing plants.

The huge linen mills in Belfast interest us more than any other industry, and they are indeed the most important. There are many of these mills, and they produce enormous quantities of linen cloth. In the mills of one of the great companies, enough linen thread is produced each day to circle the earth five times at the equator.

In our ride through Ireland, we saw flax fields covering many acres. The linen industry in Belfast, however, is so immense that, in ordinary years, millions of dollars' worth of flax, chiefly from Russia and Belgium, must be imported annually to keep the mills running.

You are probably wondering what role the United States plays in the flax and linen industry. We grow a great deal of flax and rank, alongside Argentina, Russia, and India, among the leading flax-producing countries in the world. However, flax is grown in the United States not so much for the fiber as for the seeds, which are highly valuable. You have probably heard of linseed oil, which is made in immense quantities from flaxseed. There is no other oil that, when mixed with paints and varnishes, dries so quickly and leaves such a fine surface. Millions of gallons of linseed oil are spread every year on our houses, leather goods are treated with it, sailors' oilskin clothing is soaked in it, and it is even present in the ink used to print newspapers.

The flax seeds are crushed in much the same way as cotton seeds are crushed to make cottonseed oil. After the oil has been extracted, the crushed seeds are turned into cakes, which are considered a valuable food for cattle. Millions of bushels of flaxseed are produced annually. Argentina, India, Russia, and the United States produce nearly all of this vast quantity.

TOPICS FOR STUDY

I.

1. Description of Cobh.
2. A trip to Blarney Castle.
3. Cattle and dairy products.
4. Emigration.
5. Peat.
6. Description of Dublin.
7. Northern Ireland.
8. Cultivation of flax.
9. Manufacture of linen.
10. Description of Belfast.
11. The flax industry in other countries.
12. Flaxseed.

II.

1. Trace the voyage and name the waters sailed on during a voyage from Cobh to New York.

2. Sketch a map of Ireland. Locate all cities mentioned in the chapter. Write the names of the surrounding waters. Trace our route from Cobh to Belfast. Add the map of Scotland and indicate the coal and iron regions of that country.

3. Write the story of the formation of peat and its preparation for use.

4. Write a list of the markets to which exports from Belfast may be sent. Locate each city.

5. Name the processes involved in the preparation of flax. Describe each process.

6. Make a list of the industries of Belfast. Try to think of reasons why each industry is located in that city.

7. What countries produce the best flax fiber and the most flaxseed?

8. Add to your school collection by bringing samples of flaxseed and linseed oil, as well as samples of articles made from jute, flax, and hemp.

9. Why was there such a linen shortage during the World War? What very important use did linen serve during the war?

III.

Be able to spell and pronounce the following names. Locate each place and tell what was said of it in this and any previous chapters. Add any other facts you can find.

Argentina	Scotland	New Orleans
Belgium	United States	Portland
Connecticut		San Francisco
Great Britain	Belfast	
India	Chicago	Lagan River
Ireland	Cobh	Lee River
Maine	Cork	Liffey River
Russia	Dublin	North Channel

CHAPTER IV

JUTE, HEMP, AND OTHER FIBERS

Other fibers besides flax are of great value in the industrial world, and many new ones, unknown to-day, will be used in the future. In the deep forests of tropical lands, there are varieties of trees and plants, the names of which are as yet scarcely known, but which, at some time, will supply much of the demand for fibers used in textiles and other manufactures.

You have all seen the brown bags — gunny bags, they are called — in which grain is sometimes shipped, or the coarse bagging in which bales of cotton and wool are wrapped. Perhaps you have on your floors at home some of the fiber rugs, which are now so popular. All these and many other articles are made of jute.

Jute is one of the fibers whose original home was in a tropical jungle. To-day, it is widely used in manufacturing. To see the plant growing and to learn how it is raised, we shall have to take a long journey to the southern part of Asia. We will go to the province of Bengal in India, for nearly all the jute used in the world comes from that region. There, we shall see fields upon fields of the tall, slender plant swaying in the tropical breeze. It grows in single stalks to the height of ten or twelve feet, and the jute fields in the province of Bengal alone cover an area half as large as the state of Massachusetts.

The crop is sown, cared for, and reaped by the dark-skinned natives of India, who also work in large numbers in the great jute mills of Calcutta. These workmen are very unlike the mill operatives in the United States and in Europe. They live in villages made up of huts built of mud or bricks, or of palm leaves woven into sheets and tacked onto bamboo poles. The huts are thatched with a long, tough grass used for the purpose throughout India. The floor is of clay, covered in places with matting made of bamboo grass. There may be a few rough benches, possibly a rude bed, but little other furniture. The natives eat on the floor, squatting around a pot or pan containing the food, which is probably a preparation of rice, vegetables, and curry. No knives, forks, or spoons are used, as the fingers answer all purposes. As the climate is so warm, the people wear but little clothing. The men in the jute fields are dressed in what looks to us like a shrunken bathing suit, while the women are draped with many yards of thin muslin.

About blossoming time, the jute is cut close to the ground, and the leaves and branches are trimmed off. The stalks are retted in a manner similar to the retting of flax. They are then beaten to remove the woody matter, after which the fiber is cleaned, dried, and made into bales of four hundred pounds each. Several millions of such bales are produced each year, many of which are sent to Calcutta for manufacture, and many more to Scotland, the remainder being scattered among different countries. Most of that bound for Scotland is shipped directly from Calcutta to Dundee, a fine port on the Tay River, about eight miles from the sea. It is the chief center in Great Britain for the manufacture of coarse linen fabrics and is the birthplace of jute manufacturing.

A greater variety of products than most people realize is made in Dundee from this coarse fiber. Among them are burlap, wadding, sailcloth, curtain and furniture hangings, imitation tapestries and fancy goods, and mixtures of linen, cotton, and silk.

There are more than fifty jute mills in Dundee, in which enough jute cloth is made annually to stretch a layer of more than thirty thicknesses entirely across the United States from Boston to San Francisco. In these mills, many thousands of people, three-fourths of whom are women, find employment. Jute is raised and manufactured very cheaply in India, and in order to compete with that country, manufacturers in Dundee must keep their prices as low as possible. Women can be hired more cheaply than men, and more than half of the seventy-five thousand women and girls who live in the city of Dundee earn their own living, and perhaps that of relatives dependent on them, by working in the mills and factories.

Many of the families of the operatives live in houses of one or two rooms, sleep in the kitchen, and have little leisure for fun. The schools are good, and the boys and girls are obliged to attend them until they are fourteen years of age, when most of them go to work. Their food is plain — porridge and milk for breakfast, a soup made of meat, leeks, carrots, turnips, and barley for dinner, and bread, butter, and tea for supper, with perhaps a piece of fish or meat for the men.

The world's entire crops of cotton and coffee, and much of the grain, sugar, and rice, are shipped in jute bagging. Its manufacture is a very important industry. Not alone in Dundee, but in other cities of Great Britain, in other European countries, and in the United States, there are many jute mills. To supply the looms in our country, we buy each year many millions of dollars'

FIG. 22. THE TRUE HEMP IS A TALL, SLENDER PLANT WHICH
GROWS TO A HEIGHT OF FROM FIVE TO FIFTEEN FEET
(Courtesy of Mr. T.R. Bryant, College of Agriculture, Lexington, Kentucky)

worth of the fiber. Brazil is the best customer for British-made jute yarn, which is manufactured in the great South American Republic into millions of bags to hold her immense coffee crop.

Calcutta, however, takes highest rank for both the export and the manufacture of jute fiber. In one year, there is shipped from India, largely by way of Calcutta, enough jute fiber to fill more than twenty-five thousand freight cars, enough yards of gunny cloth to wrap between fifteen and twenty times around the earth at the equator, and more than two hundred million gunny bags.

There are many other fibers used in the manufacture of

FIG. 23. COMBING HEMP (Courtesy of the International Harvester Company)

articles which we should surely miss if we were to be deprived of them. Did you ever think of the value of rope and other cordage as an article of commerce, and of the great variety of uses to which it is put? By its aid, the sailor adjusts his sails, the fisherman reaps his ocean harvest, the soldier fastens down his tent, the workman arranges his staging, and the farmer binds up his sheaves of grain.

Rope has been used for many centuries. Pictures on the tombs of Egyptian mummies buried hundreds of years ago illustrate the making of rope. Most savage peoples manufacture rope of some sort, and many different kinds of fiber are used for this purpose.

Rope is made chiefly of hemp, and a number of plants are included under this name. The true variety is a tall, slender plant with a single hollow stalk, which grows to a height of from five to fifteen feet. Russia has produced more hemp than all the rest of the world. It is also grown in Central Europe, Italy, France, Germany, in certain parts of Asia and Africa, and to a small extent in the United States — in Kentucky, California, and in some other sections.

FIG. 24. ONE FIRM MANUFACTURES TWINE ENOUGH EVERY YEAR
TO STRETCH TO THE MOON AND BACK MORE THAN THIRTY
TIMES (Courtesy of the International Harvester Company)

FIG. 25. "MANILA FIBER IS OBTAINED FROM A PLANT SIMILAR TO THE BANANA"

If any of you own a canary, you have probably noticed how fond he is of hempseed, and large quantities are sold each year to be used as bird food. The newly sown fields of hemp have to be carefully watched, lest the birds should get more than their share.

The hemp is cut, and the fiber is separated from the woody part of the stalk in much the same way as the flax is treated. The fibers of the hemp are much longer and coarser and cannot be easily bleached. Hemp is not so useful, therefore, for fine, delicate articles as for rougher materials, such as ropes and twine.

Hemp is grown all over Russia, except in the extreme north. Nearly two million acres are covered with this tall, graceful plant, and an enormous quantity of the fiber is produced. More than half of this is used in Russia itself, and the remainder is sent to different European countries and to the United States for making various kinds of cordage, which, as different industries of the world are developed, is made in increasing quantities each year.

There are many firms in the United States that make immense quantities of rope and twine. Since our wheat crop has grown to such enormous proportions, and those wonderful harvesting machines, which cut, thresh, and tie up the bags of grain, have been invented, we use and sell to other grain-producing countries immense quantities of twine. One firm in Chicago, which manufactures harvesters and the twine to use on them,

FIG. 26. "SISAL HEMP RESEMBLES AN OVERGROWN CENTURY PLANT"
(Courtesy of the International Harvester Company)

makes in one year enough to stretch to the moon and back more than thirty times.

You must not think, however, that these enormous quantities of rope and twine are made from the true hemp, such as grows in Russia and other European countries, for comparatively little is made from that material. Most of the cordage made in the world today is manufactured from Manila fiber and sisal fiber, neither of which is related to the real hemp. The Manila fiber is obtained from a plant similar to the banana, which grows chiefly in the Philippine Islands. The sisal hemp, produced chiefly in Mexico, resembles an overgrown century plant.

A train of more than three thousand cars would be required to carry our annual imports of either sisal or Manila fiber. The true hemp fiber imported from European countries could be easily loaded onto a few hundred cars.

TOPICS FOR STUDY

I

1. The jute industry of India.
2. Jute manufacturing in Dundee.
3. Uses of jute.
4. The hemp industry.
5. Varieties of fiber used for rope.

II

1. Name the waters sailed on in a voyage from Calcutta to Dundee.
2. Write a list of places in Scotland mentioned in Chapter II. Add those in this chapter. Sketch a map and show these places.
3. Sketch a map of India. Show its land and water boundaries, the province of Bengal, and the city of Calcutta.

III

Be able to spell and pronounce the following names. Locate each place and tell what was said of it in this and in any previous chapter. Add other facts if possible.

Bengal	India	Mexico	Boston
Brazil	Italy	Philippine Islands	Calcutta
California	Great Britain	Russia	Chicago
Egypt	Kentucky	Scotland	Dundee
France	Massachusetts	Tay River	San Francisco

CHAPTER V

THE BRAVE LITTLE COUNTRY OF BELGIUM

For many years Belgium has been famous for her flax, for her fine linen lace, for her carpets, named for the capital, Brussels, for her wonderful bulbs and seeds, for her great commerce with many different parts of the world, and for the thrift and industry of her people. Since the World War, however, Belgium is remembered, more than for anything else, for her heroism in the face of overwhelming odds, for the terrible suffering of her people during the four long years of fighting, and for the awful devastation and ruin left behind by the German invaders.

In 1914, Belgium saved the world from a German victory and all the horrors which such a victory would have meant. Through Belgium lay the easiest route from Germany into France. For years, Germany had been planning for the war and had everything in readiness. France was not so prepared, nor England; and Germany planned to march her armies quickly through Belgium into France and take Paris before the French could be ready to stop her. This done, an attack on England would come next. With these two western nations at her mercy, Germany would then turn her attention to the East and hurl her full strength against Russia. The carrying out of these plans meant victory. They all depended, however, on haste, on the capture of Paris before the French army was ready to defend it. The Germans never anticipated that their well-made plans would be upset by little Belgium.

Some years before, the Great Powers of Europe had signed a treaty to the effect that they would respect Belgium's neutrality; that is, that they would not take their armies through her territory to attack another nation. In case any one of them did so, it was Belgium's duty to do her best to prevent it. Few people thought that Germany would be so dishonorable as to break her word, which she had solemnly pledged in this treaty, but when the treaty interfered with her plans, she regarded it only as a mere "scrap of paper" and started her army through Belgium into France.

Belgium, in her turn, might have broken her pledge, might have kept still and allowed the German army to go on its way unmolested and so saved herself the awful destruction and suffering which came to her. But Belgium was too honorable to do this. She knew that her little army could not long hold back the hordes of German soldiers, but she prepared to do her best. One after another, her strongly fortified cities — Liège, Namur, Antwerp — fell before the German attacks and the awful onslaught of her big guns, but the little Belgian army, inspired by their hero-king, Albert, who preferred ruin and death to dishonor, fought on. By the time that the Germans had succeeded in conquering the Belgians, the French were ready, the English were ready, and Paris was saved. Germany never forgave Belgium, however, for the delay to her armies and the consequent upsetting of her plans.

Throughout the war, Belgium was terribly punished for what she had done. With the exception of a very small area, near Ostend, all of brave King Albert's country was in German hands, and for four long years they committed every kind of atrocity on cities, industries, and people. Under the name of indemnity, they levied blackmail on the cities; they set fire to the towns, destroyed priceless treasures, killed old men and women and little children, and sent others away into Germany to toil in factories and on farms until they died. The German occupation of Belgium during the World War was one long horror. It will be many years before some of the Belgian villages and towns are rebuilt, before her industries flourish as they did before 1914. Can you imagine returning to your home and finding not one single building standing in the town? Can you imagine yourself

FIG. 27. SUPPOSE THIS WERE YOUR HOME

unable to find where the streets were or to locate the place where you had lived all your life? Yet this was the condition of some Belgian and French towns and villages which lay in the path of the Germans. Perhaps you remember some woods where you liked to play. Imagine returning to them after a short absence and finding not a single green tree in sight. If you live on a farm, you can picture the smooth cultivated fields, the growing crops, and the waving grain. Imagine these fields all rough with hills and holes, covered with barbed wire, and the rich soil saturated with poison gases. The holes are of all sizes, from those big enough for you to play in to some large enough for your house to stand in. So you see it will be long years before all the villages of Belgium and northeastern France will once more resound with the happy voices of the people and the play of the children. It will be many returning seasons before the fields in some localities are again green with growing crops.

Massachusetts is one of our most densely populated states. Belgium contains about twice as many people as Massachusetts in an area less than one and one-half times as large. Before the war, it was the most densely populated country of Europe, and though it is so small, it held fifth place among the commercial nations of the world.

The northern and southern parts of Belgium are as different from each other as the fertile plains of Kansas are different from the mining regions of Pennsylvania. In the days of its prosperity, someone called southern Belgium a great factory district, smoky, dusty, and disagreeable, and the northern half a market garden, flat, fertile, and green. Is it not terrible that war should lay waste so prosperous a region?

Southern Belgium is the industrial part of the country. Here there are rich deposits of coal and iron, and important manufactures are carried on in the cities and towns. Coal is the principal product of Belgium, and in the mountainous southern part, mining has long been a leading occupation. When the Germans retreated from southern Belgium, they wreaked such destruction on some of these mines that it will be years before they can be worked again.

The people in northern Belgium are very different from those in the south. In the northern part live the Flemings, a light-haired, blue-eyed race, more like the people of Holland than those of southern Belgium.

In the northern half of the country, most of the people earn their living from their tiny farms, which in some cases seem scarcely larger than good-sized lawns. Long before sunrise, they begin their day's work in the fields, the women wearing heavy, clumsy wooden shoes, called sabots, with coarse woolen stockings, short, full skirts, and linen sunbonnets, each with a sort of hood which falls over the forehead. The men wear wooden shoes, short trousers, and dark blue smocks or blouses.

Their simple breakfast consists of rye bread and coffee. For dinner, they have more rye bread spread with butter or butterine, and perhaps a piece of cheese or bacon. For supper, the rye bread is supplemented by a soup made of vegetables and meat. If they live near a city, the men usually find work in some mill or factory, while the women tend the cow, feed the pig, and raise the vegetables on the little farm.

It is in northern Belgium that many interesting old cities are located. One of these is Ghent, with its picturesque gateway, its curious old buildings dating from the Middle Ages, its rambling streets, and its dark canals. The city of Ghent is not so important now as it was in the bygone days, when it was the proud capital of ancient Flanders and one of the chief cities of Europe.

Brussels is the capital of Belgium. Its broad boulevards, its avenues lined with ancient lime trees, its parks and forests, its fountains and statues, its magnificent Palace of Justice, and its Grand Place, or public square, make it one of the most beautiful cities in the world. On one side of the Grand Place stands the Hôtel de Ville, or City Hall. It was built a half century before America was discovered and is one of the famous buildings of Europe. On the Grand Place, there are other interesting buildings several centuries old. In the square enclosed by these buildings, markets are held in the early morning hours. You would like to visit the bird market. Such a chirping and trilling and whistling and singing as you never before heard comes from the hundreds of canaries, thrushes, parrots, mockingbirds, and nightingales. The flower market is fully as interesting. Enormous quantities of roses, pinks, lilies, violets, and other exquisite blossoms fill the air with their fragrance.

The Palace of Justice in Brussels is the finest building in all Belgium, perhaps in all Europe. It stands in the newer, higher part of the city, and its central tower rises nearly four hundred feet above the low hill on which it is located. The building cost more than ten million dollars. It is in the form of a square which measures six hundred feet on a side. Find out how far six hundred feet would extend from your schoolhouse and estimate how much space this splendid building covers.

In the great World War, the Belgians realized the impossibility of defending Brussels from German invasion. Therefore, they surrendered the city in order to preserve its beauties and treasures for future generations.

Brussels is a popular residence for the well-to-do people of Belgium, and it is also important as a manufacturing city. It has long been noted for the making of exquisite linen lace and the manufacture of carpets. Printing and all other departments of bookmaking give employment to many of its people, and breweries, distilleries, sugar refineries, foundries, mills, and factories make it a busy industrial city. It is connected by canals with other Belgian cities and with the North Sea. These waterways help in its commerce with other parts of Belgium and with other countries.

About fifteen miles from Brussels lie the ruins of the old university city of Louvain with its record of five hundred years of learning. Its town hall was one of the gems of Gothic architecture. Its university was founded half a century before America was discovered and was, up to the time of its destruction in 1914, the most famous Catholic university in the world and attracted students from every country. Louvain was a peaceful, quiet, undefended city, yet, by order of a German official, it was systematically destroyed. The men were made prisoners, the women and children were deported, and the German soldiers were given bombs with which to demolish the buildings.

Bruges is another interesting old place. Three centuries ago and more, Bruges was wealthier and of greater importance than Antwerp. Vessels from the far distant East and from the then powerful Italian cities of Venice and Genoa unloaded their rich cargoes on its wharves. Today, the city is of much less importance but is still a center of some canal commerce. More than fifty bridges span the waterways. The word *Bruges* means "bridges," and the city received its name from the number which it contains.

Longfellow wrote a beautiful poem about the famous old belfry of Bruges, which, though "thrice consumed and thrice rebuilt, still it watches o'er the town." In the poem, he sees in imagination the former grandeur of the city, its busy life, and the great traffic which was once carried on through its doors.

Some one has called Antwerp the window of Belgium. A better name for it would be the door, for through it passes nearly all the seagoing trade of the country. This is so great that Antwerp ranks as the second commercial port on the continent of Europe, Hamburg alone surpassing it.

We sail about fifty miles up the Scheldt River, which is more

FIG. 28. MANY OF THE CARTS ARE DRAWN BY DOGS

like an arm of the sea than a river, before we arrive at the city. We are astonished at the amount of shipping, and at the many acres of docks and quays crowded with vessels whose masts rise like a forest and whose flags represent nearly all the important nations of the world. They have brought to Antwerp products of every clime — ivory and rubber from Africa, oil and breadstuffs from the United States, wheat from Russia, coffee from Brazil, lumber from Scandinavian countries, and many other luxuries and necessities. These same vessels will carry to far-away countries the products of the mines, the farms, and the factories of Belgium and the imports from her colonies.

A network of canals connects Antwerp and the Scheldt River

with other cities and waterways. We can go by boat to the Rhine or Meuse rivers, or even find our way by water to the Rhone River and thence to the Mediterranean Sea.

To reach the famous flax-growing district of Belgium, we follow the Scheldt River down to Ghent. Many canals, shaded by endless rows of Lombardy poplars, lead off from the river into the flat, fertile country, which is dotted with low cottages with red-tiled roofs.

Many of the milk and vegetable carts in Belgium are drawn by dogs. These are sometimes driven between the shafts or three abreast like horses. Sometimes they are harnessed behind the cart or beneath it. Most of the dog teams that we see are driven by women, and there are many women and girls, as well as men, working in the fields.

Continuing on our way, we follow the valley of the river Lys, a branch of the Scheldt, down to Courtrai, where the banks are

©Underwood & Underwood
FIG. 29. THE FIBER IS RETTED IN THE RIVER LYS

crowded with factories and warehouses. This is the famous flax-growing region of Belgium. Nearly every farmer in the valley raises flax, which is of so fine a quality that the annual product is often of more value than the land on which it was grown. The water in the river Lys, in which the fiber is retted, contains just the right elements to make it clean, silky, smooth, and of a lustrous color.

TOPICS FOR STUDY

I

1. Belgium in the World War.
2. Devastation in Belgium.
3. Contrast between northern and southern Belgium.
4. Cities of Belgium.
5. Destruction of Louvain.
6. The port of Antwerp.
7. The flax industry in Belgium.

II

1. Sketch a map to show the waters sailed on in a voyage from Belfast to Courtrai.
2. Name the waters sailed on in sending to Belgium ivory and rubber from Africa, oil from the United States, wheat from Russia, coffee from Brazil, lumber from Scandinavia. Name the shipping port in each country.
3. Contrast in appearance and occupations the northern and southern parts of Belgium.
4. Study your map and find why the easier route from Germany into France lay through Belgium rather than farther south.
5. On the map of the Western Front (p. 11), find some of the river valleys that the armies followed and in which many battles took place.
6. What historic battleground is located in Belgium?

III

Be able to spell and pronounce the following names. Locate each place and tell what was said of it in this and in any previous chapter. Add other facts if possible.

Africa	Massachusetts	Courtrai	Lys River
Brazil	Pennsylvania	Ghent	Mediterranean
East Indies	Russia	Hamburg	Sea
England	Scandinavia	Liege	Meuse River
Flanders		Louvain	North Sea
France	Antwerp	Namur	Rhine River
Germany	Bruges	Ostend	Rhone River
Kansas	Brussels	Paris	Scheldt River

CHAPTER VI

MANUFACTURING ENGLAND

Before we leave the British Isles for our tour of the Continent, we wish to see something of England, a great manufacturing and commercial center of the world. It is such a small country, only about one sixtieth of the size of the United States, that one wonders why it has developed so greatly in these directions. Let us search for some of the reasons.

If all the productive land of the United States were to be divided equally among its people, each person would receive about fifteen acres of farmland or forests. This is more than enough to raise the products necessary to feed, clothe, and shelter the entire population. Therefore, we are not dependent upon other nations for our supply of life necessities. Let us see how it is in some European countries.

If all the productive land of France were divided in the same way, every man, woman, and child living in the country would receive about three acres apiece; in Germany, each person would possess nearly two acres; while in England, the people are so many and the island is so small that less than one acre could be given to each person. This small amount of land makes the people dependent upon other countries for their food and clothing supplies, for in such a country there is little room for large farms.

It is said that if all outside food materials were shut out from England for six months or less, her people would starve. So, to a degree entirely unknown to us, with our immense wheat and corn farms, our large cotton plantations, and our great cattle and sheep ranches, European nations, and especially England, must depend on other parts of the world for raw material for food and clothing.

Unless she would see all her money slowly drift to other shores, England must pay for her imports by selling manufactured goods and must give her people employment in making them. England exports enormous quantities of manufactured goods, and it is by means of these exports that she is able to supply three times as many people as could be fed from the products of her own soil.

For these great industries, nature has given to England every advantage, and first among them is her position. The country is situated in the northern part of the temperate zone, in a latitude where there are long hours of sunshine during the summer months. The cold of winter might interfere with the carrying on of some industries, but the westerly winds, warmed by the Gulf Stream, temper the climate to such a degree that England's harbors are ice-free, her rivers are navigable all year round, and her climate is a moist one, favorable for the spinning of flax, cotton, and wool.

To the people of ancient times, Britain lay upon the very edge of the great Sea of Darkness, and to venture on this was to expose oneself to all sorts of unknown dangers. The voyage of Columbus and the discovery of a continent to the west put England in the center, rather than on the edge, of the world, and she forthwith began to earn her title of the "Mistress of the Seas."

Separated from the Continent by water, she was disturbed less than other European nations by the many wars that ravaged the mainland, and she was therefore freer to develop her industries.

Look at the map and see how deeply the coast of Great Britain is indented. Some of her river mouths are really bays penetrating the land, and though the rivers are small, the tide makes most of them navigable for some distance.

Notice also that the indentations made by the rivers are in several cases opposite one another, thus bringing the coasts and the important seaports much nearer together. The most important of such pairs of rivers are the Severn and the Thames, with Bristol and London near their mouths; the Mersey and the Humber, with Liverpool and Hull only about one hundred miles apart; the Clyde, with the city of Glasgow, and the Forth, with Edinburgh and its port of Leith linking the east and the west coasts together.

Favored thus by a genial climate, by a convenient separation from warring nations, by a long water boundary of some two thousand miles, by good harbors, and by navigable rivers, England has another incentive for commerce in the great number of her foreign colonies. Though England itself is only one sixtieth as large as the United States, the entire British Commonwealth of Nations is large enough to cover an area nearly four times that of the United States and contains nearly five times as many people. In all these countries, England finds a market for a great variety of manufactured goods, which she can supply to better advantage than any other nation.

No nation, however, can become great in manufacturing and commerce unless nature has favored her in yet another way. Stored deep in her soil, there must be fuel to supply her factories and mills, and there must also be rich deposits of iron for the manufacture of machinery and other necessary articles. Although other countries connected by trade may possess iron in great abundance, the cost of transporting so heavy a material, and one that must be used in such quantities, is too great to allow for extensive manufactures.

The forests with which England was at one time largely covered furnished fuel for her manufactories, which sprang up in any place where charcoal could be easily supplied. Great stretches of forests have disappeared in this way. The discovery of coal, however, in large measure decided the location of the manufacturing districts of England, and her great industrial cities have grown up near the deposits of coal and iron. On account of the size of the country and the indented coastline, the mineral deposits and the manufacturing cities lie near together and near the great seaports. This gives to England a great advantage over those countries whose deposits of coal and iron and whose manufacturing centers lie a long distance away from their seaports.

Many of the inventions which have revolutionized great industries were made in England and used in her manufacturing districts for years before other nations obtained the secrets. Among the more important inventions which have had an influence in developing important industries are the spinning jenny, which makes it possible for a person to operate more than one spindle at a time, and the power loom, in which, at first, water power and then steam was applied to the weaving of cloth. The invention of the steam engine and the perfecting of Stephenson's model have also had a great effect in stimulating English manufactures. Thus, because of her great colonial market, her rich coalfields, and her power machinery, England obtained a tremendous start in manufacturing and commerce over other European nations.

The greater part of our products shipped to England enter the country by way of Liverpool. Let us follow our wheat, cotton, wool, cattle, and beef into the country through the door of this great seaport and learn, by visiting the chief industrial centers, what manufacturing England can tell us.

Every Cunarder, every White Star liner that docks at Liverpool

FIG. 30. "THE DOCKS OF LIVERPOOL ARE THE MOST WONDERFUL IN THE WORLD"

leaves on the wharves its hundreds and thousands of passengers. Most of these take a hurried meal, or possibly spend the night, and then rush off from the busy port by express to London or to other scenes. We will make a longer stop and discover, if we can, what it is that has made this city one of the greatest seaports in the world.

Our liner steams slowly up the Mersey to the docks of Liverpool, which extend in a semicircle along the left bank of the river, three miles from its mouth. We see forests of masts and funnels, and pass tugs pouring out clouds of black smoke as they pull along some giant of the deep. We glide slowly by dozens of arriving or departing steamers anchored in midstream. There are vessels loaded with wheat from Montreal and Duluth, steamer loads of cotton from Galveston and New Orleans, and from far-away Bombay and ancient Alexandria. The holds of the steamers from South America and Africa are filled with wool from the alpacas of Peru and from the Angora goats of Cape Colony. We should find wine from Portugal, olive oil and silk from Italy, fruits and vegetables from France, cork from Spain, sugar from the Bahamas, lumber from our Southern states, and wool from the great sheep ranches in the West. We are bewildered as we look at the crowd of tramp steamers, schooners, ocean liners, and barges, and try to guess their cargoes and their sailing ports. More than twenty thousand vessels of all kinds and descriptions, from every corner of the world, enter and leave the harbor annually.

The docks of Liverpool are the most wonderful in the world. They extend for six or seven miles along the river and are lined with warehouses, elevators, derricks, and cranes. Vessels from all over the world stop at them, but those from America far outnumber all the rest.

Truly, Liverpool is a city of ships and sailors, but as we go from the wharves up into the city, we see that it is a city of manufactures as well. Great quantities of flour are made here from the wheat that grew on Canadian farms and on our Western plains. Sugar refineries convert the raw sugar from far-away islands into the pure, white article, which is shipped away in

FIG. 31. THE MANCHESTER SHIP CANAL IS LARGE
ENOUGH TO ACCOMMODATE OCEAN STEAMERS

great quantities. There are also rope, leather, soap, paper, and glass factories, and iron and steel works, the products of which add greatly to Liverpool's commerce.

You are doubtless wondering why it is that Liverpool has grown to be such an important commercial city, why it is that great steamers, with their heavy loads, seek this harbor rather than others on the coast of England, and why it is that thousands of vessels find cargoes here awaiting them to be carried to the ends of the earth.

Other things besides a good harbor are necessary in order that a city may grow to be a great commercial port. The goods brought to her doors must be disposed of, and cargoes must be supplied for the vessels to carry away. Therefore, much of the importance of a seaport depends upon the surrounding country. Let us go farther into England and see what the interior supplies to aid Liverpool in her trade.

If we continue our journey up the Mersey as far as Eastham, we shall find there the beginning of a great canal, one of the most important in the world. It is twenty-six feet deep and

FIG. 32. THE DOCKS AT MANCHESTER ARE LARGER AND MORE
NUMEROUS THAN MANY AN OCEAN PORT CAN BOAST OF

twice as wide as the Suez Canal, large enough, as you see, to accommodate ocean steamers. It follows the valley of the Mersey and, later, of the small tributary called the Irwell. After a trip of about thirty-five miles, our boat stops at the docks in the heart of the great city of Manchester, the center of the textile-manufacturing district of England.

We are astonished at the docks of this inland city. They are larger and more numerous than many an ocean port can boast of. All around, we see every facility for loading and unloading freight and for handling goods — grain elevators, warehouses, electric and steam cranes, stockyards, cold-storage buildings, great spaces for timber, iron, and other materials not requiring cover, and oil tanks with a capacity of millions of gallons, so situated as to permit steamers discharging directly into them. The docks and wharves are completely covered with a network of railways.

We are in the county of Lancashire, famous the world over for cotton spinning and weaving. This industry, which furnishes such a large part of the cotton goods needed in the world, has been built up over rich coal deposits and near the seaport of Liverpool, through which the raw material can be imported and the finished goods shipped away. In "Cottonopolis," every town and city is more or less dependent upon cotton manufacturing, and five hundred fifty thousand people, a number about equal to the population of Baltimore, Maryland, find employment in the numerous occupations connected with it.

Not one of the principal railways of England could earn a dividend if disaster were to overtake the cotton-milling industry of Lancashire. Such a calamity would bring poverty to the people, paralyze Great Britain's ocean commerce, and work immense damage to all the industrial interests of the country.

More of the actual manufacturing of the cotton is carried on in the smaller places around Manchester than in the city itself, and the goods are carried by rail or by canal to the Manchester docks for shipping. Some of the towns specialize in the kinds of goods made. One place, perhaps, makes shirtings, another muslins, while another manufactures chiefly heavy cotton dress goods. Many of the workmen have been trained for generations in some particular line. Frequently, they are doing the same work today that their fathers and grandfathers did before them, and as a consequence, they have become highly skilled.

All the towns in the Manchester district are of modern growth, and the cotton industry feeds, clothes, and furnishes employment for the entire population. Each town is made up of the warehouse where the cotton is stored, the great factories, the cottages of the workmen, and the finer houses of the manufacturers. Manchester, the center of "Cottonopolis," is about as

FIG. 33. COTTON GOODS ARE CARRIED BY RAIL OR CANAL TO THE MANCHESTER DOCKS FOR SHIPPING

large as St. Louis and, since the building of the Ship Canal, is increasing in size very rapidly.

A large part of the cotton used in the district comes from the United States. Much of this is now shipped without unloading from Galveston or New Orleans to the Manchester docks. Great quantities are carried to the different mills or warehouses in huge drays drawn by some of the largest horses you ever saw, and the rattling of the heavy teams over the cobble-paved streets keeps up a continual racket.

The "double-decked" streetcars, or trams, look queer to our American eyes, but the seats on top make sight-seeing easy, and we climb to our places there for a ride through the city. We pass great warehouses where bales of cotton are being unloaded from the heavy drays. We see the busy factories filled with whirring machinery. One of these buildings is so large that in it between thirty and forty miles of cloth a yard wide are woven every day. We ride by rows of small brick houses in which mill operatives live, and which seem more comfortable than tall tenement blocks.

Our ride takes us out into the residential part of the city, filled with the beautiful houses of well-to-do families, and past several pretty parks where children are enjoying the shade and the green grass. Manchester has more than thirty such breathing spaces for the use of her people.

We pass some of the fine buildings of the technical schools, which the city maintains at great expense. Many skilled workmen are needed in her industrial establishments, and hundreds of them are trained in these schools.

As we come back to the center of the city, we stop at the Cotton Exchange — a great building with a beautiful portico, dome, towers, and an immense hall, said to be the largest in England. Its floor covers an area of more than four thousand square yards. Can you reckon the number of square yards in your schoolroom floor and then find how many times larger this great hall is? On Tuesday and Friday of each week, more than half of the ten thousand members of the Exchange meet and transact an enormous amount of business. On those days, we could see cotton merchants, manufacturers of yarn and cloth, dyers, finishers, printers, packers, builders of mill machinery, and representatives of every industrial activity related to the cotton trade.

In the galleries are telegraph instruments and telephones, and the Exchange is in constant touch with Liverpool and New York. By an electrical device, the prices and sales of cotton at those two controlling points, as well as the condition of the market at other places, are promptly displayed on an immense blackboard that extends across one end of the great room, in figures large enough to be easily read from every part of the floor. The business of the Exchange is transacted without confusion or excitement, and without noise other than a continuous hum natural to conversation being carried on by several thousand persons.

Looking at the map, you notice that the Pennine Mountains extend north and south through the northern half of England. On the slopes of this range lie two of the great coal fields of the country. The third important deposit is in the northeastern part of England, around Newcastle, and as a consequence, a great manufacturing center has grown up in that section.

Near the coal field on the western slope of the Pennine Range, around Manchester, the great cotton industry has been built up; and over the deposits of the eastern slope has grown up the wool-manufacturing center.

The woolen industry is one of the oldest and most important of the country. At the time that the Pilgrims were fighting their Indian battles in the little towns of New England, and the colonists of Virginia were beginning to find the wealth of their soil in tobacco, the English farmers were largely engaged in raising sheep. At that time, this was their chief source of wealth, and England was the only important wool-producing country of northern Europe. Most of the wool was sent across the water to Flanders, then the chief manufacturing center of Europe, now a part of Belgium, Holland, and France. Bruges and Ghent, cities which still have a flavor of their old history, manufactured most of the English wool.

It seems queer to us in these days of freedom of thought to learn that religious quarrels had a tremendous effect on English industries. But so it was. Three or four centuries ago, Protestants were persecuted when sovereigns of the Catholic religion were on the thrones of different countries, and when the Protestants came into power, they persecuted the Catholics. The Catholics were the ruling class in Flanders and France when England had a Protestant government; therefore, many Protestant workmen, skilled in various trades, fled from the persecutions in the Catholic countries to England. Here they could live and work safely. Before that time, England had been almost exclusively an agricultural and pastoral country, exporting its raw wool and importing manufactured goods. Gradually, this state of things changed, and more and more manufacturing was done at home until, in time, manufactured cloth and yarns were exported, and as the home supply became insufficient, raw wool had to be imported. At the present time, more than nine hundred million pounds of wool are sent annually by other nations to Great Britain. Two-thirds of this comes from the British colonies, and the remainder from other wool-producing countries in Europe and other continents. It is estimated that from this immense quantity of wool, enough cloth can be made to stretch a curtain more than three yards wide to the moon.

The wool-manufacturing industry was, at first, scattered over the country, but the introduction of steam meant the use of coal, and gradually, the factory districts became centered north of the River Trent, where the richest coal deposits lie.

The cities of Bradford and Leeds, with the surrounding towns in the county of Yorkshire, make up the most important wool-manufacturing district in the world. Through Liverpool and London, millions of pounds of wool from Australia, Africa, South America, and the United States, besides great quantities from England and Scotland, are brought to the wool centers.

Bradford is the center of the raw wool and the worsted trade. Probably five-sixths of all the wool used in England is handled in that city, and the greater part of the worsted yarns and cloth are made there. Most of the woolen cloth is made in Leeds. Both woolen and worsted cloths are made of wool — the woolen of the shorter fiber, the worsted of the longer. The processes in preparing the fiber differ also. Fiber for woolen cloth is carded, while that for worsted cloth goes through the additional process of combing.

From your study of the great textile industries of the United States, you are probably familiar with the spinning and weaving of both cotton and wool, so we will not stop here for a long description. You remember that the first process through which the wool goes, after sorting, is the washing, or "scouring," as it is sometimes called. Wool is very dirty and greasy as it comes to the mill, and in the cleansing, it often loses half or more of its weight. So much wool is scoured in Bradford, and so much fatty and other matter is washed out, that it is said that the sewage is harder to dispose of than that of any other city in the world. Bradford, like some other English cities, owns a large establishment where great quantities of fertilizer are made from the sewage. This is sold in considerable quantity, and an income to the city is thus derived from the waste matter.

Bradford, like many other manufacturing centers, is not very attractive. Great, dingy mills, in which many of the women, as well as the men of the city, find employment, are everywhere. As we pass by dozens of mills and factories and think of the yards and yards of cloth and yarn made in each one, we wonder what can become of it all. Hundreds of great ships, sailing every week from Liverpool and London, carry it to all parts of the world, and thousands and millions of people have coats and trousers and dresses, carpets and blankets, made from Bradford yarn and cloth.

Leeds is only eight miles east of Bradford. It is situated on the little River Aire, a branch of the Humber. These two streams and the North Sea furnish water communication with the continent of Europe, while the Leeds and Liverpool Canal opens the way to the west through the Mersey River and the Atlantic Ocean.

The old forest, in which centuries ago the barbarians from the Continent fought the Saxons, has long since disappeared, and in its place have risen factories and foundries, fine public buildings, statues, and churches. In the great factories, which border some of the streets of the city and which form the most conspicuous feature of the towns around, is made the plain cloth for the use of the army and navy, uniforms for the police, and greenish-drab khaki cloth for the soldiers stationed in tropical countries. In the shipping rooms of the factories, we should also find numberless packages of rainproof cloth, serges, and tweeds, besides quantities of rugs, carpets, and blankets.

From Leeds, the fifth city in size, our trip through industrial England takes us southward twenty-five or thirty miles to smoky Sheffield, the sixth city in population. As we pass through the towns and villages, we are reminded of the Bible story which tells us how the Israelites were guided in their long journey through the wilderness by a pillar of cloud by day and a pillar of fire by night. Heavy smoke darkens the blue heavens in the daytime, and the flames from hundreds of furnaces and foundries light the sky at night. Sheffield is situated near coal and iron mines, and where sandstone, especially good for grinding, is found. It is at the junction of the Don and Sheaf rivers, branches of the Humber, and the name "Sheffield" is probably shortened from "Sheaf-field." The city is the great manufacturing center of the northern portion of the so-called "Black Country," just as Birmingham, which we will visit later, is of the southern part.

While Sheffield is one of the largest and most important towns of the county of Yorkshire, it is also one of the blackest, dirtiest, and most disagreeable. But iron and steel cannot be manufactured without smoke and dirt, and the words "Sheffield" and "iron and steel" have been connected since the earliest times. The city is picturesquely situated on hills, on whose wooded slopes are old estates and mansions of the nobility. A ride through Sheffield shows us fine public buildings, libraries, churches, parks, and gardens. But these do not impress the visitor so much as the hundreds of chimneys rising like a dead forest, the pall of smoke like a thundercloud overspreading the sky, and the enormous works where everything that one can think of, made from iron and steel, is produced—saws, razors, knives, scissors, plates for the great ironclad warships, and immense shells strong enough to pierce them, railroad rails, cannon, and delicate watch springs. Sheffield ware has been used since those early days when the Romans invaded England, when wood was the only fuel, and when the workshops were situated in the great forests. And Sheffield ware will be used until the time, far in the future, when the coal pits and iron mines will no longer yield the necessary material.

From Sheffield, we go southward through the Black Country to Birmingham. Everywhere are the tall chimneys and the smoky sky, for in all the towns and cities through which we pass, there are manufactures of iron and steel or cotton and wool. At the foot of the Pennine Hills, we pass through Derby, famous for its silk manufactures. The peculiar properties of the water of that region make a fast, lustrous dye, which has given to the Derby silks their high reputation.

Ten or a dozen miles east of Derby is Nottingham, the great industrial center for stockings and lace. So famous is it for machine-made laces that Calais, across the English Channel, another of the great lace-manufacturing cities of Europe, is often called the Nottingham of France.

Farther south, we see on our right the smoke from the woolen mills of Leicester, and soon after, we arrive in Birmingham. An old historian says of Birmingham:

"The Arab eats with a Birmingham spoon, the Egyptian takes his bowl of sherbet from a Birmingham tray, the American Indian shoots with a Birmingham rifle, the Hindoo dines on a Birmingham plate and sees by the light of a Birmingham lamp. The South American horsemen wear Birmingham spurs and gaily deck their jackets with Birmingham buttons. The West Indian cuts down his sugar cane with Birmingham hatchets and presses out the juice into Birmingham vats and coolers. The German lights his pipe on a Birmingham tinder-box, and the emigrant cooks his dinner in a Birmingham saucepan, over a Birmingham stove."

A historian of today might add that astronomers study the stars at night through telescopes fitted with Birmingham lenses;

FIG. 34. IN THE NEWER PORTION OF BIRMINGHAM THERE ARE FINE STREETS AND
SPLENDID PUBLIC BUILDINGS

architects decorate churches and other buildings with Birmingham stained glass; armies are supplied with Birmingham
swords. Women in many parts of the world wear Birmingham
jewelry and sew with Birmingham needles the cloth which they
have fastened together with Birmingham pins. Men in different
countries drive Birmingham nails, use Birmingham screws, and
carry watches containing Birmingham springs. In your school,
very likely you use pens which were made in this English city,
for Gillott's pens, which are used by the millions all over our
own and other countries, are manufactured there.

This "Metalopolis" is smoky and dirty. In the old part of
the city, there are narrow, crooked streets, dingy houses, and
huge factories everywhere. But in the newer portion, there are
fine streets and splendid public buildings. Birmingham has the
enviable reputation of being one of the best-governed cities in
the world.

Situated near rich iron mines and in the heart of a great forest, Birmingham, centuries ago, was well known for its metal
manufactures. A history of the city tells us that as early as 1727,

fifty thousand people were employed in them. Since the use of steam and the introduction of coal, of which there are rich beds near, the city has grown very rapidly. The following curious old verses, published in 1828, tell of its rapid growth. An old name for Birmingham is used:

> "Full twenty years and more are past
> Since I left Brummagem,
> But I set out for home at last,
> To good old Brummagem.
> But every place is altered so,
> There's hardly a single place I know:
> And it fills my heart with grief and woe,
> For I can't find Brummagem.
>
> I remember one John Growse,
> A buckle-maker in Brummagem.
> He built himself a country house,
> To be out of the smoke of Brummagem.
> But though John's country house stands still,
> The town itself has walked uphill,
> Now he lives beside a smoky mill,
> In the midst of Brummagem."

London is one hundred twelve miles away to the southeast, and of course, we must visit that city before leaving England. The ride from Birmingham takes us through a beautiful, rolling country where the fine, white roads are bordered with linden trees, and the fertile fields are fenced with green hedgerows. These hedges are typical of English scenery. You remember Priscilla, when sick with longing for her old English home, says to John Alden:

> "I have been thinking all day,
> Dreaming all night, and thinking all day, of the hedge-
> rows in England,
> They are in blossom now, and the country is all like
> a garden."

Once in a while, we catch a flying glimpse of a fine old estate and see, in the beautiful green park shaded by grand old oak trees, several deer raise their startled heads as we fly by.

We pass near Stratford-on-Avon, where, if we were visiting literary fields instead of industrial centers, we should stop for a while to see Shakespeare's birthplace, the school he attended, and the memorial erected by a man from Philadelphia who appreciated his genius. We could walk through the very path in which the great poet walked when he went to call on Anne Hathaway, who afterwards became his wife. We could visit her cottage and sit on the very oak settle beside the fireplace where William and Anne probably passed many long, happy winter evenings.

Near by is Warwick Castle, one of the few old feudal buildings now in repair. It is still occupied by descendants of the noble family to whom it was given by the ruler of England. Only a few miles away is Kenilworth Castle, whose ruins have been immortalized in the novel of the same name by Sir Walter Scott.

Before we go to London, let us visit the two famous university towns of Cambridge and Oxford. Our institutions are so young that it seems strange to think of English young men going to school today in the old buildings, climbing the worn stairs, and playing in the green courts in which English boys worked and played before America was discovered. The oldest of the buildings connected with Oxford University dates back to 1264, and the most ancient college in Cambridge is but twenty years younger.

At last, we reach London, next to New York, the largest city in the world. It is hard to imagine how immense it really is. It contains as many people as the New England States and covers seven hundred square miles. Find the area of your hometown and see how many times larger London is.

Enough babies are born within its boundaries every year to make a city with a population larger than that of Kansas City, Missouri. It is said that London contains more Irishmen than Dublin, more Scotchmen than Edinburgh, and more Jews than Palestine. Its streets, if laid out in a straight line, would reach from New York to San Francisco and thence across the Pacific Ocean to Japan.

It would take you nearly two years to walk through all the

highways of London, and you would see many interesting and wonderful sights in the course of your journey. On many of the streets, your progress would be slow because of the crowds. As we drive through some of these busy thoroughfares, we wonder whether we shall ever gain sufficient courage to cross them on foot, so full are they of heavy drays, lumbering motor "busses," innumerable carriages, automobiles, and hosts of other vehicles. When we make the attempt, however, we find it much easier than it looks. All the teams on one half of the street are going in one direction. In the middle of the street, we discover that there is a raised walk where we can take refuge before we

© Underwood & Underwood

FIG. 35. THE ROYAL EXCHANGE AND BANK OF ENGLAND, LONDON

attempt the other half, where the vehicles are all going in the opposite direction.

The streets are lined with buildings, representing such a variety of occupations that it would be impossible to name them all. There are streets bordered with banks, and streets with newspaper and printing offices; there are some with business houses, and some with clubs and hotels. Many streets are lined with great stores, which make such a fine display of goods that it is a temptation to linger and look into the windows.

London is situated farther from the coal and iron mines than other English cities and is therefore more handicapped in its manufactures. Still, judging from the large mills and factories that we see on many of the streets, it carries on a great variety of industries. The largest breweries, distilleries, and sugar refineries of the British Isles are located in London. The city is also noted for the dressing of sealskins and other fine furs. The sealskins are brought from both Alaskan and Russian waters, and in the great establishments, they are transformed from hard skin into the soft, beautiful fur used for coats and muffs. Machinery of all kinds is made in great quantities. Manufactures on a large scale — of watches, jewelry, brass, books, prints, and boots and shoes — are carried on. There is also much cabinetmaking, coopering, coach-building, leather-working, hat-making, shipbuilding, rope-making, and mast-making.

Before the Suez Canal was opened, London was a great distributing center for oriental goods, and it is today the principal world market for tea. Though little or no wine is made in England, London is the greatest market in the world for that product. It is the chief money center of the world, and business in many countries is affected by the condition of finances in the mammoth city. Money from London banks supports great enterprises in all parts of the world; it helps build bridges in Africa, develops silver mines in Peru, constructs railroads in China, and makes possible the carrying out of irrigation projects in Australia. The Bank of England, an immense gray stone building, is the heart of the entire financial world.

You have learned that the importance of a city depends to

a great extent upon its situation. Let us notice the location of London and see whether it has aided the city in its growth. It is on a small but navigable river, about forty miles from its mouth. Therefore, it has free passage to the ocean, yet is so far inland that it is in easy communication with the rest of England. It is separated by only a narrow channel of water from continental seaports, the outlets of the most developed and densely populated countries of Europe — countries which need the manufactures of England and which send her in return many of their own products.

There are many famous buildings which you must surely see before leaving the city. The great Tower of London is one of these. During the centuries since it was erected on the bank of the Thames, it has served as a prison, a palace, and a fortress. In it, we can see crowns and scepters set with wonderful jewels that have been worn by English sovereigns, and robes in which kings and queens have been crowned. There are rooms

© Underwood & Underwood

FIG. 36. "THE HOUSES OF PARLIAMENT ARE AMONG THE MOST BEAUTIFUL BUILDINGS OF LONDON" filled with figures of horses and men in all kinds of armor. One room contains the instruments of torture used in those awful days which we do not like to think about. There are dungeons and prisons, and so many rooms to visit and so many things to examine that we could spend days at the Tower before we could see it all.

The Houses of Parliament are among the most beautiful buildings of London. They are situated on the Thames River and extend more than nine hundred feet along its bank. We wish that we might visit them when the House of Lords and the House of Commons are in session and listen to some of

© Keystone View Co.

FIG. 37. "THE BRIDGE IS STRONGLY BUILT OF STONE AND WILL DOUBTLESS ENDURE FOR CENTURIES" the interesting debates and eloquent addresses which are often given by famous statesmen.

One of the buildings in London which perhaps the people love better than any other is Westminster Abbey. In it, for many years, their rulers have been crowned; and in it are the tombs of many famous soldiers, statesmen, inventors, authors, and poets. We find there monuments to such men as the Duke of Wellington, Sir John Franklin, William Pitt, David Livingstone, Sir Isaac Newton, Alfred Tennyson, Robert Browning, and Charles Dickens. In the poets' corner is a bust of our dearly loved Longfellow.

There are several bridges across the Thames River, but the one called London Bridge is the most important of them all. You have all played "London Bridge" and have sung the old refrain:

> London Bridge is falling down, falling down, falling down,
> London Bridge is falling down, my fair lady!

There is little danger, however, of such a disaster ever occurring, as the bridge is strongly built of stone and will doubtless endure for centuries.

TOPICS FOR STUDY

I.

1. Density of population in European countries and the results.
2. Natural advantages of England.
3. Description of Liverpool.
4. The cotton industry.
5. Description of Manchester.
6. The wool industry.
7. Description of Bradford and Leeds.
8. The iron and steel industry.
9. Description of Sheffield and Birmingham.
10. Places passed in our trip: Stratford-on-Avon, Warwick Castle, Oxford, and Cambridge.
11. Description of London.

II.

1. Boundaries of England. What separates it from France? From Germany? From Ireland? From Scotland?

2. Name the important indentations on the coast of England. Make a map showing the chief indentations on opposite coasts, the rivers which flow into them, and the cities at their mouths.

3. What was said of these rivers in Chapter II?

4. Name the foreign colonies of England. Ship a cargo from each colony to England; tell what is carried, the shipping port, and the waters sailed on.

5. Write a list of the causes which have helped England to become such an important manufacturing nation; an important commercial nation.

6. Tell the waters on which a vessel would sail in bringing the following cargoes to Liverpool: wheat from Duluth, cotton from New Orleans, wool from Callao and from Cape Town, wine from Lisbon, olive oil from Naples, fruits from Marseille, cork from Barcelona, sugar from the Bahama Islands.

7. What does the Suez Canal connect? What does it separate? What particular interest has England in this canal?

8. Do you know any cities in other countries noted for iron and steel manufactures? Which one holds first rank in the world in this industry?

9. Write a list of the different kinds of woolen cloth that you have ever heard of. See how large a collection of samples you can get.

10. Read, if possible, the chapters on Cotton, The Sheep and Wool Industry, and Iron in "Industrial Studies - United States," Vol. I.

11. Make a list of the buildings in London which are spoken of in this chapter. Tell one fact about each. See if you can find pictures or descriptions of them or of any other important buildings in that city.

12. Tell why each of the men spoken of on page 89 is famous.

13. Name the places in the United States that you can think of that are named for places in England. In what part of our country are most of these situated? Why?

III.

Be able to spell and pronounce the following names. Locate each place and tell what was said of it in this and in any previous chapter. Add other facts if possible.

Alaska	Alexandria	Nottingham
Australia	Baltimore	Oxford
Bahama Islands	Birmingham	Philadelphia
Belgium	Bombay	
British	Bradford	St. Louis
Commonwealth	Bristol	San Francisco
British Isles	Bruges	Sheffield
Canada	Calais	Stratford-on-
Cape Colony	Cambridge	Avon
China	Derby	
England	Dublin	Aire River
Flanders	Duluth	Clyde River
France	Eastham	Don River
Germany	Edinburgh	Forth River
Great Britain	Galveston	Gulf Stream
Holland	Ghent	Humber River
Italy	Glasgow	Irwell River
Japan	Hull	Leeds and
Lancashire	Kansas City	Liverpool
Palestine	Leeds	Canal
Pennine	Leicester	Manchester
Mountains	Leith	Ship Canal
Peru	Liverpool	Mersey River
Portugal	London	Severn River
Russia	Manchester	Sheaf River
Spain	Montreal	Suez Canal
United	Newcastle	Thames River
Kingdom	New Orleans	Trent River
Yorkshire	New York	

CHAPTER VII

PORTUGAL AND ITS CORK FORESTS

Our next visit will take us to a country which, though only a little larger than the state of Maine, was once rich and powerful, and famous for exploration and conquest. The great kingdom of Brazil was one of her colonies, and the riches of the East poured into her treasury. To-day, she is one of the least important of European countries and is famous, not for her colonies (for she has lost most of them), not for her wealth (for her treasury is low), not for her commerce (for in this many European nations outrank her); but for two products known and used in many countries — cork and port wine.

We will enter Portugal through its capital, Lisbon, which some one has said is "the kernel around which the country has crystallized." It is situated about twelve miles from the mouth of the Tagus River, which divides Portugal into two nearly equal parts. Our first glimpse of Lisbon gives the impression of great beauty as it rises from the water, terrace upon terrace, with masses of white buildings gleaming in the sun. As we enter the city and climb the hills, much of the beauty disappears. There are few really beautiful buildings. Perhaps the people feel, because of the earthquakes from which, in times past, the city has suffered greatly, that it is not wise to put their money into expensive houses. Many of the streets are narrow, crooked, steep, and dirty. The modern part of the city lies in the valley. Here, the streets are broad, straight, and well-paved. Modern conveniences, such as electric cars and electric lights, are found side by side with bullock carts and springless ox teams.

© Underwood & Underwood

FIG. 38. MANY OF THE STREETS
IN LISBON ARE NARROW

What queer names the streets have! Nine out of every ten of them are named for some saint. There are also such names as Rua do Ouro, or Gold Street; Rua da Prata, or Silver Street; and Chiado, or Noisy Street. Let us walk up the Rua do Ouro, for this is a popular promenade. The shop windows are gay with fine lace, silks, and the gold and silver filigree jewelry for which Lisbon is famous. At the head of the street is the Praça do Comércio, a large square, bounded on three sides by public buildings and on the fourth by the Tagus River.

After exploring other parts of the city, we will go down to the wharves, for we are more interested in what the people are doing than in their houses, parks, and gardens. See that long line of brick buildings stretching along the river. As we come nearer, the smell of fish and of hot oil tells us that they are sardine factories. Many of the people of Portugal, who live near the coast, are engaged in sardine fishing, and great quantities are packed and exported each year. If all the people in the United States were lined up in a long row, we could give every other one a can of sardines, caught and canned by Portuguese fishermen.

Fish, either fresh, salted, or dried, is a common food of the poor and is eaten by all classes on the many fast days which occur during the year. Every day, there is consumed in Lisbon an average of half a pound each for every person in the city.

The fish girls, or *ovarinas*, as they are called, are one of the characteristic sights of Lisbon. Bareheaded except for the huge baskets of fish, and barefooted, two thousand of them, of all ages and degrees of beauty, travel many miles each day through the streets of the city, crying their wares in tones no more musical than the creak of the oxcarts.

The river and harbor seem full of vessels of all kinds and sizes. At the dock on our left is a small, dirty-looking steamer which plies up and down the Tagus, stopping at the small towns along the shore. At another pier is a large vessel with the flag of Brazil flying from her mast. Portugal carries on more trade in wine, salt, cheap cotton goods, and other products with this old colony of hers than with any other country except Great Britain.

That vessel flying the Union Jack is from England. Lisbon and Oporto, the chief ports of Portugal, are situated on the Atlantic Ocean near where English vessels must pass in their voyage to the Mediterranean Sea and Asia, and to West and South Africa. So, it is natural that much trade between the two countries should spring up. As Portugal has few factories, many manufactured goods, such as cotton and woolen cloth, machinery and tools, as well as coal, oil, and other goods, are brought by these English ships. Dried herring, cod, and other varieties of fish are also brought from northern cities, of which you will read in another chapter.

Vessels from other European countries — France, Holland, Denmark, Italy, and Sweden — may be seen in the harbor, and perhaps one from the United States. Our trade with Portugal is not very important. We send her a few million dollars' worth of cotton, corn, petroleum, tobacco, wheat, and staves, and receive in return comparatively little except cork.

We will take a train at Lisbon for southern Portugal, for it is in that part of the country that the forests, which produce more than one-half of all the cork used in the world, are chiefly found.

The country through which we pass on our journey is not very beautiful. In some places, there are naked plains, shallow rivers, and broad marshes, stretching as far as we can see. The northern part of the country has many rugged mountains, deep, fertile valleys, and clear streams, but the landscape south of the Tagus

River is, for the most part, flat and uninteresting. The farms here are not so attractive nor so well kept as in the northern part of Portugal. This is owing partly to the nature of the country and partly to the fact that many of the peasants are the tenants of larger landowners and do not own their little farms as do the people in the north. Consequently, they seldom have the same pride and ambition as their more fortunate northern brothers.

There is a thrifty-looking place, however, in the fields off to the right. Let us delay our trip to the forests for a little in order that we may see how the Portuguese peasant really lives. The low, square, one-story house is built of stone and is whitewashed without and within. The roof has broad overhanging leaves, gay underneath with bright vermilion paint. As we enter the door, we are greeted graciously by a dark-haired peasant, who, with a graceful bow, tells us that his time, his house, his family, and all his possessions are ours. This is the hospitable way of the Portuguese, who, however, would be very much surprised if we were to accept their generous offers. Travelers, not understand-

FIG. 39. STRIPPING THE COBS WITH THRESHING FLAILS IN
PORTUGAL FROM "WORLD'S COMMERCIAL PRODUCTS"

ing the custom, have sometimes been placed in embarrassing positions by accepting in good faith some admired article, which the kindly host, though it was his most valued possession, urged upon them.

The house consists of one central room, with the smaller bedrooms opening out of it. Over the small charcoal fire hangs a kettle containing a savory soup made of beans, cabbage, rice, and gourds. Sometimes beef or bacon takes the place of one of the vegetables or is added to them. Various kinds of soup, dried codfish or sardines, olives and olive oil, and dark bread made of rye, or maize, or both, supply the needs of the Portuguese peasants.

The fuel of the poorer classes consists of charcoal or small branches and sticks of wood, which are sold at very low prices. Scattered through the mountain forests are charcoal burners, who look like bandits and who live miserable, lonely lives, preparing this cheapest of all fuels for the peasants.

The forests yield other harvests, for pine cones are gathered for the fire, and pine needles for bedding the cattle. The forest products are brought down from the mountains on the backs of mules, while the dark muleteer, in his dusty cape and wide-brimmed hat, walks beside the mule down the narrow path. Portugal is famous for its fine mules, which, with bullocks and oxen, are used much more than horses. The farmer's oxen can be seen in the cattle shed near at hand — great, shaggy fellows with widespreading horns five or six feet from tip to tip. These make them look very fierce, though the owner tells us that they are really quite gentle and would not harm us.

We admire the yoke, which the farmer has skillfully carved for the oxen. Centuries ago, the old Romans tilled the soil with just such oxen, wearing a similarly shaped yoke, harnessed to a plow like the ones used by the peasants today, made of a crooked branch of a tree with a small iron share, which turns up but a few inches of soil. Things move slowly in some of the countries across the water. Although one might see in Portugal a few modern plows and some other up-to-date machinery, agriculture, for the most part, is carried on in the same fashion as

© Underwood & Underwood

FIG. 40. BULLOCKS AND OXEN ARE
USED MUCH MORE THAN HORSES

it has been for hundreds of years. The men and women out there in the fields beyond the cattle sheds are bending low to the ground and cutting the grass, a few blades at a time, with reaping hooks, while a man with a pile of fragrant hay on his head is carrying it across the fields to the barn.

The farmer's life is a busy one, with the care of his fields, his crops, and his cattle. In August, he must harvest his grain and vegetables, his gourds and grapes in September, his corn in October, and his olives in December. He raises flax for his linen and sheep for his wool. His wife and daughters spin the fiber into yarn, and the village weaver weaves the yarn into strong, durable cloth. His farm yields him most of his food — bread, butter, cheese, meat, wine, vegetables, and olives. The village carpenter makes his cart, and the blacksmith his plow and simple tools. He plows and reaps in the same way as his ancestors. Neither he nor his family, perhaps, ever see books or papers or know how to read and write. The great world is a dream to him. Yet his house is warm and comfortable, his cattle well-fed, his storehouse supplied for the winter with materials for food and clothing, and he lives contented and happy the whole year through, for, as the old saying goes, "Though winter lies outside, he has summer in the barn, autumn in the cellar, and spring in the heart."

Leaving the farm, we continue our journey southward until the dim stretches of the cork forests come into view. Soon we are in the midst of them. Interspersed with dark firs and great oaks are hundreds and thousands of wide-spreading, evergreen trees, from twenty to sixty feet high, and with rough trunks from one to four feet in diameter, covered with thick, gray bark. If our visit were later in the fall, we should find the ground strewn with acorns, and droves of pigs contentedly chewing the bitter fruit, while the barefooted Portuguese boys who tend them have a gay time among the gnarled old trees. The acorns are considered very valuable as food for swine, as they are said to give to the ham a flavor superior to that produced by any other food.

You notice in the picture that the trees look like old veterans that have braved the winter storms and the summer heat for years. Many of them are nearly one hundred years old; they had lived nearly twenty years before they yielded their first crop of bark, which was so rough and coarse as to be of very little use. The second stripping, eight or ten years later, was of better quality but not so good as that of still later harvests. When about forty years old, the trees yield their best bark, and continue to

© Armstrong Cork Co., Pittsburgh

FIG. 41. "IT IS INTERESTING TO WATCH THE CORK STRIPPERS AT WORK" do so every ten years until they are about one hundred years old, and sometimes even longer.

It is interesting to watch the cork strippers at work and to see how the bark is removed. With a sharp knife or hatchet, the peasant makes a cut around the trunk near the base of a fine old tree, and another just below the point where the branches put out. He must make these cuts deep enough to go through the outer coating of bark, but not deep enough to touch the inner layer. When the outer coat is stripped off, the inner one, if not injured, will grow thicker and will, in turn, be removed, when the same process will be repeated. If the inner bark is injured, no more will form, and the usefulness of the tree is destroyed. So the workmen are very careful that their knives go just deep enough and no deeper. The two crossway incisions are then connected by lengthwise cuts, which follow, when possible, the

© Armstrong Cork Co., Pittsburgh

FIG. 42. THE FIRST CROP OF BARK (AT THE LEFT) IS SO ROUGH AND COARSE AS TO BE OF LITTLE USE. THE SECOND STRIPPING (AT THE RIGHT) IS OF BETTER QUALITY

deepest cracks in the bark. Then, by inserting the wedge-shaped end of his hatchet handle, the workman pries off the sheets of bark. The larger branches of the trees, as well as the main trunk, are stripped of their gray coats, the branches yielding a thinner layer, but one of fine quality.

Not only in Portugal, but also in Spain, France, Italy, and across the blue Mediterranean in Tunis and Algeria, we should find, could we visit these countries during the summer, thousands of peasants in the cork forests stripping the bark from the trees. In Spain alone, whose output of cork ranks next to that of Portugal, nearly ten thousand men are engaged in this work. Here in Portugal, where the forests cover an area more than one-fourth the size of Massachusetts, hundreds of men find work in their deep shade.

The stripping from the trees is only the first of several processes through which the cork must be put before it is ready for use. The men leave it in piles for a few days to dry, after which they weigh it and carry it in ox teams or on the backs of mules to the boiling stations, which sometimes are long distances away. Here, after seasoning in the open air for some weeks, it

FIG. 43. THE MEN LEAVE THE CORK IN PILES TO DRY, AFTER WHICH THEY WEIGH IT

is put into vats and boiled. This softens the outer coating of woody matter, which makes up nearly one-fifth of the weight of the bark, so that it can be easily scraped off.

The bark is then sorted according to quality and again loaded on ox or bullock teams, or piled so high on the backs of mules that, as they walk away, the loads look like moving woodpiles.

© Armstrong Cork Co., Pittsburgh

FIG. 44. "IN FORMER DAYS ALL CORKS WERE MADE BY HAND"

Arriving at the seaport, the bark is again carefully sorted and done up in large bales bound with steel or wire hoops, and loaded onto vessels bound for different ports in England, Germany, Japan, the United States, and other countries. You may be surprised to learn that we import annually several million dollars' worth of cork bark and cork products. Some of the bark comes from Spain, but her contribution is much smaller than that sent by little Portugal.

In former days, all corks were made by hand, and in every peasant's house in the cork district, we could have found whole families engaged in slicing the bark into strips, then cutting the strips into blocks, and finally shaping the cork from the block. This house industry is still carried on to some extent, but most corks are now made by machinery. A skillful workman with his sharp knife can make perhaps two thousand a day. The machines which are used can each do the work of twenty or more men and are so simple that skilled labor is not required to operate them. Out of nearly one hundred thirty million pounds of cork produced in Portugal, only about one-third is manufactured there.

We buy from Spain nearly a million and a half dollars' worth

FIG. 45. WHEN THE BARK ARRIVES AT THE FACTORY IT
IS PLACED IN WAREHOUSES UNTIL NEEDED

of manufactured corks, but most of our imports from Portugal come in the large sheets of cork bark.

When this arrives at the factory, it is placed in warehouses until needed. In Portugal, the bark was sorted into twenty-five or thirty grades. In the sorting room of a great factory, skilled workmen divide the cork into one hundred fifty different grades, depending on the quality and thickness and on the uses to which it is to be put.

It is then softened by steaming, after which the slabs are sliced into strips from which machines bore out stoppers at a daily rate of thirty thousand to fifty thousand an operative. These stoppers are straight-sided. If tapering ones are desired, they are put through a machine which holds them against the edge of a circular knife that revolves so rapidly that it appears to be standing still. The corks are then washed and dried and finally reach the sorting room. In a large manufactory in Pittsburgh, the largest one in the world, five million corks of all shapes, sizes, and qualities are made each day and sorted into more than twenty grades. An expert sorter can handle from fifteen thousand to fifty thousand daily, the number depending on the size and quality.

© Armstrong Cork Co., Pittsburgh

FIG. 46. IN PITTSBURGH, IN THE LARGEST CORK MANUFACTORY
IN THE WORLD, FIVE MILLION CORKS ARE MADE EACH DAY

Cork is used not only for stoppers but in many other ways. It is used for floats and fishing nets, for buoys, and for life preservers. The optician uses small cork strips on the nosepieces of eyeglasses; the plasterer uses cork floats; the glass manufacturer polishes his wares with cork wheels. The finest pieces of bark are made into cork paper, so thin that five hundred sheets measure but one inch in thickness. This velvety material is used in making cigarette tips. When you push the cork into a bottle, buy a pair of inner soles, use a cork penholder at school, or grasp the handles of your bicycle, just remember that some peasant in the green forests of Spain, Portugal, or Algeria labored to procure the material for you.

In cutting the cork, the dust and small shavings accumulate in large amounts. More than half of the cork bark which started out on its journey through the factory may be found later in the scrap heaps. None of this is wasted; it is carefully collected, and the small pieces are ground. Perhaps you have seen in some

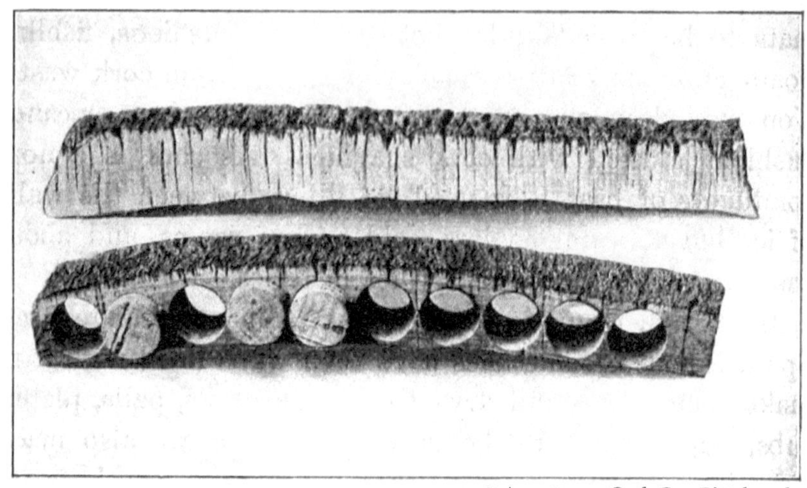

FIG. 47. "THE SLABS ARE SLICED INTO STRIPS FROM
WHICH MACHINES BORE OUT STOPPERS"

grocery or fruit store the Malaga grapes from Spain packed
in ground cork. That very durable floor covering, linoleum, is
made from a preparation of cork powder and linseed oil spread
on strong cloth. Table mats to be placed under hot dishes,
pincushions, fishline floats, and many other articles are made
from cork waste. You may sleep on a mattress or use in your
boat or canoe cushions stuffed with cork shavings. As cork is a
non-conductor of heat, it is used for filling between the walls
of iceboxes, water coolers, cold-storage rooms, and about the
sides of freezing tanks in ice factories.

In foreign countries, cork is put to many strange uses. Spanish houses sometimes have their walls lined with it to make
them warm and dry. Cooking utensils, pails, plates, tubs, cups,
furniture, boats, and beehives are also made from it. In Turkey,
this useful bark is made into huts for the cork cutters while alive
and coffins for them when they are dead. One writer has said:

"There are three trees in the world which yield that
which is of more real value to man than all the jewels
and precious stones ever dug from the earth: a South
American tree yields the liquid which is caoutchouc or

India rubber, the Peruvian cinchona gives us quinine, and a species of live oak supplies the world with cork."

TOPICS FOR STUDY:

I.

1. Former power of Portugal.
2. Description of the Tagus River.
3. Description of Lisbon.
4. Commerce of Portugal.
5. Southern Portugal.
6. The cork forests.
7. Obtaining cork.
8. Manufacturing cork.
9. Cork areas and production.
10. Uses of cork.

II.

1. Find the area of Portugal. Compare it with that of England or some state in the United States.
2. Ship a vessel from Portugal to Brazil. Name the waters sailed on, the cargo carried each way, and the shipping and receiving ports.
3. Can you find a description of the great earthquake at Lisbon?
4. What colonies of England does she reach through the Mediterranean and Red Sea route? Name the waters sailed on.
5. With what colonies in West and South Africa does England trade? What cargoes are taken each way? How long is the voyage? How many miles is it?
6. Sketch a map of Europe. Show routes from Lisbon to some port in Germany, France, Denmark, Italy, Sweden, and England. Write the name of each port.
7. Imagine yourself a Portuguese boy or girl and write a story of your life.
8. The Portuguese use charcoal for fuel. How is it prepared?
9. Sketch a map of Portugal. Show in it the area where cork is obtained. Show also all places mentioned in this chapter.

10. Write a list of the processes in the manufacture of cork and
    of the uses of cork.
11. Add to your school collection anything you can find which
    is made of cork.
12. What is linseed oil? What is it made from? What are its uses?

III.

Be able to spell and pronounce the following names. Locate
each place and tell what was said of it in this and in any previous chapter. Add other facts if possible.

Algeria	Japan	United States
Brazil	Maine	
Denmark	Massachusetts	Lisbon
England	Peru	Oporto
France	Spain	Pittsburgh
Germany	Sweden	
Great Britain	Tunis	Mediterranean Sea
Italy	Turkey	Tagus River

CHAPTER VIII

A TRIP THROUGH RUSSIA

Our next trip will take us from little Portugal to great Russia, a country many times larger. In this, the largest country of Europe, we shall also visit great forests, but they are of a very different kind from those we saw in Portugal. We shall feel more at home in the deep woods of Russia, for they are made up of trees that are common in the United States — birch, oak, pine, fir, and others.

We can reach Russia by sailing from Lisbon either to the north or to the south. We will choose the northern route, as this will bring us much nearer to the forest region which we wish to visit. This route takes us past the coast of France, where the sardine fishermen are gathering their ocean harvest, and through the English Channel and the Strait of Dover, where the white chalk cliffs of England gleam in the sunshine.

Instead of going around the coast of Denmark, through the Skagerrack and Kattegat with their treacherous shallows and difficult passages, we will choose a shorter, much safer route from the North Sea to the Baltic Sea by means of the Kiel Canal, which was built by Germany to connect these waters.

There are several ports on the Baltic Sea at which we might stop and begin our journey into Russia. Riga, the capital and chief city of Latvia, is one of these. Riga is a great timber and flax port, situated about seven miles from the mouth of the Düna River, a deep, navigable stream which leads into the heart of Russia.

We pass Reval in Estonia, where, in ordinary years, we might see vessels loaded with cotton from the United States. Most of the cotton shipped from our Southern states enters Russia through the city of Reval, as this port is open the year-round, while Riga, being situated on the Düna River, is often frozen for two or three months during the winter.

We desire, however, to make our entrance into the country through "the eye" which Peter the Great made, so that he might, as he said, "look out on the rest of Europe." Consequently, we steam past other ports and sail through the Gulf of Finland to Petrograd.

The "eye" of Russia is, of course, very precious and must be well protected. This protection is provided by the fortress of Kronstadt, which is built on an island in the narrowest part of the Gulf, about twenty-five miles west of Petrograd. Except for the fact that it is frozen over for some months of the year, the harbor of Kronstadt is a fine one. The portion designated for merchant vessels is large enough to hold several hundred of them at the same time. The part devoted to the use of war vessels is protected by forts built on two small islands.

Most of the trade of Petrograd was formerly carried on through Kronstadt, as the Neva River is too shallow to carry large vessels to the capital. Now, however, a canal large enough for ocean steamers has been built between the two cities, and very little commerce is carried on at Kronstadt anymore.

In the seventeenth century, the land where Petrograd now stands was a low marsh, peopled only by a few miserable fishermen living in rudely constructed huts. Peter the Great, the most famous of all Russian rulers, was wise enough to know that before Russia could become the great nation that he thought she was destined to be, she must have knowledge of and communication with other countries. The waters of the Baltic Sea, washing the shores of other nations, furnished a highway to the rest of Europe. Therefore, Peter decreed that a seaport should be built upon its borders. "There is no lumber," said his nobles. "Bring it from the forests!" replied Peter. "There is no rock or building stone," objected the courtiers. "No vessel shall land here unless it brings some!" retorted Peter. "But it is only a marsh; there is no solid land," pleaded his ministers. "Make some!" thundered Peter. And the nobles, courtiers, and ministers dared say no more.

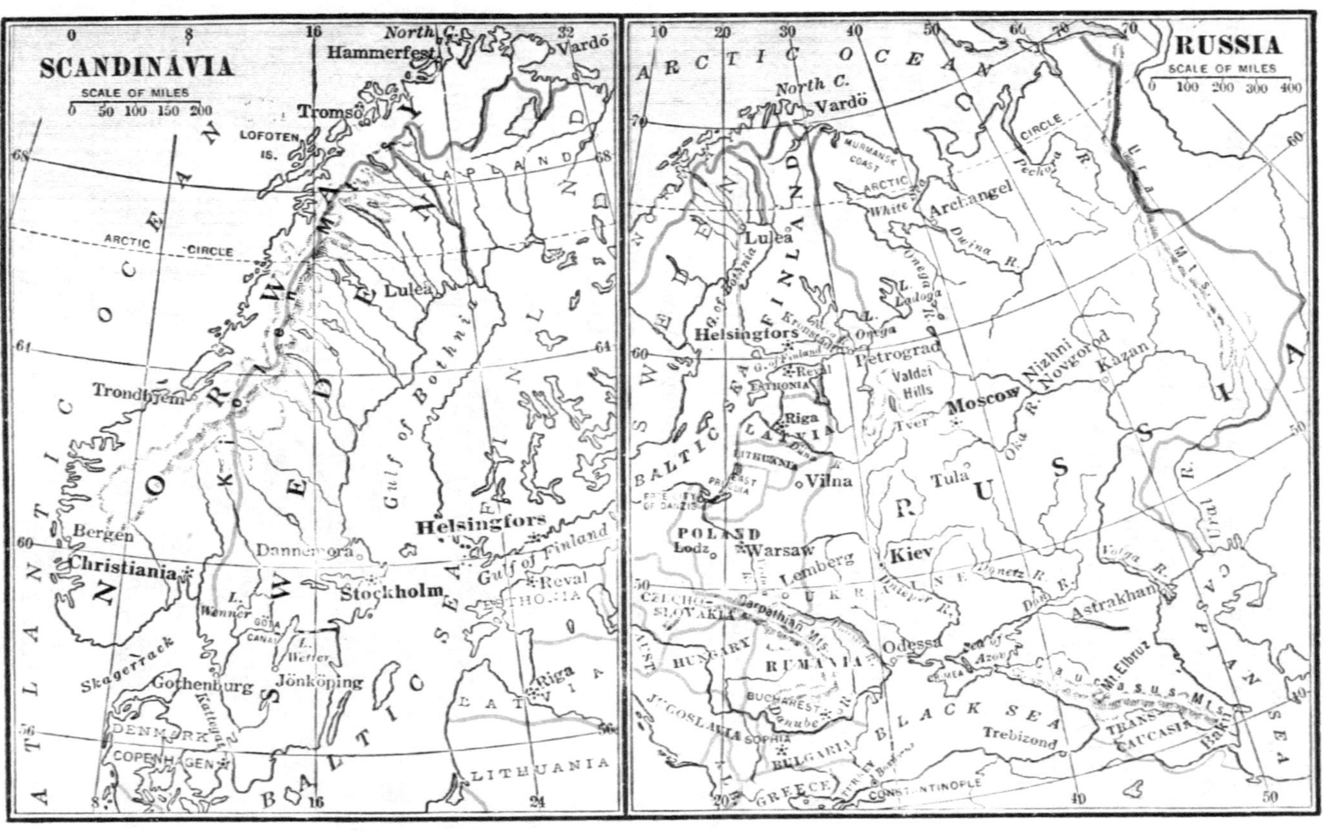
SCANDINAVIA
SCALE OF MILES
0 50 100 150 200

RUSSIA
SCALE OF MILES
0 100 200 300 400

North C.
Hammerfest
Vardö
Tromsö
LOFOTEN IS.
LAPLAND
ATLANTIC OCEAN
ARCTIC CIRCLE
NORWAY
SWEDEN
FINLAND
Luleå
Gulf of Bothnia
Trondhjem
Bergen
Christiania
Dannemora
L. Wenner
GÖTA CANAL
L. Wetter
Stockholm
Helsingfors
Gulf of Finland
Reval
ESTHONIA
Skagerrack
Kattegat
Gothenburg
Jönköping
DENMARK
COPENHAGEN
BALTIC SEA
Riga
LATVIA
LITHUANIA

ARCTIC OCEAN
North C.
Vardö
MURMANSK COAST
ARCTIC CIRCLE
White Sea
Archangel
Dwina R.
Pechora R.
Ural R.
URAL MTS.
FINLAND
Luleå
G. of Bothnia
Onega
L. Ladoga
L. Onega
Helsingfors
Petrograd
Valdai Hills
Moscow
Nizhni Novgorod
Kazan
Oka R.
Volga R.
Tver
Riga
LATVIA
LITHUANIA
Vilna
Tula
RUSSIA
BALTIC SEA
FREE STATE OF DANZIG
POLAND
Lodz
Warsaw
Lemberg
Kiev
UKR.
Dnieper R.
Donetz R.
Don R.
Odessa
Sea of Azov
CRIMEA
Astrakhan
Volga R.
CZECHO-SLOVAKIA
Carpathian Mts.
HUNGARY
RUMANIA
BUCHAREST
Danube
SOPHIA
BULGARIA
JUGOSLAVIA
GREECE
CONSTANTINOPLE
BLACK SEA
Trebizond
CAUCASUS MTS.
Mt. Elbruz
TRANSCAUCASIA
Baku
CASPIAN SEA
AUST.

Piles were driven, foundations were laid, and houses were built. Workmen died by the hundreds and by the thousands, but more were brought from other parts of the country, and the work went on. There were no masons to build the houses. An order from Peter, and all stonework and brickwork over the entire kingdom stopped. Masons everywhere could find no work; and so they flocked to Petrograd, and the buildings grew like magic. In one year, thirty thousand houses were built in the city, and one hundred thousand workmen died.

Once more the nobles objected, "There are no people for your city." "I will bring them!" declared Peter. And he did. Whole families, whole towns, were ordered to take their goods and live in the emperor's new capital. Peter himself defied the unhealthy climate and built his palace there. All court functions and festivities were held there, and the nobles and officers of the court were obliged, therefore, to reside in the city. Thus, Petrograd grew and flourished. Today, it is the second-largest city of Russia, but it is no longer the capital, for during the World War, the seat of government was changed to Moscow.

The houses in Petrograd are built chiefly of brick or rubble, often covered with stucco and showily decorated. The streets are broad and straight, and the finest of all is the Nevsky Prospekt. It is broad, straight, and well-paved. The electric cars occupy the middle of it, and on either side, there are spaces for private carriages, while beyond these limits, public carriages and heavy teams may drive.

A walk down the

© Underwood & Underwood

FIG. 48. "A WALK DOWN THE NEVSKY PROSPEKT FURNISHES PLENTY OF ENTERTAINMENT"

Nevsky Prospekt provides plenty of entertainment. Crowds of people of so many different nationalities throng the sidewalks that a secret whispered in any language would hardly be safe. On either side of the street are shops with fascinating windows. Here is one showing beautiful jewelry and glittering gems of all colors and sizes. Beyond the Ural Mountains in Siberia are regions very rich in precious stones, and many of those displayed here have come from places thousands of miles away.

In the next store, there is a magnificent display of furs — rich, brown sables worth almost their weight in gold; black fox, soft and fine as feathers; white, curly, Tibetan goat; velvety otter; heavy bearskins, wolfskins, and warm, serviceable reindeer skins. The houses in Petrograd are kept very warm, and people do not wear heavy clothing indoors. When they go out, however, into the biting cold, thick clothing and warm furs are a necessity and are sometimes worn as late as May.

There are many market gardens around Petrograd which supply the city with delicious summer vegetables and fruits — strawberries, raspberries, plums, gooseberries, and currants. Mushrooms are eaten in great quantities in Russia, and a special dainty of the peasants is a fresh cucumber covered with honey. Country housewives have many ways of preserving fruits and vegetables. Were it not for this, their food during the long winter would be very monotonous.

It would seem quite strange to us to buy milk in a solid block. Not so to the children of Petrograd, for during the winter, many of the provisions, including milk, are kept frozen. The fish market, too, with its piles of frozen fish, is interesting, and we wish we might hear some of the thrilling stories of storms and suffering which that weather-beaten fisherman from Archangel, at yonder stall, might tell us.

Though the cold is intense, it is in the winter that you would most enjoy Petrograd. The houses have walls two or three feet thick, and double windows which are seldom opened.

A huge stove made of clay or brick and reaching nearly to the ceiling is commonly used. It is generally built into the wall so that it projects into the rooms on either side and warms both of them. A great fire is built, and when the wood has burned down to a pile of coals, the drafts are shut, and the walls of the stove become hot enough to keep the high-ceilinged rooms warm for twenty-four hours or longer.

You would not care to spend your time inside the house in Petrograd, even though it is so very cold outside. Low sleighs, carrying people wrapped up to their noses in furs, are dashing hither and thither through the streets. The Russian drivers never go slowly but urge their willing horses until we hold our breath for fear of an accident.

Notice in the picture below the peculiar wooden arch over the horse. The duga, as it is called, is fastened to the ends of the shafts and is used on all Russian teams. Three horses are often driven abreast, as you see in the picture. The middle one is trained to trot, while the outside ones usually gallop.

The canal leading from Petrograd to Kronstadt, which is twenty-five miles away, is frozen over for several months each year. A roadway for teams is marked on it by a row of evergreen trees fastened in the ice on either side. As the horses dash down this frozen highway between the green trees, it seems as if it

FIG. 49. THE MIDDLE HORSE IS TRAINED TO TROT, WHILE THE OFFSIDE ONES USUALLY GALLOP (Courtesy of Mr. B. E. Baker, Boston)

were Christmas time, and that this must be the place where Christmas trees for all the world are sold.

In the summer, ferryboats ply from one shore of the Neva River to the other. However, in the winter, passengers are taken across in chairs furnished with warm robes. These chairs are propelled by skaters, who push one swiftly across the river for less than a penny.

It is fascinating to watch the skaters in the skating gardens on the canal. Have you ever seen such graceful figures? Every one, old and young, knows how to skate, for the winter is so long that there is plenty of time for practice.

The boys and girls have great fun making snow houses, which they people with snow boys and girls. Water poured over them freezes them into solid statues, which remain as playthings for the children for several months.

Throughout almost its entire area, Russia is one vast plain. The Ural Mountains, which form the backbone of the country, divide it from Siberia, and the lofty Caucasus lie near its southern border. Nowhere else within its vast boundaries, from the Arctic Ocean to the Black Sea and from the Caspian to the Baltic, are there mountains worthy of the name. The only exceptions to this are the Valdai Hills in the west-central part of the country, the highest of which are only about a thousand feet. These hills serve as the center where many of the rivers of Russia have their source. Winding southward through forests or through fields of wheat, rye, potatoes, and blue-eyed flax, or making their way slowly toward the desolate Arctic waters, are the Volga, Don, Dnieper, Dvina, Onega, and many smaller streams, all of which — through the means of communication they furnish and the commerce they facilitate — give union and strength to this great country. These long, navigable rivers serve as the best roads in Russia. Many canals connect these rivers and their branches, so that it is possible to travel by water from the White Sea to the Caspian, or from the Baltic to the Black Sea.

The northward-bound rivers flow for hundreds of miles through forests of dark pines, where the gloomy shades are lightened by clusters of silvery birch. In the regions farther

FIG. 50. WE ARE SURPRISED TO FIND IN A LATITUDE AS FAR NORTH AS
THE KLONDIKE REGION IN CANADA THE PORT OF ARCHANGEL

north, the trees become smaller and smaller until only a stunted
growth dots the wide plain, which stretches, bare of all vegeta-
tion, to the lonely Arctic Sea. The rivers wind slowly through the
desolate frozen marshes, or tundras, until they lose themselves
in the northern ocean.

We do not expect to see cities and towns in such a region,
and we are somewhat surprised to find at the mouth of the
Dwina River, in a latitude as far north as the Klondike region
in Canada, the port of Archangel, a city of twenty thousand or
more inhabitants. For many weeks in winter, the sun cheers the
lonely town for only a few hours each day, but the bright moon,
the glittering stars, and the gleaming northern lights make the
long nights radiant.

In the Dwina River, during the few months that it is open,
you would see great rafts of lumber, which have come from the
forests hundreds of miles away to the south. This lumber may
later be found in the shipyards on the Clyde River or at some
lumber wharf on the Thames. Before Petrograd was built, much
more lumber, fish, wheat, flax, and hemp were sent to England
and other places by way of Archangel than is sent now.

We are glad to leave these desolate regions behind us and
follow the river southward toward the great forests. These forests stretch through central Russia, from the Baltic Sea to the
Ural Mountains, and cover nearly half of the country — an area

FIG. 51. "RUSSIAN VILLAGES ARE ALL VERY SIMILAR IN APPEARANCE"
(Courtesy of Mr. B. E. Baker, Boston)

large enough to include California, Nevada, Utah, Arizona, New Mexico, and Texas.

There are few real roads through the forests, only open spaces where one may drive for hours and days and even weeks without reaching the open plain. Perhaps you have seen pictures or read stories of travelers through the woods being attacked by wolves. This is not uncommon, for the wolves and bears sometimes become fierce from hunger and attack cattle in nearby farmyards, or even children from some of the villages on the outskirts of the forest.

In a visit to one of these villages, we should probably find at home only the very old people, the women, and the children, for the men are away cutting timber in the forests, fishing in the polar seas, or trapping in the deep woods. Russian villages are all very similar in appearance, and having seen one, we will know what most of them are like.

In the forested area, the little one-story houses of one or two rooms are made of logs or rough boards plugged with moss, and they have wooden roofs. In the southern plains, far away from the forests, the cottages are usually made of clay, brick, or stone, and the roofs are thatched with straw. Three small windows, with their frames painted red or green, are in the

FIG. 52. "THE LITTLE ONE-STORY HOUSES OF ONE OR TWO ROOMS
ARE MADE OF LOGS" (Courtesy of Mr. B. E. Baker, Boston)

front, and the door, reached through a yard littered with farming
tools, chickens, and pigs, is on the side. Each house has near it a
wattled shed for fodder and stores or for shelter for the animals.
In the coldest weather, the cow and horse are often taken into
the house for warmth and occupy one of the two rooms. In the
very poorest houses, the family and animals sometimes live in
the same room during the coldest part of the winter.

Our eyes gradually become accustomed to the dim light
of the room in which we are standing, and we look curiously
around. There is very little furniture. A bench extends around
three sides of the room against the wall; two or three rough
chairs, and a rude table on which are a few wooden bowls
and spoons, occupy most of the space. A loom stands near
the window and shows signs of hard use, for in the villages
far from towns and cities, most of the coarse cloth used for
clothing is woven by hand.

The stove interests us more than any other piece of furniture.
It is a huge, clumsy affair, reaching nearly to the ceiling and
occupying one-quarter of the whole apartment. The cooking
is done by placing the pots among the glowing coals after the

FIG. 53. NEAR THE HOUSE IS A WATTLED SHED FOR FODDER AND STORES
OR FOR SHELTER FOR THE ANIMALS (Courtesy of Mr. B. E. Baker, Boston)

roaring wood fire has burned down. The coarse, dark rye bread
is baked after the coals are raked out.

These Russian boys and girls would be very much surprised
at our food and astonished at the many different kinds of things
which we eat. They have little besides their black bread, cabbage
soup, and perhaps a piece of dried or salted fish. How would you
like black bread spread with sunflower oil for your supper, or
sunflower seeds to eat instead of peanuts? You have probably
never seen a sunflower farm, but to the Russian children, these
farms are familiar sights, for thousands of acres are covered with
the tall waving plant and the big sunny blossoms.

The little village which we are describing consists of thirty
or forty houses, a small church, and a two-story building which
contains a store. The houses are all similar to the one which
has been described, and they stand in two long rows along the
wide street — if such it can be called. It is frozen in deep ruts in
the winter, ankle-deep in dust in the summer, and is well-nigh
impassable because of the mud in spring and fall.

Whether our journey takes us into the forested area of Russia,
or into the treeless, fertile "black-earth" region farther south,
or into the more arid lands to the southeast, we will find villages similar to the one described. The muddy or dusty streets,
the rows of houses on either side with the windows facing
their opposite neighbors, the littered farmyards, and the wide,

spreading plain around, with its cultivated fields and pasture lands, can be found in thousands of Russian villages. In no other country in the world, probably, is there such a similarity of life over such a wide area.

Of course, there are in Russia people who live in a different fashion; but nearly all of the population is made up of these peasants, whose life you have just read about. Someone has said, "The Russian peasant is the Russian nation. He tills the fields, fills the factories, consumes the tea, pays the taxes, equips the army, fights the battles, mans the ships; he holds in his breast the destiny of the Slav race."

Lumbering in Russia is carried on in much the same way as it is in our country, except that it is done for the most part without the aid of machinery. The men have their logging camps, river piles, log jams, log rafts, and river drivers, all much the same as in the United States. Nearly every stream flowing from the lumber region carries with it its share of the lumber harvest. One can hear the shouts of the men as they break the jam or the scream of saws in the busy mills, just as in Maine, Minnesota, or Washington.

Some one has said, "What coal is to Great Britain, the forests are to Russia." If the wood which is cut every year were sawed

FIG. 54. RUSSIAN PEASANTS (Courtesy of Mr. B. E. Baker, Boston)

into four-foot lengths and stacked up four feet high, the pile would extend more than eighty-two thousand miles, or nearly three and one-half times around the earth at the equator. Most of this wood is used in Russia alone. What a great variety of articles, and what enormous quantities of them, may be made from it! Of course, an immense amount is used for fuel, as coal is unknown throughout the greater part of Russia, and the huge stoves need ample fuel during the long, cold winter. Then, too, as in Sweden, much of the smelting of iron is done with charcoal instead of coal or coke, and as a consequence, a very superior quality of iron is produced.

Another use of charcoal is for making tea. Russians are great tea drinkers and consume nearly one-fourth of all the tea raised in the world. Tea is usually made in a samovar. This peculiarly Russian dish is of brass or copper. In the center of it is a cylinder filled with burning charcoal, and around this is a space for the water, which is thus always kept hot and ready for use.

The Russians are skillful workers and make out of wood nearly everything one can think of. Each village has its specialty, at which the men, between harvests or in the winter, work in groups of half a dozen or more. In one village, barrels are made; in another, spoons, tubs, chairs, spinning wheels, sledges, or pails; or, perhaps, dugas, the arches which are worn over the horses' heads. Sometimes different parts of the same article are made in different hamlets. For instance, in the case of wheels, one village makes the hubs, another the spokes, and a third the rims.

It is said that even if all the many great factories of Russia were closed, the thousands of peasants in the little villages far from the railroad would not be inconvenienced, for most of the articles used by them in their simple lives are made not in the factories, but in the hamlets and towns by the peasants themselves. Not only wooden articles are made, but those of metals and fibers — cotton, hemp, flax, and silk. Around Nizhni Novgorod, fifty or more villages are engaged in making hemp fishing nets. Thousands of families dress hides and skins and prepare sheepskin for clothing.

FIG. 55. GREAT QUANTITIES OF THE PRODUCTS OF THE FACTORIES
AND HOUSEHOLDS ARE SHIPPED DOWN THE VOLGA RIVER

Great quantities of the products of the factories and the busy households are shipped down the Volga River, for through this important water route, Russia furnishes many necessary supplies not only to her own people on the plains of the south but also to the people of Siberia, Turkestan, and other countries of western and central Asia.

A voyage on this largest of all European rivers is very interesting. We pass huge rafts of lumber, as high as a house, floating down to the treeless regions of the south. On each is a rough log hut in which the rivermen live, for a trip from the forest region to the Caspian Sea on such slow craft takes some weeks.

Should we examine the cargoes of some of the vessels which glide slowly along with the current, we should find a greater variety of wooden articles than we ever saw before. There seems to be everything on board — from bowls and spoons, chairs and tables, to ready-made houses. Some of these things may be found later in the cottages on the southern plains, and some will be used by the people in far-away Bokhara, Persia, and Turkestan.

Ships loaded heavily with corn, oats, rye, barley, and other grains drift slowly down the great river to furnish food to the animals and people in the barren regions of the southeast. Cargoes of flax will supply the material for Russian blouses, Persian robes, and Turkish garments. There are barges of cattle, which gaze calmly at their four-footed relatives on the shore, and boats laden with rich furs from the wealth of animal life in the forest belt.

Even more interesting are the craft ascending the river. We meet many barges loaded with petroleum from the oil fields of Baku, an interesting place situated on the western shore of the Caspian Sea. This region is one of the greatest oil-producing areas of the world. Wheat from the "black-earth" region is carried up the Volga and thence by canal to Petrograd, or even to Archangel, whence it is shipped to other countries. There are loads of salt from the barren steppes, and cargoes of furs and skins from the plains in the southeast and from Siberia, Persia, and Turkestan. Among them are great piles of coltskins, many of which will be shipped from Petrograd or Riga to the shoe factories in the United States. There are also pony skins, which will follow the same route to our country and will be made up into fur coats.

Little Mother Volga, as the Russians call the river, is about as long, as placid, and as majestic as our great Mississippi. Notice on the map the sharp turn in its lower course, where it bends abruptly to the east. A layer of hard rock lay in its way, causing it to flow toward the southeast and into the landlocked Caspian rather than into the Black Sea. The river is therefore

FIG. 56. RUSSIAN PEASANT
ON A VOLGA BOAT

of less importance commercially, as all the goods destined for ocean freight have to be taken by railroad across to the Don River, just at the place where the two streams come the nearest together. Sometime a canal may connect them at this point so that goods can be taken from one river to the other without unloading. Notwithstanding its disadvantage in flowing into a landlocked sea, much more traffic is carried on the Volga than on any other Russian river.

As we near the lower Volga, we see many fishing boats, and we pass ships going north, loaded with quantities of isinglass, dried and salted fish, and a delicacy known as caviar, which is made from the eggs of the sturgeon. The lower Volga and the Caspian Sea are among the most important fishing grounds of the world, and the yield of these waters is worth more than that of Norway and Newfoundland put together.

Astrakhan, situated about twenty-five miles from the mouth of the Volga, is very attractive when seen from the water. The tall, slender minarets of numerous mosques gleam among the cupolas and domes of its many churches. In the outskirts are neat-looking vineyards and flourishing fruit and vegetable gardens, where grow the ever-present cucumber and delicious watermelons. But if you wish to hold the illusion that Astrakhan is an interesting city, do not enter it. "An ancient and fishlike smell" fills the place, while dust and dirt and badly paved streets do not invite one to a long stay.

Of all its cities, Moscow, the capital of Russia, is the most interesting to visitors, for, removed as it is from foreign influences, it is more purely Russian than are the coast cities. If Petrograd is the eye of Russia, Moscow is the heart. It is situated almost in the center of the great country on the little river Moskva, which, though navigable for small vessels only, gives the city, through its canal connections, water communication with the Black, Caspian, and Baltic seas and with the Atlantic Ocean. Moscow is the chief railroad center of Russia, and all main routes converge here. From the great white railroad station, one may start over the Trans-Siberian Railroad on a two- or three-week journey to far-away Vladivostok on the Pacific coast.

© Underwood & Underwood

FIG. 57. THE TALL TOWER OF IVAN THE TERRIBLE AND THE GREAT BELL AT ITS BASE

A view of Moscow from an airship would be most interesting. Mixed with the foliage of the many trees and the varied colors of the houses, rise hundreds of towers and domes, brilliant in gilt, spangled with stars, or blue as the sky above. Great chimneys, rivaling in number the domes and towers, pour forth their dark clouds of smoke. Around the city stretches an ancient wall, twenty-six miles long, useless now for purposes of defense. In the center of the city, we can see, in the shape of a triangle, a higher wall broken by great towers and massive gates, some of which date back to a time before the discovery of America. Within the enclosure are many buildings—the cathedral where the czars of the great empire have been crowned, the royal palace where they lived, other churches and palaces, and the tall tower of Ivan the Terrible, a former ruler of Russia, whose character may be imagined from the title given to him by his subjects. In the tower hangs the largest bell which has ever been rung in the whole world, and at the base stands a much larger one, the Great Bell of Moscow, as it is usually called. This bell has never been hung or rung. While it was being raised to the tower, it fell, and a great piece was broken out of the side, making a hole so large that a person much taller than you might walk through it without bending his head. Moscow is a city of bells. All of its four hundred churches contain several, and some of them are ringing most of the time.

This collection of churches, palaces, monasteries, towers, and fortifications is called the Kremlin. Every Russian city has one, but the Kremlin of Moscow is the most celebrated.

Let us alight from our airship and explore those parts of the city where the great chimneys are thickest. In ordinary years, Petrograd ranks first among Russian cities in commerce, while Moscow leads in manufacturing and population. There are nearly fifteen hundred factories in the city, among them many large silk, woolen, and cotton mills. The situation of Moscow, in the most thickly populated part of the country, and its railroad and water connections all help in the development of trade and manufacture.

There are cotton and woolen factories in the city in which the machinery is as modern as that which may be found in the mills of Manchester, England, or in Lowell, Lawrence, or Fall River, Massachusetts. There are large factories, too, where very beautiful silks and velvets are made. There are also sugar refineries, for the neighboring farmers raise great quantities of sugar beets. Those long, low buildings with the sparks flying from the chimneys are iron foundries, rolling mills, and other establishments for the manufacture of iron and steel, for rich iron and coal deposits lie not far from Moscow. Tula, situated about a hundred miles farther south, manufactures many articles of iron and steel, and is sometimes called the Sheffield of Russia.

The leather industry of Russia is very important. In spite of the enormous production of hides and skins, many of which are exported to other countries, Russia imports, for home manufacture, in ordinary years, millions of dollars' worth, chiefly from Germany and other countries of Central Europe, France, the British Isles, and Persia. Perhaps some of you may own a pocketbook or a cardcase made of the so-called Russia leather, which has such an agreeable odor. The smell is given to the leather by the birch oil and bark which are used in the tanning process.

Many years ago, before the time of canals and railroads, merchants and producers carried their goods miles and even hundreds of miles overland or by river to great centers, where they were sold or exchanged for other merchandise. There were many such markets in olden times, in both Europe and Asia, where large fairs were held, and in some places, the custom still prevails.

Of all these cities, Nizhni Novgorod is to-day the most important. Its situation at the junction of the Volga and Oka rivers is similar to that of Lyon on the Saône and Rhône, or of St. Louis near the meeting place of the Mississippi and the Missouri, the influence of the two navigable rivers in each case contributing to the importance of the city.

For the greater part of the year, Nizhni Novgorod is a city about the size of Albany, the capital of New York State; but for six weeks every summer, it is more than twice the size of that city, and contains more goods for sale than a great many large cities put together. During the time that the fair lasts, one can meet in the streets of Nizhni, merchants from all over Russia, as well as turbaned Turks, swarthy Armenians, slant-eyed Chinese, dark-skinned people of India, tall Persians, vivacious Frenchmen, light-haired Germans, dignified Englishmen, and businesslike representatives from the great firms of the United States.

The wholesale merchant asks more for his goods than they are worth; the customer offers less than he knows he will have

FIG. 58. SHEEPSKINS AND GOATSKINS FROM SOUTHEASTERN RUSSIA AND THE NEIGHBORING PARTS OF WESTERN ASIA BEING UNLOADED ON THE SANDS AT NIZHNI NOVGOROD (Courtesy of Mr. B. E. Baker, Boston)

to pay. After much discussion, during which many cups of the ever-present tea are consumed, a bargain is made in which both parties are satisfied. In many cases, the amount paid for goods at the fair decides their price for the coming year all over the world.

As we stroll through the streets, we are astonished at the amount of merchandise. We certainly never saw so much in one place before. The wharves are piled high with iron from the rich Donetz valley to the south; the granaries near the river are filled with wheat from the fertile, "black-earth" region, oats from the north, and rye from all over the kingdom. The streets in that part of the town where the fair is held are laid out at right angles, and each one has its own particular article for sale. The fur exhibits are especially interesting. One finds piles of bear, wolf, and fox skins from the Far North; sable, marten, and ermine from Siberia; otter from the peninsula of Kamchatka; and beaver from the streams of Canada. There are pony furs

FIG. 59. "THERE ARE HUNDREDS OF BELLS OF ALL SIZES AND TONES"

and colt, sheep, and goat skins from the plains in southeastern Russia and in the neighboring parts of Asia, and great piles of soft lambskins which have been brought overland from Asia to the Caspian Sea and shipped up the Volga from Astrakhan.

We are amazed at the quantity of tea which is displayed in Chinatown. Many merchants buy at the fair their supply for the entire year, which, because of the tea-drinking habits of many of the Russians, has to be a generous one. Some of the tea has been brought by water from Canton, China, but great quantities have come on the long trip overland from Kiakhta, a journey of more than a year.

There are piles of beautiful rugs from Persia, millions of yards

© H. C. White, No. Bennington, Vt.
FIG. 60. CLOTH MARKET, NIZHNI NOVGOROD

of silk, cotton, linen, and woolen goods from the factories in great Russian cities, and rolls of hand-woven linen crash from the homes of the peasants.

There are many tons of dried and salted fish from Archangel and Astrakhan; there are hundreds of bells of all sizes and tones which will later, in scores of towns and cities, call the peasants to worship; there are thousands of samovars, the making of which has kept whole villages busy for months. In one province of Russia alone, the people make annually more than forty thousand of these dishes.

The stores where jewelry and precious stones are for sale are extremely fascinating. From beyond the Ural Mountains have come glowing rubies, deep-yellow topazes, rich red garnets, and sapphires blue as the skies. Then there are metals, wonderful enamel work on silver, and arms and cutlery from Russian workshops. There are barrels of sugar from Far Eastern countries, and gaudily painted chests which country merchants will buy to pack their goods in and then sell to peasants to store clothes in. There are laces and ribbons and silks from France and Germany, perfumes from France, gems from India — in short, everything that one can think of to eat, drink, wear, or use is here displayed. The goods are not sold by sample, but are bought, packed, loaded, and shipped during the few weeks that the fair is in progress. The Volga is full of steamers and barges, and the railroad station is piled high with freight.

The bustle, noise, and confusion last until about the middle of September, when the city settles down into its usual sleepy condition, from which it is roused again the following summer by the arrival of the crowd.

Russia is an immense country containing millions of people. For many years, the peasants were serfs or slaves. An edict from the Czar in 1861 abolished slavery, but though freed from their masters, the mass of the people have been ever since the slaves of ignorance and, therefore, nearly as helpless as they were before. The ruling classes have done little to educate and uplift the peasants, but, on the other hand, have tried in every way to keep them in ignorance and poverty. They have made unjust laws which increased the wealth and power of the officials and nobles but which made the life of the peasants harder.

For some years during and after the World War, Russia was in a state of revolution. The peasants realized more fully than ever before the injustice and oppression under which they were living and made an effort to change their condition and make such things impossible in the future. Led by dreamers and visionaries, they began to look forward to a wonderful change of conditions, to a time when all classes of people should be equal, when there should be no rich and no poor, no crime, no greed, no poverty and hunger, no "bosses or overseers or proprietors." The people were to own everything and run everything. Just how mills and factories were to run with no owners, with no responsible person at the head of affairs, this great child nation was not sure. But everything would come out all right. Surely nothing would be as bad as it had been. They were free. Nothing else mattered much. The excited mobs did not realize that they were bound just as surely by the bonds of ignorance, prejudice, superstition, and lack of experience as they had been by the old chains of slavery. They did not know the best ways of carrying on this great work of uplifting the people and developing the country, nor did they have wise leaders to help them.

Russia has had the sympathy of the whole world in her struggle, and all civilized nations have wished to help her. The difficulty has been in knowing how to do it. Soldiers and armies would be of but little use, for the mass of the people would look upon them as enemies come to make their state worse rather than better. Other nations can best aid poor Russia by helping her to develop her industries, to increase her commerce, to improve her methods of farming, and above all, to build up her system of education. Knowledge is power. Russia needs schools for the common people, and also wise teachers and honest rulers. When she possesses these things, we shall see a tremendous development in this great Slav nation.

UKRAINE

In southwestern Russia is the region known as Ukraine. The people who live here are often called "Little Russians," in contrast with the "Great Russians" of the Moscow and Petrograd regions.

The surface of Ukraine is, like most of Russia, a wide-stretching plain. The great forest region of Russia lies farther north, and these southern plains are treeless and, where uncultivated, are covered with tall grass.

In a trip through Ukraine, we shall find the same monotonous level land, the same desolate-appearing villages, and the same primitive ways of life that prevail in the rest of Russia. Yet this

FIG. 61. "ODESSA IS THE GREATEST WHEAT PORT IN THE WORLD"
From "World's Commercial Products"

is one of the richest parts of Europe. So fertile is the soil that, even with the backward methods of agriculture which are common among the people, large crops are produced.

Ukraine includes most of the famous "black-earth" region, where grain is such an important crop. Russia is one of the most important wheat-producing countries of the earth. A freight train long enough to carry the crop would reach from Boston to San Francisco. Much of this great crop is raised in Ukraine.

Thousands of peasants from the little villages dotting the great plain plow the rich soil with a small homemade plow which just scratches the top of the ground they sow, reap, and thresh the grain by hand, and draw it in their small wagons or low sleds for long distances to the nearest railroad station, canal, or river, whence it is shipped to Riga, Petrograd, or other ports, but chiefly to Odessa. The peasants reserve but little for themselves, as the coarse, dark bread which is one of their chief articles of food is made largely from rye.

The villages and towns in which the peasants live are separated from one another by great distances. Each one is sure to be located by some meandering stream where the villagers can find water for their flocks and herds in case of drought. As one approaches one of these villages, he can see, while yet a long way off, the church towering above the little low houses, and the gray old windmills waving their arms in the breeze. Around the windmills are the wagons of the farmers who have come from miles away bringing their grain to the mill to be ground. As soon as they receive their grist, they will start on their long homeward journey to some little village far out on the great plain.

The rich soil is not the only resource of Ukraine. The celebrated Donetz coal fields, which are among the richest in Europe, are in this region. Much of the coal used in Russian factories comes from these Donetz mines. Iron too is found, as well as copper and mercury.

Find on your maps the city of Kiev, once the capital of all Russia and now an important city of Ukraine. It is a holy city, and hundreds of thousands of pilgrims with staves in

© Underwood & Underwood

FIG. 62. GREAT STAIRCASE, ODESSA

their hands and wallets on their backs visit it annually. So much does this pilgrimage mean to these poor people that they will travel on foot for days and spend their last penny for the sake of visiting this holy place.

As the legend runs, a thousand years ago, a very holy monk came to Kiev and made his home in a cave. Other holy men followed him and made their homes in caves. Many of them, it is said, never came out again into the daylight, but lived on the food left at the entrance by brother monks. When the food remained where it was placed, it was known that the cave monk had died and his niche was then walled up. It is these tombs that the pilgrims come to visit.

Odessa is the greatest wheat port in the world. It is situated on a high bluff, on the edge of which is a fine boulevard overlooking the water. The great stone buildings, the wide streets, the public squares, the fine railroad station, the electric cars and lights, all tell us that Odessa is a modern city. Near the water are large flour mills, oil mills, sugar refineries, soap works, tanneries, and other factories, which show that it is a manufacturing center as well as a commercial port.

In the harbor, which is finely protected by strong forts, there are vessels from many countries, bringing to the city coal, tea, fruits, agricultural implements, machinery, iron and steel, and raw cotton. They reload with fish, timber, oil, flour, leather, sugar, and other products and manufactures. But they carry greater quantities of wheat than of anything else — wheat for the macaroni makers of Italy, for the silk weavers of France, for the factory hands of England.

TOPICS FOR STUDY

I

1. Route from Lisbon to Petrograd.
2. Russian ports on the Baltic Sea.
3. Kronstadt and Petrograd.
4. Winter sports in Russia.
5. Surface and drainage of Russia.
6. The port of Archangel.
7. Description of a Russian village.
8. Description of a peasant's home.
9. Forests of Russia.
10. Lumbering in Russia.
11. Household industries.
12. A trip down the Volga River to Astrakhan.
13. Kiev and Odessa.
14. The old city of Moscow.
15. Nizhni Novgorod and its great fair.
16. Ukraine.

II

1. Sketch a map of Russia and show in it:
    (a) The forest region
    (b) The "black-earth" region and Ukraine
    (c) The Valdai Hills and the chief rivers which have their source in them
    (d) All the cities mentioned in the text
    (e) All the mountains mentioned in the text
2. Sketch a map of Germany and Denmark and show in it:
    (a) The North and Baltic Seas
    (b) The Skagerrack and Kattegat
    (c) The Kiel Canal
3. See if you can find any further facts about the life of Peter the Great.

4. Name the three greatest oil-producing countries of the world.

5. Write a list of all the products of Russia that you know.

6. Why is Tula called the "Sheffield of Russia"? Where is Sheffield? What does it manufacture?

7. Write a list of all the kinds of furs, hides, and skins produced in Russian lands.

8. Write a list of articles sold at the great fair of Nizhni Novgorod. Tell where each was produced and the route followed in bringing it to Nizhni.

9. Write as many differences as you can between the life of an American and a Russian.

10. Write a list of all the likenesses that you can think of between the Volga and the Mississippi River; the differences.

III

Be able to spell and pronounce the following names. Locate each place and tell what was said about it in this and in any previous chapter. Add other facts if possible:

Albany	India	Klondike
"Black-earth"	Italy	Maine
region	Kamchatka	Manchester
Arizona	Reval	Massachusetts
Armenia	Riga	Minnesota
Bokhara	St. Louis	Nevada
British Isles	San Francisco	Newfoundland
California	Sheffield	New Mexico
Canada	Tula	Norway
Central Europe	Vladivostok	Persia
China	Caucasus	Portugal
Denmark	Mountains	Siberia
England	Ural Mountains	Sweden
France	Valdai Hills	Texas
Germany	Clyde River	Tibet
Great Britain	Dnieper River	Turkestan

Ukraine
Utah
Washington
Don River
Donetz River
Düna River
Dwina River
Mississippi
  River
Missouri River
Moskva River
Neva River
Oka River
Onega River
Rhône River
Saône River

Thames River
Volga River
Archangel
Astrakhan
Bakn
Canton
Fall River
Kiakhta
Kiev
Kronstadt
Lawrence
Lisbon
Lowell
Lyon
Manchester
Moscow

Nizhni
  Novgorod
Odessa
Petrograd
Baltic Sea
Black Sea
Caspian Sea
English Channel
Gulf of Finland
Kiel Canal
Kattegat
North Sea
Skaggerack
Strait of Dover
White Sea

CHAPTER IX

FINLAND AND LAPLAND

North and east of the arms of the Baltic Sea lies the country of Finland. It is, indeed, a "fen-land," a region of swamps, marshes, and lakes, of deep forests, short and cold winter days, and long, hot summer ones.

Finland is often called "The Land of a Thousand Lakes." In reality, there are probably five thousand or even ten thousand lakes, which would be closer to the actual number. In some parts of Finland, the lakes form a network, separated by deep forests and impassable marshes. This unique feature of its landscape has been a hindrance to the development of the country, but the patient, energetic Finn has gradually overcome these disadvantages by draining large areas of land and connecting the lakes with canals, thus forming continuous waterways that serve as the chief highways of the country. Villages and industries have sprung up in places once remote and inaccessible. Thanks to the canals and lakes, during the summer season, one can explore a large part of Finland, and in winter, it is possible to travel for many miles over their frozen surfaces. Some of the poorer people of southern Finland, where the lakes are the most numerous, find their chief occupation in fishing. Most of the rivers in Finland are unnavigable and are primarily used for water power and for transporting logs from the inland forests to the large sawmills near the sea.

From the earliest times, Finland had to fight against the desires of both Russia and Sweden to possess her territory. She was annexed, first by one and then by the other of these two countries, until, in 1808, she was permanently separated from

FIG. 63. THE WINTER SPORTS ARE VERY ENJOYABLE

Sweden and came under Russian rule. Since the World War, Finland has declared her independence from Russia.

Because of the rigorous climate in which they live, the Finns are a sturdy race. The winters in this northern land are long and hard, with very little sunshine. During December and January, there are days and weeks when the sun does not rise above the horizon, and the people in the northern part of the country live in perpetual twilight. Despite the short days and lack of sunlight, it is the winter season that the Finn loves the most.

The cold is not as severe as one might imagine, given the country's northerly position. This is due to the warmth brought by the Gulf Stream, which is carried to the continent by westerly winds. The weather is cold enough, however, to keep the country covered with a white frozen blanket of snow all winter long. This is the time for skating parties, gay sledge rides, and merrymaking on skis and snowshoes.

If you lived in Finland during the summer, you would scarcely know when to go to bed, for there are weeks when the sun barely dips below the horizon, and some nights, it can be seen at midnight as a low, red ball shining in the northern sky. Crops grow very quickly during the long hours of daylight, and although spring is late and frosts arrive early, considerable crops of grain and vegetables are raised.

Most of the people in Finland are farmers. The great glacier that once covered the country smoothed off the hills and dug the valley beds for the lakes, leaving behind many boulders on the land's surface. These do not make the farmer's work any easier. Much of the land is better suited for pasturage than for crop production, which is why dairying has become an important industry. Large quantities of butter are exported, and the Finnish product is considered as good as any made in other countries worldwide.

Finland has little natural wealth. The soil is not very rich, the climate is not favorable for agriculture, and the mineral wealth is limited. However, the water power of the rivers, sometimes referred to as "white coal," is more valuable than any deposits of black minerals found beneath the surface. Finland's forests are more valuable than any other natural resource. More than half of Finland is covered with trees, and the chief industries of the country are connected to them. Little coal is used, and the people would hardly know how to get by without wood for fuel. Thousands of men work in the forests, and dozens of sawmills, situated along swift streams and near waterfalls, operate using water

FIG. 64. DAIRYING IS AN IMPORTANT
OCCUPATION IN FINLAND
THE pails are full of milk

power. Lumber is produced and exported in large quantities. In connection with nearly all the sawmills, there are factories for making wood pulp, paper, cardboard, and other forest products.

We should not expect a country with few natural resources like Finland to have very extensive manufactures. Yet in some of the southern cities and towns, there are cotton and flour mills, tobacco and glass factories, machine shops, and other industries. In part of southwestern Finland, there are splendid granite quarries, and the cities present a more dignified appearance because many of the buildings are made from this material. Numerous bridges, monuments, and large buildings in Petrograd are constructed using Finnish granite.

Helsingfors, the capital of Finland, is a very attractive city in spite of the fact that its harbor is closed by ice from November to May. Pine-clad hills surround it, and the deep-blue sea, studded with green islands, makes a pleasing approach. As we walk

FIG. 65. HELSINGFORS IS A VERY ATTRACTIVE CITY

down the main boulevard and note the fine shops, handsome buildings, comfortable hotels, open-air restaurants, and listen to the music of the band, we can almost imagine ourselves in Paris or some other lively capital of a more southern country. Despite the short days and cold winters, Helsingfors is no less lively in winter than in summer.

Should you like to visit a Lapp village? You might enjoy it for a short time, but I am sure that you would not like to make a long stay, for neither the people nor their homes are very clean.

In the northern part of Finland, as in Norway, the only inhabitants are Lapps. They live in a barren, desolate region that is almost impassable in summer due to the deep forests, pathless swamps, and persistent mosquitoes. For a month or two during the summer season, the sun never sets below the horizon, and for an equal amount of time in winter, the people of Arctic Lapland never see it in the sky. Their only means of travel during the long summer days is by the network of lakes and rivers. During the dark winter days, their low, fur-filled sledges are drawn by reindeer across the vast, frozen wastes of untrodden snow. Near their villages, you might see large herds of reindeer, as a Lapp sometimes owns two or three thousand of these useful animals. A Lapp woman might be seen milking one of them, while a man holds it with a kind of lasso drawn tightly around the horns. Without reindeer, the Lapp could not survive in these cold Arctic lands. He relies on the animal for its skin and fur, which he uses to make his clothes, as well as for meat and milk for food. The reindeer also serve as a substitute for a horse and draw the low sledges over the snow at tremendous speeds.

Reindeer feed on Arctic moss, which often lies buried under several feet of snow. Using their horns and hooves, they dig away the snow to reach the moss, enabling them to survive where other animals would starve.

Some Lapps use reindeer skins to cover their tents, while others live in low stone huts with sod roofs. In the center of the hut or tent, a fire built on a circle of flat stones provides warmth, and above it, there is a hole in the roof through which the smoke

Fig. 66. "WERE IT NOT FOR THE REINDEER THE LAPP COULD NOT
LIVE IN THESE COLD ARCTIC LANDS"

escapes. The earth floor is covered with hay and spread with reindeer skins, on which the Lapps sit. On the floor, or leaning against the walls, there are cradles containing babies, of whom there are usually several in a Lapp house. Adding to the confusion and odor are the dogs, trained to assist their masters in guiding the reindeer herds, much like the shepherd dogs of Scotland herd sheep.

In their filthy snow huts in winter and skin tents in summer, living on reindeer meat and fish, these people of the Far North drag out a miserable existence that can hardly be called living. They cannot read or write and are not skilled in any form of handwork. All their strength and energy are concentrated on the effort to obtain food and clothing.

TOPICS FOR STUDY

I

1. The situation of Finland.

2. Surface and climate.

3. History of Finland.

4. Occupations of the people.

5. Resources of the region.

6. Forest industries.

7. Helsingfors, the capital.

8. Life of the Lapps.

II

1. Boundaries of Finland.
2. Find the latitude of Helsingfors. Through which one of the United States possessions does this parallel run?
3. The forests of Finland are part of the great wooded belt of Russia. What other great forests exist in the northern hemisphere around the same latitude?
4. Ship a cargo of lumber from Helsingfors to London. On which waters will the vessel sail?
5. How is Finland governed?
6. Hudson Bay is nearly the same latitude as Finland. Which place is colder? Why?

III

Be able to spell and pronounce the following names. Locate each place and describe what was said about it in this and any previous chapter. Add other facts if possible.

Finland	Russia	Helsingfors	Baltic Sea
Lapland	Scotland	Paris	Gulf Stream
Norway	Sweden	Petrograd	

CHAPTER X

SWEDEN AND HER FORESTS

Before we leave our study of the countries that are particularly noted for their forest products, let us go to Sweden. Like Finland, Sweden contains numerous bodies of water, and it is often called the "Land of the Three Thousand Lakes."

We sail from Helsingfors through the Gulf of Finland and across the open Baltic Sea. Then, for many miles, we steam through the winding passages between the islands on the eastern coast of the peninsula. The water is a deep blue, and the islands are green with grass and are shaded by beautiful trees, behind which peep many charming country houses, the summer homes of people from Stockholm. Small steamers dart from island to island, sailboats show their white wings, and lumber boats steam slowly southward, laden heavily with the products of the northern forests. A writer has said:

"Some cities are situated like Berlin on a plain, others like Edinburgh on hills, others like Copenhagen on islands. Stockholm unites all three. Parts lie on the islands, parts on the rocky hills several hundred feet high, and parts are as level as a prairie. In nearly every direction, water, interspersed with islands, lies around it."

Stockholm has been called the Venice of the North, but it is even more attractive than its southern sister. The wide streets, the splendid stone buildings, and the many bridges connecting the islands with one another and with the mainland add greatly to its beauty.

The oldest part of the city, with its irregular streets and quaint buildings, is situated chiefly on two or three islands. The newer portion occupies others. Ship Island is the headquarters

FIG. 67. "STOCKHOLM HAS BEEN CALLED THE VENICE OF THE NORTH"

for a part of the Swedish navy and contains shipbuilding yards and marine repair shops. In a part of the old city, situated on another island, is the royal palace, one of the finest buildings in Europe. We should have difficulty in finding our way in it without a guide, for it contains more than eight hundred rooms. On other islands are the zoological gardens, parks, and pleasure grounds.

The hills around Stockholm afford many fine views. One can ascend to the heights by means of the zigzag streets, flights of steps, or elevators. We take the Katrina elevator, which, for a penny, lifts us high above the tops of the buildings on the plain and allows us to look down in wonder at the scene spread out below us.

Nearly forty miles away to the east is the blue Baltic Sea, while between it and the city are hundreds of islands set in the clear blue water. To the west is Lake Mälar, with its thousand and more islands dotted with beautiful mansions and smaller summer homes. Where the waters of the lake enter the bay of the Baltic Sea lies Stockholm, gleaming in white and yellow at our feet. Away to the north, we can see the smoke of a freight train drawing its heavy load from the rich iron region, the streams and highways of which converge toward the city. In the harbor,

© Underwood & Underwood

FIG. 68. THE KATRINA ELEVATOR LIFTS US
HIGH ABOVE THE TOPS OF THE BUILDINGS

there are vessels bound for different countries, waiting for their cargoes of iron and steel.

Leaving the beautiful view, we reluctantly descend from the heights and take a train from Stockholm, heading northward toward the great forests. On our way, we shall pass through the iron region of Dannemora, from which the freight train we saw was crawling southward. The deposits of Dannemora are very famous, and iron of a quality that has made the Swedish product known over the whole world has been mined there for many years.

Everything around seems smoky and dirty, not clean, fresh, and beautiful as we had imagined Sweden to be. As we continue our ride, however, the country justifies all our expectations. Though the scenery is not so grand as that of Norway, it is, in a different way, equally beautiful. There are fresh green fields dotted with farms, and groves of oak, beech, and fragrant pines. There are dashing streams, sparkling waterfalls, and clear blue lakes, whose deep waters are studded with islands and whose green shores are brightened with dull-red cottages.

The best farms are found in the southern part of the country on the fertile plains, and the rich iron deposits are in the south-central part, just north of the region where the lakes are largest and most numerous. In recent years, still richer seams have been discovered in the extreme northern portion. Thousands of tons

FIG. 69. FARM SCENE IN NORWAY

of ore from this region are sent by rail to Luleå, a city in northern Sweden, and from there, by steamer, to many different countries in Europe and to the United States.

The great forests of birch, pine, spruce, and other trees cover nearly all the rest of the country, from the mountains on the west to the Baltic Sea on the east. In the winter, the woods in the northern portion are half buried in snow, and in their depths wander bears, wolves, elk, and deer. In traveling through the country on the hard-beaten roads of snow, we meet farmers driving to market with their sleds full of game, or sledges filled with merry passengers wrapped warmly in furs and drawn by small but speedy horses. We may come upon an endless line of timber sledges, or a woodsman on his long snowshoes, or, in the forest depths, a charcoal burner, for these are all common sights in this region.

If you look at the map of Sweden, you will see that nearly all the rivers flow southeastward through the forest region, from the mountains to the sea. Every river is a lumber stream, and many have sawmills along their banks or near their mouths. There are between fifteen hundred and two thousand sawmills in Sweden, some of them small, while others are among the largest in Europe, and there are thousands of men at work in them. The lumber is made into boards, beams, masts, staves, window sashes, doors, sleepers, props to be used in mines, paper and paper pulp, matches, charcoal, and many other articles. Not many of these products remain in Sweden. Her forest exports

FIG. 70. SOME OF THE PEOPLE OF SWEDEN GO TO CHURCH IN BOATS

are worth more than all the other goods sent out of the country and are of more value than the forest exports of most of the other countries of the world. The great importance of the industry is largely due to the wide extent of the forests and to the fine quality of the timber, resulting from its slow growth. The great output is made possible by the numberless watercourses, on which the logs may be floated to the sawmills; by the snow and the frozen lakes and marshes, which make winter transportation easy; by the many good harbors on the coast; and by the convenient situation of Sweden for communication with other nations.

Of all the articles manufactured in Sweden from wood, the most important are paper, paper pulp, and matches. Great Britain is Sweden's best customer, not only for these products but for others, and in some years she takes more than half of all the Swedish exports. Nearly all the butter, much of the timber, and great quantities of paper, wood pulp, matches, and iron and steel products are sent from Gothenburg direct, or by way of Copenhagen, to English ports. The vessels bring back coal and coke for the factories, cotton and woolen yarn for the mills, besides cloth, oils, leather, and other manufactures. Other nations of Europe light their fires with Swedish matches, build their houses with Swedish timber, make their machinery from Swedish iron, and spread their bread with Swedish butter. The people of the United States are especially interested in the forests of Sweden, for we pay her each year many thousand dollars for matches alone, and an amount several times larger for the large quantities of wood pulp, which we buy from her to supply our numerous paper mills.

© Underwood & Underwood

FIG. 71. PRINCIPAL STREET IN JÖNKÖPING

One of the places in Sweden we should like to visit before leaving the country is Jönköping, perhaps the most beautifully situated of all Swedish towns. It lies at the southern end of Lake Vättern and is surrounded by hills on the east, west, and south. But beautiful as the scenery is, it is not that which has brought us here. No, it is those large buildings in the western part of the town where, for more than sixty years, matches have been manufactured. A Swede invented friction matches, and Johan Lundström, whose name is still seen on match boxes, started and built up an immense industry in Jönköping, where they have been manufactured ever since in such great quantities that the town has become famous for the product.

Most of the factories in Sweden manufacture safety matches, which can be lighted only on the box in which they are put up. The matches are made chiefly of aspen wood, much of which has to be imported from Finland and Russia, for the supply in Sweden has diminished rapidly in recent years.

When the manufacture of matches first began, each little stick was made and dipped by hand. Now, however, machines do the whole work. And such wonderful machines! One of them takes blocks of wood as wide as a match is long and two inches thick, cuts the blocks into splints the size of a match, forms the head, puts the finished matches into boxes, which are fed into the machine, and thus turns out, untouched by the human hand, forty to fifty thousand boxes a day.

© Underwood & Underwood

FIG. 72. FARMING NEAR JÖNKÖPING

There are more than twenty factories in Sweden, now united into one corporation, which turn out annually immense quantities of matches. Besides the great number consumed in the country, from twenty to twenty-five thousand tons are exported annually. Though this seems a great amount, the United States manufactures many more. It is estimated that the factories of our country produce from two hundred seventy-five to three hundred billion matches every year. If these were fastened together end to end, the line thus made would be long enough to stretch to the moon and back nearly twenty times.

Some one interested in problems has figured that the nations of the civilized world use about three million matches every minute, and that one half of this immense quantity is consumed in the United States.

TOPICS FOR STUDY

I

1. The trip from Helsingfors.
2. Description of Stockholm.
3. A journey to northern Sweden.
4. The forests of Sweden.
5. Lumbering in Sweden.
6. Exports of the country.
7. Jönköping and the manufacture of matches.
8. World product of matches.

II

1. Sketch Sweden, showing the mountain, forest, and plain regions. Show the direction of the rivers. Indicate the cities mentioned.
2. Write a list of the reasons why Sweden ranks so high in the lumber industry.
3. Trace the route of a vessel bringing Swedish iron to Philadelphia.
4. Load a vessel with Swedish products for England. Name the products carried, the waters sailed on, the shipping and receiving ports, and the return cargo.
5. Make a list of the addresses which you can find on match boxes. Locate these places.

III

Be able to spell and pronounce the following names. Locate each place and tell what was said of it in this and in any previous chapter. Add other facts if possible.

Finland	Copenhagen	Stockholm
Great Britain	Dannemora	Venice
Norway	Edinburgh	
Russia	Gothenburg	Baltic Sea
United States	Helsingfors	Gulf of Finland
	Jönköping	Lake Mälar
Berlin	Luleå	Lake Wetter

CHAPTER XI

GERMANY AND THE WORLD WAR

Our next trip will take us into Germany, a country of Central Europe bordering on the North and Baltic seas. It is less than twice the size of Colorado, while its population is nearly two-thirds that of the entire United States.

For many years, Germany was a strong military country. As the years passed and her military and industrial strength grew greater and greater, her ruler and her "war-lords" became more and more obsessed with the idea of dominating the world: of creating a Germany that should extend through middle Europe southward into western Asia and eastward across the dominions of the Czar of Russia to the Pacific; of absorbing the little countries to the north; of conquering France, then England; and, in due time, of reaching across the Atlantic even to our own United States and to the countries south of us. Such were the plans of the Kaiser of Germany and his advisers, and for years prior to 1914, everything within the mighty empire was directed to their accomplishment.

In 1914, Germany was ready, and the great war began. Never in the history of the world had there ever been such a war. It was not a struggle between two countries or between two continents, even. Nearly the whole world took part in the conflict. At first, the people of the United States were divided in their opinion as to whether our country should join the Allied Nations against Germany and the other Central Powers, and it was nearly three years after the beginning of the fighting before we entered the war. Our strength, our resources, and our brave boys, added to those of France, England, and the other Allies, proved too much for the foe, and from the time we entered the conflict, the German cause was lost, and the world freed from fear of German rule.

The war had many results. Some of them were awful ones. Millions of men were killed; hundreds of towns and cities were laid completely in ruins; thousands and thousands of people lost homes, household goods, farms, cattle — everything in the world that they possessed. In the fighting zone, mills, factories, mines, machinery, and industries of all kinds were laid in ruins. Wonderful art treasures and ancient buildings were forever lost to the world. Forests of splendid trees, hundreds of years old, were laid waste in a few weeks. What had taken man and nature centuries to accomplish was destroyed in four years.

Some of the results of the war were as beneficial as others were harmful. In some of the countries of Europe and other continents, the people had few rights and privileges. They had been oppressed for centuries and governed by autocratic rulers of other races or religions who hated them and forbade them to use their native language, to have schools with teachers of their own race, to make their laws, or to choose their officials.

The war changed many of these conditions. New nations, people happy in a new freedom, and new boundary lines drawn by a higher law than greed and selfishness were some of the results. To guard the liberties of peoples, to help to prevent wars and all their disastrous results, there was planned the greatest organization the world has ever yet known—the League of Nations. Powerful, just, far-seeing, ready to defend the right, to repress the wrong, and to see that law and order, justice and mercy, should prevail.

The industrial changes brought about by the war have been many and great. Before 1914, Germany controlled the world's markets in certain important products. Chief among these were optical and surgical instruments which required a high degree of skill in the making, chemical manufactures, such as dyes and drugs, and potash and other substances which help in making the world's fertilizers, without which large crops cannot be produced.

Soon after the war commenced, it became impossible to obtain these and other products from Germany. Therefore, other nations began experiments in their manufacture. The results of these experiments in building up new industries have been very successful. In the future, neither Germany nor any other country will hold a monopoly on those products which are essential to the welfare of the world.

For many years, few people from the United States or from other countries will care to travel in Germany for pleasure. We should be giving to that country, however, a great advantage over us if we knew nothing of her people, her land, and her industries. It is as important now as it ever has been that we have considerable knowledge of the country of Germany.

For many years, Germany had been an important country in the production of iron and coal. She ranked first among European nations in her iron output and next to Great Britain in the amount of coal mined. It was largely due to these two products that she was able to build up her manufacturing industries and prepare herself for the great war. A large part of the iron ore was mined in Alsace-Lorraine. Now that this territory has been given back to France, Germany will no longer hold first rank in Europe in iron production.

When the German armies retreated from northern France, they wrecked the coal mines of the region, destroying and carrying away the machinery and flooding the mines. Many years must pass before some of these mines can be worked; some of them are permanently damaged. One of Germany's richest coal fields lay in the valley of the Saar River, a branch of the Moselle. To make up partially for the great industrial loss to France, the treaty of peace at the close of the World War provided that she should be given control of the Saar Valley coal mines in western Germany. At the end of fifteen years from the signing of the treaty, the people there are to be given the opportunity of deciding to which nation they desire to belong.

Although Germany has many large cities and important

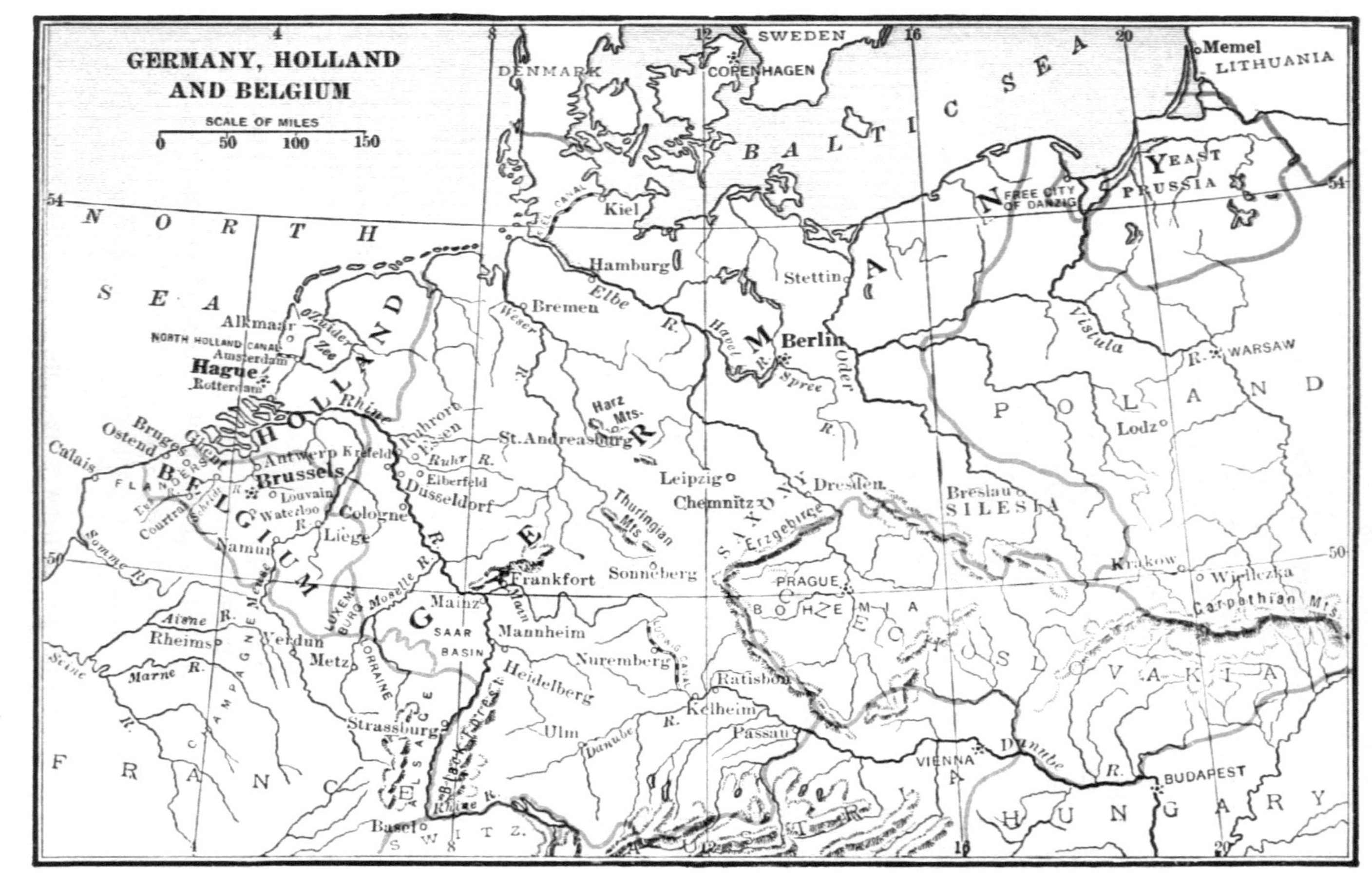
4
GERMANY, HOLLAND
AND BELGIUM
SCALE OF MILES
0 50 100 150
NORTH SEA
BALTIC SEA
DENMARK
SWEDEN
COPENHAGEN
Memel
LITHUANIA
EAST PRUSSIA
FREE CITY OF DANZIG
Kiel
KIEL CANAL
Hamburg
Elbe R.
Weser R.
Bremen
Stettin
Havel R.
Spree
Berlin
Oder
Vistula
R. WARSAW
POLAND
Lodz
HOLLAND
Alkmaar
Zuyder Zee
NORTH HOLLAND CANAL
Amsterdam
Hague
Rotterdam
Rhine
Ghent
Bruges
Ostend
Calais
FLANDERS
Antwerp
Krefeld
Ruhrort
Essen
Ruhr R.
Elberfeld
Brussels
Louvain
Waterloo
Cologne
Düsseldorf
Liège
Namur
BELGIUM
Scheldt R.
Meuse R.
Harz Mts.
St. Andreasburg
Leipzig
Chemnitz
Thuringian Mts.
Dresden
SAXONY
Erzgebirge
Breslau
SILESIA
Sonneberg
Frankfort
Mainz
Main R.
SAAR BASIN
Mannheim
Nuremberg
Heidelberg
Ulm
LUXEMBURG
Moselle R.
LORRAINE
ELSASS
Black Forest
Rhine R.
Strassburg
Basel
SWITZ.
PRAGUE
BOHEMIA
LUDWIG CANAL
Ratisbon
Kelheim
Passau
Danube R.
Krakow
Wielicka
Carpathian Mts.
CZECHOSLOVAKIA
VIENNA
Danube R.
BUDAPEST
HUNGARY
Aisne R.
Rheims
Verdun
Metz
CHAMPAGNE
Marne R.
Seine R.
Somme R.
FRANCE
N O R T H   S E A

manufactures, a fourth of all her many million people depend on agriculture for a living. Though most of the farms are small ones, the owners cultivate them so carefully that there are immense quantities of grain, sugar beets, grapes, potatoes, and other products raised on them. In ordinary years, Germany raises more potatoes than any other country in the world. They form one of the chief foods of the people and, with coarse rye bread and buttermilk or sour milk, are eaten daily by the peasants.

If we could look down upon Germany from an airship, we should see acres and acres of sugar beets waving their green tops in the sunshine, for Germany is one of the leading countries of the world in the production of beet sugar. We should also see from our airship the browner green of the hop vines twining around tall poles twice as high as your head. Thousands of acres of hops are raised to be used in the making of beer, which German people drink in large quantities.

© Underwood & Underwood

FIG. 73. IN GERMANY WE CAN SEE MANY ACRES OF SUGAR BEETS

Flying low in our airship over the valley of the Rhine River, we should see below us the terraced vineyards—the fruit from which yields the famous Rhine wines. In fertile meadows and on green hillsides, we should catch a sight of many sleek-looking cattle, for Germany is an important dairying country.

Agriculture, in a great variety of forms, is one of the leading industries of the country. Yet, Germany is better known as an important manufacturing and commercial nation. She is noted not only for the great amount but for the variety of her productions, and is famous also for the science and skill displayed in

FIG. 74. "THOUSANDS OF ACRES OF HOPS ARE RAISED"

their manufacture and use. The making of indigo is an illustration of this. Formerly, and to a slight extent at the present time, the indigo plant yielded the dye, large quantities of which were imported at great expense. Today, an artificial product, discovered in coal tar by a German chemist and manufactured in great quantities, is cheaper than the natural product of the indigo plant. Its use saves the cost of importation, and its sale to other countries increases the value of Germany's exports.

This is only one of the many brilliant dyes which scientific men have discovered can be made from the dirty-looking coal tar. Great quantities of fertilizers, artificial camphor, drugs, powders, perfumes, and other chemicals are also made here. Germany is noted for the number of expert chemists connected with her manufacturing industries, and chemicals rank among the most important manufactures of the country.

The discovery of a method by which beet sugar could be manufactured cheaply enough to make it commercially profitable was the work of a German chemist. By painstaking experiments, beets have been developed which yield several times the amount of sugar formerly obtained from the vegetable.

To feed and clothe her millions of people, Germany must

import many million dollars' worth of raw material to furnish occupation for them. She must manufacture; and to pay for her imports, she must export these manufactured goods. The growth of the nation, therefore, depends to a great extent upon her commerce.

Let us see if the situation of Germany favors this commercial development. It occupies a central position in Europe, with other nations on every side, and her land routes, therefore, are short ones. This, in itself, is favorable, for land routes are usually expensive for transportation purposes. If we measured her entire boundary line, we should find it to be about four thousand miles. Rather more than a fourth of this borders on the sea — about eight hundred miles on the Baltic and nearly three hundred miles on the North Sea. The Baltic, being farther from the ocean and separated from it by the Scandinavian peninsula, is colder than the North Sea, and the ports on it are closed by ice for a part of the year, while the North Sea ports remain open. The Kiel Canal, which connects the waters of the two seas, extends from the city of Kiel to the mouth of the Elbe River, a distance of sixty-one miles. It was built by Germany largely for military and naval purposes, in order that she might move her war vessels at will in and out of the Baltic Sea. Since the Peace Treaty was signed in 1919, at the close of the World War, the Kiel Canal has been open to vessels of all nations.

Because of the disadvantages connected with the carrying on of commerce on the Baltic Sea, most of Germany's trade is carried on through the

© Underwood & Underwood

FIG. 75. THE KIEL CANAL EXTENDS FROM KIEL TO THE MOUTH OF THE ELBE RIVER

North Sea ports. This traffic is greatly increased by the position of these cities opposite the great markets of England, and also by the surface and drainage conditions of the country, for however favorably situated a seaport may be, its importance depends largely upon its means of communication with the country which furnishes the goods for export.

If, from our airship, we could view at once the whole area of Germany, we should see four long, navigable rivers, which rise in or break through the mountains in the southern part of the country and flow northward across the great German plain to the North and Baltic seas. These are the Rhine, the Weser, the Elbe, and the Oder. A fine canal system connects these rivers with one another, and with the Seine, the Rhone, and the Danube, which flow to the west and south. By means of this system of waterways, Germany has been able to draw her commercial

FIG. 76. THE RHINE RIVER IS FAMOUS FOR ITS CASTLES AND VINEYARDS

products from the fields and factories of many countries to the east, west, and south.

At or near the mouth of each of the great northward-flowing rivers is a large commercial port. Rotterdam in Holland is located near the mouth of the Rhine, Bremen on the Weser, Hamburg on the Elbe, and Stettin on the Oder. Through each of these ports pass not only the products of the river basin which it controls but those also which have come by canal and railroad from other sections.

The Rhine River, famous for its castles and vineyards, is the most westerly and the most important of these commercial streams. A ride through this section of Germany and along the Ruhr River would remind us of a visit to Pittsburgh, for it is as full of foundries, rolling mills, and steel works, with their tall chimneys and roaring furnaces, as is the "Smoky City" of Pennsylvania. In this district is Essen, a city famous for its iron and steel manufactures. Before and during the World War, it was a most important center for the manufacture of munitions. In Elberfeld, a city larger than New Orleans, we should see many large cotton mills and factories. At Krefeld, which is about the size of Lowell, Massachusetts, there are many factories in which are made silk goods of all kinds and descriptions.

In ordinary years, many boats descend the Rhine from these and other busy manufacturing cities, carrying all kinds of silk, cotton, woolen and linen goods, cloth, yarn, ribbons, braids, laces, trimmings, and embroideries. Others are heavily loaded with coal and iron and with a variety of iron manufactures — cutlery, hardware, machinery, needles and pins, and guns and rifles.

Besides these products, the Rhine boats carry many goods of the finest workmanship, among which are musical, optical, and surgical instruments, and thermometers such as physicians use to tell the temperature of a patient. These have come from the great factories and splendidly equipped laboratories, and also from the little houses of the peasants, where only one or two workmen find employment. Many of the products of Germany, as well as of other European countries, are made in the homes of the people rather than in large manufacturing plants.

The center of the chemical industry for which Germany is famous lies on the upper Rhine between Frankfort and Mannheim. Millions of dollars' worth of fertilizers, drugs, acids, and powders for use in manufacture and medicine are made in this section of the country.

The busy peasants from the small, well-kept farms of the upper Rhine valley send great quantities of wheat, barley, rye, potatoes, grapes, and tobacco down the river in barges. Much of the tobacco will go by canal to the Weser River and thence to Bremen, which is one of the largest tobacco ports of the world.

In a trip down the Rhine, we should notice that all the more important cities along the river — Ruhrort, Düsseldorf, Cologne, Mainz, Mannheim, and others — have the best modern conveniences for carrying on commerce: quays, sheds, warehouses, granaries, petroleum tanks, cranes, and other devices for handling heavy goods.

The mouth of the Rhine River is in the Netherlands, and the great city of Rotterdam, situated near the coast and connected with the sea by a ship canal, is the natural port of the whole valley. By means of canals, which cut the city into many islands and stretch off through the low plains, we can reach any part of the Netherlands, for the network of waterways extends to all parts of the small kingdom. On them, one can see every imaginable variety of canal boat and barge, in such numbers and so close together that they touch one another for long distances along the sides of the canal. Every boat is named, many of them after the dearly loved Queen Wilhelmina.

Rotterdam is not a beautiful city, nor is it thoroughly Dutch, for it carries on commerce with too many countries of the world and is visited daily by too many foreigners for it to keep its Dutch characteristics. If you do not like sailors and sailor ways, do not go to Rotterdam, for they are everywhere, and hundreds of ships lie at the docks, are towed or poled slowly through the dark water of the canals between the rows of boats on either side, or sail proudly out of the harbor toward distant lands. Those bound for the United States carry great quantities of hides and skins, spices from the Dutch colonies in the East Indies, cheese, rice, and many other things. Among the important exports are bulbs, seeds, roots, and plants, for the Netherlands is famous for these products.

Thomas Hood has well described Rotterdam in a rather humorous poem written to a friend in England. It runs as follows:

> Before me lie dark waters
> In broad canals and deep,
> Whereon the silver moonbeams
> Sleep, restless in their sleep;
> A sort of vulgar Venice
> Reminds me where I am;
> Yes, yes, you are in England,
> And I'm in Rotterdam.
>
> Tall houses with quaint gables,
> Where frequent windows shine,
> And quays that lead to bridges,
> And trees in formal line,
> And masts of spicy vessels
> From western Surinam,
> All tell me you're in England,
> But I'm in Rotterdam.

Before the war, some of Germany's strongest fortifications lay along the Rhine River and in its valley. By the terms of the Peace Treaty, Germany is not allowed to maintain the forts in this area or to send any armed forces there. It is intended that this unarmed corridor of the Rhine Valley shall help protect France from any future invasion of the Germans.

The next important stream east of the Rhine is the Weser, with Bremen, the second-largest port of Germany, situated about fifty miles from its mouth. The part of the city on the right bank of the river is very old. As we wander through the narrow, crooked streets lined with the quaint old houses of the Middle Ages, and visit the ancient cathedral and the old council house with its famous wine cellars, we feel as if we must be separated by hundreds of years and hundreds of miles from the newer

© Underwood & Underwood

FIG. 77. GERMAN EMIGRANTS

part of the city, which rises from the opposite bank of the Weser with its broad, straight streets, fine business blocks, lovely parks, and attractive gardens.

The docks at Bremen extend along the banks of the Weser River. The waterfront is usually crowded with vessels from many lands in different parts of the world. They are anchored in the harbor, loading at the docks, or departing on long voyages to far distant countries. In a single year, more than two thousand vessels have arrived at this busy port of Germany. From Bremen, also, have sailed more than half of all the emigrants who have left the Fatherland to seek their fortunes in other parts of the world.

As our airship floats slowly eastward, we find ourselves above a great river as crowded with boats and barges as the Rhine. This is the Elbe, one of the most important rivers of Germany, for on it, goods can be carried entirely across the country, and thence, by means of the Moldan River, southward beyond the German border into the new country of Czechoslovakia. Vessels called express transports make the trip of nearly four hundred miles from Hamburg to the frontier in five or six days, and the return trip down the river in about half of that time.

Canals connect the Elbe with the Weser and Rhine on one side and with the Oder and Vistula on the other. One of these, on which much of the great trade between Hamburg and the capital city of Berlin is carried on, follows the course of the Spree River for some miles and then joins the Oder, thus connecting the waters of the North and Baltic Seas.

Hamburg is the largest seaport on the continent of Europe.

It is situated at the head of ocean navigation, sixty-five miles from the mouth of the Elbe River. There are larger and finer docks, quays, warehouses, granaries, and elevators crowded on the waterfront than we have seen in any other city of Germany. The machinery for loading and unloading vessels probably equals that in use in any seaport of the world.

Large quantities of foodstuffs and much of the raw material for manufacture enter Germany through the port of Hamburg. It is admirably situated at the head of the North Sea, across the water from the great markets of England, and near the entrance to the Kiel Canal, which connects it with the Baltic Sea. By the aid of this canal, the Elbe River and its connections, and the numerous railroads which enter the city, Hamburg has become a great distributing center, scattering the products received by its ocean commerce all over Germany and into many parts of Central Europe.

Much of the trade of the great city of Berlin is carried on through the same port, and goods are conveyed by rail, by canals, and by the Havel and Spree rivers to the capital city, from which they find their way by rail, river, and canal to waterways and cities farther east and south.

A list of the exports which Hamburg has sent to other countries would include nearly everything that has been produced or manufactured in Germany, as well as imports from other countries. Millions of dollars' worth of these goods are shipped annually from this busy port. Vessels bound for different parts of the world carry hides and skins, oils, seeds, ore, wood pulp and paper stock, toys, chemicals, dyes and drugs, India rubber, fertilizers, cloth, laces, embroideries, and gloves. From different parts of the Elbe valley, boats are continually arriving at Hamburg, bringing mineral products, silver, lead, copper, tin, nickel, and iron from Erzgebirge, or ore mountains, on the southern frontier. Other boats bring all kinds of manufactures from Saxony, the most densely populated and the chief manufacturing section of Germany - china from Dresden; books, furs, and skins from Leipzig; and all kinds of cotton goods from Chemnitz. There are also cargoes of toys, dolls, trimmings, embroideries, laces,

© Underwood & Underwood

FIG. 78. WE PASS THE ODER RIVER,
WITH STETTIN AT ITS MOUTH

artificial flowers, tobacco, thousands and thousands of postcards, real and artificial silk, seeds, salts, and so many other things that if we were to attempt to name all of them, the chapter would be a very long one.

As our airship takes us still farther east, we pass over the Oder River, with Stettin, a city the size of St. Paul, Minnesota, at its mouth. Stettin has one of the finest harbors in Europe and is connected by the Oder River and numerous canals with the Elbe on the west and the Vistula on the east. It is, therefore, a great trading center for those southern countries that can be reached by these water connections and for central and eastern Germany. Both of these regions include fine agricultural areas, and thousands of tons of freight come to Stettin by way of Berlin, and from Czechoslovakia. Chief among these exports is beet sugar, and following this in importance are flour and starch, products of the great potato crop in which Germany is one of the leading countries of the world. The composition of the soil in this part of Germany favors the manufacture of cement, of which large quantities have been exported.

If, in our tour through Germany, instead of looking down from our airship at the traffic on the rivers and at the great manufacturing cities and seaports, we had examined the quaint little houses in the country regions and in the smaller towns and cities, we should have seen many of the people engaged in an industry that would have interested us more than any of those carried on in great factories or mills. You wonder how any industry of importance can be carried on in small houses of two or three rooms, such as many of the peasants live in, but when thousands of families — father, mother, and children — in homes all over the country are working at the same occupation, they accomplish a great deal, even if they do not work together in a few large buildings.

Thousands and thousands of the people of Germany live in the country and depend for a living on the products of the farm and on the work which they do in their own homes during their spare hours. Many of these peasants are engaged in making toys — woolly dogs, teddy bears, Noah's Arks, tin soldiers, coaches, engines and trains, ducks that float, dolls that cry, sheep that bleat, and scores of others. Many also work on wooden articles, such as kitchen goods, boxes, toothpicks, frames for brushes, carved wood, and barrels. In their own homes, hundreds of families are engaged in making ribbons, laces, silks, and embroideries, besides knitted and crocheted goods. There are also glass workers, straw plaiters, and glove, basket, and violin makers.

Of all these home industries, the making of toys is more interesting than any other. Many of these come from Sonneberg, a quaint little town which nestles quietly in the long valley of the Thuringian Mountains, which you will find on the map opposite page 154. We will plan our visit so that we may arrive in the town on Saturday, for that is the day when the people from the outlying districts bring to the town the toys which they have been making during the week, and we shall find the scene at the railroad station very interesting. Some of the peasants have heavy loads. See that woman with a basket nearly a yard deep fastened to her shoulders, while an oblong box a yard wide rests on the top of that. Both are filled with woolly dogs which every member of the family, from the aged grandfather down to the seven-year-old girl, has had a hand in making.

The Thuringian Mountains, as you see on the map, lie on the borders of Saxony. Were it not for the difference in the appearance of the people and their homes, we might think we were in one of the pleasant valleys of the Green Mountains of Vermont. The German mountains, however, are darker, for

FIG. 79. "IN ONE HOUSE NOTHING IS MADE BUT DOLLS"

their slopes are covered with deep forests of evergreen trees. The Germans take excellent care of their forests. The cutting is very carefully done, the undergrowth and brush are removed so that the forest areas are as clean as a picnic grove, and a tree is planted for each one felled.

Sonneberg is a queer old town of nearly fifteen thousand people, where the tall, quaint houses topple toward one another across the narrow streets leading from the marketplace up the slopes of the mountains. The farms are small, for most of the land is wooded. The peasants raise the rye for their bread, the corn for their meal, and the flax for their linen. The men cut wood in the forests and work on the farms; the women spin and weave the flax into clothing for the family, and the children gather berries or tend the cattle and sheep in the mountain pastures. While the animals feed on the green hillsides, the little keeper knits the warm woolen stockings or mittens which will be needed when the mountains are covered with snow and the drifts lie deep in the valleys.

If you were to walk through the village in the long, cold winter months, you would find nearly every family — mother, father, chubby-cheeked girls, and sober-faced boys — sitting around the table in the small, low room working on some kind of toy. In one house, nothing is made but dolls. The father makes the heads, and the mother cuts out and stuffs the body; a little girl, only eight years old, sews on the arms and legs; her brother, eleven years old, fastens on the hair, while the elder sister paints the eyebrows and cheeks.

In another house, the whole family is making figures of Santa Claus. Each child has his own particular part of the work to do — perhaps making the legs or arms, perhaps painting the cheeks or fastening on the hair or beard, or the white wool hat — and he will continue at this same work day after day and year after year.

The reason that the peasants work so quickly and skillfully is because their fingers, like those of their ancestors, have been trained to do just this special work. But how monotonous it must be! In the summer, the work on the small farms makes some variation, but in the winter, when the cold winds blow and the snow is piled high around the little house, the workers sit from early morning till late at night painting lips, fastening in eyes, cutting out bodies, sewing on limbs, or doing some other detail, over and over, the whole day through.

We must not leave "Toyland" without visiting its capital, Nuremberg. Toys have been made there for many, many years and are manufactured in great numbers both in large factories and in the homes of the peasants. Nuremberg is about as large as our capital city, Washington, but it would be hard to imagine two cities more unlike.

Nuremberg represents in great measure the old life of some hundred years ago, while Washington stands for the most modern life of the twentieth century. The old wall still surrounds the city, with some of the towers and gates remaining. The quaint old houses, with their steep-pitched roofs and the second story projecting over the first, the ancient marketplace, and the narrow streets of the older parts of the city, make one feel as if he were living in the seventeenth century, in spite of the fact that we see also modern factories for the manufacture of chemicals, machinery, electrical apparatus, and scientific and musical instruments.

You have all read of the Black Forest and its stories of goblins, witches, and fairies. In parts of it, the woods are so dense that it is no wonder that the Germans call it Schwarzwald, or "Black Woods." Other parts of the forest are very pleasant. The sun flickers through the trees, and the pine needles make a clean, dry carpet underneath; birds nest and sing there; and silvery brooklets trickle between mossy banks.

Many peasants live in the more open spaces and till their small farms. During the long, cold winter, the men and boys work at wood carving. They make many toys of various kinds and also the cuckoo clocks which many of you have seen. The cases of these clocks are of wood, often very beautifully ornamented with carvings of animals, fruits, or birds. There is a little door on the front, just above or below the face of the clock. When the hour sounds, this door opens, and a little cuckoo springs out and calls his name or warbles some short strain of music.

One very interesting region of Germany which we must be sure to visit before leaving the country is the Harz Mountains. As we walk through the little villages or climb the steep slopes of the mountains, at whatever door we chance to stop, we are greeted by such a chorus of chirps and trills and calls and whistles as only Birdland can furnish. And we are really in the canary center of the world, where, in ordinary years, many thousands of

© Underwood & Underwood

FIG. 80. THE CASES OF THE CUCKOO CLOCKS ARE OF WOOD, OFTEN VERY BEAUTIFULLY ORNAMENTED WITH CARVINGS

the beautiful yellow songsters are raised.

To see the finest singers, let us go up the mountain to St. Andreasburg, a little village high on the slope. The air is so clear and pure that people suffering from throat or lung troubles are often advised to go there. The birds also become strong and hardy and develop fine voices, and the St. Andreasburg "rollers," as they are called, are considered the finest songsters in the world.

To assist in their training, larks, nightingales, and specially trained canaries with soft, sweet voices are used. There are also various mechanical devices that produce long trills, water bubbles, flute notes, and other pleasing sounds. Amid such surroundings, the young birds begin to sing. Only those with pure, soft voices capable of high training remain here long. The poorer singers are removed to another room where, though they never will make first-class singers, their training still continues. Most of the birds, however, which are raised in St. Andreasburg and the vicinity are better than those bred in the valley.

There are many other cities in Germany that we would like to visit — Heidelberg with its old castle ruins; Cologne with its marvelously beautiful cathedral; Leipzig with its great book binderies and establishments for dressing hides and skins. Time will not allow for all these trips, but we must make a flying visit to Berlin, the capital of the country.

Berlin is one of the three largest cities in all Europe. Its situation helps somewhat to explain why this is so. It is the most central city of Europe, situated in the middle of the great plain, where important routes of travel from Paris to Petrograd, and from northern Europe to Italy, cross each other.

On these highways of traffic, it was natural that a great city should spring up. Many railroads radiate from Berlin, and canals stretch eastward to the Oder River and westward, by the Spree and Havel rivers, to the Elbe.

Berlin is a great manufacturing center as well as an important commercial city. You would soon be lost in the industrial section among the foundries, machine works, locomotive works, electrical works, and silk, cotton, woolen, and linen mills, unsurpassed in Europe.

This is not the part of the city, however, which most visitors like to see, not the part which has earned for Berlin the title of the cleanest city in Europe. There are other sections where we can drive through one wide, shaded street after another and see no dirt, no dust, and no disorder.

There is one very beautiful avenue which, because of the linden trees which border it on either side, the Germans call Unter den Linden. On this wide boulevard are separate divisions for heavy teams, for light carriages, for bicycles, for horseback riders, and for people on foot. This avenue is about a mile long. At one end is the palace, and at the other, a lovely park, called the Tiergarten, or "animal garden." Should you like to go into the park for a while? We enter it through the Brandenburg Gate, a fine stone structure of five entrances, the middle one surmounted by a splendid statue of the Goddess of Victory. In former years, only the royal family might pass through this middle entrance.

We should like to remain for hours in this beautiful place, in the deep shade of the trees near one of the lovely lakes, watching the horseback riders, the children playing in the green grass, and the splendid carriages with liveried coachmen and footmen. We must leave much of the country unseen and many interesting cities unvisited, and hasten on to its southern neighbors where scenes equally beautiful and industries equally interesting await us.

TOPICS FOR STUDY

I.

1. Area and population of Germany.
2. Germany and the World War.
3. Some results of the war.
4. Mineral products.
5. Agriculture in Germany.
6. Manufacturing in Germany.
7. The situation of Germany.
8. Surface and drainage.
9. The Rhine River and its port of Rotterdam.
10. The Weser River and Bremen.
11. Hamburg and the Elbe River.
12. Stettin and the Oder River.
13. The canal system of Germany.
14. Home industries in Germany.
15. Toys and canaries.
16. Berlin, the capital of Germany.

II.

1. Sketch a map of Germany. Write the names of all the land and water boundaries. Which ones are different from what they were before the World War? Is the country of Germany larger or smaller than it was before the war?
2. On your map of Germany, trace the courses of the principal rivers and write their names. Write also the names of all the cities mentioned in the text. Be able to state one fact about each of the cities you have named.
3. Sketch a map showing the Baltic Sea, the arms of the sea, and the surrounding countries. Show the Kiel Canal. Why was this canal internationalized at the close of the World War?
4. Have you ever read *The Pied Piper of Hamelin*? Tell the story to the class. With what river of Germany is it connected?

5. Name the waters on which goods would be carried in going from New Orleans to Bremen and from New York to Berlin.

6. Tell the advantages of the situation of Hamburg. Why has Stettin not grown to be as important a city?

III.

Be able to spell and pronounce the following names. Locate each place and tell what was said of it in this and in any previous chapter. Add other facts if possible.

Alsace-Lorraine

Czechoslovakia	Heidelberg	Black Forest
Colorado	Kiel	Danube River
East Indies	Krefeld	Elbe River
England	Leipzig	Erzgebirge
France	London	Green
Netherlands	Lowell	Mountains
Russia	Mainz	Harz Mountains
Saxony	Mannheim	Havel River
Scandinavia	New Orleans	Kiel Canal
United States	Nuremberg	Moldau River
	Paris	Moselle River
Berlin	Petrograd	North Sea
Bremen	Pittsburgh	Oder River
Chemnitz	Portland	Rhine River
Cologne	Rotterdam	Rhone River
Dresden	Ruhrort	Saar River
Dilsseldorf	St. Andreasburg	Seine River
Elberfeld	Sonneberg	Spree River
Essen	Stettin	Thuringian
Frankfort	Washington	Mountains
		Vistula River
Hamburg	Baltic Sea	Weser River

CHAPTER XII

THE COUNTRIES OF CENTRAL EUROPE AND THE DANUBE RIVER

If you look at any map of Europe printed before 1919, you will find, in the center of the continent, the country of Austria-Hungary. Though smaller than Texas, Austria-Hungary contained about half as many people as the whole United States. Its population was made up of more nationalities than could be found in any other European country except, possibly, Russia and Turkey. There were Germans and Magyars, Poles, Czechs, Serbs, and other members of the Slav race, besides other peoples whose names you might find it hard to pronounce. Each of these races differed from the rest as much as a Greek differs from an Italian, or a Frenchman from a Norwegian. There was little in customs, religion, language, or character to bind these different nationalities together. Each was jealous of the others and looked down upon them in scorn as inferior peoples. Many of the people of the part of the empire known as Austria were of the same race as the Germans, resembled them in appearance and character, and used to a great extent the German language.

About half the inhabitants of Hungary are Magyars, a people of the same ancestry as the Turks, though there is little resemblance between the two nations today. Each of the three races — the Germanic Austrians, the Slavs, and the Magyars — had little love for the others and no desire to be ruled by them. For years, it was the strong hand of the old emperor, Francis Joseph, that held together these quarrelsome elements.

It has long been the desire of the people of the Slav race who

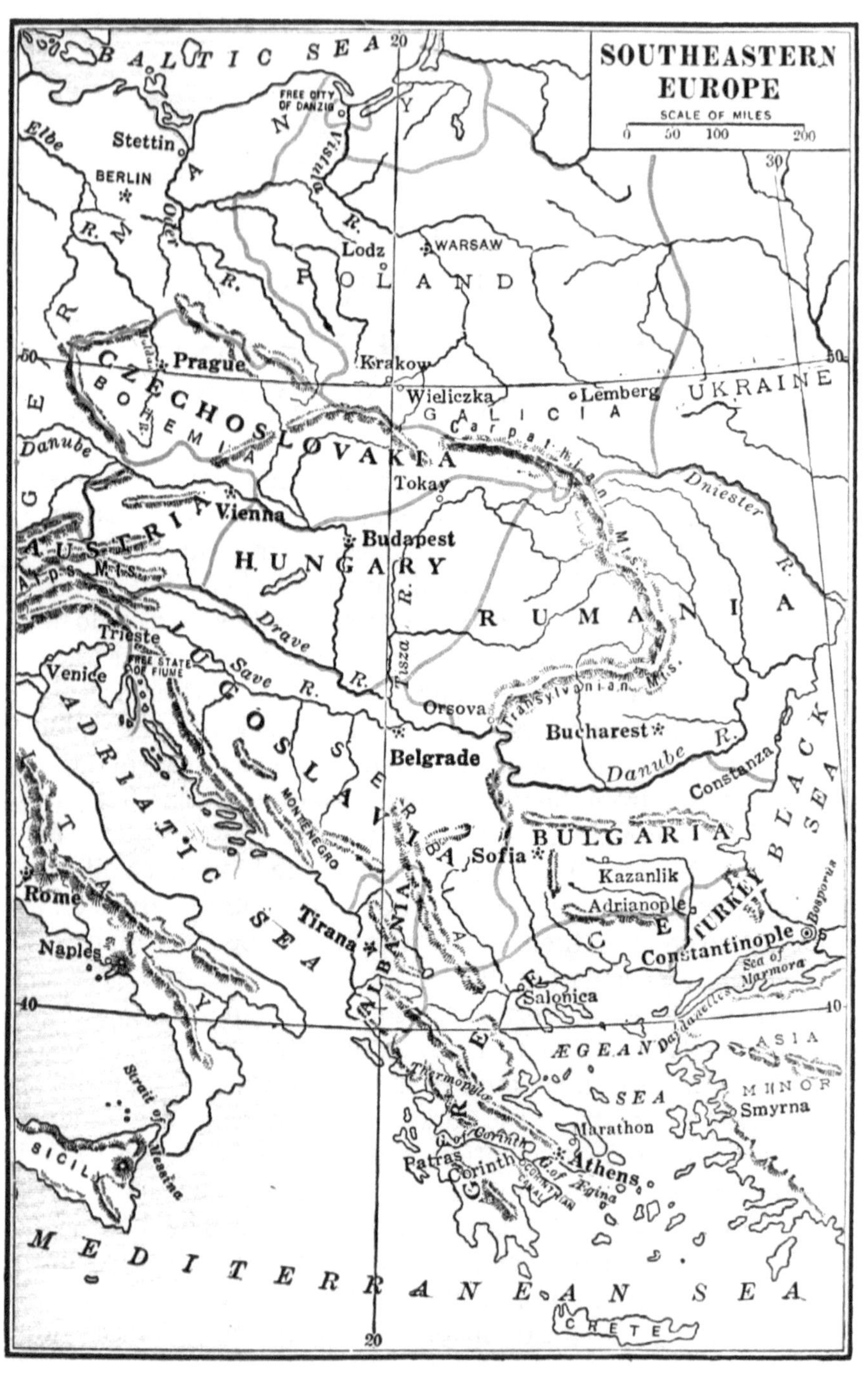

SOUTHEASTERN EUROPE
SCALE OF MILES
0   50   100   200
BALTIC SEA
FREE CITY OF DANZIG
Elbe
Stettin
BERLIN
Oder R.
Vistula R.
Lodz
WARSAW
POLAND
GERMANY
Prague
CZECHOSLOVAKIA
BOHEMIA
Krakow
Wieliczka
Lemberg
UKRAINE
GALICIA
Carpathian Mts.
Danube
Tokay
Dniester R.
AUSTRIA
Vienna
Alps Mts.
Budapest
HUNGARY
RUMANIA
Drave R.
Tisza R.
Save R.
Transylvanian Mts.
Trieste
FREE STATE OF FIUME
Venice
YUGOSLAVIA
Orsova
Bucharest
Danube R.
Constanza
ADRIATIC SEA
SERBIA
MONTENEGRO
Belgrade
BLACK SEA
Rome
BULGARIA
Sofia
Kazanlik
Adrianople
Naples
ITALY
Tirana
ALBANIA
Constantinople
Bosporus
TURKEY
GREECE
Salonica
Sea of Marmora
SICILY
Strait of Messina
AEGEAN
Dardanelles
ASIA MINOR
Marathon
Smyrna
SEA
Thermopylæ
G. of Corinth
Patras
Corinth Canal
Athens
G. of Ægina
Sea of Ægina
MEDITERRANEAN SEA
CRETE
20
30
50
50
40
40
20

lived in the southern part of Austria-Hungary to unite with those of the little countries of Serbia and Montenegro farther south and set up an independent nation. Serbia's chief aim in joining in the World War was to free those people of her race who were living under the rule of Austria-Hungary and thus enlarge the kingdom of the Serbs. Thus, the new country of Yugoslavia came into being. The word *Yugoslavia* means "Southern Slavs." Most of the people in Czechoslovakia, another new country of Central Europe, are also Slavs who live farther north. Between these two new Slavic countries lie Hungary, populated largely by Magyars, and Austria, most of whose people are Germans. Therefore, the greater part of Central Europe today, instead of being largely occupied by one great empire as it was before the war, is made up of four countries — Yugoslavia, Czechoslovakia, Austria, and Hungary.

Czechoslovakia is a country about as large as Alabama. It is an inland region, with its southern part drained by the Danube and its branches, and the northern portions by German rivers.

FIG. 81. THE LIFE OF THE PEASANT IN CZECHOSLOVAKIA IS A SIMPLE ONE

Much of the commerce of the country will be carried on by these rivers and their connecting canals.

Notice the western part of Czechoslovakia, where it juts northward toward Germany. This part, known as Bohemia, occupies about a fourth of the entire country. It is surrounded by mountains where many valuable minerals are found. The interior of Bohemia is the basin of an old inland sea, about the size of Lake Michigan. The soil of this old basin is very fertile, as such valleys usually are, and farming is important. The population is dense, and consequently, the farms are very small. Grains, vegetables, fruits, hops, sugar beets, and grapes are the principal crops. Cattle-raising and hog-raising are also important. The life of the peasant is very simple, his needs few, and his food cheap. Yet, he is often unable to supply his few needs from his small farm. During the winter months, many of the farmers and their families, like those of Germany and other European countries, work at a variety of occupations in their own little homes. Large quantities of tools and kitchen utensils are made in Bohemia in this way, and buttons, bags, lace, embroideries, gloves, hairnets, beads, linen, and many, many other things are made in the peasants' houses during the cold months when there is little to do on the farms.

Before the war, Bohemia was the most important part of the old empire of Austria-Hungary. It is blessed by nature with almost every kind of agricultural and mineral resource. The great sugar

FIG. 82. WILL THE BUTTER EVER COME?

industry of the empire was centered in Bohemia. The guns of the Austro-Hungarian artillery were made here. About half of the enormous quantity of beer manufactured in the country was brewed in this section. Its textile industries were most important, and its production of embroideries, lace, linen, leather, chemicals, hardware, and machinery was very large. The Elbe River, of which you read in the last chapter, drains much of Bohemia, and most of the foreign trade is carried on by rail and water through the great port of Hamburg at its mouth.

All tourists in Bohemia like to purchase gloves while in this country, and some of the supply in our stores has come from this part of Czechoslovakia. The leather for the gloves is cut at the factories, but the making is done largely in the homes. One of the family does the ornamental stitching on the back, another stitches the seams, another makes the buttonholes, or fastens on the snaps. In parts of Bohemia, there are thousands of women and girls who spend all their time at home working on gloves.

You have all heard of Bohemian glassware, which has been famous for centuries. The china and porcelain made there is almost as well-known, and in ordinary years, much fine tableware is exported from this part of Europe into the United States.

The mineral springs of Bohemia have brought her much fame and money. The hot water of these springs is thought to be helpful in curing many diseases, though the wry faces of some of the drinkers indicate that the taste is not always pleasant. Millions of bottles of mineral waters and salts have been sent out of the country annually, and thousands of people each year have visited the springs.

What kind of bath will you take while you are at the springs? You may have your choice of a mud bath, a mineral water bath, a carbonic acid bath, or a Russian steam bath. These are only a few of the many varieties that the visitors at the bathing establishments connected with the springs may experiment with.

While we are in this part of Czechoslovakia, you will enjoy a visit to the old city of Prague, which, next to Vienna and Budapest, is the largest city in Central Europe. Prague is really

FIG. 83. SHEEP RAISING IN CZECHOSLOVAKIA

a cluster of towns connected by as many bridges over the little river in whose valley the city has grown up.

Prague is an old city. Its ancient town hall was built one hundred and fifty years before Columbus sailed across the Atlantic. Its moat, once filled with water, protected the place from invasion, but it has since been changed into a splendid street. Its Jewish burying ground is eight hundred years old.

You remember reading in the chapter on Russia about the Kremlin of Moscow, and the wonderful collection of buildings inside the historic enclosure. Prague has a Kremlin also — a collection of castles, cathedrals, monasteries, and arsenals — which forms the most interesting part of the city. Much of the history of the ancient place centers around these buildings.

Now let us go to the new city—the modern Prague— as different from the older part as our modern Washington is different from some historic New England village. Here is one of the finest museums in Europe, a splendid modern theater, an art gallery, a university, banks, street railways, and hotels such as one might find in any up-to-date city of the world. Here are also many manufacturing establishments — car shops, machine works, breweries, and paper mills — and many other industries that you would expect to see in a busy manufacturing city.

The country of Yugoslavia, sometimes known as the Kingdom of the Serbs, Croats, and Slovenes, extends along the eastern shores of the Adriatic Sea. It is about as large as Italy and is made up of Serbia, Montenegro, and some of the southern provinces of the old country of Austria-Hungary. Of these different divisions, Montenegro is the most rugged and mountainous, and Serbia is the largest and most important.

Like the other countries of the Balkan Peninsula, Serbia and Montenegro were once parts of the great Turkish Empire. Like the other countries also, they revolted from Turkey because of the cruelty, the oppression, and the backwardness of their Mohammedan rulers.

FIG. 84. IN THE SERB CITY OF ÜSKÜB
A shoe salesman in the market place

Owing to wars, oppressive government, and consequent poverty, the Serbs have not as yet progressed very far in civilization. They had made a good start in this direction when the World War broke out in 1914. What they suffered during this war has set them back many years. More than a fourth of the people of Serbia were killed in the war or died from disease or hunger. Many of her towns and villages were destroyed, three-fourths of her livestock killed and driven away, and half of her tools and machinery stolen or broken up by the retreating enemy. Knowing these facts, we can understand that it must be a long time before the villagers will be tilling their small farms and living comfortably and happily again in their little homes.

The part of Yugoslavia that is occupied by Serbia is rich in the gifts bestowed on it by Mother Nature. The soil is fertile, the climate good, the water supply abundant, the rivers numerous, the mineral wealth great, and the forests large. Before the war, none of the people were very rich, but neither were any very poor. Perhaps one reason for this is the fact that most of

FIG. 85. YUGOSLAVIA HAS MANY TOWNS SIMILAR TO THIS ONE

the peasants owned their little farms. The land was divided among the people, and there were few large estates held by the wealthy and worked by the peasants as tenants. Nine-tenths of the people were farmers and raised on their farms most of the things that they needed in their daily life. Their crops of grain and vegetables and their cattle gave them food, and their flax and flocks supplied materials for clothing. If a Serb acquired a little extra money, it was securely hidden in an old stocking or invested in tools or machinery for his farm.

From the little villages clustered under the plum trees, the men carried their wheat and corn in rough wooden carts for miles to the mills along the rivers. Here the grain was ground much as it is in the river mills along the Danube. Every peasant had and, as the country recovers from its great losses, hopes to have again his cattle, sheep, goats, and pigs. There is much fine pasture land in the country, and many heads of livestock can be raised. Some of these wander through the forests of oak and beech and feed on the nuts under the trees.

There are two chief reasons why Serbia suffered so greatly in the World War. One is because of its position. The Balkan Peninsula forms a great highway of trade between European countries, with their extensive manufactures and dense populations, and undeveloped Asia, with its riches of raw materials and its people just awakening to new needs and desires. Most of the Balkan Peninsula is mountainous. The ancient trade routes and the modern railroads must follow the valleys of the rivers. These connect Belgrade on the northern border of Serbia with Constantinople, the key to Asia. Study a good map on which these valley routes are shown. Find also another valley route which runs south to the port of Salonica on the Aegean Sea. The two chief railroads of the Balkan Peninsula follow these valleys. You can readily see that if Germany wished to get possession of Central and Southern Europe and thence expand into Asia, it was necessary for her to control these railroads and have possession of the through lines from Belgrade to the waters at the south. It was in the campaigns directed to this end that Serbia suffered most.

FIG. 86. A POTTER IN YUGOSLAVIA

The other chief cause for much of the destruction and suffering in Serbia was her natural wealth. The Central Powers needed the grain, the cattle, and the minerals of both Serbia and Romania. Serbia is very rich in mineral deposits, and some of her mines have been worked since the time of the Romans. Lead and copper were very necessary in the carrying on of the war, and neither Germany nor her tool and ally, Austria-Hungary, produced these minerals in abundance.

Belgrade is the chief city of Yugoslavia. It was larger than Duluth, Minnesota, but in the World War scores and hundreds of its buildings were destroyed, and many of its industries were crippled. We all hope that never again will war cause so much suffering and loss. The city is situated on the Danube River near the mouths of both northward-flowing and southward-flowing rivers. Thus, its position is of great importance, as it

FIG. 87. A VILLAGE IN YUGOSLAVIA

controls routes in all directions. For this reason, it has been for ages an object of warfare between nations on all sides and has been captured and recaptured many times. Belgrade has but few manufactures, but as you can see from its position, it is an important distributing center for nearly all the exports and imports of the region.

The present country of Austria, once a part of the empire of Austria-Hungary, is a hilly and mountainous land in which much of the soil is unfit for agriculture. It has comparatively few resources of importance. The greater part of the chief industries of the old empire were carried on in other parts of the country.

Vienna, once a city of more than two million people, and the gay, proud capital of a prouder empire, is today the capital city of a little country of perhaps nine or ten million people. Before the World War, Vienna was very wealthy, but its wealth came chiefly from people nearly all of whom made their money in parts of the kingdom now included in Czechoslovakia, Poland, and other independent nations. Vienna was the center of art, of science, of government, of education, of commerce, of banking, of sports and amusements, and of wealth and fashion. During the war, Vienna lost much of its wealth. Today, instead of being the capital of a great empire, it is only the capital of a small, poor country with few resources and industries. What will be the future of the city? Will Prague, Budapest, Warsaw, or some other metropolis take its place as the gay center of Central Europe? Only time can answer the question.

The countries of Central Europe have very little seacoast, but they possess one of the greatest rivers of Europe, the beautiful blue Danube. A sail down this wonderful river takes us into the heart of Hungary, a region famous for its grain fields. The Danube is about the same length as the St. Lawrence but bears very little resemblance to it in other ways. Unlike the American river, which has its source in one of the Great Lakes, the Danube has its beginning in two tiny streams, the Brigach and the Breg. They start in the foothills of the Black Forest Mountains and come tumbling over the rocks, gathering strength from little streamlets which hurry down the slopes.

It seems hardly possible that this small, muddy stream is really the mighty Danube. But as it flows along, now through smiling valleys and now in the shadow of towering mountain

FIG. 88. ULM, THE HEAD OF NAVIGATION ON THE DANUBE

peaks, now spreading its blue waters around green islands and now receiving swift streams from wooded highlands and from the high Alps, it grows in volume from the tiny brooklet to the mighty river, the second largest in Europe.

Not many miles from the source of the Danube, you will find the city of Ulm, the head of navigation on the river. Ulm is a very old city with crooked streets and narrow houses, many of which have stood since the days, centuries ago, when the crusaders passed down the Danube valley on their way to Asia to rescue the burial place of Christ from the hands of Turkish Mohammedans.

Below Ulm, in place of the acacia trees which lined the banks of the river farther upstream, we see long rows of willows. Beyond them, in the fields, some peasant women are digging potatoes with curious-looking spades. Central Europe produces enormous quantities of potatoes. The crop is so immense that if it were loaded on freight cars of the ordinary capacity, the train would

FIG. 89. THE SOIL IS RICH, AND MUCH GREATER CROPS
THAN ARE NOW HARVESTED MIGHT BE RAISED

be more than long enough to fill three tracks stretching from London across Europe and Asia to Peking, China.

Farther down the river, we see the people working in the hayfields and bending over the long rows of sugar beets. There are many factories where immense quantities of beet sugar are made, and this product is one of the chief exports of the region. Both men and women are at work in the fields. The women and girls can do nearly as much work as the men, but their pay is much smaller, in some cases amounting to only twenty-five dollars a year.

Some heavy, lumbering wagons filled with hay and drawn by cows or oxen are waiting for the ferry to cross the river. The animals show no hesitation in going aboard the large, flat boat and stand quietly chewing their cud while the boat is slowly pulled across the stream by means of wire guys.

Kelheim, where we next stop, is a town of little importance save for the fact that it is the terminus of the Ludwig Canal. This important waterway extends to the Main River and thus joins the waters of the Danube and the Rhine and of the Black and North Seas.

We see many large, flat boats being towed by horses up the stream. These were filled farther up the Danube with grain or with lumber from the mountain forests and were drifted downstream with the current, carrying the horses on board. After the freight is unloaded, the horses drag the empty boats back to the starting place. Most of the long-distance traffic of this part of the Danube Valley is carried on by rail, but the local trade from town to town is carried on in this primitive way on the river.

We are approaching Passau, a queer old town where the houses cling to the steep rocks, and the roads zigzag back and forth up the steep hills. When we consult our maps of the region and find that the city is situated almost on the boundary line of Germany, we understand better the reason for the great fort which crowns the heights.

Just below the city of Passau, the boundary line is marked by a great rock which stands in the middle of the river. As we pass this ancient landmark, we can see on its summit a shrine

FIG. 90. "WE ARE APPROACHING PASSAU, A QUEER OLD TOWN"

with a crucifix and a rude figure of a saint, which, as one author says, "gazes eternally on the flowing river as if looking forward to the time when peace shall dwell between all nations and there shall be no need of the frowning fortress on the heights."

Thus far in our trip, we have seen freight boats, barges towed by horses, and a few small skiffs, but no steamer traffic. The regular steamboat service extends no farther up the river than the city of Passau, but at that place, we can take a comfortable boat, much like those steamers which ply on lakes and rivers in the United States, for places farther downstream.

Many of the small streams which enter the river from the mountains are filled with logs. These are floated down into the Danube, where in places they line the banks, while waiting to be towed down to Vienna. Little villages of quaint houses like those of Switzerland, with broad balconies and overhanging roofs, can be seen in the sheltered valleys and on the more gentle slopes.

This part of the Danube above Vienna rivals the Rhine in beauty. On either side are dark, wooded mountains, and steep

FIG. 91. THERE ARE STEEP CLIFFS WITH RUINED CASTLES CLINGING
TO THEIR SIDES OR PERCHED UPON THEIR SUMMITS

cliffs with ruined castles clinging to their sides or perched upon their summits. Many a gallant crusader and thrifty merchant lost his wealth and perchance his life to the robber knights who lived in these gray old castles and preyed on the travelers who dared attempt the journey down the Danube. The legends of brave knights, cruel robbers, lovely maidens, and horrible witches are as numerous and as fascinating as those of the Rhine.

Soon, the broadening river full of boats and the opening plain surrounded by hills tell us that we are nearing Vienna.

The city stands on the shores of the Danube just where the river enters its way between the Alps on the west and the Carpathians on the east. This natural water highway thus furnishes a route from western Asia into northern and western Europe. Other natural routes of travel lead through passes in the mountains and through river valleys from northern Italy to Germany and Russia. Railroads always follow the easiest routes; therefore, they radiate from Vienna through these natural highways like the spokes of a wheel. The rivers of this section do not lead to open ocean ports, so that most of the ocean-bound freight is carried by rail, and Vienna has thus become a great railroad center.

We should like to remain in the city for some days, to visit the great university, to see the royal palace, to drive between the long rows of linden trees on the Ringstrasse, the beautiful boulevard which has been built around the city where the ancient moat once lay, or to walk in one of the finest of all the parks of Europe, the Prater. This beautiful pleasure resort contains stately forests of oaks, elms, and chestnuts, lovely gardens, sparkling lakes, and wide avenues. There are games and shows and animals and merry-go-rounds, and so many interesting sights that we should find plenty of entertainment for many hours. But we finally decide to turn from these and the other attractions to another part of the city, where the great cotton and silk mills and other factories are located.

We are interested in the glove manufactures and buy several

© Underwood & Underwood

FIG. 92. THE PRATER IS ONE OF THE FINEST PARKS IN EUROPE

pairs, for they are of fine quality and cheaper than they are in America. Skins from the sheep and lambs which feed on the plain of Hungary, and from the goats which wander over the pastures of the Balkan Peninsula, are used in great quantities in the leather manufactories of Vienna, and many gloves are exported from the city.

We see also in the stores musical and scientific instruments and glittering displays of china and glassware. Many railroads branch out from Vienna, carrying these and other products to all parts of Europe and to the seaports to be shipped to other continents.

With regret, we leave the gay city behind us and continue our sail down the river. This part of the trip is made in a large steamer which reminds us of those used on the Hudson River. Pleasure boats, carrying merry Viennese crowds, are flying up and down. The river is full of craft passing and repassing the huge rafts of lumber - heavy boats filled with grain, and puffing tugs towing vessels many times larger than themselves.

Some thirty or more miles from Vienna, the hills close in on either side of the river, and we know that beyond them lies the object of our sail - the great plain of Hungary. The Carpathian Mountains encircle it for nine hundred miles, forming a natural boundary from the northwest around to the east and south. Besides the opening in the mountains through which the river enters from the west, and the narrow gorge in the south where it works its way through the heights out of Hungarian territory, the only means of communication between the enclosed plain and the outside world is through a few difficult mountain passes. The Danube, as you can see, is the only natural waterway which connects the valley of Hungary with other countries. There is only one river in the whole plain, a small branch of the Vistula, which does not finally join the Danube on its way to the Black Sea. For more than six hundred miles, a distance about equal to that from Duluth to St. Louis, winding in and out across the level plain, bordered by cornfields and waving wheat, the great river flows on, the ill-remembered remnant of an immense lake which once filled the whole valley. Through long ages, the basin has been gradually filled by the fine, rich soil brought by the streams from the mountains around. This deposit, which in places is several hundred feet thick, is the secret of the great fertility of the region. There are a few barren tracts, but nearly all of this great Hungarian plain is capable of producing immense crops much larger than the peasant of today, in his ignorance of scientific agriculture, has dreamed of raising. For miles and miles on either side of the river, one can see fields of nodding wheat, yellow corn, climbing hops, blue-eyed flax, stalky hemp, grapes ripening in the sun, tobacco plants hiding the ground beneath their great leaves, and acres of mealy potatoes such as a Maine farmer might well envy. We must not picture this whole region, however, as a plain. Though there are large areas as level as a floor, there are also great stretches of rolling, hilly land much like parts of New England. In the pastures of the upland region, large numbers of horses and cattle feed, and in the oak forests, thousands of hogs live on the acorns. In every village, you can hear the cackling of hens and the crowing of roosters.

A ride through the Danube Valley furnishes many odd, interesting sights. Down by the river is a swineherd tending the hogs from the village yonder; he makes a curious appearance in his long blouse and full trousers. He has a staff to aid him in

FIG. 93. ON SOME LEVEL PIECE OF LAND NEAR THE WHEAT FIELDS THE GRAIN IS STACKED TO AWAIT THRESHING

guiding his squealing charges, and he carries a long, curiously shaped pipe from which he enjoys his afternoon smoke. When the sun gets low, he drives the hogs back to the village and sees that each animal finds its way to its own sty, which is nearer to the family quarters than we should think pleasant.

The country is very different from a farming area in the United States. There are no farmhouses dotting the landscape, surrounded by orchards, green fields, and ripening crops. The peasants live in villages and often go several miles to their work. During the day, the villages are deserted except for a few old people and babies. In the early morning, the entire population walks, or perhaps rides in springless wagons along the uneven track, which serves as a road, to the farmlands, where they work until nearly dusk. At nightfall, the rattle of the wagons and the merry chatter of the boys and girls herald their return to their homes.

The scattered buildings in the village often cover an area large enough for a good-sized city. The houses are low, one-story, whitewashed structures on either side of wide, unpaved streets, which are deep with dust in summer and gullied with rains in winter. Every house has its loom, which is heard continually throughout the winter months when the women are weaving the cloth with which the family is clothed. Not many moments are wasted. Even the time they spend on the long ride to and from the farms is often occupied in knitting some warm garment for the cold winter days.

A harvesting scene in the Danube valley is very different from one on the great plains of the United States, where harvesting machines thresh, bag, and process the grain. On the Hungarian plain, old-fashioned methods prevail for the most part, though the number of up-to-date farming implements is increasing rapidly. We see in many places men beating out the grain with pitchforks and flails; others are driving horses round and round over the straw spread out upon the ground, to loosen the seeds. With the introduction of more modern methods of cultivating and harvesting, the crop raised in the Danube valley will be greatly increased.

As we continue our trip on the Danube, we find the scenes on the water fully as interesting as those upon the land, for the peasants use the river and its branches for many purposes.

FIG. 94. MANY OF THE WOMEN OCCUPY THEIR TIME DURING
THE DAY BY WASHING ON THE RIVER BANKS

Whole families come to spend the day on the banks. The children watch the pigs and fowl on the shore, while at the same time their fingers are busy with some piece of embroidery, for the peasants do beautiful work and like to decorate their garments with fine needlework.

The women occupy their time by washing on the river banks. On the flat rocks, they pound out the dirt from the clothes with a wooden mallet and carry them to the shore in rude tubs on their heads. Some of the men tend the cattle, while others take the corn to the mill to be ground. It is chiefly for this latter reason that they have come to the river, for in Hungary, most of the mills for grinding the grain are situated in the water. All along this part of the Danube, near the banks where the current is swift, these curious structures may be seen. The water wheels are supported by two boats of different sizes. The larger one contains the mill and the home of the miller, while the smaller boat, farther out in the stream, contains the rest of the machinery.

A great deal of the grain raised in Hungary is ground in these river mills. In the harvest season, the peasants drive their slow, lumbering carts, drawn by oxen or buffaloes, across the plain to the Danube and camp on its banks, awaiting their turn for the grinding of their grain. The journey often takes many days, for the teams are slow and the roads are rough. The peasants carry no tents or extra clothing, and but little food. When night comes, they eat their coarse bread, then lie down on the ground beside the tired oxen, and sleep under the stars until daylight awakens them. The carts are rude affairs, made of rough wood and held together for the most part by wooden pins. Centuries ago, the army of crusaders might have seen just such teams crawling over the plains to the river towns, for customs change slowly in interior countries.

Besides the grain which is ground in the mills on the river, a great deal is floated down to the Black Sea and there loaded onto steamers to be carried to different European countries. Great quantities are also taken down as far as Budapest or towed

FIG. 95. THE PEASANTS DRIVE THEIR SLOW,
LUMBERING CARTS ACROSS THE PLAIN

FIG. 96. "THE WHITE WALLS OF THE ROYAL PALACE GLEAM FROM THE HILLTOP"

upstream to Vienna, where many large modern mills, similar to those in Minneapolis, are situated.

Budapest, splendidly situated in the heart of the country and at the lowest place on the Danube where it can be easily bridged, is the center of Hungarian trade. It is made up of two cities, Buda and Pest, the one on the right bank of the Danube, which here is wider than the Thames at London, and the other on the left. Buda, on the west bank, is the older, the smaller, and the more hilly of the two. On the rocky heights above the city stands an old fortress, keeping watch over the river at its feet. The white walls of the royal palace gleam from the hilltop. The parliament houses of the capital are in Pest, which is situated on the low plain on the eastern bank of the Danube. Here also are most of the business blocks and fine business houses.

Budapest has been a rapidly growing city. Today, it is larger than St. Louis and ranks high in commerce and industry. Because of its situation on the river, it carries on a great trade in grain, wine, wool, cattle, and other goods.

Though Budapest is modern in all its aspects, scenes of a very different life lie very near. You could not go far from the city without meeting many gypsies, for in Hungary, there are thousands of these thriftless, ignorant, superstitious people. They usually live on the outskirts of the villages and towns,

FIG. 97. "BUDAPEST IS MODERN IN ALL ITS ASPECTS"

and although the location is often beautiful, the houses and people are filthy. Sometimes, the houses are half buried in the ground, and only the thatched roofs are visible.

The gypsies seldom engage in any regular occupation. The women sometimes tell fortunes, and the men often do blacksmithing, basket-making, or whitewashing, but there is little skilled labor among them. They are very fond of music, and no village festival is complete without the gypsy band.

Besides the grain from the borders of the Danube, great quantities are brought from the valleys of the Tisza and the Drave rivers. In their basins are the same level stretches, the same straggling villages, the same rich soil, and the same abundant crops as in the valley of the Danube. Thousands of Magyars, Jews, Russians, Bulgarians, and Serbians, each with a different language, different customs, and different dress, are engaged in raising the same kind of crops. Down the winding Tisza and the muddy Drave, and through the canals connecting them with the Danube, come barges loaded deep with grain and rafts of lumber from the distant forests. Whole families live in the tiny houses on both barges and rafts. The children play, and the women attend to the cooking and washing as if they were on land, while the men guide the heavy craft on its slow journey.

At the junction of the Save and Danube Rivers lies Belgrade, the capital of the new country of Yugoslavia. Due to its strategic location as the key to the rich plain of Hungary, it has, for ages, been an object of warfare between the countries to the north and south. It has been captured and recaptured many times by these nations.

Beyond Belgrade, the river flows on — now through fertile plains, now between green foothills, across smiling valleys rich in yellow grain fields — straight on to a narrowing gorge, beyond which loom lofty mountains. The gorge becomes narrower and darker, the scene wilder and more gloomy, the cliffs higher and straighter, until the Danube finally makes a wild dash between them and emerges swirling, hurrying, dashing, and tumbling over the rocks at Orsova, the Iron Gate.

The most dangerous part of this stretch of water is now avoided by a canal, while other sections have been improved through deepening of the channel and the removal of rocks, allowing vessels drawing nine feet of water to safely pass. The Iron Gate has been, since ancient times, a place of great importance, forming a natural barrier on this vital water highway that connects East and West.

At one time, Russia controlled the mouth of the Danube and imposed restrictive laws on river traffic to benefit its own trade. However, this is no longer possible, as an international commission, composed of men from all interested countries, now regulates and controls its navigation. The commission has surveyed and made detailed maps of the delta, improved one of the mouths by constructing canals to bypass dangerous areas, deepened the channel, shortened the route through cuttings, and generally supported the commerce of the countries within the Danube Valley.

TOPICS FOR STUDY

I.

1. The former empire of Austria-Hungary.
2. The new countries of Central Europe.
3. Czechoslovakia.
4. Life and industries in Bohemia.
5. The old city of Prague.
6. Yugoslavia.
7. Life in Serbia.
8. The city of Belgrade.
9. The present country of Austria.
10. The Danube River and its valley.
11. Vienna and Budapest.

II.

1. Sketch Central Europe, showing the boundaries of the countries before the war.
2. Sketch another map of Central Europe, depicting the countries as they are today.
3. Identify the names of countries that have disappeared from the map of Central Europe and note the new ones.
4. Explain the importance of Serbia's position.
5. Discuss why Belgrade has become such an important city, and the significance of Vienna and Budapest.

III.

Spell and pronounce the following names, locate each place, and recount what was mentioned about it in this and any previous chapter. Add any additional facts if possible.

Austria	Duluth	Drave River
Austria-Hungary	London	Elbe River
Balkan	Moscow	Great Lakes
Peninsula	Orsova	Hudson River
Bohemia	Passau	Ludwig Canal
Czechoslovakia	Peking	Main River

Germany
Hungary
Italy
Yugoslavia
Montenegro
Russia
Serbia
Turkey
Belgrade
Budapest
Constantinople

Prague
St. Louis
Salonika
Ulm
Vienna
Washington
Adriatic Sea
Aegean Sea
Black Sea
Danube River

North Sea
Rhine River
Save River
St. Lawrence
  River
Thames River
Tisza River
Vistula River
Alps Mountains
Black Forest
  Mountains
Carpathian
  Mountains

CHAPTER XIII

THE NETHERLANDS AND OTHER DAIRYING COUNTRIES

Our next visit will be to the Netherlands, a country vastly different from any other we have studied. The land is lower than the ocean and nearly as level as a classroom floor. There are no hills, stones, or rushing waterfalls. Instead, the fences are ditches filled with water rather than wire or wooden barriers. The people even wash their sidewalks, scrub their barns, and blanket their cows to shield them from flies and cold. Surely, this visit to such an unusual land will be fascinating.

All of the Netherlands, most of Denmark, and the northern part of Belgium collectively form what is termed the "Low Countries." Of these, the Netherlands is most renowned for its dairy products, so we will start there. This small country is only one and a half times the size of Massachusetts but has about twice its population. However, it differs greatly from Massachusetts, as it has neither hills nor stones, while Massachusetts has an abundance of both. More than half of the Dutch population lives on farms, whereas most people in Massachusetts reside in cities. The Netherlands has over two million cattle, in stark contrast to Massachusetts, which has only about one-eighth that number. To truly see the heart of the Netherlands' main industry, one must visit its farms, small villages, and towns, not its cities or large factories.

Before embarking on this visit, it is essential to understand why the Netherlands has become a major dairying country. From your studies of the United States, you know that the industrial life of any place largely depends on the natural forces at work around it. The story of these forces and their impact on this part of Europe is compelling.

Long ago, the area now known as the Netherlands was part of a vast ocean. The Rhine, Scheldt, Meuse, and smaller rivers scoured the land and carried northward their loads of silt, much of it originating from the lofty mountains to the south. This silt gradually built up the land. The winds and waves washed sand back and forth from the ocean bed, creating dunes near what is now the shoreline. Between these dunes and the mainland, water still lay. Over time, the rivers deposited so much silt in this basin that the land began to rise above the water's surface, extending the coastline and leaving large lakes in the deepest parts of the basin.

The mighty ocean did not surrender this land easily and often surged over it, destroying farms, cattle, and entire villages. A catastrophic flood in the 15th century, for example, submerged thousands of acres and destroyed numerous villages. After each disaster the sturdy Dutch people tried harder than before to protect their precious land. Strong earth walls called dikes were made to keep out the ocean, and windmills were built to pump out the water which accumulated in the inclosed land. These reclaimed areas were called polders, and every polder which was made was a victory of the persevering people over the mighty ocean. The work went on little by little; every year more dikes

FIG. 98. WINDMILLS PUMP WATER FROM CANALS; OTHERS GRIND GRAIN

were built, more windmills pumped out the inclosed water, and more acres of fine farming land were added to the area of the country.

If you look at the map of the Netherlands, you will see in the northern part a large indentation called the Zuider Zee. This is a part of the ocean basin that has never been entirely filled by the wash from the rivers whose courses lie farther to the south and west. The name Zuider Zee means "Southern Sea" and was given to the inlet in contrast to the larger body of water beyond, known as the North Sea.

The Zuider Zee has existed only since the twelfth century, for before that time, the part of the country where it now lies was covered by lakes and marshes. The Zuider Zee is about eighty miles long from north to south and about forty miles wide at its widest part. The Dutch people have now set themselves the gigantic task of reclaiming the southern part of this great basin.

The entire work will take between thirty and forty years and will be done step by step, as the task is far too great to complete as a whole. The undertaking has been so well-planned that all the nearby cities and the rivers of the region will remain undisturbed. The work will be so gradually carried out that the people engaged in the fisheries of the Zuider Zee will have time to adjust themselves to the changed conditions.

The entire cost of this great project will be nearly one hundred million dollars—an immense sum for a small nation to raise. But the Dutch people are willing to make the investment, knowing that the eight hundred square miles of fertile land added to their country will yield rich returns.

Having learned something of how the country was made, let us see how it looks. We can travel the entire length and breadth of it without seeing a high hill or finding a large stone. The whole surface is as level as a floor and covered with the thickest, greenest grass imaginable. Everywhere throughout the country, scattered over the flat meadows, are large, fat, clean, contented-looking black-and-white cows. You might look for a long time without seeing a red cow such as is common in the United

© Underwood & Underwood

FIG. 99. IN RECENT YEARS LARGE DAIRIES HAVE BEEN ESTABLISHED WHERE CHEESE IS MADE IN GREAT QUANTITIES BY MODERN METHODS

States, though a few such are now owned in the Netherlands.

If good care, cleanliness, and nourishing food can make a cow happy, then the Dutch herds are certainly to be envied above all others. Their food is of the best quality and is very carefully prepared. They are blanketed to protect them from flies and from the cold winds of autumn, and they live in stables as clean as soap and water can make them. Indeed, many houses in our country would suffer by comparison.

Cattle tended with such care and given such nourishing food naturally yield great quantities of milk. The greater part of this milk is made into butter and cheese, both of which are noted for their excellence. Formerly, both products were made by hand on the small farms, much as they are today. However, in recent years, large dairies have been established, as in most dairying countries. The farmers sell their milk to these dairies, where butter and cheese are made in great quantities using modern machinery.

The cheese markets of the Netherlands are very interesting. We could find such a market in many towns in the northern part of the country, but the largest and most important is in the small town of Alkmaar, so we will choose that one for our visit.

The square where the market is held is surrounded on three sides by tall, narrow buildings, and on the fourth side by a canal. The market is held every Friday, and on Thursday afternoons, the canal is filled with boats and barges piled high with round, yellow balls. Queer-looking wagons painted bright red, green, or blue come in from the country loaded with nothing but cheeses.

Until late in the evening, the streets resound with the voices of young men and maidens, who make a celebration of the occasion, and the wagons rattle over the pavements throughout the entire night.

Having selected a good spot for his product, the farmer tosses the golden balls from the boat or wagon to an assistant, who catches them as skillfully as a baseball player would and piles them carefully on the ground. Once all the cheeses are unloaded, they are covered with sailcloth until the market opens. The piles are usually eight or ten cheeses wide, thirty to fifty long, and only two layers deep.

Before market time, some of the sellers can be seen carefully rubbing their cheeses with oil until they shine. The market opens promptly at ten o'clock. A little before that hour, a number of men in white suits, with hats of red, yellow, blue, or some other bright color, begin to gather in the market square. These are the porters who carry the cheeses to the weighing house. The men who do the weighing wear similarly colored hats, and each porter must take his load to the corresponding weigher.

When the clock in the old church tower announces the opening of the market, the country people remove the covering from their shining products, and the merchants begin their inspection of the wares. The seller stands quietly with an unconcerned air while the buyer feels, smells, and perhaps tastes some of the cheeses in the pile. The bargain is quickly made and is confirmed by a striking together of the hands of the two parties. To an outsider, this handshake might look like a cordial morning greeting between the merchant and the farmer.

As the buyer moves on to another pile, the farmer who has closed his deal hires some of the porters to carry his cheeses to the weighing house. By eleven o'clock, the market is nearly over, and when the chimes ring at twelve, the square is empty, the cheeses, merchants, and farmers having disappeared as if by magic, leaving the square deserted until the next market day.

The number of cheeses sold at Alkmaar each Friday is astonishing. It is not unusual for one hundred thousand to change hands during the morning. There are many cheese markets scattered across the country, primarily in the northern region, although none handle as much business as Alkmaar. The quantity of cheese produced annually in the Netherlands is truly impressive. If divided among the population, each person would have around thirty pounds, but fortunately for their health, more than two-thirds of the product is exported.

More than three thousand freight cars are needed to transport the annual cheese exports from the dairies to Amsterdam. Six or seven hundred of these cars carry England's share, while the rest are shipped to various other countries.

Some of you may be wondering what cheese is and how it is made. When rennet, a substance obtained from a calf's stomach, is added to milk, it curdles the milk. In this process, the casein and fat, two of the primary elements in milk, separate and form a solid called curds, while the remaining liquid is known as whey.

When the curds are pressed, more whey is removed. Salt is added, and the mixture is worked over. It is then placed into molds of the desired shape and pressed again, after which the cheese is left to ripen for days or weeks. During this ripening process, certain types of mold grow, giving each cheese its distinct flavor.

The Dutch do not use all their milk for cheese-making. In the southern part of the country especially, great quantities are used for butter. A freight train long enough to carry the entire cheese product of the Netherlands would stretch about twenty

© Underwood & Underwood

FIG. 100. CHEESES IN A MODERN DAIRY

miles, while one carrying the butter product would be only four miles shorter.

Let us leave the dairy farms and the flat, green meadows dotted with black-and-white cows, and follow the butter and cheese to the shipping port of Amsterdam, so that we may see what a Dutch city is like.

Amsterdam has often been compared to Venice. Both cities have numerous canals which serve as streets, and both are connected by hundreds of bridges. Both cities are also commercial centers, but Venice, for the most part, belongs to the past, while Amsterdam thrives in the present. In the northern city, as well as in the southern, the visitor will notice that the water in the canals is very dirty, and there is an abundance of various smells arising from it. However, it is where the resemblance ends. Amsterdam, in contrast to Venice, is cold, practical, and matter-of-fact. Venice, on the other hand, is warm, romantic, and full of poetry. Venice boasts of its beautiful, historic palaces, while Amsterdam is filled with solid, dignified, but not necessarily beautiful houses. Most of the buildings in Amsterdam are constructed on foundations of piles that are driven deep into the loose soil. It is said that constructing the part of the house below the ground costs as much as building the part that stands above.

In some of the older streets, the piles have settled unevenly in the swampy soil, so that the houses tilt forward as if they were trying to make it possible for the people living in the upper stories to shake hands across the narrow streets. These old houses are tall and narrow, often with very slanting roofs, and are usually built with the gable end facing the street. In many of these houses, fastened close to the window on the second floor, is a small mirror that can be tipped in various directions. By looking into this mirror, the Dutch housewife, while busy with her knitting, can watch the activities in the street or see who her visitor is without having to go to the door.

Though the water in the canals of Amsterdam is dirty, the houses themselves are spotlessly clean. The Dutch housekeeper is known for being constantly scrubbing. Furniture, walls, win-

FIG. 101. AMSTERDAM HAS MANY CANALS WHICH SERVE AS STREETS

dows, doorsteps, and sidewalks are all as clean as soapsuds and strong arms can make them, and one writer even declares that the trunks of the trees are scrubbed as well. Whether or not this is true, all other things around the house certainly get their weekly bath. It is possible that the fine quality of Dutch butter and cheese is, at least in part, due to the exceptionally clean conditions in which the cows are kept, as well as the cleanliness of the stables, pails, and tubs used in their care.

If we could look down upon Amsterdam from an airship, we would see a dense collection of dull-red peaked roofs, with here and there a church tower rising above them. Winding through the city in and out, among the buildings, are broad, dark canals, crossed by many bridges and filled with low, flat barges, or ships carrying masts taller than some of the houses. The larger vessels are found on the two most important canals: the North Holland Canal and the North Sea Canal, both of which connect Amsterdam with open water and make the city a crucial commercial port of the North Sea.

In the smaller canals, we would see hundreds of broad, flat barges. Would you like to live on one of these, creeping slowly day after day up and down the winding canals? If you were a Dutch boy, you would take your turn walking on the bank, pulling the boat along by a stout rope, while your father sat at the stern, smoking the long pipe that is rarely out of a Dutchman's mouth and steering the heavy craft.

Hundreds and thousands of families in the Netherlands know no other home than these barges. They have their own tiny rooms in the stern of the boat, their cages of songbirds, and their neat little flower gardens. They live happily and contentedly in their moving homes.

One of the industries we may wish to explore in Amsterdam is that of diamond-cutting. Amsterdam is one of the chief centers of the world for this work, and many precious stones are cut and polished in its workshops. When diamonds are extracted from the mine, they are rough and dull, requiring skilled artisans to cut them in such a way that no pieces of the precious gems are wasted, and to polish them until they glitter and glisten in the light.

A diamond is the hardest of stones and can only be cut by another diamond, while it can only be polished with diamond dust. That which gathers from polishing the stones is so valuable that every grain is carefully collected and stored in metal

© Underwood & Underwood

FIG. 102. A FAMILIAR SIGHT IN
PARTS OF THE NETHERLANDS

boxes. The United States is the largest customer for the diamond merchants of Amsterdam, with more than half of the sparkling gems cut in the city being bought by Americans.

The colonial possessions of the Netherlands are more than fifty times the size of the country itself, and much of its commerce is conducted with these faraway lands. At the docks in Amsterdam, we can observe vessels from both the Dutch East and West Indies. Some of these ships have brought cargoes of coffee and linseed oil, as Amsterdam is one of the world's greatest markets for both of these products. Other ships from these rich islands in the East carry tea, sugar, spices, and cinchona bark, which is used to make quinine, a bitter medicine. There are also grain ships carrying rye from Russia and wheat from the United States, along with many other vessels from nearby European countries and faraway lands. These ships are loaded with manufactured goods such as leather, sugar, pottery, tiles, bricks, glassware, fish, cattle, dairy products, and bulbs and seeds for the return journey.

In the Netherlands, more people, in proportion to the whole population, are engaged in dairying than in any other country in the world. However, in many other countries, the dairy industry remains very important. Across the Channel in the British Isles, enormous quantities of butter and even larger amounts of fine cheese are produced in ordinary years. The quantity produced is enough to provide every person in London with between thirty and forty pounds of both items each year. Despite this,

England still imports large amounts of butter and cheese, as there are many other large cities to supply. Great quantities of dairy products come from Siberia, a region in which the dairy industry has grown faster than people realize. In typical years, fast freights run from Siberia across the Russian plain, carrying nothing but butter destined for the London markets. Both butter and cheese are also imported from Norway, Sweden, Denmark, the Netherlands, Belgium, and Switzerland. Ireland's exports of butter, nearly all of which are sent to England, are, after cattle, of greater value than any other product exported from the Emerald Isle. The government has played a role in establishing large dairies in Ireland, and it is common to see barefooted boys or girls driving scores of donkey carts, loaded with fresh milk for the dairy, or carrying skimmed milk back to the farm to be fed to the calves or pigs.

Denmark is also an important dairying country. It is low, flat, and fertile, much like the Netherlands, and farming is the primary occupation of the people. Butter is Denmark's largest export by value, surpassing all other items combined. Danish butter is considered by many to be the finest in the world, and it is shipped in sealed cans to all parts of the globe.

Most of Denmark's butter is shipped from Copenhagen, the only truly large city in the country. Copenhagen is about the same size as Buffalo, New York. Perhaps the chief reason for Copenhagen's importance lies in its position at the entrance to the Baltic Sea, where it has the only good harbor on the Danish coast. Copenhagen has historically been a "Merchant's Haven" where Russian ships bound for the open sea, along with ships from Norway and eastern Germany, stop at its port. Today, many vessels from the Baltic Sea shorten their route by taking the Kiel Canal, and some from Sweden opt for the shorter voyage through the Göta Canal. Despite these shorter routes, more than fifteen thousand ships, carrying large quantities of grain, dairy products, beef, cattle, wool, and hides, leave Copenhagen's harbor annually. The city is considered one of the principal ports of Northern Europe.

It is not alone its commerce that has made Copenhagen the

© Underwood & Underwood

FIG. 103. COPENHAGEN IS ONE OF THE PRINCIPAL PORTS OF NORTHERN EUROPE

most important city of Denmark, for being the only large city, most of the manufacturing also is done there. We might visit porcelain works and piano factories, watch the fine processes of clock and watchmaking, or see in our walks about the city great sugar refineries, distilleries, and tobacco factories. Copenhagen is also a center of literature and art, not only of Denmark but of northern Europe. It contains a fine library and a wonderful museum of northern antiquities in which the customs of the people of Denmark from earliest times may be traced. Weapons, pottery, jewels, facsimiles of dwellings, clothing, and many other interesting exhibits dating back to the Stone and Bronze Ages are preserved there.

In the little country of Switzerland, nestled among the high Alps, there are many cattle, sheep, and goats that feed in the mountain pastures. On a summer trip through the country, you would wonder where all the animals were, for you would see scarcely any in the valleys. If they were kept in the lower fields,

© Underwood & Underwood

FIG. 104. THE LITTLE COUNTRY OF SWITZERLAND IS
NESTLED AMONG THE HIGH MOUNTAINS

they would eat so much of the grass that there would be but little hay for their winter food; so in the early summer, the boys and girls drive them high on the hills and mountains, where they remain until cold weather approaches. During the summer, the young people remain in the high pastures tending the animals, making butter and cheese, cutting the grass which the cattle do not need, and spending their spare minutes knitting warm socks for the coming winter. Cold weather comes early in the mountain pastures, and there is a great holiday in the fall when the cattle and sheep come down the steep paths to the valleys.

Those boys and girls who do not go to the mountains in the summer find plenty of other work to keep them busy. Switzerland has sometimes been called the Playground of the World, for between four and five hundred thousand tourists visit the country in normal years, most of them in the summer months. Some of the young Swiss people work in the hotels scattered over the country. There are so many of these, and they do such a thriving business, that hotelkeeping has been called one of the chief industries of Switzerland. Many of the tourists wish to climb the mountains, but this is usually dangerous work unless they are accompanied by a guide thoroughly acquainted with the region. No one knows the Alps so well as the sturdy young Switzers who have spent their lives among them, and hundreds of young men find occupation in this way, while during the winter months, many of the men and boys spend their time carving out of wood chairs, tables, picture frames, paper cutters, umbrella holders, and boxes of all kinds, which the tourists buy in great quantities.

In driving through the quaint little Swiss villages, we should see the girls and women sitting in front of their neat chalets, as the Swiss houses are called, doing exquisite embroidery or tossing the bobbins in and out, in and out, as they add inch by inch to the beautiful lace which each worker is making on a hard pillow in her lap. This work furnishes occupation for all the spare minutes during the summer months and for the long hours in the winter when there is no work to be done outside on the little farm. Great quantities of embroideries are also made by machinery, and this industry is one of the most important in Switzerland, employing more than seventy-five thousand people. Wonderful machines have been invented, and the work that they do is so fine and beautiful that it is hard in some cases to tell whether or not it is done by hand. American manufacturers of embroideries are equipping their plants with Swiss machinery, and a majority of the factories in St. Gall, the center of the industry in Switzerland, are either owned outright or controlled by Americans. It seems hardly possible that little Switzerland, a country only about twice the size of Massachusetts, can furnish more than thirty-five million dollars' worth of hand-worked and machine-made embroideries, but this immense quantity is exported every year.

Making articles for the tourist trade, working on the farm, doing the housework, tending the cattle, and making butter and cheese keep most of the Swiss people busy throughout the year. Not all of the people, however, live on farms, for there are large, important manufacturing cities in Switzerland. The country is so centrally located that, since the mountains have been tunneled, it is easy to import materials and to send away manufactured products. In the chapter on silk, you will read of Zurich, the largest city and the center of the silk industry. Of the eighty silk mills in Switzerland, the majority are in and around Zurich, where this old industry flourishes with most up-to-date machinery and inventions. Basel, another important Swiss city, is noted the world over for its manufacture of ribbons.

Perhaps some of you may own or may have seen a Swiss watch. These are made in the city of Geneva, which has long been famous for the manufacture of watches and jewelry. To many people, the shop windows with their fascinating displays prove as attractive as the blue waters of the Lake of Geneva with its border of rugged mountains. Watchmaking is one of the oldest industries in Switzerland and is carried on today in several cities besides Geneva.

Another industry in Switzerland in which every boy and girl who likes candy will be interested is the making of sweet chocolate. Thousands of tons of cakes of chocolate and cans of cocoa, worth millions of dollars, are made in Switzerland every year. Most of it is of a very superior quality and is sold in large quantities to other European countries.

All these and other industries were greatly interrupted by the four years of the World War. Switzerland was not one of the fighting countries, but she was surrounded by nations at war. Her trade was entirely cut off and her industries crippled.

Of course, no tourists visited Switzerland during the war, and her big hotels were all closed except a few which were used as hospitals for soldiers of the Allied armies.

About four-fifths of Switzerland is very mountainous. Few people live in these parts except tourists and hotelkeepers who stay during the summer months. Most of the people live in the lowlands. Here the soil is good, but the area is too small to support many of the population. Hence, the people have turned to other occupations. The mountains, which have proved such an obstacle in many ways, have been of great help in others. Tourists in large numbers have been attracted by their beauty. Many of the slopes are covered with forests. The people use the wood in making toys and various articles of furniture and have become very skilled in such work. In some towns and cities, woodcarving is taught in the schools. Tumbling down the steep mountain sides, there are hundreds of streams which furnish an enormous amount of water power for manufacturing. This power is one of Switzerland's most important resources, and each year sees more and more of it being utilized. The electricity generated by this power runs trolley cars and many railroads. Another use which is made of it is the taking of nitrogen from the air and making it into fertilizer. About four-fifths of the air is nitrogen. Plants are very dependent on it and must have it in certain forms to help their growth. The nitrate beds of Chile, South America, are very valuable and for years have furnished a large part of the world's supply. These deposits will not last forever, and so, as they have done in other ways, the chemists have come to the help of the farmer. They have experimented in taking nitrogen from the air and getting it to unite with other substances so that it might be used in fertilizers. Switzerland, Norway, the United States, and Germany have gone ahead of other countries in this industry and have been for some years perfecting machinery and methods by which this important work may be done. Both Switzerland and Norway are mountainous countries and have been greatly aided by the immense amount of water power which they possess. Their "white coal" enables them to run their machinery more cheaply than those countries which depend on the black mineral mined in the earth.

Before we leave the dairying countries, we must visit the little mountain village of Roquefort, in the southwestern part of France, where cheese-making has been carried on for eight hundred years. The region around is of limestone formation, which is easily worn away by water, and consequently, the mountains contain many deep caves and dark passages. In the town, there are less than a thousand people. Their tall, narrow houses clinging to the steep slopes look very queer to us, for they have only one or two rooms on a floor and are from two to four stories high. The wealth of these village people is in the awkward, long-legged sheep, which find their food in the scanty herbage of the mountain sides. The milk which is obtained from them forms the chief support of the villagers; it is sold to the large firms which control the dairy industry of this region, and is made in their great factories into cheese. This is put to ripen into the cool caves in the mountains, where the peculiar form of mold which develops in Roquefort cheese gives it its special flavor.

The United States raises more cattle than any other country. Our great area gives us plenty of room for pasture land, and our fertile soil yields quantities of grass for hay; so we are not surprised to learn that the United States ranks first in the world in the amount and value of its dairy products. We produce enough milk every year to fill a tank fifty feet in diameter and one hundred miles high. The butter made annually in the United States would make a square pile one hundred feet on a side and half a mile high. To appreciate better this immense quantity, measure the length and width of your school building and compare its dimensions with those of the pile of butter. If the cheese manufactured every year in this country were spread out six inches deep between the rails of an airline railroad, it would reach from Chicago to Charleston, South Carolina.

The manufacture of such immense quantities of butter and cheese as are produced in our country and in other lands furnishes occupation for thousands of people. Thousands more find employment in caring for the cattle which produce the milk. In making both butter and cheese, great quantities of salt are used, and the production of this necessary article gives work to other thousands in various parts of the world.

Let us leave the green, fertile plains of the Netherlands, the mountain pastures of Switzerland, and the cool caves of Roquefort for Poland, one of the most interesting countries of the new Europe.

TOPICS FOR STUDY

I

1. The Low Countries.
2. The Story of the Formation of the Netherlands.
3. Floods and Dikes.
4. Reclaiming the Zuider Zee.
5. Appearance of the Netherlands.
6. The Cheese Market of Alkmaar.
7. How Cheese is Made.
8. Butter-making in the Netherlands.
9. Description of Amsterdam.
10. Dairying in the British Isles.
11. Butter-making in Denmark.
12. Description of Copenhagen.
13. Dairying in Switzerland.
14. Other Industries in Switzerland.
15. Cities of Switzerland.
16. Roquefort Cheese.
17. Dairying in the United States.

II

1. What is said in Chapter III of Ireland as a dairying country? What facts are added in this chapter?
2. Sketch a map of Europe and color all the countries where dairying is an important occupation.
3. Add to your map the names of all the cities, rivers, and other bodies of water mentioned in this chapter.

4. Do you know Phoebe Cary's poem, "The Leak in the Dike"? Tell the story as told in the poem.

5. Write a list of the chief colonial possessions of the Netherlands. What early settlements were made in America by the Dutch?

6. Ship a cargo of dairy products from Amsterdam to each of the Dutch possessions. Tell the waters sailed on in each voyage, the destination, and the return cargo.

7. Where do the diamonds which are cut in Amsterdam come from?

8. Trace the route on which the diamonds are taken from the mines to the city of Amsterdam.

9. Name the causes which have made Copenhagen an important city.

10. By what route do goods come from Zurich to New York? From Basel? From Geneva?

11. Write a list of the industries of Switzerland. Give the reasons for the carrying on of each industry. Which one would you best like to see?

12. Write a list of the chief dairying states in the United States. What states raise cattle for beef?

III

Be able to spell and pronounce the following names. Locate each place and tell what was said of it in this and in any previous chapter. Add other facts if possible.

Belgium	Norway	Basel
British Isles	Russia	Copenhagen
Denmark	Siberia	Detroit
East Indies	Sweden	Geneva
England	Switzerland	London
France	United States	Roquefort
Germany	West Indies	St. Gall
Ireland		Venice
Italy	Alkmaar	Zurich
Massachusetts	Amsterdam	

Baltic Sea
English Channel
Göta Canal
Kiel Canal
Meuse River

North Holland
  Canal
North Sea
North Sea Canal
Po River

Rhine River
Scheldt River
Zuider Zee

CHAPTER XIV

THE COUNTRY OF POLAND

The next place which we will visit is Poland, one of the countries of new Europe. We cannot call it one of the new countries of Europe, for Poland is a very old country. Centuries before the explorers set sail from western Europe to discover and colonize a new world, the kings of Poland were ruling over a large kingdom. At the time of its greatest power, in the latter part of the sixteenth century, Poland was considerably larger than Germany is today and was one of the greatest powers in Europe.

For many years since that time, however, though there were millions of Poles in Europe, there was no Poland. A Polish poem says,

> "The wild dove has its nest, and the worm a clod of earth,
> Each man has a country, The Pole has but a grave."

The downfall of the ancient and powerful kingdom of Poland was due largely to two causes. The first one had to do with the surface of the land. Ancient Poland was a great plain with few natural boundaries to separate it from her ambitious neighbors, no high mountains, no great rivers, no wide expanse of sea or desert. Such boundaries are always a great protection to a country. In the absence of such natural defenses, Poland, however, could be easily invaded by the armies of her enemies.

The other reason for the downfall of Poland was connected with the people. The Poles have always been noted for their courage and their love of independence. Among the nobles, this love of liberty was carried so far that the freedom of the individual counted for more than that of the nation. The nobles were unwilling to sacrifice anything of their own wealth or power or privileges in order that the nation as a whole might become strong and powerful. This soon led to such selfishness and other evils that the kingdom was weakened and so became a prey to the stronger nations around it. Three times Poland has been partitioned among its neighbors—Russia, Austria-Hungary, and Germany. Now these different parts of Poland are united, and the country stands again among the independent nations of the world. The people are once more free to speak their own language, to make their own laws, and to run their own schools.

When Poland was divided among her conquerors, Austria was given the part next to the Carpathian Mountains. In this area lies the interesting old city of Krakow, the early capital of the kingdom before the seat of the government was transferred to Warsaw. Krakow is perhaps the best-beloved city of the Polish people. It is an ancient place. Its university is between five and six hundred years old, and ever since the year 1400 has granted degrees to the students who have attended it.

On a rock overlooking the Vistula River is the Wawel (vah-vel), a fortified part of the city. Here, according to the old legend, is the ancient castle in whose deep dungeon Krak, the mythical founder of the city, slew the dragon which had long lived by human sacrifices.

Within the walls of the Wawel is the old cathedral, dating back nearly five centuries before Christopher Columbus set sail on his eventful voyage across the Atlantic. Here lie the bones of famous Polish statesmen, heroes, and poets. Here also are the tombs of her kings, and here, before the high altar, her rulers were crowned.

In the old market place, we can see much of the life of the city. The electric cars, the well-lighted streets, and the passing automobiles are of the twentieth century. But the old market and the ancient buildings are of much earlier years. The barefooted peasant women bring in from the country on their broad backs their loads of vegetables and fruits, or their chickens and geese, as Polish women have done for centuries.

FIG. 105. THE PEASANT WOMEN STILL DRIVE THEIR GEESE IN FROM
THE COUNTRY AS POLISH WOMEN HAVE DONE FOR CENTURIES

Farther north on the Vistula River is a city larger than St. Louis. This is Warsaw, another city of ancient Poland, founded in 1269. Four hundred years later, it succeeded Krakow as the capital of the country, and for many years was one of the gayest, most brilliant capitals of all Europe. Warsaw today is an important industrial center. Everywhere we see signs of its growth and development. In the manufacturing part of the city, among the foundries, the cotton, linen, and woolen mills, the breweries, and distilleries, there is little to remind us of the fact that we are four thousand miles from home in an ancient city that was vainly fighting for its life at a time when we were struggling to become independent.

The new Warsaw is a very beautiful city. It has attractive stores, splendid streets, fine parks and boulevards, and numerous open-air cafés like those of Paris. Leaving this part of the city, we soon find ourselves in an entirely different section, where the effects of age, war, and poverty are seen on every side. The mean, low houses are huddled together with no apparent effort at order or arrangement, and the streets twist and wind as if trying to get by the buildings which stand in their way. It seems queer to think that into such a city and into the country which lies around it have gone many tools and machines from our most up-to-date factories. We have sent to Warsaw saws, planes, augers, chisels, axes, hammers, hatchets, padlocks, meat choppers, clothes wringers, and other hardware. From our manufactories have gone also binders, reapers, mowing machines, rakes, and harrows for the farms on the fertile plains of Poland. The goods sent to us are chiefly the agricultural products of the country — beet seed, flax, tow, and wool.

For the most part Poland is an agricultural country and most of the people are farmers. Around Warsaw and Lodz, however, there are rich beds of coal and iron, and the deposits of these useful minerals account for the development of these cities into important industrial centers.

In the World War, when Russia was fighting against the Central Powers, the eastern battlefront for a long time lay in Polish

©Brown Bros.

FIG. 106. THE NEWER PART OF WARSAW IS BEAUTIFUL

territory. Parts of her area were fought over again and again, and the sufferings of her people were terrible. Their farms and factories were destroyed, their cities and towns laid in ruins, and men, women, and children, homeless and starving, died in great numbers. These things set back for many years the development of Poland.

The commercial importance of the great city of Warsaw lies not in its trade with us or with any other distant country, but in the traffic which is carried on with Danzig up and down the Vistula River. In our trip down the Vistula, we shall certainly wish to visit this queer old city which is built on the slopes of the hills overlooking the delta. Before the war, Danzig was a German port. By the terms of the treaty in 1919, it has been internationalized — that is, made free to the vessels of all nations.

During the Middle Ages, Danzig was one of the chief commercial centers of the world, and many of the quaint old buildings, narrow and tall, with odd stone porches, still remain. There

FIG. 107. POLAND IS AN AGRICULTURAL COUNTRY

are also great granaries down by the river, still known by such queer names as "Golden Pelican," "Whale," "Milkmaid," and "Patriarch," which were given to them in those far-away days when Danzig merchants sent their grain ships to Venice and brought back spices, gums, perfumes, silks, and other luxuries of the East.

Down the Vistula, from the peasants' farms to the southward, come clumsy barges full of wool and lumber, and wheat, corn, and other grains. These are sold and stored in the granaries, the barges taken apart, and the lumber disposed of. The boatmen trudge back on foot through the valley or find passage on some of the vessels ascending the river. If we were to examine the cargoes of some of these vessels, we should find the products of many countries. There is coal from England, oil from the United States, coffee from Brazil, fish from Scandinavia, as well as salt and breadstuffs for the peasants.

The display of amber in the stores in Danzig is fascinating, for the beads look like great drops of crystallized sunshine. Amber is often called the "tears of the daughters of the sun," who wept beside the river, mourning the death of Phaethon, who attempted to drive the sun chariot across the sky in place of his father, Apollo.

The true story of the origin of amber is as wonderful as the myth. Ages ago, the continent of Europe was not of its present shape. Northern Germany, now a low plain, was covered by the waters of a sea much larger than the present Baltic. On its borders grew luxuriant forests of oak, beech, birch, cedar, cypress, chestnut, and many other familiar kinds of trees. There also grew in great numbers a species of pine unlike any found in the world today. A thick, sticky sap, or resin, exuded from these trees in much the same way as it does from our common pitch pine, only in much greater quantities. Sometimes it was shed in drops from the branches; sometimes it trickled to the ground, leaving long threads behind. At certain seasons, it flowed in such quantity that it completely covered whole cones and twigs or even branches and trunks. Queer insects, which lived in those far-off days, were often trapped in the gummy mass, just as flies are caught on sticky paper.

These pine forests must have flourished for many centuries, for immense quantities of the yellow resin accumulated. During long ages, this resin became buried deeper and deeper under accumulating soil, and slowly changed from a sticky gum into a hard substance as yellow as gold and as clear as crystal.

As centuries passed, some of the hardened gum was washed by streams and storms into the great sea to the north. Some remained where it had fallen and became buried under the masses of branches, needles, and decaying wood which, as generations of forests lived and died, were deposited upon it.

Danzig is the chief amber market of the world, and near the shores of the Baltic, to the east of the city, most of the world's product is obtained. In one small town not far from Danzig, nearly all the inhabitants are engaged in the amber industry. We should find a visit there very interesting, for amber fishing is different from any other kind of fishing. It is after the heavy storms that the amber fishermen reap their greatest harvest, for the waves and the winds do part of their work. The sand and boulders are loosened from their beds and roll up and down in the shallow waters. The fishermen wade out almost up to their shoulders and, using their nets or long-pronged forks, pull great masses of seaweed inshore. These are passed on to the women, who examine them to see if any pieces of amber may be entangled.

After the winds and the waters are more quiet, the Baltic fishers go out in their boats with dredges, which they drag along the bed of the sea. These become filled with seaweed and stones, among which small pieces of amber may be concealed. To recover the larger masses, divers are employed. While these men are fishing for amber in the depths of the ocean, other men on land are searching for it in mines. The amber is brought to the surface, separated from the rock that encloses it, and sent to the quaint old city of Danzig to be cut and polished.

One of the minerals found in Poland in large quantities is salt, and some of the mines where salt is obtained are among the most interesting in the world. But before we visit them, let us think for a few minutes about this most useful product. What should we do without it? It is so common and so cheap that we do not appreciate its value. If we were to be deprived of it for a long time, however, we should realize how necessary it is to our health and to our enjoyment of food. Where it is scarce, people will often exchange their most valued possessions for a little of it. In some regions, it is used for money, while in other places the most cordial greeting one can give is the offer of a small piece of salt.

Salt has many uses aside from seasoning food. It is used in preserving fish and meats, in curing hides and skins, and in making butter and cheese. It is necessary in other manufactures, especially in those of washing, cleaning, and baking powders, dyestuffs and extracts, soap, glass, fertilizers, and fireworks.

In what form is salt found, and how is it obtained? Mother Nature usually furnishes very plentifully those things which are necessary to life, and in the supply of salt, she has been very generous, for it is found in great quantities not only in the earth but in the ocean water too. You know how salty a mouthful of sea water tastes. It is estimated that, on average, a hundred pounds of sea water, if evaporated, would yield about three pounds of salt. The ocean is the final home of nearly all the thousands of rivers that flow over the earth's surface. Journey-

© Underwood & Underwood

FIG. 108. LARGE QUANTITIES OF SALT ARE REQUIRED

ing through the long ages, they collect from the soil and hold in their waters great quantities of mineral matter. Salt is one of the most important of these minerals, and the accumulated loads of centuries are deposited in the ocean depths, where they remain, increasing with the passing years. Only the pure, fresh water evaporates, and therefore, the ocean is slowly but constantly growing more salty.

During the long, long ages since the ocean first existed, such enormous quantities of salt have been carried to it that today, if it could be extracted and piled up, it would cover the whole continent of Europe with a layer considerably deeper than the height of the highest mountains.

© Underwood & Underwood

FIG. 109. THE WATER IS LED INTO SHALLOW, ARTIFICIAL PONDS

In many warm countries, where the heat of the sun makes evaporation rapid, the people obtain much of their salt supply from the ocean. At high tide, the water is led through pipes or channels into shallow, artificial ponds. Evaporation takes place rapidly, and as the brine becomes stronger, it is led to a still more shallow pond. This process is continued in several pools until, in the last one, the salt crystallizes on the bed and banks.

© Underwood & Underwood

FIG. 110. "THE SALT CRYSTALLIZES ON THE BED AND BANKS. IT IS THEN RAKED UP AND STORED IN PILES"

It is then raked up and stored in piles for the sun, rain, and air to purify and whiten it. In some places, it is redissolved and again evaporated by artificial heat to obtain a finer grade of salt.

Inland countries often produce greater quantities of salt than those which border on the ocean. Let us see how this can be.

In many places, there once existed rivers, lakes, or arms of the ocean whose waters, long ages ago, evaporated, leaving deposits of salt in their dry beds. Changes in the earth's surface have buried these deposits under deep masses of soil and rock, and the salt has, in time, become as hard as coal. This formation is called rock salt, and it is from such deposits that most of the world's supply comes. The easiest way to obtain salt, and the one most used today, is by brine wells. A pipe is driven into the salt deposit, and water is forced down to dissolve it. A strong brine is thus formed, which is pumped to the surface and there evaporated either by the sun or by artificial heat, leaving the crystallized salt in the pans. In some of the most up-to-date salt works, a double-tube pipe is driven, through the outer opening of which the fresh water is forced down, while the brine is pumped out through the inner one.

Salt is sometimes obtained from natural brine springs. Underground water, percolating through the soil, has collected in the salt deposits and has formed a strong brine, which is pumped out and evaporated, as in the brine wells.

A third method of obtaining salt is by mining, which is carried on in a manner not very different from the mining of coal. To see something of this method of production, we will visit the largest and most beautiful salt mine in the world.

A few miles from Krakow is the little town of Wieliczka, which is built on the roofs of the great salt caverns beneath. These deposits are among the most wonderful in the world. The beds are nearly a quarter of a mile thick in places and extend beneath the surface for a distance equal to that between London and Cologne or between New York and Buffalo. The mines here have been worked for nearly seven hundred years, and at one time were the chief source of revenue for the Polish kings.

As we ride through the village of Wieliczka, we see few men, for they are all at work below the surface of the earth, whither we will follow them.

We can descend into the mine either by elevators or by a grand staircase carved out of the solid salt. As we wish to go to the lowest floor of this seven-storied cave, we choose the elevator, which drops us quickly through the nine hundred feet to the deepest levels of the mine. We pause for a moment at the foot of the elevator before we begin our tour and try to realize that we are more than a sixth of a mile below the surface of the earth. The air seems cool and singularly fresh and invigorating. We are told that it remains at about the same temperature during the entire year, and that it is very healthful.

As we wander through the great galleries, with the roof and walls of solid salt, we wonder how such great tunnels and rooms have ever been made. It has taken centuries to do it, for peasants have been working in this underground world for more than six hundred and fifty years. Formerly, all the supporting columns were of salt, but now many of these have been wholly or partially removed and wooden supports substituted.

The gallery in which we are walking suddenly opens out into a magnificent ballroom. A ballroom in a mine? Impossible! Nevertheless, it is true, and furthermore, it is not only in a salt mine, but it is made entirely of salt! A ballroom three hundred feet long, ninety feet high, with a dull-gray ceiling, glistening pillars, and flashing chandeliers—all of hard, crystalline salt! Can you imagine a chandelier thirty feet high and sixty feet in circumference, all gleaming and glittering as the lights fall on the sparkling white surfaces?

Statues carved from salt, representing Vulcan, Neptune, and other mythological and historical persons, ornament this magnificent room, and a gleaming throne has been erected at one end. Real balls are held here from time to time. What else is a ballroom for? Whenever all old workings are closed or a new street is opened, the event is celebrated in true Galician style. Peasant women from the village above dance with the miners to the sound of shrill pipes and noisy violins, whose music is magnified a hundred times by the wonderful echoes of the cavern.

Only a short distance from the ballroom is a cathedral, which is fully as magnificent. Here is the great organ, and the high altar with its crucifix, its twisted pillars, and its statues of saints carved in pure, glistening white. Nearby are the figures of two monks made from blocks of ruby-red salt.

Leaving the cathedral, we walk on through several streets to a room two hundred feet long. This contains two immense pyramids carved and ornamented in commemoration of a visit of the emperor and empress of Austria-Hungary when this part of Poland belonged to that empire.

One of the most thrilling adventures for visitors is a sail on the black waters of the lake far in the depths of the mine. Our boat holds about twenty-five people, and the man in charge pulls it along by means of ropes that extend across the lake. The water is like strong brine—no fish ever swam in it, and no bird ever came to drink from it. The torches fastened into the crystal walls throw a weird light out over the black water, and the splashing made by the boat is echoed and re-echoed from point to point along the walls. The flickering shadows, the strange echoes, the awful solitude, and the deep, black water beneath us make us shudder, and we are glad to step from the boat to the solid rock again.

But what about the miners? They are the peasants of the region around and have worked in the mine all their lives. There are several hundred of them, and they mine two or three hundred million pounds of salt annually. This amount might be much increased by the use of modern methods and up-to-date machinery.

The salt industry in Germany is important, and its history is very interesting. Ages ago, a large portion of Germany was covered by the ocean waters, and in the course of time, as these grew more and more shallow, great quantities of salt were deposited. Before the middle of the last century, the production of salt was too small to supply the demand, and the Prussian government undertook some borings in search of new deposits. At one place near the Elbe River, after boring for more than eight hundred feet, salt formations were reached, but to the disappointment of those in charge, they were found to be not pure salt but what is known as potassium salts. At that time, these were supposed to be worthless, so the borings were abandoned, and a further search was made a few miles away. Here more potassium salts were found, but on boring deeper, rich beds of pure salt were also discovered. Further work with the first deposits showed this to be true in that locality as well.

The potassium salts were thrown out as waste material, and the rock salt was mined for some years. Finally, the waste piles became so large that they interfered with the working of the mine. The superintendent then began some experiments to see if he could discover any uses for the potassium salts. To his surprise, he found that they contained substances very useful in fertilizers, in medicines, in photography, and in various manufactures. So valuable, indeed, were the products obtained that in less than twelve years, thirty-two factories were in operation. Potassium salts have been, for some years, one of the most important products of Germany, and many tons of manufactures worth millions of dollars are made from them.

In both England and Germany, salt is obtained from mines, from natural brine springs, and from brine wells. France obtains some salt from these sources, but most of her large supply comes from the evaporation of ocean water.

We have said that the United States is the greatest salt-producing country in the world. The mineral is obtained in several ways — by mining, by pumping from brine springs and brine wells, by evaporating ocean water, and by collecting that already deposited in the dry beds of salt lakes.

By far the greatest part of the enormous quantity of salt produced in our country is obtained from brine wells, where the fresh water, which is let into the salt deposit, dissolves all the mineral possible and is then pumped up again as a strong brine. The evaporation of the brine is carried on in a scientific way, for the kind of salt produced depends upon the speed with which it is done. When the evaporation is slow, the grains are large and coarse, and they grow finer in proportion as the heat is increased and the process hastened.

Among the many uses of salt, the curing of fish is very important. Were it not for some such method of preserving fish, it would not be possible to furnish this cheap, nourishing food to inland portions of Europe, and the peasants would be deprived of a staple article of diet on which they are dependent. Our next visit will take us to some of the most important fishing countries, where the industry furnishes occupation for many of the people.

TOPICS FOR STUDY

I.

1. History of Poland.
2. The old city of Krakow.
3. Warsaw and its industries.
4. The effect of the World War on Poland.
5. The seaport of Danzig.
6. The story of amber.
7. Uses of salt.
8. Salt in the ocean.
9. Methods of obtaining salt.
10. The salt mines of Wieliczka.
11. Potassium salts in Germany.
12. The United States product.

II.

1. Sketch a map of Poland. Write the names of the countries which bound it. Show its cities.
2. Find the names of some famous Poles. For what are they noted?
3. Write a list of the uses of salt.
4. Account for the saltness of ocean water.
5. Name the countries which produce the most salt.
6. What are the most important salt-producing states of the United States?

III.

Be able to spell and pronounce the following names. Locate each place and tell what was said of it in this and in any previous chapter. Add other facts if possible.

Austria-Hungary	Buffalo	Venice
Brazil	Cologne	Warsaw
England	Danzig	Wieliczka
France	Krakow	
Galicia	Lodz	Baltic Sea
Germany	London	Carpathian
Russia	New York	Mountains
Scandinavia	Paris	Elbe River
United States	St. Louis	Vistula River

CHAPTER XV

A TRIP TO NORWAY AND THE FISHING GROUNDS OF EUROPE

In the northern part of Europe lies the long, narrow country of Norway, stretching from the desolate, frozen north to a latitude somewhat farther south than Petrograd, Russia, or Sitka, Alaska. Forests of pine, spruce, and birch trees cover one fourth of its area. The largest glaciers of Europe fill its mountain passes. Hundreds of waterfalls splash in the sunshine. Thousands of lakes lie in the valleys. Deep bays, called fiords, fringe its coast and penetrate, in some places, a hundred miles into the interior. On either side of these inlets, bare, rocky walls rise perpendicularly to a height of two thousand feet or more, and extend for an equal distance below the surface of the blue water. One eighth of the whole population of Norway lives on the one hundred fifty thousand islands which dot its shores. These vary in size from those only a few feet across to some nearly as large as the state of Rhode Island.

Norway is smaller than California, yet its complete coastline, measured in all its irregularity, would, if extended in a straight line, reach halfway around the world at the equator. In the northern part of this strange country, for a period of nearly two months during the summer, the sun never sets. Even in the southern portion, one can read by light at ten o'clock in the evening. In the winter, there are several weeks when the people of the northern towns do not see the sun at all. The long, cold night is made radiant by the glittering stars and by the northern lights, which gleam and flash and sparkle and send long rays of light streaming up to the very zenith.

© Underwood & Underwood

FIG. 111. "DEEP BAYS, CALLED FIORDS, FRINGE ITS COAST"

If upon a map of the United States, you should place one of Norway, with its most northern point upon the city of New York, its southern end would reach nearly to the southern extremity of Florida. It is so narrow, however, that the very widest part, from east to west, would not reach from New York to Buffalo. As Norway borders upon the ocean for its entire length of eleven hundred miles, many of the people find employment on the water instead of on the land.

The old Norse sagas tell us that more than a thousand years ago, brilliantly painted ships with gay-colored sails carried fish from Norway to England. Though the ships of today differ from those of ancient times, and the sails lack the bright colors, they still carry to Great Britain the product of the Norwegian fisheries. The annual sales amount to millions of dollars. So important and valuable is the fishing industry to Norway that one tenth of the national income is derived from the fish exports.

Cod, herring, and mackerel are caught in the greatest numbers — more than sixty million cod being taken annually. Haddock, sole, flounder, and other varieties are also plentiful, while from the cold Arctic waters, whales and seals are obtained. In the late winter and early spring, between forty and fifty thousand Norwegians find employment in the cod fisheries, which are carried on chiefly from the Lofoten Islands. As we approach these islands in a steamer, we see, rising abruptly from the sea, long lines of bare mountains with sharp peaks, and with snow patches on their slopes. The land looks cold and desolate, and it is indeed a lonely, barren waste.

Along the shores of many of the islands, we notice groups of low, dark houses. These are the stations from which fishing is carried on. Some of the buildings are warehouses of traders, some are storehouses for the fishing tackle, and still others are the huts

© Underwood & Underwood

FIG. 112. AS WE APPROACH THESE ISLANDS WE SEE LONG LINES OF BARE MOUNTAINS

for the fishermen. They look dreary and uncomfortable to our eyes, but they are a welcome sight to a Norwegian fishing crew who have perhaps been battling for hours with the winter storm.

You may wonder why the men fish during the awful Arctic winter instead of in the warm season. It is at that time that the cod leave the waters of the deep ocean and come to the shallows nearer the coast to lay their eggs, and it is then that the greatest catch can be made. Later, in April or May, the fishing is carried on nearer the coast of Norway, whither the cod go for food. A small fish called the capelin frequents the coast waters at that time, and immense numbers of the cod follow to prey upon them.

The fishing is done either with nets, sometimes more than half a mile long, or with lines to which many hundred short lines with hooks and bait are attached. A catch of three or four hundred cod in the net, and less than that number on the lines, is considered a good day's work. When the fleet reaches shore with the slippery cargoes, a busy time ensues. Many merchant

© Underwood & Underwood

FIG. 113. MORE OF THE HERRING THAN OF ANY OTHER SPECIES ARE CAUGHT ON THE DIFFERENT FISHING GROUNDS OF THE WORLD

vessels are waiting at the docks for loads of fish, and the bargaining quickly begins. Many of the cod are salted and then dried on the flat rocks near the shore. The heads, bones, intestines, and all other parts not useful for food are made into fertilizer; the eggs, called roe, are sent to France to be used for bait in the sardine fisheries; the livers are used for cod-liver oil, thousands of barrels of this medicinal oil being made each year in Norway.

Next in importance to the cod fisheries of Norway come those of herring — King Herring, it is sometimes called, for more of these small fish than of any other species are caught on the different fishing grounds of the world. The Norwegian herring are considered the best, and the people of Norway might live on them the whole year through, for the product of their fisheries is sufficient to give every man, woman, and child in the country one third of a barrel annually.

The herring leave the deep waters of the ocean twice every year and are caught at these times all along the western coast of Norway. A few are exported fresh, but most of the catch is either salted or smoked. The poorer classes in nearly every European country eat herring in some form, for they are not only a cheap food but a nourishing one as well. Many of the people of Europe are Catholics, and on certain days, do not eat meat. This is one of the reasons why the Norwegian sales of fish are so enormous. The extent of coastline, the great numbers of fish which come to these waters, the large cities situated on the southern shores of the North Sea, which serve as distributing centers — all help to make the fisheries of Norway among the most important of the world.

The fishing grounds for mackerel lie a little south of the region where cod and herring are most plentiful, and comparatively few are caught in the waters north of Trondhjem.

Another branch of the fishing industry is that carried on in the Arctic Ocean for seals and other fur-bearing animals, and for whales. Norwegian whalers are also found not only in different parts of the Arctic Ocean, but in the far southern waters of the Antarctic and in the Pacific as well. The catch of the fleet which sailed one year from Tromsø, Vardø, and Hammerfest included

© Underwood & Underwood

FIG. 114. "WE SHOULD EAT FISH,
SEE FISH, AND SMELL FISH"

several thousand seals, many hundred polar bears, whales, reindeer, foxes, and a few musk oxen.

All the cities on the western coast of Norway are interested in the fishing industry and export from their harbors large quantities of fish products. Tromsø and Hammerfest in the far north and Trondhjem and Bergen in the southern part are the chief centers. The harbors of these places are filled with vessels unloading their slippery cargoes, while others are storing away in their holds great quantities of salted, smoked, or canned fish. On the shore are the frames on which to dry the fish, the houses for curing, packing, and canning it, and the factories in which oil and fertilizer are prepared. In such fishing centers, we should eat fish, see fish, and smell fish so much that we should long for other food and sights and odors.

Long before Columbus discovered America, Bergen was a wealthy city. For years, it was the largest in Norway and was then, as now, the center of the fishing industry. When fishing was the only industry of importance in Norway, the port that directed and controlled the trade naturally became the largest city. Since other industries have risen in importance, other cities have grown in proportion, and Bergen today no longer holds the first place. However, no other city rivals it in the collecting and shipping of fish. Vessels loaded with cod, herring, mackerel (pickled, smoked, and salted), sardines, whale oil, cod-liver oil, and cod roe sail from the harbor to England, Scotland, Germany, France, and other countries.

The United States buys large quantities of sardines from Bergen every year. These purchases, together with larger fish, oil,

© Keystone View Co.

FIG. 115. NO CITY RIVALS BERGEN IN THE COLLECTING AND SHIPPING OF FISH

and other articles, amount to nearly a million dollars. Goods sent to this Norwegian port are worth many times that value, including flour, oatmeal, petroleum, cottonseed oil, dried, canned, and fresh fruits, machinery, tools, and meat.

Though Bergen lies as far north as central Labrador, the winters are not very cold, and the harbor never freezes. The westerly winds bring much rain, making the climate rather disagreeable, as it rains or snows more than half of the year. Nonetheless, grass, grain, flowers, and trees flourish well in this damp climate, and the abundant moisture enhances the country's natural beauty.

About three hundred miles north of Bergen lies the old Norwegian town of Trondhjem. You might think that a town as far north as southern Iceland, and the most northerly city of any importance in the world, must be cold and lacking in modern conveniences, with few places of interest. However, a visit to Trondhjem would change that opinion. After the unification of the petty kingdoms of the Norse into a single state, Trondhjem became the capital and held that status for many years. All Norwegian kings have been crowned in its old cathedral, built of gray stone. The crowning of King Haakon VII and Queen Maud in 1906 was a brilliant ceremony held within its walls.

Today, Trondhjem has about forty thousand residents and ranks next to Christiania and Bergen in importance. Aside from a few small branch lines, it serves as the northern terminus of the Norwegian railway system and has a splendid station that surpasses many found in more southern cities.

The city streets are wide and well-paved, flanked by quaint wooden houses with red-tiled roofs and gardens that add bright patches of color. Surrounding the city are scenic walks and drives, with views of the fiord that are simply grand. In the nearby hills and mountains, waterfalls cascade down from green heights to the blue waters below.

Like other Norwegian cities on the western coast, Trondhjem's harbor is always bustling. Despite being farther north, it remains ice-free throughout the year, unlike the harbors in the Baltic Sea, which are closed to commerce for many weeks annually. Immense rafts of lumber await their turn at the busy sawmills, which, along with buildings for salting, curing, and packing fish, line the shores.

As we walk up from the wharf we find that this arctic town, though farther north than Iceland, has hotels, churches, a telegraph office, schools, and a bank. The main street is very wide, and the houses even in this far northern town are gay with little gardens and window boxes. The furs offered for sale are very attractive. We see many fine bearskins and wolfskins and some warm cloaks of eiderdown. Eider ducks are very plentiful along the shores of Norway, and the down, from which quilts, muffs, and many warm garments are made, is obtained from their nests. The female duck plucks the down from her own body to line her nest in order that the young birds may have a warm, comfortable home. Many Norwegians find employment in gathering and selling the down, which is used in great quantities in these northern countries and is exported also to those farther south.

We then board a steamer at Trondhjem to continue our journey north. The voyage along the coast is pleasant, as the route is sheltered by a chain of islands that protects it from the rough ocean waters. The scenery is spectacular, with cliffs hundreds of feet high rising almost vertically along the narrow fiords, where the deep, dark water lies in shadow. Our first stop is Tromsø, a city on an island with a harbor open year-round. In the streets, we encounter short, greasy-looking Lapps dressed in blouses of coarse cloth or reindeer skin with the fur inside. They live outside the town and come in during summer to sell tourists handmade spoons and knives from reindeer horns, moccasins, and bright-colored caps.

As we leave Tromsø and continue our way northward the country grows more and more barren and desolate. Cliffs gray and bare rise abruptly from the water. The shore seems uninhabited save for the gulls, eider ducks, and other sea fowl which, alarmed by the whistle of the steamer, rise in swarms from the rocks. Our next stop is at Hammerfest, the most northerly town in the world. In this bleak arctic town, far removed from the land of trees, flowers, and warm sunshine, we are surprised to find gay geraniums peeping out of the windows of the rough wooden houses. This touch of brightness is needed, for the region is dreary and desolate. No green trees relieve the somber gray of the rocks and soil, and no roads stretch away from the town to friendly villages, for the country around is uninhabited. During the long winter months no visitors come to break the monotony of the cold and darkness. From Thanksgiving time to the latter part of January not even the sun cheers the people with its light and warmth. The stars glitter in the cold sky, and the Aurora Borealis sends long lines of rosy light far up toward the zenith, but every one looks forward to the time when the bright yellow rim of the sun will be first seen at noon, just peeping for a moment above the southern horizon. Every day it rises higher and higher until the middle of May, when it describes a complete circle in the sky, higher in the south at noon and lower in the north at midnight. For many weeks it does not go below the horizon, but shines continually unless hidden by clouds. It is hard to tell when to go to bed and when to get up, or to decide whether it is supper or breakfast one is eating. Finally, near the last of July the ball of light dips for a moment below the northern horizon. It is lost to sight each night for an increasing length of time until the last of November, when it disappears entirely for the long winter.

The houses of Hammerfest are close to the shore; behind the town rise bare, rocky hills, down which avalanches of rock, loosened by the winds and storms, roll with terrific force. Most of the three thousand inhabitants of Hammerfest are fishermen. Near their homes are the frames for drying the fish and the buildings for curing and packing it, and a fishy

© Keystone View Co.

FIG. 116. "THE HOUSES OF HAMMERFEST ARE CLOSE TO THE SHORE"

smell pervades the town. In the harbor, vessels from Russia, Germany, England, and other European countries are docked. One is unloading coal, another wheat, while others are taking on cargoes of fish and oil.

In one part of the town, we notice the low stone huts of a Lapp village. In the stores of Hammerfest, we see costumes, furs, moccasins, carvings, and reindeer skins, which the Laplanders have brought in to sell.

Leaving the town of Hammerfest behind us, we steam farther on our way into the bleak, dreary Arctic world. On our left stretches the blue-gray water; on our right rise bare, steep cliffs, from the summits of which desolate plateaus stretch off into the distance, brightened by no sign of human life. The cry of the gulls and the whirring of the wings of sea birds are the only sounds, save the splashing of water against the prow of the vessel.

Seven hours after leaving Hammerfest the dark gray promontory called the North Cape comes into view, standing in solitary majesty, with its bold front facing the wild waste of waters. The scene reminds us of the words in which Longfellow describes this lone rock:

FIG. 117. "THE DARK GRAY PROMONTORY CALLED THE NORTH CAPE"

> "So far I live to the northward
> No man lives north of me;
> To the east are wild mountain chains
> And beyond them meres and plains;
> To the westward all is sea."

The promontory rises about a thousand feet from the water, and tourists climb a steep, zigzag path, sometimes assisted by ropes. From the summit, there is nothing to see but the gray sky, cold sea, and rock. On a clear night, however, the sight of the midnight sun — a golden ball near the northern horizon — is a remarkable reward. Yet, such clear nights are rare, and many travelers leave disappointed after their long climb.

Though so many Norwegians spend much of their life upon the ocean, many more are employed on land. Thousands are engaged in lumbering or in the making of paper pulp, for the forests of Norway, you remember, cover nearly one-fourth of its surface. The country is so mountainous, lies so far north, and is so rugged and barren that comparatively little of the land is adapted for farming. Yet, the arable portion is divided into farms so small that more people are engaged in agriculture than in any other occupation.

Hay is the most important crop. The farmer is dependent on his cows for milk, butter, and cheese. The winters are long and cold, and great quantities of hay are needed to feed the cattle until the coming of summer. Each nook and corner, each steep slope and sheltered valley, yields its small harvest to the thrifty Norwegian. The first mowing is done with a scythe, but the second crop is so short that it is cut with a kind of sickle. Everybody works in the hayfields — men and women, boys and girls. In the western part of the country, the season is so damp that the grass is hung on long poles to dry, as you see in the picture, instead of being left on the ground. On hillsides too steep for horses to draw loads, the grass is tied up with ropes into huge bundles. Below, on the steep slope, a man stands ready to receive it on his shoulders. One of the haymakers rolls it onto his back, and down the hill he goes, completely covered by the huge pile of hay, which looks as if it were slowly moving

FIG. 118. "THE GRASS IS HUNG ON LONG POLES TO DRY"

down of its own accord. Sometimes a stout wire is stretched from some high slope to the valley below. The hay is tied up in bundles, fastened to rings on the wire, and sent whizzing on this "hay-trolley line" down to the farm.

Though nearly every farmer owns cows, we see but few of them during our summer tour through the country. As in Switzerland, they are driven to the high hills and the mountains to remain through the warm weather. If they were fed in the valley during the summer months, there would be little grass left to make into hay for their winter food. Ten, twenty, or even fifty miles from the farm, in some sheltered place in the mountains, is the *saeter*, or dairy house. It is built of logs or of rough stones, and there, during the summer, the people from the valley come to pasture their cattle and goats on the scanty grass.

On some pleasant June morning, everyone at the farm is busy, for on that day, the cattle are to be driven to the *saeter*. Many things must be packed for the trip — the milk pails, the churn, the cheese presses, coffee, bread, warm blankets, a few dishes, a frying pan, and many other necessary articles. Bells are tied to the necks of the cows, and the mark of the owner is fastened into the ears of the sheep and goats. They will wander

FIG. 119. "IN SOME SHELTERED PLACE IN THE
MOUNTAINS IS THE *SAETER*, OR DAIRY HOUSE"

many miles on the mountains and, perchance, become mixed with the herds of other farmers.

If you were going away for the summer, you would hardly expect to take with you bread enough to last until you return, but the Norwegian housewife bakes her *fladbrod* only three or four times a year. She makes a dough of water mixed with rye meal and barley and rolls this into round, flat cakes, perhaps as large as the bottom of a pail or a small washtub. This is baked over the fire and then put away to last through the coming months. It is not eaten until it is some days or weeks old. It is hard and not very appetizing, but it is wholesome and nourishing, and the people thrive well on it with their other simple food. Milk, usually sour and changed to a firm mass as thick as blancmange, and porridge are often found on the tables of the poorer classes, who also eat a great deal of fresh, salted, and smoked fish.

The boys and girls at the *saeter* find plenty to do to keep them busy during the long, bright summer days. They watch the

FIG. 120. "THE NORWEGIAN HOUSEWIFE BAKES HER
FLADBROD ONLY THREE OR FOUR TIMES A YEAR"

cattle, drive them to new pastures when necessary, and call them home when they stray by blowing on a long birch-bark horn. They make butter and cheese and, in their few spare minutes, knit warm socks and mittens, which they will need during the winter. The people at home on the farm seldom visit the *saeter*, for they are too busy haying, and the distance is too great; so the whole summer passes with only one or two trips from the home people, who come to bring provisions and to carry back the butter and cheese and perhaps some small bundles of hay. The life is a lonely one, and the boys and girls are glad when the time comes to pack up the things and start the cows and goats down the steep path toward home.

We do not wish to leave this northern land without a peep at its capital, Christiania. This city is finely situated at the head of a fiord sixty miles long. To the north are high wooded hills, beautifully green in summer and covered with snow in winter. These afford splendid opportunities for tobogganing, skiing, and other sports.

The city is clean and well-built, and the people live in a

FIG. 121. "WE DO NOT WISH TO LEAVE THIS NORTHERN LAND WITHOUT A PEEP AT ITS CAPITAL, CHRISTIANIA."

healthy, happy way, enjoying their homes and their home life. They show the kindly, honest disposition characteristic of Norwegian folk.

The winter sports in Christiania are very enjoyable, and everyone, old and young, takes part in them. There are skating and sleighing parties and fine opportunities for coasting. Horses draw the people and the heavy sleds to the tops of the long hills, and the merry coasters come flying down the steep slopes, which are often four or five miles long.

Norwegians are very expert on snowshoes. The skis, as they call them, are from four to seven feet long and from three to five inches wide. If you should try a stand-up slide downhill with them fastened securely to your feet, you would very likely get

FIG. 122. SKIING IN NORWAY

a tumble before you reached the bottom; but a Norwegian boy guides himself very easily and comes down the steep hills at a terrific pace, showing great skill in dodging trees and rocks. When going at full speed, he sometimes, when coming to a sudden drop in the hillside, leaps into the air out over the tops of the trees on the slope below. We watch breathlessly, expecting a mishap when he touches the ground again, but he lands safely on his skis and continues his slide to the bottom of the hill.

We must leave Norway, however, and visit some of the other countries where fishing is carried on to a great extent. Little Japan ranks first in this industry, while the United States, England, and Russia are important fishing countries.

FIG. 123. WHEN GOING AT FULL SPEED HE SOMETIMES LEAPS INTO THE AIR OUT OVER THE TOPS OF THE TREES

In Great Britain, the services of nearly a hundred thousand men and between twenty-five and thirty thousand vessels are needed to carry on the industry. Even the secondary industries connected with the ocean harvests, such as the importation of ice and salt for preserving the fish, are of great importance. Every weekday, several thousand tons of fish are carried ashore to the fishing centers along the coast. This immense quantity is packed, salted, cured, and distributed over the island kingdom and sent to other countries as well. London is an important center, receiving and distributing daily many tons of fish. Billingsgate, the famous fish market of London, is the largest in the world. The best time to see it is early in the morning when the fish dealers of London come to buy their daily supplies. From the noise, the confusion, and the piles of fish, you would surely think that all of Europe was quarreling over its Friday dinner.

Hull, Grimsby, and Yarmouth, on the eastern coast of England, are important fishing centers. Thousands of vessels sail from these places to the fishing grounds of the North Sea. They may be gone for a few days or for a few weeks, or they may never return. The news from a fishing fleet after a severe storm reminds one of the news from an army after a battle. The life is hard, but it develops strong, brave men, many of whom become sailors in the British navy.

Grimsby is one of the most important of the English fishing towns. One of the American consuls in England describes a scene on the wharf at Grimsby when the vessels come in loaded with fish:

"No sooner has the last knock of the auctioneer's hammer betokened the successful bidder than the fishermen are busy swinging the baskets of herring from their vessel to the 'slip,' where the purchaser's men are ready with empty boxes and with barrels of salt to pack the 'king of fish.' A never-ending string of wheelbarrows convey the boxes, when packed, to another portion of the market, where carts are waiting to run them to the railway wagons, to the Scotch curing girls, or to the steamship which is to take them over to Hamburg. Over five thousand boxes of herring are often thus exported, and when the stevedores of the vessel have to cry, 'Enough, we can take no more,' the quay side is at times covered with another four thousand boxes.

"One feature of the herring season at the different ports on the east coast is the arrival of the 'Scotch lasses,' who follow the fishing fleets down and who clean and 'pickle' the fish on the piers as they are brought in by the trawlers. In a good season, these lasses will earn from eight to ten dollars, but in a poor season, they will receive little more than their board, which is guaranteed them on engagement."

Most of the people who live on the eastern coast of Scotland are fishermen. Aberdeen, one of the largest cities of Scotland, is the center of trade in that country. It is sometimes called the "Granite City," for nearly all of the buildings are made of that material, giving the city a very handsome and dignified appearance. Granite is found in great quantities in eastern Scotland, and Aberdeen contains the largest polishing works in the British Isles.

Much of the fishing from Aberdeen, as well as from other centers, is done at night. In the early morning, hundreds of boats come in from the banks. The fish are unloaded, sorted, cleaned, and packed so quickly that, before sunrise, most of the catch has been put aboard the long train standing beside the dock, and it has started with its ocean cargo for London. Part of the fish will be reloaded there and distributed throughout the country.

The other countries near the North Sea — Germany, Sweden, Denmark, and Belgium — are engaged in fishing to a considerable extent, but in none of them does the industry rank in importance with that of Great Britain and Norway.

The fisheries carried on in the northern part of Russia are of comparatively little importance, but those in the Caspian Sea and in the Volga and Ural Rivers are of great value. The amount caught annually in these waters is enough to give nearly a pound apiece to every man, woman, and child in the world.

In many of the markets of Russia, one is sure of procuring fresh fish, as they are kept alive in tanks of water and killed after the customer has made a selection. Immense quantities of fish are consumed by the poorer classes, for it is one of their chief articles of food.

In the Ural River are the most famous sturgeon fisheries in the world. The sturgeon is a fish five or six feet long that lives in salt water for most of the year, and in the spring, it comes up the rivers to lay its eggs. This is the harvest time for the Russian peasants of that region. When the migration begins, a gun announces the opening of the fishing season. The sturgeon is caught in nets, by harpooning from boats, and by lines. In some places on the lower Ural, a long line is fastened on one bank of the river, and the other end is anchored to a boat in midstream. From this line hang hundreds of shorter ones, six or seven feet long, with a large hook at the end of each. As a sturgeon comes up the river, it is caught on one of the hooks. In its wild efforts to escape, it becomes more and more entangled with other hooks, which hold it fast while the peasants kill it.

The fishing season lasts only three weeks, but during that short period, thousands of sturgeon are captured. The flesh is used by the peasants for food, and the skin sometimes serves them as window glass. From the eggs, or roe, a delicacy known as caviar is prepared. This is much nicer when eaten fresh, but as it does not keep well, it is often preserved by salting. The Russians are so fond of caviar that more than one hundred thousand dollars' worth is often prepared in a single season.

The swimming bladder of the sturgeon is used in the preparation of isinglass, the name itself coming from two Dutch words that mean "sturgeon's bladder."

One of the smallest fish that is commercially valuable is the sardine. When we think of the quantities sold by grocers all over the United States and the great numbers eaten in other countries, we wonder where they all come from and who the people are that catch them.

Several varieties of small fish are caught, preserved in oil, and sold as sardines. The industry is carried on in Maine and Norway, but the very best sardines come from France, so we will visit that country to see how they are caught and prepared for market.

In the northwestern part of France is the province of Brittany, which someone has called a "land of granite and rocks." There are meadows, fields, and forests as well, but for the most part, the province is dreary and uninteresting. The people are as different from other inhabitants of France as the land they dwell in. The monotonous landscape, the lowering sky, the gray rocks, and the sound of the ever-restless ocean are reflected in the character of the silent, dreamy, persevering Breton. Far removed from the great highways of the mainland, these people know little of the advance of civilization but live on in the simple ways of their forefathers, clinging to a multitude of old customs and superstitions.

In the center of Brittany, the people are engaged in cattle breeding, beekeeping, and raising grain, vegetables, and other products for their food and clothing. They live simply — on cabbage soup, porridge, rye or barley bread, and fish. Meat is seldom seen on the table. Their houses are usually built of stone, with only one story, and often only one room, which is sometimes shared by the pig or occasionally occupied by the cow. From the ceiling hang provisions such as gourds, onions, and other vegetables, and bunches of herbs. The people on the coast spend much of their time fishing. Some of the men go on long voyages to Newfoundland for cod and mackerel, some to the coasts of Iceland, while others fish nearer home for herring, sardines, lobsters, and oysters.

The sardine fishing begins in March or April and lasts into November. The early run of fish is not good for canning and is not commonly used for that purpose. In the height of the season, there are twelve to fifteen hundred boats engaged in sardine fishing off the coast of Brittany, and millions of fish are caught in a single day.

The town of Concarneau is one of the chief fishing centers,

and nearly all its five or six thousand inhabitants are engaged in fishing or in preparing the fish for market.

If we wish to accompany the sardine fleet to the fishing grounds, we must start very early in the morning, between two and three o'clock, in order to begin the catch by daybreak. With good luck, we may be back in port by ten o'clock in the forenoon.

Our boat has two masts and carries two pairs of very long, heavy oars and twenty nets. The nets are made of fine cotton twine with small meshes. They are about one hundred thirty-five feet long and five hundred meshes deep. They are usually dyed a dull blue to render them more nearly invisible in the water. When the boats are at the wharves, these greenish-blue draperies are hung from the masts to dry. The blue nets, the brown sails, the dull-colored boats, the gray beach, and the shimmering water create a wonderful scene that artists love to paint. The women, with their full, short skirts, bright bodices, and white caps, and the men in their dark blue smocks and wooden shoes, give a touch of life to the picture.

Out on the fishing grounds, a streak of silver in the water some distance away reveals the location of a shoal of sardines. The men lower the net from the stern of the boat. It is buoyed up by corks on the upper side and kept in a vertical position in the water by weights on the bottom. The crew lower the sails and take their places

© Underwood & Underwood

FIG. 124. "THERE ARE TWELVE TO FIFTEEN HUNDRED BOATS ENGAGED IN SARDINE FISHING OFF THE COAST OF BRITTANY"

at the oars. The captain, giving directions, stands at the stern with the bait nearby.

Sardine bait consists of the eggs of fish and peanut meal. The roe of the cod is used more than that of any other fish and comes chiefly from Norway, though some is shipped from the cod-fishing grounds of America and the Netherlands. Immense quantities are needed, and between forty and fifty thousand barrels are used in Brittany every season.

The bait scattered on the water attracts the sardines, and they make an eager rush toward it. At just the right moment, more bait is thrown on the opposite side of the net, and the fish swim after it in greedy swarms. As they strike the net, their heads pass through the small meshes, but as they draw back, they are caught behind the gills by thousands. The net, with the struggling mass entangled in it, is pulled into the boat, and another is put out to be filled in the same manner. When the catch is over, the men carefully remove the fish from the meshes, as the flesh is easily bruised. The boats then return to port immediately so that the sardines can be delivered to the canneries as soon as possible. On arriving at the wharves, the fishermen begin to unload their catch. The fish are counted by hand into wicker baskets with round bottoms and sides, each basket holding two hundred fish, plus ten additional ones to allow for any imperfect fish. Though the baskets could hold three to five times as many fish, the desire is not to crowd them.

Before the baskets of sardines are sent to the canner, the fishermen move them rapidly up and down in the water to remove dirt and loose scales, making the fish appear bright. Many scales come off, and after a day's fishing, the shores of the harbor are lined with them. The water near the shore is usually quite foul, making the rinsing of the fish in it seem objectionable.

The baskets are then taken by the fishermen to the agent to whom the cargo has previously been sold, and the contents are poured into flat boxes or trays, which are carried in wagons to the cannery. From the time the sardines are first caught, everything that could bruise, mash, or otherwise impair the soundness of the flesh is carefully avoided.

We follow the wagonloads of fish up the narrow streets to the canneries — large stone buildings surrounded by high stone walls and enclosing a courtyard. There are about a hundred of these establishments in Brittany, each with a yearly output ranging from three hundred thousand to four or five million boxes of sardines.

Here, the fish are first cleaned and then soaked in a strong brine. Women remove them from their salt bath and place them in wicker baskets, which are dipped in water to remove all loose dirt, scales, and other matter. After this, the sardines are carefully packed for drying in shallow, oblong wire baskets. The more modern establishments are equipped with drying rooms heated with steam pipes; however, in many canneries, the drying is done outdoors in yards where the baskets are hung or placed on wooden frames.

After drying, the fish are taken in the same wire baskets to the cooking room and lowered, basket and all, into boiling oil. Olive or peanut oil, sometimes adulterated with cottonseed oil, is generally used.

© Underwood & Underwood

FIG. 125. "THE SARDINES ARE CAREFULLY PACKED FOR DRYING"

After cooking in the boiling oil, the fish are drained and cooled. They are then packed by hand in the small boxes that are such familiar sights in our grocery stores. Spices and other flavoring matter are often added, sometimes to the boiling oil and sometimes to the fish when they are packed. After covering and sealing, the boxes are placed in iron vessels large enough to hold several thousand at a time and immersed in boiling water for two hours. This completes the cooking, kills any germs that would otherwise cause the fish to spoil, and reveals any leaks in the boxes.

Think of the enormous quantities of tin plate and boxes that must be made every year to supply these canning establishments! The sardine industry is not one of the most important industries of the world, yet thousands of people are engaged in it. In one Breton town, three thousand men, women, and children are employed in the canning factories, not to mention the hundreds of fishermen who catch the sardines.

TOPICS FOR STUDY

I.

1. Description of Norway.
2. Vikings and modern Norwegian sailors.
3. Cod, herring, and mackerel fishing.
4. Fishing in the Arctic Ocean.
5. Description of Norwegian cities.
6. North Cape and the midnight sun.
7. Lumbering and farming in Norway.
8. Norwegian sports.
9. Other fishing countries.
10. The sardine industry.

II.

1. Through how many degrees of latitude does Norway extend? How far would this distance reach on a map of the United States?
2. What is the area of Norway? The population? How many people are there per square mile? Compare both area and population with some states in our country. Compare the population density with that of England, Germany, and France. What effect may the position of a country have on the density of its population?
3. Locate the great fishing grounds of the world. Name the countries in which the fishing industry is very important.
4. Sketch a map of the North Sea and show all the countries bordering it. Indicate the cities that serve as distribution centers

for the fish exported from Norway. Show the regions where cod, herring, and mackerel are caught.

5. Sketch a map of the Atlantic Ocean showing the eastern coast of North America and the western coast of Europe. Show the Gulf Stream and indicate by arrows the direction of the prevailing winds. What would be the effect on the climate of both North America and Europe if the prevailing winds were in the opposite direction? Explain the difference in climate between the eastern and western coasts of the Scandinavian Peninsula.

6. What part of North America is in the same latitude as Hammerfest? Write out a comparison of the two places.

7. On a map of Norway, locate the four chief cities. Write beside each its latitude and the names of places in North America that are equally far north.

8. Name several causes that have contributed to the importance of the Norwegian fisheries.

9. Describe the Norwegian city you would like most to visit.

10. See if you can find any information about the sardine industry in Maine.

III.

Be able to spell and pronounce the following names. Locate each place and explain what was said about it in this and any previous chapter. Add other facts if possible:

Belgium	Lapland	
Brittany	Maine	Aberdeen
California	Netherlands	Bergen
Denmark	Newfoundland	Buffalo
England	New York	Christiania
Florida	Norway	Concarneau
France	Rhode Island	Edinburgh
Germany	Russia	Grimsby
Iceland	Scotland	Hammerfest
Japan	Sweden	Hull
Labrador	United States	London

New York
Petrograd
Sitka
Tromsø
Trondhjem

Vardø
Yarmouth

Arctic Ocean
Caspian Sea

Lofoten Islands
North Cape
North Sea
Ural River
Volga River

CHAPTER XVI

SPAIN AND OLIVES

Cottonseed oil is made from the seed of a plant, peanut oil from a nut grown in the ground, but olive oil is made from the fruit of a tree — the only fruit that yields oil from its pulp in sufficient quantity to be of great commercial value, though coconut oil is now of considerable importance.

The gnarled, twisted olive trees, with gray-green foliage, can be found in great quantities in all countries bordering the Mediterranean Sea. They are especially numerous in Spain, Italy, and France, where the fields and hills would seem bare without them. In these three countries, as well as in Greece, across the Mediterranean in Algeria and Tunis, and in those parts of Asia near the eastern end of the great blue sea - olives are raised in sufficiently large quantities to meet domestic needs and for export. The home use is significant, as the fruit is a common food among the poorer classes.

Nearly every family in southern Spain keeps a small barrel of pickled olives on hand; they are eaten not as a relish, as with us, but as a main dish. Olive oil is one of the first necessities of life for the peasantry of southern Europe. In a trip through southern Italy, you would see dark-eyed boys and girls munching a piece of bread spread with oil with as much enjoyment as an American child would eat a slice of bread and butter. Olive oil is used in place of lard for frying, and from every open door where cooking is going on comes the smell of hot fat.

Besides its use for food, olive oil is used in significant quantities in soap-making, and you will find this product among the manufactures of many cities located in the olive-producing countries. The oil used for soap, lighting, and lubricating pur-

SOUTHWESTERN EUROPE
SCALE OF MILES
0 50 100 200 300
ATLANTIC OCEAN
Land's End
English Channel
ENGLAND
LONDON
Thames R.
Dover
Strait of Dover
Calais
Ostend
HOLLAND
Antwerp
BRUSSELS
BELGIUM
Cologne
Rhine
GERMANY
Nuremberg
PRAGUE
CZECHOSLOVAKIA
WARSAW
POLAND
Rheims
Seine R.
CHAMPAGNE
Metz
LORRAINE
ALSACE
Strassburg
Paris
Versailles
BRITTANY
Concarneau
Loire R.
CÔTE-D'OR
BURGUNDY
VIENNA
AUSTRIA
BUDAPEST
HUNGARY
Danube
BAY OF BISCAY
FRANCE
Berne
SWITZERLAND
Basel
Zurich
Gall
Geneva
Simplon Tun.
St. Gothard Tun.
Munich
Arlberg Tunnel
Trieste
FREE STATE OF FIUME
BELGRADE
Gironde R.
Bordeaux
Garonne R.
Lyon
St. Etienne
MT. CENIS TUNNEL
Mont Blanc
Pass
Isselle
Milan
Venice
Po R.
Genoa
Carrara
Lucca
RIVIERA
ADRIATIC SEA
YUGOSLAVIA
Roquefort
Pyrenees
Rhone R.
Grasse
Nice
Cannes
Pisa
Leghorn
Florence
Arno R.
ITALY
Marseille
Cantabrian Mts.
Oporto
PORTUGAL
Douro R.
SPAIN
Madrid
Barcelona
CORSICA
Rome
Vesuvius
Naples
Torre del Greco
Tiber R.
SARDINIA
BALEARIC IS.
Lisbon
Tagus R.
Sierra Morena
Cordoba
Seville
Guadalquivir R.
ANDALUSIA
Jerez
Sierra Nevada
Cadiz
Strait of Gibraltar
Malaga
Almeria
Gibraltar
MEDITERRANEAN SEA
AFRICA
GREECE
Strait of Messina
SICILY
ALBANIA

poses is not suitable for food but is produced after the pure, edible oil has been extracted from the crushed pulp. The medicinal qualities of olive oil, known for centuries, are appreciated by modern physicians. The early Grecian athletes used to run along the sandy beaches of the Adriatic Sea until they perspired freely. They would then rub their limbs with sand, irritating the skin, and immediately afterwards rub olive oil into the pores to lubricate their muscles and limber up their joints.

Important as olive oil is in the homes of the people of Southern Europe, it is also exported in great quantities. The olives and oil shipped from Spain rank higher than the orange in value. In Italy, only the silk exports exceed those of the olive tree. Not only the oil, but the pickled green fruit as well, is sent in great quantities to America, England, and, in fact, to all parts of the world. The large olives seen in the bottles at the grocery stores

FIG. 126. "THE OLIVES AND OIL SHIPPED FROM SPAIN RANK HIGHER THAN THE ORANGE IN VALUE"
Courtesy of H. C. Newcomb, Philadelphia

are called queen olives and are produced only in a small circle, not twenty-five miles in diameter, around the city of Seville in southern Spain. Of the fine large olives grown in this region, ninety-five out of every one hundred come to the United States, where they are placed in bottles by American laborers. Millions of the tall, slender bottles are now made annually in the United States for this purpose.

To see how the fruit is raised and prepared for market, let us visit an orchard in Spain, where more land is covered with olive orchards and more oil is made than in any other country. It is claimed that of every one hundred pounds of olives produced in all the world, Spain produces more than forty. The land in Spain devoted to the cultivation of olives is nearly equal to the area of the state of Connecticut. This land bore more than three billion pounds of fruit in a year. Four-fifths of this amount was used in the manufacture of oil, of which such a great quantity was made that a tube three feet in diameter stretching the entire distance across the United States would not hold it all.

Our trip will take us through the southern part of Spain to the province of Andalusia, which lies between the Sierra Morena and Sierra Nevada mountains. This is the most important olive-producing section of the country and, in many ways, the most attractive portion of Spain, with snow-capped mountains, fertile valleys, and the famous old cities of Seville, Granada, Cordoba, and Malaga. The Guadalquivir River, which drains much of this region, is the most important river in Spain, for it is the only one in the country which is navigable for any considerable distance from its mouth. The city of Seville is at the head of navigation, about one hundred miles from the ocean.

The olive grove which we will visit lies not far from the river and near the city of Seville. In this famous olive-producing section, the orchards cover a vast territory. Some of them are very small and are owned by Spanish peasants, but often several estates are controlled by one proprietor. One house in Seville owns seven estates comprising six thousand acres, all devoted to the culture of queen olives. In the region around this city are located many olive-oil factories and pickling establishments.

FIG. 127. "IN THIS FAMOUS OLIVE-PRODUCING SECTION THE ORCHARDS COVER
A VAST TERRITORY"
Courtesy of H. J. Heinz Company

Cultivated olive trees are divided into two classes, according to the use made of their fruit. The queen olive and the manzanilla are the most popular for pickling. The former is the large heart-shaped fruit sold in great quantities in the United States, while the smaller, stronger-flavored manzanilla is more generally used in Europe.

The peasants who work in the orchards are very poor and live in a way which would seem impossible to us. We should not rest well upon their beds of straw on the hard floor, nor should we enjoy the presence of the goat, the pig, or the hens in the same room with us; but these things do not trouble the Spanish peasant, for he has known nothing else all his life. Gay and happy by nature, he comes cheerfully out of the low stone cottage and, in the early dawn, starts for his day's work in the orchards, perhaps several miles away. He eats his breakfast as he goes—some hard, dark bread, with an onion or perhaps some pieces of tough, salted fish. Sometimes he is fortunate enough to have in his pocket a bottle of wine and a few olives. He may not have anything else to eat until the end of his long day's work. This is hard and tiresome, for in the region around

© Keystone View Co.

FIG. 128. "THE SPANISH PEASANT IS POOR"

Seville, during July and August, the temperature sometimes rises as high as one hundred twenty degrees.

The Spanish peasant is poor, but he is also polite, hospitable, and cheerful. No matter how small or mean the home, in entering the door we should be greeted with cordial wishes in the musical Spanish language. Though the fare be poor, we should be given an invitation to share it. In traveling the country roads, should we meet a peasant on muleback, we should hear the kindly salutation, "May God go with you."

The gathering of the olives for pickling is done when the fruit is still green, and the object of pickling is to take out the bitterness and make them more pleasant to the taste. The pick-

FIG. 129. "THE PICKING OF THE GREEN OLIVES BEGINS ABOUT THE MIDDLE OF
SEPTEMBER."
Courtesy of H. J. Heinz Company

ing of the green olives begins about the middle of September and lasts about six weeks. They are picked from the trees one by one with great care, for a bruise or a scratch shows very plainly after they are cured and injures their appearance in the bottles. Hundreds of pickers, carrying long ladders, work together in the fields, for the fruit must all be gathered before it changes color.

Each workman is supplied with a light basket, which is hung around his neck or shoulders in order that both hands may be free for picking. The fruit is carefully heaped in piles scattered over the ground, to be roughly assorted before it is taken from the orchard; it is then loaded on donkeys, horses, and large two-wheeled wagons, and taken to the factory, where it is properly cured. Few owners of orchards prepare the pickled olives; the fruit is generally cured by merchants who make a specialty of that work. The curer of olives contracts with the farmer for his entire product and sends his own pickers to gather the fruit. When the olive is first picked from the tree, it is light green in color. After it has been pickled, it is a very dark green; and after its bath of six

FIG. 130. "THE FRUIT IS GENERALLY CURED BY MERCHANTS WHO MAKE A SPECIALTY
OF THAT WORK"
Courtesy of H. J. Heinz Company

or seven weeks in brine, it takes on the bright, golden-green color of commerce and is ready to be assorted into fourteen different sizes. The difference in diameter of the middle sizes is only a small fraction of an inch, and the girls of the region who do the sorting become very skillful at this work.

The making of oil is a much more important industry than pickling the fruit. After the picking, the olives are taken either to some large factory or to a press on the farm. There are today in Spain thousands of small presses worked by hand or mule power, and, in the case of some of the larger factories, by steam. In many places, the old-fashioned horse power is used as it was hundreds of years ago, and in other sections, mountain streams run the presses. It is a well-known fact among makers of olive oil that the slower the process used in crushing the pulp, the better the quality of the oil. Modern machinery is more rapid, but it has the bad effect of heating the pulp, and the oil produced has a greater tendency to grow rancid.

FIG. 131. "THE CURER OF OLIVES CONTRACTS WITH THE FARMER FOR HIS ENTIRE
PRODUCT"
Courtesy of H. J. Heinz Company

We will follow the donkeys with their loaded baskets from
the orchard to the oil mill. The olives are placed on a large, flat
stone, and other circular or conical stones move around upon the
flat one until the pulp is crushed. The juice which is pressed out
runs off into large tanks and looks very much like New Orleans
molasses. Seventy-five percent of this juice is water, not more
than fifteen percent is oil, while the remaining ten percent
consists of pulp, stems, sticks, and little particles of sand which
have embedded themselves in the skin or pulp of the olives. After
this mass has been allowed to stand for a time in the crocks or
tanks, the heavier particles sink to the bottom, and the lighter

FIG. 132. CIRCULAR OR CONICAL STONES MOVE AROUND OVER THE
FRUIT UNTIL THE PULP IS CRUSHED
Courtesy of H. J. Heinz Company

oil bubbles to the top, where it is siphoned off and afterwards
filtered for bottling purposes. The pulp is crushed again two
or three times between straw mats. The first pressing of oil —
which is considered the best — is called virgin oil; the second
and third may also be edible, but the fourth pressing, which is
made after soaking the pulp in hot water, is used only in the
manufacture of soap and for lubricating and lighting purposes.

Nearly every port of Spain exports olive oil. From Barcelona,
the chief industrial center, very large quantities are shipped.
This city, nearly the size of Boston, is the largest city in Spain
next to Madrid and is built in a crescent shape on the coast of
the Mediterranean Sea. Its manufactures are as important as its
commerce. Nearly one hundred million dollars' worth of cotton,
woolen, and silk goods are made here annually, besides great
quantities of machinery, paper, glass, chemicals, soap, dyes,
and many other articles. These manufactures, together with

FIG. 133. THE PULP IS CRUSHED AGAIN BETWEEN
STRAW MATS
Courtesy of H. J. Heinz Company

wine, brandy, oil, and fruit, form its principal exports.

If you could examine the cargoes of the steamers which leave Seville on the Guadalquivir River, which lie in the Bay of Cadiz, or which steam out of the harbor of Malaga, you would find stowed in their holds, besides almonds, cork, licorice, wine, grapes, and raisins, immense quantities of olive oil and pickled olives. There are steamers sailing once a month from Seville to New York, which carry thousands of gallons of pickled olives, and our annual importation from this one Spanish city is worth many thousands of dollars.

We should like to stop in some of the queer old Spanish towns, for they are very different from our American cities. The streets are narrow and crooked; the windows of the lower stories of the houses are barred and look forsaken, but we might catch sight of a dark-eyed Spanish beauty peering shyly at us from the balcony above. We should miss many of our ordinary comforts and luxuries, and the tiny stove with its small fire of charcoal does not look as if it would keep us sufficiently warm when the cold wind del Norte blows from the snow-capped Pyrenees.

The oil produced in Italy is of a finer quality and is in much greater demand in the United States than that produced in Spain. The product of the country, however, is not large enough to meet the requirements of the Italian home and export trade, and the merchants of Italy, therefore, purchase annually large

© Underwood & Underwood

FIG. 134. BARCELONA IS BUILT IN CRESCENT SHAPE ON
THE COAST OF THE MEDITERRANEAN SEA

quantities of oil from Spain, the amount varying with the crop
of the two countries. This oil they blend with the Italian oil and
pack in tins, glass, and barrels for export.

We must not lose sight of the fact that great quantities of olive
oil are manufactured on the southern as well as on the northern
borders of the Mediterranean Sea. Both Algeria and Tunisia make
considerable amounts each year, most of which is sent to France,
generally to Marseille. The product of those two countries is crude
and can scarcely be called edible oil; a small percentage of it,
however, is successfully blended with the better oils of France and
Italy. The olive tree flourishes in portions of Tunisia where there
is little rainfall and where the climate is similar to that of Texas
and Arizona. The United States government has sent experts to
northern Africa to study the industry in these dry regions and to
obtain seeds which may be tested in our arid states.

In addition to the olive oil which goes to Marseille and Bor-

© Underwood & Underwood

FIG. 135. THE STREETS OF THE QUEER
OLD SPANISH TOWN ARE NARROW

deaux, Algeria sends considerable quantities to Brittany, the province in the northwestern part of France where live the quaint fisher folk whom artists love to paint. The oil is used in the canning of sardines, of which you read in the chapter on ocean harvests.

A very excellent quality of olive oil is manufactured in northern Italy and on the Riviera, that beautiful French coast on the Mediterranean shore so noted for its healthful climate and its beauty. The olive oil produced in those two sections, from the very nature of the climatic conditions, is the finest in the world, because the nearer the cultivator reaches the point where the olives cannot be grown, the finer becomes the quality of the oil, just as New England and Canada apples are finer than those grown in the Southern states. The very best olive oil comes from near Nice, France, and next to that is the product of Lucca, a city of northern Italy near the Mediterranean Sea.

We have not mentioned thus far the olive industry of the United States, although in recent years this has grown to considerable importance. Neither the acreage nor the product of California equals that of France, Italy, or Spain, yet it is the only state in our country in which, as yet, olives are produced in any quantity. The oil is considered very good, and there seems to be a market for all that is produced. The olives not used in the

© Underwood & Underwood

FIG. 136. BULLOCK TEAM USED IN SPAIN

manufacture of oil are cured ripe and preserved in tins. They are different both in appearance and taste from the green, pickled olives of European countries.

Until recent years, the people of the United States have always used animal fats and mineral oils for food, for lighting, for lubricating, and for the manufacture of soap. Vegetable oils are much cheaper and are used in Europe in immense quantities for those purposes. Consequently, there are many plants cultivated in Europe for the oil obtained from their seeds, and immense quantities of oil-producing seeds and nuts are imported from far-away countries and islands. Chief among them are hemp, flax, and cotton seeds, those of the gorgeous sunflower, and great quantities of peanuts and other nuts. Hundreds of thousands of tons of flaxseed from the plains of Argentina, oil seeds and nuts from the East Indies and West Africa, and cotton seeds from Egypt and the United States are imported into Europe and manufactured into oil. England imports two billion pounds of such seeds for her oil factories. The city of Marseille alone imports annually enough seeds to fill a freight train one hundred seventy-five miles long. More than ten thousand of the

FIG. 137. WASHING CLOTHES BY THE RIVERSIDE IN A SPANISH TOWN

cars will be filled with peanuts, of which Marseille imports, chiefly from the East Indies and Africa, more than any other city in the world. From these, a great quantity of oil is made in her factories; this is used in the manufacture of soaps and perfumeries, and undoubtedly a limited quantity is used for the adulteration of olive oil.

Have you ever heard of a sunflower farm? In Russia, there are hundreds of them covered with tall green stalks and immense yellow blossoms. What a sight it must be! More than one hundred fifty mills turn out millions of gallons of sunflower oil every year. This is eaten as salad oil by the Russians, who prefer it to the oil of the olive.

Until the value of the seeds of the cotton plant was discovered, the United States never ranked very high as a producer of vegetable oil. To-day, however, from the millions of pounds of cotton seeds produced every year, we make such immense quantities of oil that this country holds first rank in vegetable-oil production.

As cottonseed oil is healthful and nourishing, and cheaper than the oil of the olives, it is used by the European peasants as a food by itself or for mixing with olive oil. After all the oil possible has been extracted from the cotton seeds, they are pressed into cakes or ground into meal. Both of these products furnish excellent food for cattle and are used in large quantities not only in this country but abroad. Few people realize what a great trade in cottonseed products is carried on today, for not very many years ago these seeds were considered a waste material of which it was difficult to dispose.

In very recent years, a new source of oil has been discovered in the soya bean, which grows in great quantities in Manchuria, China. The peppery sauce called "soy," which the Japanese like so much and which they consume in such large amounts on different articles of food, is made from these beans. Large quantities of them are shipped to Japan, where the oil is extracted. The imports into Europe are also large, and considerable quantities of the oil are used for the manufacture of soap, for lubricating purposes, and for the adulteration of other oils, while the cake and meal are sold as cattle food.

TOPICS FOR STUDY

I.

1. Spain's product of olives and olive oil.
2. Area of olive production.
3. Uses of olive oil.
4. Olive orchards.
5. Picking the fruit.
6. Pickling olives.
7. Making olive oil.
8. Shipping ports.
9. Other oil-producing countries.
10. Some important oil-producing seeds and nuts.

II.

1. On a map of Europe, color the olive-producing countries.
2. Look at bottles of pickled olives and find, if possible, from what place they come. Examine, in a similar way, bottles of olive oil.

3. What interesting building is in Granada? Why is it famous?

4. Look up some facts about Cordoba.

5. Sketch a map of Spain. Show all the places mentioned in the chapter.

6. Tell the route from Malaga to New York City. What will be the cargoes of vessels sailing between these ports?

7. What name is given to the four countries of Africa bordering on the Mediterranean Sea? To whom does each country belong? Name their principal products.

8. Read the chapter on Fruit in "Industrial Studies - United States," and tell what was said in it about the production of olives in California.

9. Name all the different kinds of oil mentioned in this chapter. From what seed or nut are they manufactured? Where are these obtained?

III.

Be able to spell and pronounce the following names. Locate each place and tell what was said of it in this and in any previous chapter. Add other facts if possible.

Algeria	New England	Malaga
Andalusia	Riviera	Marseille
Argentina	Russia	New York
Arizona	Spain	Nice
Brittany	Texas	Seville
California	Tunis	Adriatic Sea
China	United States	Bay of Cadiz
Connecticut		Guadalquivir
East Indies	Barcelona	River
Egypt	Bordeaux	Mediterranean Sea
England	Boston	Pyrenees
France	Cadiz	Mountains
Greece	Cordoba	Sierra Morena
Italy	Granada	Sierra Nevada
Japan	Lucca	
Manchuria	Madrid	

CHAPTER XVII

GRAPES AND WINE AND THE COUNTRIES WHICH PRODUCE THEM

The raising of grapes and the manufacturing of wine are very important industries in most of the countries of central and southern Europe. To become acquainted with the real everyday life of the peasants, one must see them at work in the vineyards or wineries, for hundreds of thousands of men, women, and children find employment in tending the vines and in the manufacture and sale of wine.

From its original home, probably somewhere in Asia, the industry has spread westward through Europe, and thence across the Atlantic Ocean to the United States and South America, until at the present time, large vineyards may be found in nearly all countries of the world where the climate is favorable. Throughout all southern Europe, in the United States, in the northern and southern parts of Africa, in several of the South American countries, and in far-away Australia, the grape industry and the making of wine have become of much importance.

The grapevine is naturally a great climber, and if left to itself, it will twist and twine high in the branches and even reach the tops of the tallest trees. A noted historian of Italy tells us that, in olden times, the vine climbed so high that the grape gatherer always inserted a clause in his contract to the effect that in case he lost his life by falling from such heights, the master of the vineyard was to pay all funeral expenses.

In modern vineyards, however, the plants bear little resemblance to their ambitious ancestors, and it is hard to recognize

FIG. 138. THE LARGEST GRAPEVINE IN THE WORLD IS IN CALIFORNIA

the rambling, twisting climbers in the short, closely pruned vines tied to poles no taller than our heads. In many parts of Italy, the vine is allowed to grow in a more natural way and is hung from pole to pole or from tree to tree. In riding by acre after acre of these festooned fields, one feels as if the whole country were decorated for some great holiday.

During the vintage season, from September to October, great fêtes or festivals of the vine, witnessed by thousands of people, are held in France, Germany, and Italy. There are long days of hard work in the vineyards for old and young, but there are also days of merrymaking, and with them, dances, tableaux, and processions with gayly decorated floats. In all of the vine-growing countries of Europe, the vintage time is looked forward to as the pleasantest part of the year, and much fun and frolic are mixed with the long days of hard work in the vineyard.

The variety of grapes raised usually differs according to the use which is to be made of them. Raisins and wine are not often made from the same kind of fruit, and different varieties must be grown for the different kinds of wine. Grapes which are to be used in the manufacture of wine are raised in immense quantities in France, Italy, and Spain. These three countries produce the greater part of the whole European product. The industry is important also in Central Europe, Portugal, Germany, and the small countries of the Balkan Peninsula. Germany is the most northerly country where the grape can be grown successfully for wine manufacture. In a sail up the Rhine River, we should hardly know which to admire the more: the gray old castles crowning the cliffs, or the miles of vineyards which, on either side, stretch from the river up the steep slopes to the very tops of the hills. These are so steep that the slopes are terraced like flights of stairs to hold the soil in place; otherwise, it would be washed down into the river by heavy rains. Some of the terraces, such as you see in Fig. 76, are built up with stone walls which are hundreds of years old. The soil for the upper terraces has been carried up in baskets by the peasants themselves, as no farm animal could pull a load up such steep grades. The little terraced gardens are so small that all the work must be done by hand, as there is no room in which to turn a plow. Yet, from these steep slopes, come the famous Rhine wines, which are considered among the best in the world.

Let us take a trip to the southwestern corner of Europe and visit the vineyards of Spain and Portugal. In both of these countries, the making of wine and the curing of raisins are the most important industries. The wine which is shipped to other countries equals in value one third of all the other exports put together. Nearly half of the enormous quantity of wine which Spain produces annually is sent to France, where it is mixed with French wines, which are considered superior.

In our tour through Spain, we shall find many peasants at work on farms, for more than half of the people are engaged in agriculture. The farms look poorly cared for, and the crops are scanty, for the methods of farming are backward. The plow is a rude affair, which only scratches the surface of the ground, and the tools which they use are of the simplest kind.

On the terraced hillsides of rich, red soil in southern Spain, the vineyards stretch for miles, and here, in the autumn, we shall find nearly all the inhabitants at work. The dark-eyed, barefooted children, half hidden behind baskets of luscious fruit, look shyly at us as we pass. We meet donkeys with huge baskets of grapes swung from either side, and clumsy oxcarts filled to overflowing with the juicy clusters. These will probably be put through the wine press and made into wine. "Sherry" is the English name given to the kind of wine originally made in the vicinity of Jerez, which you may find on the map, on the coast of southwestern Spain.

On the southern coast, a little farther to the east, lies the city of Malaga. This name reminds us of the Malaga grapes and raisins, which are shipped in great quantities from that city. Here, and also at Almeria, we may see the peasants picking great bunches of the delicious, greenish-white fruit. These grapes are packed in powdered cork, which resembles sawdust, and are placed into small kegs for shipment. In the sunny harbor, we see vessels bound for many different countries, all of

© Underwood & Underwood

FIG. 139. "ON THE TERRACED HILLSIDES OF RICH RED SOIL IN SOUTHERN SPAIN THE VINEYARDS STRETCH FOR MILES"

FIG. 140. PERHAPS SOME CLUSTERS MAY FURNISH A PART
OF THE DESSERT AT YOUR THANKSGIVING DINNER

them carrying, as part of their cargo, great quantities of Malaga grapes, some clusters of which may furnish part of your dessert at Thanksgiving or Christmas dinner.

As we go from the city of Malaga out into the country, we will pass by many fields filled with shallow trays in which grapes are drying in the sun. In this drying process, they will be changed from juicy fruit into the sweet, brown raisins for which Malaga is

© Underwood & Underwood

FIG. 141. PLANTING A VINEYARD

famous. It is possible that some of these raisins, too, in the plum pudding or mince pie, may add to the pleasure of your Thanksgiving dinner. However, it is more likely that the raisins your mother buys come from California. Not many years ago, nearly all the raisins used in the United States were brought from Europe, chiefly from Spain; now, however, California furnishes the greater part of the many million pounds used in the United States each year.

Not far distant from Malaga is the famous fortress of Gibraltar. Under its frowning walls, we will take a steamer for Oporto, the great wine port of Portugal. As we land at the pier, we see many of the small-framed, dark-complexioned natives loading a vessel bound for England with barrels of the dark red wine, which years ago was called "port" by the wine merchants of London. The name is now used for similar kinds of wine made in other countries, though that made from the grapes raised in the vineyards on the banks of the Douro River is considered superior to all others. It is only in this one area that the real port wine is made.

In the Middle Ages, the Douro was famous for the gold that was found in its bed. Today, it is far more widely known for the chief product of the country — port wine. The fruit produced in other localities does not have the same flavor. The soil and the climate peculiar to this region enable the farmers to produce a sweet, juicy grape, which cannot be equaled elsewhere. For more than twenty miles along the river, and for two or three miles back into the valley, stretch the acres of low vineyards. Everybody raises grapes. Everybody works in the vineyards.

Lofty mountains protect the valley from the damp, chill winds of the ocean to the west, and other ranges rise to the north and east. The vines, pruned to a height of four or five feet, cover the precipitous hillsides, which the peasants, by hard labor, have terraced from top to bottom.

September is the vintage time, and then the laborers from other provinces flock into the district in great numbers. Everyone is busy in the vineyards. Men and women, old people, and children help to gather the grapes. In some of the more remote villages, the young men, a dozen or more at a time, leap with bare feet into the great stone vats where the grapes have been placed. Someone strikes up a lively air, and the men, placing their hands on each other's shoulders to keep their balance, tread out the juice of the grapes to the rhythm of the music. It is tiresome work and cannot be kept up for many hours at a time.

The wine, which is stored in casks and bottles in the cellars of Oporto, is later shipped away by hundreds and thousands of gallons. Nearly all the port wine produced in the Douro valley is exported from the city of Oporto. Many other products, such as - cork, sardines, fruits, nuts, and salt, are also shipped from this city, which is the chief commercial center of Portugal.

In its course from Spain, the Douro River breaks through three ranges of mountains or hills. Oporto, a city rather smaller than St. Paul, Minnesota, is situated just where the river conquers the last obstacle and flows onward to the ocean. The city is very attractive as one approaches from the water. On either bank rise high, steep cliffs lined with houses, tier above tier, red, yellow, green, and blue, all with dull-red roofs, and overhanging leaves so wide that, in the old, narrow streets, they nearly meet. On the highest hill of all gleams the old cathedral, watching over the city whose people are its charge.

In the valley, the streets are broad and straight, with electric-car tracks, public parks, and gardens. As we ascend the hills, however, to the older parts of the city, we find narrow, crooked streets, and in some cases, stairways built to shorten the ascent.

Down near the wharves are many red-tiled, low-roofed buildings, the offices of the wine merchants. The shaggy, tawny oxen, which the peasants drive in their clumsy carts, seem to fill some of the narrow streets of this section of the city with their widespreading horns, and we are obliged to step into a low doorway to avoid them.

There are factories in Oporto where cotton, woolen, silk, and linen goods are made, also gold and silver wire, glass, leather, and lace. We should find, too, large tobacco factories and soap works. In the harbor are many vessels from different countries, bringing to the little country the materials for these manufactures and for other needs of the people, such as cotton, wool, silk, flax, machinery, tools, grain, and coal, and carrying across the water the products of her vineyards and cork forests.

Though Portugal is a small country, only a little larger than Maine, much of its surface is covered with vineyards. Nearly half of the wine product is shipped to Great Britain. If we should visit the Madeira Islands, which belong to Portugal, we would find there Madeira wine ready for shipment to the same place, for the English are the best wine customers of Portugal.

Let us next go to Italy. There are so many interesting places in this country that we hardly know which to visit first. We should like to study its wonderful ruins and beautiful cathedrals. If time allowed, we would go to Pisa and see its queer leaning tower. We would visit the quarries where the Carrara marble, the whitest, finest marble in the world, is obtained. We would go to the farms where millions of silkworms are raised, and watch them spinning their queer cocoons. We would see the peasants braiding straw for the hats, which may later be sold in your home city. We would linger again before the fascinating store windows where dainty coral chains are for sale and admire the beautifully colored Venetian beads. But we shall have no time for any of these things, for we are to visit instead the festooned vineyards and watch the merry pickers — men, women, and children — gathering the ripened clusters of fruit. The songs, the merry voices, the gay colors of the women's dresses, the golden-brown of the vine drapery, the rich purple or delicate greenish-white grapes, the full baskets, and the loaded wagons make a sight that, once seen, is never forgotten. If we follow

© Underwood & Underwood
FIG. 142. THE MAKING OF WINE CASKS IS AN IMPORTANT OCCUPATION

the loads of grapes to the waiting wine presses, we might see, in some out-of-the-way places, the peasants, bare-legged and barefooted, or perhaps with heavy, hobnailed shoes, treading out the purple juice in the old-fashioned way. But in all modern wineries, this is now done by machinery.

The proportion of land in Italy covered by vineyards is greater than in any other country, and the amount of wine produced is enormous, amounting in one year to more than a billion gallons. It is hard to imagine such an immense quantity. Suppose we try to build a tank to hold it all. You will hardly believe, unless you do the problem for yourself, that if your tank is twenty feet in diameter, you will have to make it more than eighty miles long to hold the wine that is made in Italy in one year.

A large proportion of this tankful of Italian wine is shipped to France, where it is mixed with French wines. Immense quantities, however, are consumed at home, for nearly everybody in Italy — not only men but also women and children — drinks wine. Even the poorest peasants, who drink a cheap variety costing only a few cents a gallon, look upon it as a necessary part of their daily meals.

The vineyards of France lie in river valleys or on sunny slopes of the hills. Hung with the great clusters of delicate fruit, they are as famous in story and poem as they are important in industry and commerce. France produces annually about one-third of the world's supply. If we should try to put this immense quantity into hogsheads, we should find that, before the last one was filled, we should have six rows of hogsheads end to end, stretching from Boston across the United States to the Pacific coast, with enough left to reach one-third of the distance again.

After reading these statements, you will not be surprised to learn that the wine made in southern France is of more value than all the other products of that region put together. So high is its reputation that great quantities from other countries of Europe and from Algeria are imported into France only to be exported again as French wine. Of all the wine contained in the six long rows of hogsheads, that in two rows only is shipped out of the country. The rest is consumed by the French people, for they drink it with their meals as we do milk or tea. But although you do not approve of the custom of wine drinking, you must not think, because of the amount produced and used in France or in other European countries, that the people are necessarily dissipated or drunkards. They use comparatively little of the stronger intoxicating liquors. A Frenchman and his family regard wine at meals as we do our tea or coffee, and are accustomed to it from childhood.

The vine is grown nearly everywhere in France, but three regions are especially noted for the excellence of the wine produced. One is in the upper Rhone Valley, one in the district of Champagne, in the northeastern part of the country, and one in western France, near Bordeaux, the largest wine-shipping port in the world. The city is situated near the junction of the Garonne and Gironde rivers, about sixty miles from the ocean, and is connected by canal, railroad, and river with the Mediterranean Sea and with the manufacturing cities of France.

Ordinarily, thousands of people find employment in the

French vineyards where the small, dark grapes, from which champagne is made, are grown. The champagne region, however, lies in the part of France where so much destruction was caused by the war. Hundreds of acres, once covered with thrifty vineyards, which were the chief support of the inhabitants of dozens of villages, lie barren — a mass of upheaved earth and deep shell holes. As France recovers from the awful damage done to her industries, one can see again the women and children, in their wooden shoes, short skirts, and queer-looking caps, working in the vineyards — weeding and hoeing the vines and gathering the fruit. Hundreds of men prune and tend the vines, set the poles which support them, and plant new vineyards. Many others work in the bottle and cork factories, for millions of bottles and corks must be made each year to hold the wine crop of France.

The northeastern part of France, which for four years was overrun by millions of fighting men, included about a fifth of the entire country — an area equal to that of Massachusetts, Rhode Island, and Connecticut. In this area, besides the farms which were laid waste and the homes destroyed, there were twelve hundred churches demolished, fifteen hundred schools, and more than one thousand mills, factories, and other manufacturing establishments. Such is the result of war.

In this devastated part of France lay not only some of her finest vineyards and richest farms, but here also were the coal and iron mines, from which a large part of her mineral product was obtained. Around these mineral deposits had grown up many of her most important manufacturing cities. There, too, mines and factories alike were destroyed, and many years must elapse before the prosperity of sorely stricken France returns in full.

The eastern boundary of France is different from what it was before the World War. Here, between Germany and France, lie Alsace and Lorraine. These two provinces were formerly a part of France, but at the end of the Franco-Prussian War, in 1871, they were annexed by Germany and made a part of her territory. France never gave up the hope of possessing them again, and in the treaty at the close of the World War, in 1919, they were given back to her.

Alsace and Lorraine are about three-fourths as large as Massachusetts. In this region, there are thousands of acres of deep forests, iron mines so valuable that Germany could probably never have prepared for the great war had she not possessed them, valuable potash and coal mines, splendid vineyards, and fertile farms and pasture lands.

Strassburg and Metz are the two important cities of Alsace and Lorraine. Both places are situated in river valleys on important routes between Germany and France. Strassburg is much the larger city of the two. It is located on a little river about two miles from the Rhine and commands the most important route over the Vosges Mountains between Paris and the Rhine River. For this reason, it has always been strongly fortified. Like many other European cities, parts of Strassburg are centuries old. Other parts of the city are modern, for in the war between France and Germany, which ended in 1871, the bombardment destroyed many buildings, which have since been replaced by new ones. The ancient cathedral of the city, which was four centuries in building, still stands. Its tall spire reaches more than four hundred and sixty feet toward the sky. In this famous old cathedral is the wonderful clock, parts of which were built more than five hundred years ago. This ancient timepiece contains a perpetual calendar and an arrangement that shows the position and movements of the planets. When the clock strikes the hour, the figures of Christ and the apostles come into view.

Strassburg is an important manufacturing city. You can find what its chief products are by consulting any encyclopedia. There is one very odd manufacture, not so important as others, but one for which the city is famous. Can you imagine a city making and exporting each year hundreds of thousands of dollars' worth of goose-liver pie? Strassburg is noted for this pie, which is commonly known as *pâté de foie gras*. By which name do you think you would rather call it? Many of the peasants in the country around Strassburg raise geese to supply the number needed in the manufacture of this famous pie.

FIG. 143. FACADE OF THE CATHEDRAL AT RHEIMS
From Robinson, Breasted, and Beard's "Outlines of European History," Part I

One of the important cities in the Champagne district of France is Rheims. In 1914, it contained considerably more than a hundred thousand people. Four years later, only about eight thousand inhabitants were living in the ruins of the city. Its famous cathedral, built in the thirteenth and fourteenth centuries, with its lovely rose window of stained glass, was riddled with holes, and parts of the roof and walls were demolished. The streets of the city were filled with brick and stone, and the industries of the region were destroyed.

Under the city of Rheims and in the area around it, there are deep chalk beds in which there are miles of caves. These caves are very cool all year round and have been used for many years by wine merchants to store their wine.

We have spoken of the wine, raisins, and currants made from grapes. Large quantities of vinegar are made from wine. Besides these more important products, there are many by-products, as they are called, which are manufactured in greater and greater quantities each year as people learn more about the value of

FIG. 144. JUST OUT OF SCHOOL IN ALSACE

waste material. In many industries, this material is now carefully used instead of being thrown away.

The pulp and skins left in the vats after the fermented juice is drawn off are called pomace. This is used to a considerable extent in making cheap wines and in the manufacture of brandy. In some regions, the pomace serves as food for cattle.

After the pomace is dried, the stems, skins, and seeds, from which it is composed, are separated. The seeds are the most valuable and are sometimes fed to horses, cattle, or poultry in place of oats or other grains. By crushing the seeds, a valuable oil is obtained, which is similar to olive oil and is used for many of the same purposes. There is also a substance made from the seeds that is used in tanning skins and making them into soft leather.

While the juice is fermenting, a powder known as tartar is deposited on the sides of the vats. From this, the cream

FIG. 145. IN THE REGION AROUND RHEIMS THERE ARE MILES OF
CAVES HOLLOWED OUT OF THE DEEP CHALK BEDS
From "World's Commercial Products"

of tartar and baking powder used in cooking are made. We import several million dollars' worth of this useful material annually from Europe.

It is estimated that if all the waste from the wine crop were utilized, the products made from it would equal one-tenth of the value of the wine itself. This is worth several hundred million dollars annually, so by properly using the waste, wine-producing countries could generate an additional income of many million dollars.

Though many grapes are raised in different parts of our country, it is hard for the people of the United States, even those from the chief grape-producing sections, to realize what the industry means to the peasants of European countries. In many regions, the vineyard is the sole means of support, and every member of the family feels the necessity of giving it the best care from the time when the new shoots put forth in early spring until the last cluster is gathered in autumn. The farms are small — much smaller on average than those in our country — and every inch of space is used. If not for the vines, then for the vegetables which form a large part of the peasants' food, the grain for the cattle, the flax for spinning, or the mulberry trees for the silkworms.

The French farmer is usually thrifty and saving, and he works under more favorable conditions than the peasants do in some other European countries. These comfortable circumstances are largely due to the Frenchwoman, for she is more of a helper and less of a slave in that country than in others. She works in the fields with the men, cares well for the house, and often takes complete charge of the small income. She is not only the business manager of the household but also a skilled cook, making nourishing meals out of articles that might seem of little use to others. In her spare minutes, she spins and weaves wool or flax for clothing, makes exquisite lace or delicate embroideries that fetch high prices, and in many ways, she increases the income of the household.

TOPICS FOR STUDY

I.

1. History of vine culture.
2. Manner of growth.
3. Festivals of the vine.
4. Varieties and uses of grapes.
5. Vineyards on the Rhine River.
6. The vine industry in Spain and Portugal.
7. The industry in Italy; in France.
8. Results of the war in northeastern France.
9. Alsace and Lorraine.
10. By-products of the wine industry.
11. Dependence of the peasants on their vineyards.

II.

1. Sketch a map of Europe and color all the wine-producing countries.
2. Write a list of the principal manufactures of Spain and of the principal industries of Portugal.
3. Trace the route from Malaga to London; to New York City.
4. Name the country from which you think each of the imports mentioned on page 288 will be brought to Portugal. Name in each case the waters sailed on and the shipping port.
5. Sketch a map of France and show the three great wine-producing sections. Show also the rivers and cities mentioned.
6. Reread Chapter VII and tell how the cork stoppers for the wine bottles are made.

III.

Be able to spell and pronounce the following names. Locate each place and tell what was said of it in this and any previous chapters. Add other facts if possible.

Algeria
Australia
Balkan
  Peninsula
California
England
France
Germany
Great Britain
Italy
Portugal
Spain
United States

Alsace

Champagne
Lorraine

Almeria
Bordeaux
Boston
Carrara
Jerez
London
Malaga
Metz
Oporto
Paris
Pisa
Rheims

St. Paul
Strassburg
Venice
Douro River
Garonne River
Gibraltar
Gironde River
Madeira Islands
Mediterranean
  Sea
Rhine River
Rhone River
Vosges
  Mountains

CHAPTER XVIII

ITALY AND MACARONI

If bread is the staff of life in the United States, macaroni surely holds a similar position in Italy. In that country, everyone — rich and poor, high and low — eats macaroni. Boiled in salted water, it furnishes the main food of the very poor. Served with cheese or tomato or in some other way, it is often found on the tables of the higher classes.

Though much of the macaroni imported into the United States is made in large factories, great quantities are made in the homes of the peasants. In some of the villages near Naples, before almost every door, one can see the long, yellowish-white strings of paste hanging from bars supported by two poles. A traveler in Italy describes the making of macaroni as follows:

> These towns are dependent on the manufacture of the "pastas," as the various types of macaroni are called, and hand-worked mills stand side by side with those run by steam, all squeezing out long strings of yellow paste, which are cut and hung up on poles to dry. The housetops, courtyards, narrow streets, and hillsides are covered with thousands of reed poles bending under the weight of yellow macaroni, and scattered over the ground on mats, lie different sorts of short-shaped pastas.

The process of manufacture seems exceedingly simple, but there may be, for all that, secrets of the trade. The wheat is ground into a coarse, sharp, granular product, less fine and soft than flour, called semolina. This is put through sieves to remove the undesirable parts of the grain.

The sifted semolina is then put into a square iron mixer

FIG. 146. "NARROW STREETS AND HILLSIDES ARE COVERED WITH THOUSANDS OF
REED POLES BENDING UNDER THE WEIGHT OF YELLOW MACARONI"
From "World's Commercial Products"

furnished at the bottom with screw-shaped fans, which stir the paste. Boiling water is added, and the dough is kneaded for about seven or eight minutes. The mass is then put on a flat, circular board and kneaded by two sharp-edged parallel beams, which rise and fall as the table turns, pressing into the dough as they descend. A few minutes of kneading are sufficient, and the dough is then put into a cylinder in which a piston descends upon the mass, forcing it in strings slowly through the perforated plate at the bottom. In fifteen minutes, many gallons of dough are changed into thousands of feet of yellow macaroni. The color is produced by the use of saffron, which is used in very small quantities.

As soon as the strings of fresh paste, which issue continually from the die, are of proper length, they are cut and thrown over a reed pole. They are carried into the sunlight if the weather is fair, or into sheltered terraces protected by curtains from the rain if the weather is unfavorable. On bright days, the strings of macaroni are exposed to the sunlight for about two hours.

FIG. 147. A MACARONI FACTORY
From "World's Commercial Products"

They must be dried only slightly before being put for the night into dark cellars.

For twelve hours or more, the poles of macaroni are kept in these damp places until the dough becomes moist and pliable again, and the strings lose the brittleness that the exposure to the sunlight gave them. From the cellars, the poles are carried to storehouses open on all sides to the air. Here, in great masses of millions of strings, the macaroni hangs for several days, with the time depending on the weather. This drying process toughens the brittle paste and makes it suitable for rough handling without breaking into small pieces.

When the macaroni is thoroughly dried, it is packed for shipping in light wooden boxes. On the roads around Naples, one may see many carts piled high with such boxes, all headed for the city. The mule or the small Italian horse seems not a whit discouraged by the huge load behind him, nor by the fierce heat of the bright Italian sun. When his master stops to refresh himself at some tavern on the road, the horse satisfies his hunger by nibbling at the bunch of straw, which is tied for that purpose on the end of one of the shafts.

Let us follow one of these teams along the dusty road into Naples, the largest city of Italy. It is densely populated, and the narrow streets are filled with people, loaded mules, heavy hand-carts, and queer-looking vehicles. The milkman drives his goats from house to house, milking them at his customer's doorway. The ear is deafened with the shrill cries of peddlers advertising their wares, with the high-pitched voices of loiterers, and with the screams of children at play. Black-haired, wrinkle-faced women gather on the doorsteps and in the streets, working or gossiping away the hours. The children and babies are in evidence everywhere — in the crowded streets, sprawling in the gutters, sunning themselves comfortably in the dirt. They are ragged and filthy, yet their faces are those which artists love to

© Underwood & Underwood

FIG. 148. BLACK-HAIRED, WRINKLE-FACED WOMEN
GATHER ON THE SIDEWALKS OR IN THE STREETS

paint. They have large, dark eyes, wavy black hair, and velvet cheeks such as a ballroom belle might envy. Italian children are beautiful, but the beauty soon fades, and the grown people are not very attractive. The store windows are fascinating, and we linger before them, looking at the strings of pink coral and at the combs and other articles made of the richly colored tortoiseshell, which are displayed in such profusion.

The harbor of Naples is very beautiful. The water of the bay rivals in color the clear blue of the sky. The gleaming roofs and spires of the city stand out sharp and clear in the bright Italian sunshine, while in the distance looms the ever-threatening Vesuvius. Dark smoke issues from its crater, as if the mountain were continually frowning at the city for daring to be so bright and gay in the face of its own gloomy appearance.

Many vessels sail from the harbor of Naples to the United States, and thousands of boxes of macaroni form a part of their freight. More than two-thirds of the six million dollars' worth manufactured annually in Italy, and half as much more made in the United States, are needed to supply the demands of our country. If this immense quantity were distributed among the people of the United States, it would supply every man, woman, and child with about a pound a year. This is very little, however, compared with the amount that the people of Italy eat, for in that country the average annual consumption is between five and six pounds.

You are probably wondering where all the wheat is raised from which such great quantities of macaroni are made. Good macaroni cannot be made from all kinds of wheat. A hard variety called durum wheat is the best for the purpose, and the Italians use this kind almost entirely. They do not like macaroni made from a softer wheat, and for this reason, they would not enjoy much that is made in the United States.

Durum wheat does not grow well in Italy, but it flourishes on the great plains of southern Russia, and the greater part of that which Italy imports comes from that country and from far-away Australia.

You have heard of the dreadful famines that sometimes

visit Russia when her crops fail, of the sufferings of the peasants, and of the many deaths which result. In such years, there is little wheat to ship abroad, and Italy has to look elsewhere to supply her macaroni factories. Durum wheat is now raised successfully in the United States, and large quantities are sent every year to Naples. In years of Russian famine, however, our exports are greatly increased, millions of bushels from our farms making up the shortage from Russia. Many Italians, however, do not consider our wheat as good as that which comes from the "black earth" region, and as it is more expensive, they do not as yet purchase from us in as great quantities as they do from their eastern neighbor. If we can supply suitable wheat at a lower price than Russia can furnish the same quality, we shall find a good market for it in Italy.

The making of macaroni has grown to be an industry of considerable importance in the United States. At first, it was used only by the Italian and French residents, but now it is eaten by all classes. It takes more than one hundred fifty factories manufacturing many million pounds, besides our imports of twice as much more, to supply the macaroni needed for our home consumption and for export. Many of the factories are in New York, Philadelphia, and San Francisco, and the remainder are scattered in various places throughout the country.

In wandering through the streets of Naples, we are not only fascinated by the coral and tortoiseshell ornaments, but astonished as well at the quantity displayed for sale. An animal so small that the skeletons of thousands would be required to cover a surface no larger than one's hand would seem too unimportant to mention, yet many vessels and hundreds of men sail from Mediterranean ports to obtain the skeletons of the tiny coral polyp. Coral looks more like a flower than an animal and formerly was thought to belong to the vegetable kingdom. Each polyp consists of but little more than a round, hollow body with a mouth at the top, and a fringe of feelers or arms surrounding it. It lives for a short time and only in warm, clean water where the current will supply it with the food that it needs to build its skeleton, which, at its death, settles to the bottom of the ocean. Upon this skeleton, others build, leaving theirs in turn as a foundation for still others. Thus the structure is, in time, built up near the surface of the water. The waves and storms break off much of the stony material, which, with seaweed, soil, and other ocean debris, gradually raises the formation above the surface of the water, and coral islands are built. Many of these have grown to a great size. The Great Barrier Reef of Australia, which stretches for a thousand miles along the eastern coast, with its top but a short distance below the surface of the water, is the largest in the world.

Conditions in which coral can live and work are found in parts of the Mediterranean Sea, especially near the coasts of Sicily and Sardinia, and on the North African shore. Some of the coral found in Italian workshops comes also from the Pacific Ocean, near Japan. Coral fishing in Italy is done by fleets of rather small boats, most of which start from Torre del Greco, a place of some thirty-five thousand people, located about six miles from Naples. Let us accompany the fleet to the coasts of Tunis and Tripoli, where most of the Italian coral is obtained.

The apparatus which the Italian fishermen use in obtaining coral is very simple and looks to our eyes like some worthless material fit only for the junkman. It consists of a wooden cross made of heavy beams to which are attached pieces of old nets and untwisted rope ends. The men lower this queer contrivance from the boat and drag it along the sea floor. The branching coral becomes entangled in the nets and ropes and is broken off and drawn, with the fishing apparatus, to the surface.

There is little resemblance, however, between the rough branches of coral piled on the Italian fishing boats and the smooth, delicate pink beads which you so admire. We will follow the cargo into a shop at Naples and see how coral ornaments are made.

The room which we have entered is small and poorly lit. A swarthy Italian in the farther corner is sorting out the coral from a pile before him. Though it all looks very much the same to our inexperienced eyes, he separates it into several grades, laying the finest, choicest pieces carefully by themselves. Another workman is cutting into pieces some coral from which beads are to be made and is drilling the hole for the thread. Near the door is still another worker, who, with a small, curious file, rounds each piece into shape. His work seems more difficult than the others, and his skill is greater, for the bead that he fashions out of the rough block of coral must be true and even. A wrinkled old woman near the bead-maker holds up for our inspection a dull bead which he has just handed to her. She polishes it vigorously with pumice and water until it begins to show the smooth pink surface desired. After a further polishing with a preparation of chalk and water, she holds it up again for us to see. Its surface is smooth and clear and of the most dainty pink tinge. This is a valuable bead and will be put with others of the same delicate shade to make a beautiful string, which will be sold for one hundred fifty or two hundred dollars. Much cheap imitation coral is made of celluloid and other materials, but the real coral of the best quality and color is very expensive.

Other cities in Italy, besides Naples, are interested in the coral industry, Genoa and Leghorn particularly so. In Genoa, it is said that six thousand workmen are employed in fashioning the dainty coral ornaments.

Tortoise shell is obtained from a species of sea turtle which lives in the ocean near the East and West Indies, Australia, and Africa. Thousands of dollars' worth of shell is imported into Italy each year and there made into combs, paper knives, and other articles, which are sold chiefly to tourists. The rough shell is first scraped and then sawed into pieces of the desired size and shape. If a handle of a knife or paper cutter is to be made, several pieces must be welded together. This is done by placing the pieces one upon the other, wrapping them in a wet cloth, and putting them between pieces of wood. The whole package is then placed between plates of hot iron and pressed for about ten minutes, when it looks to an inexperienced eye like a single piece of shell. After this comes the polishing with pumice and a brisk rubbing with oil to produce the beautiful, smooth finish which makes tortoise-shell ornaments so much admired.

We can hardly leave Italy without a peep at Rome, its capital, a city famous for what it has been rather than for what it is. Wherever we go, we are reminded of its ancient glory and power, when this city on the seven hills overlooking the yellow Tiber was the center of the Roman Empire, which controlled nearly all the known world.

Great triumphal arches built to commemorate Roman victories are still standing. We may also see remains of old aqueducts which carried the water to the baths where the people spent so much of their time, and the ruins of the fountains from which gushed the pure water that flowed down from the hills around the city. Ruins are everywhere. Perhaps the most interesting one of these is the Forum, where the ancient Romans held their assemblies to discuss public questions. Guides point out the very spot where Mark Antony delivered the funeral oration over the body of the great Caesar. Do you know the oration as Shakespeare gives it? It begins:

"Friends, Romans, countrymen, lend me your ears."

Very beautiful indeed are the ruins of the Colosseum, a magnificent building formerly capable of seating nearly fifty thousand people. In this, the largest theater in the world, somewhat like the modern stadium, gladiators fought; and lions, tigers, and other wild beasts tore at each other's throats or at those of the Christian martyrs, for the entertainment of the brutal Romans.

Among the three hundred or more churches in the city is St. Peter's, the very largest church in the world, yet so wonderfully planned and built that one scarcely realizes its immense size. Close at hand is the Vatican, the home of the Pope, the head of the Roman Catholic Church. His is the largest residence in the world, and one in which we might very easily be lost if allowed to wander alone through the hundreds of courts, halls, chapels, and rooms.

The Rome of today is of very little importance compared with the ancient city, and its trade and commerce are of little value. Travelers come to the city by thousands to study its ruins and to learn of its ancient splendor. Its manufactures consist chiefly of articles such as tourists fancy — mosaic jewelry, pearls, gloves, silk scarfs, ribbons, ties, and pictures.

No city is held in greater respect by any people than is Rome by the Italians. It is the home of the Pope, who is the head of the church to which most of them belong, and of the king and queen of Italy, who are dearly loved by their subjects.

Italy is one of the countries which fought on the side of the Allied Nations in the World War. You will be interested in reading stories of Italian campaigns, for they were very different from those on the other battle fronts. Much of the fighting was carried on in the high passes of the Alps Mountains, where, much of the time, the cold was bitter, the snow drifts were piled high, and marching had to be done on snowshoes. Heavy guns often had to be lifted over impassable gorges and cliffs by means of derricks and other machinery. Time and again the Austrians tried to swarm over the mountains and down upon the rich plains of the Po valley, and time after time they were driven back by the brave Italians.

The strain on the nation was tremendous. Italy is not a rich country, and two-thirds of all her wealth was spent in paying the expenses of the war. Her industries were paralyzed, her commerce was shut off, and she suffered for needful supplies. Coal was one of these necessities. Little is found in Italy, and she depends on other countries to supply her. So great was her necessity that many of her olive orchards, the chief dependence of many peasants, were cut down. The olive tree grows slowly, and it will be many years before the Italian farmers recover from their losses.

Look on the map on page 265 and find the city of Trieste. It is situated at the head of the Adriatic Sea. Before the World War it was the chief seaport of the former empire of Austria-Hungary, which is now divided into several smaller countries. Today, Trieste is an Italian port. You will be interested in visiting the old part of the city, which nestles around the Schlossberg, which, as its name tells you, is the hill on which the castle stands. We will climb some of the narrow, crooked streets to enjoy the view and to explore the old castle which stands on the site where, centuries before, the ancient Roman capitol stood. Down on the plain reaching out to the crescent-shaped bay, things are very different. We should hardly know that we were in the same city. Here are broad streets, fine modern buildings, and many manufacturing plants — petroleum refineries, iron foundries, soap manufactories, silk mills, and large shipbuilding yards. It is her commerce, however, rather than her manufactures, which has made Trieste so important. Situated at the head of the long sea, at the end of a deep gulf, it is the chief southern outlet of Central Europe and long ago outstripped its ancient rival, Venice. Ships leave the splendid harbor of Trieste bound for all parts of the world — for ports on the Mediterranean Sea, for European ports on the Atlantic, for India, China, and other countries of the Far East, and for the distant cities of North and South America. Fiume is another important port on the Adriatic Sea. This city, with a small surrounding area, forms the Free State of Fiume, but the Yugoslavs make use of the port.

TOPICS FOR STUDY

I.

1. The making of macaroni.
2. Description of Naples.
3. The Bay of Naples and Vesuvius.
4. The making of macaroni in the United States.
5. The coral industry.
6. Tortoise shell.
7. Description of Rome.
8. Italy in the World War.
9. The seaport of Trieste.

II.

1. Describe the process of macaroni-making.
2. Ask your grocer to let you see the labels on some macaroni boxes and thus find out where it was made. Make a collection of such labels.
3. Sketch a map of Italy and show all the places mentioned in this chapter.
4. Ship a cargo of wheat from Russia to Italy, from Australia, from

the United States. Tell the waters sailed on in each voyage and the shipping and receiving ports.

5. Read the poem "Horatius at the Bridge." What is said in the poem of the Tiber River, on which Rome is situated? Find out how long the river is. Compare it with some river in the United States.

6. In the days of Rome's power and splendor, the Tiber was much deeper than at the present time. How has the change in the river affected the city?

7. Sketch a map of the Mediterranean Sea. Show the coral-fishing grounds and all the Italian cities mentioned in this chapter.

8. On what waters will a vessel sail in going from the East Indies to Italy? What does Italy obtain from the East Indies? What goods might be shipped for a return cargo?

9. Find another city besides Trieste near the head of the Adriatic Sea about which there was much discussion at the close of the World War. What nation makes use of this port?

III.

Be able to spell and pronounce the following names. Locate each place and tell what was said of it in this and in any previous chapter. Add other facts if possible.

Africa	Genoa	Adriatic Sea
Australia	Leghorn	Alps Mountains
Austria-Hungary	Naples	Bay of Naples
East Indies	New York	Great Barrier Reef
Japan	Philadelphia	
Russia	Rome	Mediterranean Sea
Sardinia	Torre del Greco	
Sicily	Trieste	Mount Vesuvius
Tripoli	San Francisco	Po River
Tunis	Venice	Tiber River
United States	Fiume	
West Indies		

CHAPTER XIX

THE QUEEN OF FIBERS

Cotton is the most useful of fibers, flax the most durable, but silk is the most beautiful, and is worthy of its title, "Queen." Between seventy and eighty million pounds of this soft, lustrous fiber are used annually for making cloth, ribbon, laces, and thread. Twenty-five thousand horses, each drawing one and a half tons, would be needed to move this immense amount. Such a team, harnessed in pairs, would make a procession more than twenty miles long.

© Nonotuck Silk Co., Florence, Mass.

FIG. 149. SILK FIBER IS PRODUCED BY CATERPILLARS. THOSE SHOWN IN THIS PICTURE ARE ONLY HALF GROWN

To learn more of the origin of the silk fiber, we will visit sunny Italy again, for it is one of the principal silk-producing countries of Europe. There are many villages near Florence, that beautiful city on the Arno River, where we should find the people engaged in the silk industry. In all of them, we would see, as we did in the towns around Naples, narrow, dirty streets, dark-eyed children playing in the gutters, and chattering women around the doorways.

The little village, which we have selected for our

FIG. 150. "THE FRESH GREEN LEAVES OF THE MULBERRY TREE"

visit, is approached through orchards of mulberry trees, where dark-eyed boys and girls are chattering in their strange foreign tongue as they gather the small, tender leaves. Our guide, an intelligent Italian peasant, stops before the door of a low, rude shelter. We pause in astonishment, wondering if such a beautiful material as silk is really produced in such a place as this. As we enter the low door, we look around for the silk-making machines, but there is nothing in the building except dozens of trays filled with grayish-colored caterpillars. They are all busily engaged in eating the fresh green leaves of the mulberry tree, which the little Italian boy at our side gave them an hour or two ago. The thousands of moving jaws, which are munching the tender green leaves scattered over the trays, make a light, pattering noise, not unlike a gentle rain. It seems hard to believe that the enormous amount of silk fiber used annually for manufacturing purposes is produced by caterpillars such as these. Many millions of the small creatures are raised in China, Japan, Italy, and France.

FIG. 151. THINK OF THE THOUSANDS OF BOYS AND GIRLS WHOSE
WORK IT IS TO FEED THE SILKWORMS
From L.O. Howard, Bureau of Entomology

Though there are other countries where the industry is carried on, these four produce most of the world's supply of raw silk. Think of the thousands of boys and girls — slant-eyed Chinese, quaint little Japanese, black-haired Italians, and chattering French children — whose work it is to feed the silkworms, just as it is yours to wash the dishes, run errands, or practice your music. Think of the immense numbers of caterpillars there are in the silk-producing countries, which must be fed daily. It takes, on the average, about twenty-five hundred worms to spin a pound of fiber. To spin seventy-five million pounds, nearly one hundred ninety billion silkworms must be fed and tended. What an immense number! If distributed among the people of the United States, each man, woman, and child would receive nearly two thousand silkworms apiece.

The life of these curious caterpillars is as interesting as their work is wonderful, and an acquaintance with them is surely

© Nonotuck Silk Co., Florence, Mass.
FIG. 152. A SILKWORM CHEWS THE TENDER LEAVES OF THE
MULBERRY TREE WITH A SIDEWAYS MOTION OF ITS JAWS

© Nonotuck Silk Co., Florence, Mass.

FIG. 153. SILKWORMS LIKE STRAW OR BRUSH ON WHICH TO SPIN
THEIR COCOONS

worth cultivating. While you are watching them eat, I will tell you something of their life story.

The worm is hatched from a very tiny egg, and when it first crawls out into the sunlight, it is very small indeed—only about one-eighth of an inch long. It is almost black and is covered with dark hairs, which disappear as it grows older. It is interesting to see a young caterpillar grasp the edge of a mulberry leaf with eight of its sixteen legs, and chew the tender leaves with a sideways motion of its jaws. The young worms have to be carefully tended. The trays must be kept clean, and fresh, tender pieces of the mulberry leaves must be given to them several times a day. We must be quiet as we watch them, for they are sensitive to noise and will stop eating immediately if a loud sound is made.

The worm grows rapidly, and at the end of a month, which is the length of its life as a caterpillar, it is between three and four inches long. During these weeks, it spends most of its time eating the mulberry leaves, with which it is fed four or five times

© Nonotuck Silk Co., Florence, Mass.

FIG. 154. "BY A SIDEWAYS MOVEMENT OF ITS HEAD IT PLACES THE THREAD SO THAT IT WILL NOT PILE UP IN ONE PLACE"

a day. Four times during the month, it stops eating and takes long sleeps for nearly two days at a time. In these rest periods, it changes its skin, which has become too small for its rapidly growing body. The skin breaks at the nose, and with a peculiar, twisting motion, the worm wriggles out, tired and weak from its efforts. After resting, it begins eating again faster than ever to make up for lost time. During each molting, the worm becomes a paler shade until, when fully grown, it is a slaty or cream color.

In the last two or three days of its life, the caterpillar eats greedily and must be fed by night as well as by day. Soon after this, it stops eating, shrinks in size, and seeks some place where it may spin its cocoon. It likes straw, brush, or small branches of trees, which must be supplied at just the right time so that they may furnish supports for the silken threads that are thrown out by the busy spinner.

Thus provided, the silkworm begins spinning from its mouth a fine silk thread. By a sideways movement of its head, it places the thread so that it will not pile up in one place. When beginning the work, the worm makes about sixty movements of the head and spins about ten inches of silk in a minute. After a few

© Nonotuck Silk Co., Florence, Mass.
FIG. 155. THE MOTH LOOSENS THE SILKEN THREADS BY A LIQUID FROM ITS MOUTH, PARTS SOME OF THE FIBERS AND BREAKS OTHERS

hours, the rate is much less rapid and continues to decrease until the spinning is finished. In twenty-four hours, enough silk has been spun to hide the body entirely from sight, and in about three days, the cocoon is completed.

Inside this silken covering, the tired, shrunken worm, now little more than an inch long, slips out of its skin for the last time. Its new coat, at first yellowish in color, soon turns brown and hardens. During the next few days, a wonderful change takes place within this hard brown case. The ten front legs of the caterpillar disappear, and four small, soft wings are folded tightly against the body. Later, the brown covering breaks, and the head of a perfect moth appears. It seems wonderful that such a tiny creature should know immediately how to escape from its prison. It loses no time in setting to work, and by means of a liquid from its mouth, it loosens the silken threads which

© Nonotuck Silk Co., Florence, Mass.

FIG. 156. IT COMES OUT INTO THE SUNLIGHT, A
CREAMY, WHITE-WINGED MIRACLE

hold it captive, parts some of the fibers, and breaks others, and comes out into the sunlight a creamy, white-winged miracle.

It enjoys the warm air and the sunshine only a very short time, for it dies within two or three days after the eggs have been deposited, and with the hatching of the eggs, a new cycle of life begins for another generation.

In silk-producing regions, the mulberry tree is seldom allowed to grow more than six or seven feet high, for it is easier to pick the leaves from a low tree. It presents oftentimes a peculiar appearance, for, on account of the pruning, the trunk is very large in proportion to the top.

The Chinese call the mulberry tree the "Golden Tree," for its leaves, for thousands of years, have been a source of great income to China, which was the first country to discover the wonderful silk-making power of the caterpillar. For hundreds of years, the Chinese were very jealous of their secret of silk production. It was a crime punishable by death for anyone to carry the eggs out of the country. Finally, two monks departing for Europe concealed some in their hollow bamboo staffs, and from this beginning, the industry spread through the southern European countries.

FIG. 157. THE MULBERRY TREE OFTEN PRESENTS A PECULIAR APPEARANCE
From L. O. Howard, Bureau of Entomology

China and Japan lead all other countries in the amount of raw silk produced, making each year one-half or more of the world's

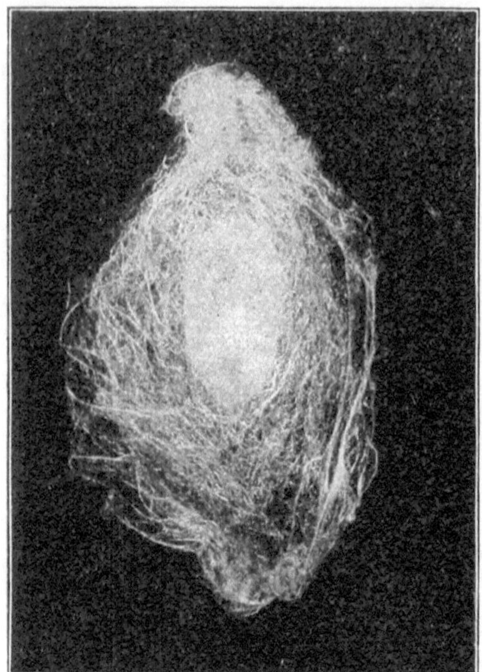

© Nonotuck Silk Co., Florence, Mass.

FIG. 158. A COMPLETE COCOON

supply. This immense production is possible not only because the climate is favorable for the growth of the mulberry tree and for the rearing of the worms, but also because hand labor is so cheap that the silk can be produced and sold at a very low price.

The climate and soil of certain parts of the United States are well adapted to the rearing of silkworms. Raw silk has been produced in small quantities for many years. But labor is more expensive here than it is in European and Asiatic countries, and manufacturers find it cheaper to buy the raw silk from abroad. We purchase from Japan about half of the forty million pounds that we use annually, while the remainder comes chiefly from China, Italy, and France.

Let us now see how the fine silk fiber of which the cocoon is made is changed into the finished cloth.

After the worms have finished spinning, the cocoons are heated in steam or hot water. This kills the moth which is inside. If allowed to live, it would in a few days make a hole in one end of the cocoon and come out into the light and air. In doing this, many threads of the delicate fiber would be broken and thus be of little value. Therefore, the moth is suffocated instead of being allowed to escape. The cocoons are then thoroughly dried before being sent to the establishments where the first process in the manufacture of silk takes place. When the caterpillar was spinning the silk for its snug hiding place, it made, at the same

FIG. 159. "AFTER KILLING THE CHRYSALIDES THE COCOONS
ARE SENT TO SOME FACTORY NOT FAR AWAY"
From L.O. Howard, Bureau of Entomology

time, a gummy substance which helped to fasten the threads
together. Before the fiber can be unwound from the cocoon,
this sticky material must be softened. This is done by putting
the cocoons into hot water. Formerly, the peasant on his own
little farm soaked his cocoons and unwound or reeled off the
silk threads by hand. By this method, the best workmen could
reel only a few ounces a day. The thread was often broken by
this clumsy work, and the fiber was not smoothly and evenly
wound for spinning. Today, after killing the chrysalides, the
cocoons are sent to some factory not far away, where the work
can be done both faster and better by power. Many women and
small children work in these reeling establishments and receive
very small pay for a long day's work.

After the soaking, the workmen brush the cocoons to find
the ends of the long fibers. Several of these ends are threaded
into a machine, which unwinds them from the cocoon and twists
them into one thread, which is wound in skeins for export. This
is known as raw silk. That which is imported into the United

States is composed usually of from six to ten strands and is much finer than the finest sewing silk.

Sometimes a fiber three-fourths of a mile long is unwound from one cocoon, though the usual length is much less. As we have said, it takes, on the average, between two and three thousand silkworms to make one pound of raw silk. This quantity, if woven into material of a medium grade, will make about ten yards of cloth. In these days, this amount is amply sufficient for an ordinary dress.

The skeins of raw silk are packed into bundles called "books," which weigh from five to ten pounds apiece. These are made up into large bales, tied up in cloth and then in stout bagging, and shipped to the manufacturers.

© Nonotuck Silk Co., Florence, Mass.

FIG. 160. THE SKEINS OF RAW SILK ARE PACKED INTO BUNDLES CALLED BOOKS. THESE ARE MADE UP INTO LARGE BALES

Let us accompany the bales of silk from Florence, Italy, to Lyon, France, for the value of silk manufactures in France is greater than in any other country. The voyage on the blue Mediterranean is very enjoyable, and were it not for the interesting sights that we know are awaiting us in France, we should be sorry to have it end.

The harbor of Marseille is wonderfully interesting and is filled with vessels of many nations. They are loaded with tea from China, corn and cattle and wine from Algeria, cotton from Egypt, grain from Russia and the United States, and silk from Italy, China, and Japan. Vessels bound for different ports are being loaded at the wharves with boxes of soap, dried fruit and oranges, and hundreds of bottles and casks of olive oil and wine.

More soap is made in Marseille than in all the rest of France, enough, we should think, to keep the whole world clean. In former days, it was said that the people of Marseille were interested in nothing but soap and oil and cared little for the appearance or healthfulness of the city. Today, however, it has beautiful streets, wide avenues, and fine buildings. Its situation is so favorable for trade with the Mediterranean countries and with the East that it has grown very rapidly, until at present it is considerably larger than San Francisco and is the leading port of France.

There are many mills and factories everywhere. We wish that we had time to inspect the large sugar refineries, where the raw beet sugar, which is made in such quantities in France, is changed into the fine white article as it appears on the table. We should like to know just what kinds of machinery are made in the noisy iron and steel works, and to peep inside the great olive-oil mills of which you read in Chapter XVI. But the bales of silk are our chief interest, and as they are already reloaded onto another vessel, we will continue our journey with them up the Rhone River.

The trip is very interesting. We find orchards of mulberry trees stretching as far as the eye can see. These trees are so numerous in this part of France that thousands of women and children are required to pick the leaves and to care for the silkworms which feed upon them. Such immense quantities of

FIG. 161. "LET US VISIT ONE OF THE GREAT FACTORIES"
Courtesy of Cheney Brothers, South Manchester, Connecticut

fiber are needed in the great silk manufactories of France that even the millions of silkworms raised in her warm valleys cannot supply the demand, and she imports many times as much as she produces.

After a trip of about one hundred fifty miles from the mouth of the Rhone, we come to the city of Lyon, at the junction of the Rhone and Saône rivers. Lyon is an important manufacturing center and makes more silk goods, including cloth, velvet, and ribbons, than any other city in the world. Seventy-five thousand people are employed in this one industry in the city itself and in the neighboring villages.

If we were making our trip by land, we should know when many miles distant from the city that we were approaching Lyon. In village after village, we should find the people engaged in some branch of manufacture connected with great Lyonese firms. In one, we might find them working at forges and foundries, in another on dainty laces, and in a third making glassware.

© Nonotuck Silk Co., Florence, Mass.

FIG. 162. THE UNWINDING OF THE SILK FROM THE COCOON IS CALLED REELING

In the vicinity of Lyon, however, more people are engaged in making some form of silk goods than in any other branch of manufacture.

Let us visit one of the great factories and see how the fine fibers of raw silk are spun into strong thread and woven into cloth.

The unwinding of the silk from the cocoon, called reeling, is usually done in the countries where the silk is produced. The great bales of raw silk as they arrive at the manufactory are first sorted according to quality. The fiber is then soaked for several hours in warm soap-suds, and after being dried, is ready for the real manufacturing processes. These are many and complicated, as you would think if you visited a silk mill, and we shall not attempt to describe them all. One of the first processes is "throwing." The word "throw" comes from an old Saxon word which means "to twist," and the throwing of silk fiber consists of a series of operations in which the thread is first wound and cleaned, then doubled to give the desired size, and twisted to give strength. The skeins are then sent to the dyer, after which the silk is ready for the weaving.

In the early days of this industry, only plain goods were made. When the making of figured patterns was first introduced, it was slow, expensive work. Two or more men were necessary to run one loom, and in order to make the pattern, there was much changing and readjusting and fixing of the machine. All this took a great deal of time and required much skill on the part of the workmen.

Near the beginning of the nineteenth century, a Frenchman, Joseph Jacquard by name, invented a machine which made the manufacturing of figured goods as easy as that of plain colors. You know how weaving is done. The long or warp threads are lifted and lowered so that the crosswise threads go in and out, in and out, over and under, over and under, thus making the firm cloth.

In the Jacquard loom, by means of an ingenious harness of wires, the warp threads of a certain color are lifted, and the right shuttle, controlled also by the wires, flies back and forth at just the proper time, more accurately and truly than if guided by the human hand. Almost miraculously, inch by inch, the pattern of plaids or checks or flowers grows. This invention revolutionized the weaving industry, for figured goods — whether silk, cotton, or woolen — could be made with the Jacquard loom as easily and as cheaply as plain goods.

The city of Lyon has been called an immense factory, and the tall chimneys, the large mills with the hum and jar of the rapidly moving machinery, the loaded boats and cars, make us realize what an important manufacturing city it is. Not only silk goods, but hats, leather boots and shoes, jewelry, articles of iron and steel, dyes, and a variety of other goods are made there in great quantities.

Why has Lyon grown to such a position in manufacturing and commerce? Study your map closely, and you will find some of the reasons. It is situated at the junction of two navigable rivers, the Rhone leading south to Marseille, and the Saône stretching northward and connecting with northern ports. The city is

FIG. 163. "THE LONG OR WARP THREADS ARE LIFTED AND
LOWERED SO THAT THE CROSSWISE THREADS GO IN AND OUT,
IN AND OUT, OVER AND UNDER, OVER AND UNDER"

a great center from which radiate railroads to Paris, Bordeaux, and Marseille, and to Switzerland and Italy. It is connected with northern waters through the canal which joins the Rhone and Rhine rivers, while other canals branching off from both the Saône and the Rhone connect it with the great interior centers.

Because of these means of communication, the freight houses

and docks are piled high with goods brought from many places — cotton from the United States, raw silk from Italy and the East, flax from Russia, and wool from Argentina and Australia — while barges bring from nearby mines the coal necessary for manufacturing these and many other products.

On the great highways of trade, boats and cars, loaded with silk, woolen, and linen goods, ribbons, flour, and machinery, depart from Lyon, carrying its manufactures to all parts of France and to other countries.

Thirty-two miles southwest of Lyon is St. Étienne. Girls, even more than boys, would enjoy a visit to that city, for more ribbons are made there — ribbons of all widths and kinds, silk, satin, velvet, brocaded — than in any other place in the world. Think of it! More people than there are in Duluth, Minnesota, or Hartford, Connecticut, or Savannah, Georgia, are engaged in St. Étienne and its suburbs in this one industry.

The city is situated near some of the richest coal fields of France, and the mines give employment to thousands of men. It is partly on account of its location near these coal deposits that St. Étienne has become extensively engaged in manufacturing. Many other articles besides ribbons are made in this busy city. One third of the steel product of France is manufactured in St. Étienne. The national gun factory, employing six thousand men, makes the weapons for the French army; the tents of the soldiers are fastened down, and the sails of many ships are raised by means of the rope made in the same city.

Paris is noted more for its art, beauty, and fashion than for its manufactures; yet the beautiful silks which are woven in other parts of France have helped the city to reach its present position as a leader of fashion. In the shopping district of Paris, one sees displayed in the stores the products of factories in St. Étienne, Lyon, and other cities. These beautiful fabrics are sent to Paris from all over France to be sold or to be made into dresses. Great quantities of silks, ribbons, and garments are sent to England and to the United States, for these two countries are the best customers of France for such goods.

Paris is one of the largest and most beautiful cities of Europe,

FIG. 164. THE ARCH OF TRIUMPH FORMS A CENTER FROM
WHICH TWELVE FINE BOULEVARDS RADIATE

and perhaps the gayest of any. Its streets are wide and brilliantly lit, and its open-air cafés, which are a part of most restaurants and many hotels, are thronged during the warm weather till late into the night with beautifully dressed people. The Arch of Triumph, or, as the French people call it, the Arc de Triomphe, the largest triumphal arch in the world, is one of the conspicuous sights of the city. It was begun by Napoleon to commemorate his victories and completed some years later by another French ruler. It forms a center from which twelve fine boulevards radiate like the spokes from the hub of a wheel. Of these, the Champs-Élysées on one side, bordered with parks and gardens and filled with carriages, motor cars, and pedestrians, is the most famous; while on the other side of the arch, nearly opposite, is the magnificent avenue called by the name of the beautiful park of more than two thousand acres in which it is situated — the Bois de Boulogne. This splendid boulevard is more than four hundred feet wide, is deeply shaded by several rows of trees, and during fashionable hours is so thronged with carriages, horseback riders, and motor cars that one can proceed only at a slow pace. There are many places in Paris which you would surely visit if you were in the city. One is the ancient cathedral, Notre-Dame. Another is the Louvre, one of the finest art galleries in the world, where priceless paintings and famous sculptures attract thousands of visitors.

There are many other European cities, however, which are more directly connected with the silk industry than is Paris, and which, therefore, we should like to visit. One of these is Milan, Italy. Most people go there to see the wonderful white marble cathedral with its marvelous carvings and its thousands of statues. Few Americans realize, as they visit the city, that it is one of the most important in Italy and has grown more rapidly than any other in the country in manufactures and commerce. This is due very largely to the silk industry, for many thousand people there find employment in spinning, throwing, and weaving silk.

People in the United States generally know little about Genoa, except that it was the birthplace of Columbus. With this far-off historical fact in mind, we are little prepared, when visiting the city, to find it as the busiest port in Italy, making and shipping not only silk goods, but also large quantities of macaroni, paper, soap, oil, and jewelry. The Genoese silks and velvets are considered very fine indeed, ranking in quality next to those manufactured in Lyon.

As Switzerland is so near Italy, where raw silk is easily obtained, the industrious Swiss have made the most of their advantages. Basel and Zurich are well-known for their silk manufactures. Basel is located on the elbow of the Rhine River, just where it leaves Switzerland and turns to the north. When the train reaches this city, you must be prepared to open your bags if the polite, well-uniformed officials demand it. This is a frontier city, on the boundary between Switzerland and Germany, and officers are on the lookout to see if any goods, on which a duty should be paid, are being smuggled into the country. In a trip through Europe, this inspection takes place whenever we pass from one country to another.

You must not think, because you have never heard of these cities before, that they are small places. Zurich and Basel are each larger than Albany, New York. Genoa, which you may have thought of as a small place, interesting chiefly for its historical connections, is the size of Minneapolis, Minnesota, while Milan, largest of all, contains more people than San Francisco.

Though the United States does not produce raw silk, we lead the world in the quantity of our silk manufactures. New Jersey, Pennsylvania, Connecticut, and New York are the most important silk-manufacturing states, and to supply the mills and factories in these and other places, we import annually many million dollars' worth of raw silk.

New England leads in the manufacture of sewing silk and twist. Look at the spools of silk in your mother's work basket and find the names of some of the important firms, and if possible, learn where the factories are located. The amount of sewing silk that is made is enormous. Twenty-five thousand miles of spool silk, enough to stretch completely around the world, are required daily to feed the sewing machines of the United States.

It is wonderful, is it not, that this valuable product is given to the world by a creature so small and so unimpressive as a caterpillar? When you use a needleful of silk, or tie the ribbon in your hair, or notice the fine display of silk in the windows of your city stores, you will think of the millions of worms in far-away countries whose patient toil gives us the delicate fiber. When you consider how very little each one of them can do and yet how valuable the total product is, you will appreciate, as never before, the value of little things.

TOPICS FOR STUDY

I.

1. The quantity of silk fiber used in manufacturing.
2. Raising silkworms in Italy.
3. Life of a silkworm.
4. Raising silkworms in China.
5. Production of silk in the United States.
6. The silk industry in France.
7. Reeling silk.
8. Silk throwing.
9. Silk weaving.
10. The Jacquard loom.
11. Description of Marseille.
12. Description of Lyon.
13. Description of St. Étienne.
14. Description of Paris.
15. Silk manufacturing in Italy.
16. Silk manufacturing in Switzerland.
17. Silk manufacturing in the United States.

II.

1. Ship a cargo of raw silk from China to France; from Japan to the United States. Send a cargo of silk goods from Switzerland to the United States; a grain ship from Russia to France. Tell in each instance the waters sailed on, the shipping and receiving ports, and the return cargo.
2. Imagine yourself as an Italian boy or girl and tell of your work among the silkworms which your father owns.
3. Sketch the group of the principal silk-manufacturing states in the United States.
4. Write a list of all the things that you can think of which are made of silk.
5. What country produces the most raw silk? What country manufactures the most silk goods? What country produces the most valuable silk manufactures?

6. On an outline map of Europe, color the silk-producing countries and show all the places mentioned in the chapter.
7. Contrast the valley of the Rhone River with the province of Brittany, of which you read in Chapter XV.

III.

Be able to spell and pronounce the following names. Locate each place and tell what was said of it in this and in any previous chapter. Add other facts if possible.

Algeria	China	England
Argentina	Connecticut	France
Australia	Egypt	Italy
Japan	Basel	Paris
New England	Bordeaux	St. Étienne
New Jersey	Duluth	San Francisco
New York	Florence	Savannah
Pennsylvania	Genoa	Zurich
Russia	Hartford	
Switzerland	Lyon	Amo River
Turkey	Marseille	Mediterranean Sea
United States	Milan	Rhine River
	Minneapolis	Rhone River
Albany	Naples	Saône River

CHAPTER XX

THE COUNTRIES OF THE BALKAN PENINSULA

TURKEY

Centuries ago, a horde of barbarians migrated westward from Central Asia. They overran western Asia, conquered it, and gradually made their way nearer and nearer to Europe. These people were the Turks. They were not a Christian people, but were followers of Mohammed, a teacher who lived about six hundred years after the time of Christ.

Before the coming of the Turks into Europe, the merchants of that continent had built up a great trade with Central Asia. This was before the discovery of America and the days of ocean travel. Their commerce was carried on over the Mediterranean Sea and by caravan routes into the trading centers of Central Asia. Here, the European merchants were met by traders from the little-known regions of eastern Asia — China, Japan, and India. Goods of great value were exchanged, after which the European merchants turned their caravans westward, bearing spices, perfumes, silks, and other luxuries for the rich nobles of Europe. The coming of the Turks stopped all this great trade, for the Mohammedans hated and persecuted all Christians. They captured and sunk their merchant vessels on the Mediterranean, and closed up their trade routes through western Asia. At the time, this seemed a great calamity, but in the end, much good came from it. It stimulated the people of Europe to find new routes to the rich lands of the East so that their trade might continue. It was this desire that started Christopher Columbus on his voyage of discovery. Believing that the earth was round, he attempted to reach India and China by sailing west. His theory was right, but the earth was much larger than he thought, and the lands of the Western Hemisphere lay in his way. Five years after Columbus set sail to the west, Vasco da Gama, with a similar object in mind, sailed around Africa and thence across the Indian Ocean toward the rich lands of the East.

Among other places in western Asia which fell into the hands of the Turks was the Holy Land, where Jesus lived and died, and the city of Jerusalem, which contained his tomb. To the Christian peoples of Europe, it seemed a terrible thing that the tomb of Christ should be in the hands of heathen who believed neither in him nor his teachings. Large armies were formed to march to the Holy Land and rescue the tomb of Christ from the hands of the Mohammedans. All the soldiers wore the cross for a badge and were known as the crusaders. One of these armies was made up entirely of boys—fifty thousand or more of them. This was known as the Children's Crusade. A few of the boys finally returned to their homes, many stopped by the way, but the large majority of them either died of their sufferings on the march, were lost at sea, or were sold into slavery.

The Crusades extended through two centuries, but they were all unsuccessful in their objective. The Turks grew stronger and spread farther and farther westward. In 1453, they captured Constantinople. Gradually, they extended their power, until, in the seventeenth century, their vast empire, distributed nearly equally in three continents, included the basins of the Danube, the Nile, and the Tigris and Euphrates rivers. In Europe, the entire Balkan Peninsula, between the Black and Adriatic seas, as well as the territory north of the Black Sea, lay under their control.

The Turks have always been a menace and a curse to the peoples over whom they have ruled. Their cruelties to the Christians whose lands they have occupied have been unspeakable, and little or no progress has ever been made by any country which formed a part of their empire.

Gradually, their power has waned, and their domain has

slipped away from them. One after another, the countries of the Balkan Peninsula — Greece, Bulgaria, Romania, Serbia, and Montenegro — have revolted from Turkish rule and started life anew as independent nations. Before the World War, all that remained in Europe of this once powerful kingdom was a small area north of the Sea of Marmara, not much larger than Vermont or New Hampshire.

Though the area of Turkey in Europe was so small, the country was important because it controlled the water route between the Black and Mediterranean seas, and the land route between Europe and Asia. The great city of Constantinople lies at the point where these important commercial routes cross each other. The Turks still hold the small area in Europe which was theirs before the World War, but they have agreed to allow the ships of all nations to pass freely between the Black and Mediterranean seas.

Only three cities in the United States are larger than Constantinople. As we approach it from the water, the gilded domes, the many turrets, and the slender minarets flash in the sunlight above the clustering housetops and green foliage. The sight is impressive, and this distant view of the city from the blue waters of the harbor is extremely beautiful. As we enter the city, however, we learn the truth of the old proverb that "all is not gold that glitters." The streets are narrow, crooked, dirty, and deep with mud or

© Keystone View Co.

FIG. 165. "LET US GO FOR A SIGHTSEEING TOUR OF THE CITY"

dust. There is no system of sewerage, and the filth in the gutters is disgusting.

Let us go for a sightseeing tour of the city. The thoroughfares are narrow and seem full of people. In them, we jostle mysterious veiled women who are accompanied by their slaves. We see tall priests in long gowns with wonderful turbans of blue, red, or green wound about their heads. Water peddlers with huge jars make loud, discordant cries to advertise their lukewarm beverage, porters carry on their shoulders huge boxes and trunks, and soldiers in gorgeous uniforms ride beautiful Arabian horses.

We stop at a bazaar, as the Turkish shops are called, to look at the long, slender bottles of perfume displayed there. A sleepy-eyed Turk, looking for all the world as if customers were a nuisance instead of a blessing, sits cross-legged on a strip of matting in a booth so small that there is no room for a customer to enter. There are no fixed prices in Turkish shops, and no shopkeeper expects to get what he asks for his goods. The word "bazaar" means "a bargaining place," and its meaning is lived up to by both dealer and customer.

FIG. 166. A STREET IN CONSTANTINOPLE

Mark Twain has described one of these great bazaars as follows:

The place is crowded with people all the time, and as the gay-colored Eastern fabrics are lavishly displayed before every shop, the Great Bazaar of Stambul is one of the sights worth seeing. It is full of life and stir and business, dirt, beggars, donkeys, yelling peddlers, porters, dervishes, high-born Turkish female shoppers, Greeks, and weird-looking and weirdly dressed Mohammedans from the mountains and the far provinces — and the only solitary thing one does not smell when he is in the Great Bazaar is something which smells good.

The shops were mere hencoops, mere boxes, bath-rooms, closets — anything you please to call them — on the first floor. The Turks sit cross-legged in them and work, and smoke long pipes, and smell like — like Turks. That covers the ground. Crowding the narrow streets in front of them are beggars, who beg forever, yet never collect anything; wonderful cripples distorted out of all semblance to humanity, almost; vagabonds driving laden asses; porters carrying on their backs dry-goods boxes as large as cottages; peddlers of grapes, hot corn, pumpkin seeds, and a hundred other things, yelling like fiends; and sleeping happily, comfortably, serenely, among the hurrying feet are the famed dogs of Constantinople.

In the World War, Turkey lost much of her Asiatic empire. In 1918, an English army succeeded in doing what Europeans in the Middle Ages vainly tried for two centuries to accomplish — they took Jerusalem and the Holy Land from their Moham-medan rulers. During the same war, the tribes of that part of western Arabia known as Hejaz declared their independence from Turkish rule and set up as an independent nation. At the end of the war, Palestine was set apart as a national home for the Jews, and Syria was put under the control of the French. More recently, the Arabs in Mesopotamia have set up the inde-pendent kingdom of Iraq. To Turkey is left only the peninsula of Anatolia, between the Black and Mediterranean seas, a mere remnant of the territory that they once possessed.

GREECE

The southernmost part of the Balkan Peninsula is occupied by Greece, a country larger than the state of Tennessee. On all sides, save the north, it is surrounded by water. Notice the coastline of Greece and the distance to which the long, deep bays penetrate into the mainland. Can you find any other country with a coast so irregular? So deeply is it cut by the long arms of the Mediterranean Sea that no other country of equal area has so long a coastline.

Greece is very mountainous and has many ranges which divide it into little plains and valleys. Thus, the surface separated the people of one part of the country from those of another part and helped to develop a spirit of independence. It also favored the growth of rival states whose jealousy of one another weakened the nation as a whole.

Greece is always thought of as the home of the beautiful. Her ancient buildings and her statues carved centuries ago come nearer perfection than those of any other land. She is famous not only for her art but for her history and philosophy. With the exception of Palestine, where Jesus lived and died, there is no country which, in proportion to its size and population, has had so great an influence on other nations of the world.

"The Glory that was Greece has passed away. The Beauty that is Greece remains." The land itself is one of the most beautiful on earth, beautiful in its skies and seas, in its blue mountains and green valleys, in its deep bays and long headlands.

Her people are, for the most part, happy, contented farmers and fisherfolk. In her southern peninsulas, we should find many little farms where figs, oranges, lemons, melons, and other fruit and vegetables are raised. There are many olive orchards also, with their gnarled, twisted trees, some of them centuries old. The fruit is one of the most important products of Greece, and the making of olive oil is one of the important occupations. Mulberry trees grow here also. If you lived in southern Greece, it might be a part of your work each day to gather mulberry leaves and feed the silkworms, for many are raised in some of the villages.

© Underwood & Underwood

FIG. 167. FARMING IN THE SIGHT OF WONDERFUL RUINS

Wandering through the country, we might hear the far-off notes of a shepherd's flute and, following the sound, find on some green, sheltered slope the player making sweet music while he tended his sheep and goats.

In the northern part of Greece, we find more fields of grain. If our visit were in the springtime, we might see the farmers plowing their fields with queer, old-fashioned wooden plows drawn by oxen with widespreading horns. In the autumn, the grain is reaped and brought to the threshing floor, which is found in every village. These hard stone floors are very old, and the grain from the fields around has been threshed on them for centuries. The grain is spread out, and the patient oxen walk slowly back and forth, back and forth, treading out the seeds from the straw.

There are many interesting things to see in a Greek village. We like to linger near the fountain and watch the women who gather there. The scene reminds us of tales which we have read about ancient Greece, for the fountain and the water jars which the women carry might be the very ones described in the story.

We have spoken of the deep bays and the many peninsulas of southern Greece. This entire part of the country was once a peninsula. Look on your map and see how near the Gulf of Corinth on the west comes to the Gulf of Aegina on the east. Southern Greece was formerly tied to the mainland by the narrow strip of land between these indentations. Today, this part of the country is an island instead of a peninsula. A waterway called the Corinthian Canal has been cut through between the two gulfs. Centuries ago, when Greece was under the control of the Roman Empire, the emperor Nero began a canal at this place. It was never completed, however, until the Corinthian Canal was made in 1893.

Find on your map the city of Corinth at the western end of the canal. The ruins of the ancient city of this name lie about four miles away. Here lived the Corinthians to whom St. Paul wrote centuries ago. You can read his very letters, his "Epistles to the Corinthians," in the New Testament.

Corinth reminds us of currants, for the word "currant" comes from *Corinth*. The vines which bear the little black grapes that your mother uses for cakes and puddings grow in this part of Greece and were formerly shipped from the city of Corinth. Hence their name. More of them are shipped today from Patras, the largest city of southern Greece, near the mouth of the gulf. Dried currants are the chief export of Greece, and thousands of the Greek people depend for a living on the vineyards that produce them. Millions of pounds are exported from Greece every year, many of them to the United States.

The world-famous city of Athens, named for the goddess Athena, lies near the end of one of the long peninsulas of southern Greece. The blue sky, the pure air, the temperate climate, the fertile soil on the plains around, the harbors, and the easy communication both by land and water, all favored the growth of the city. In ancient times, Athens was the very heart of Greece and the center of learning of the known world. If a city today is noted for the learning and culture of its people or for its educational institutions, it is often called the Athens of the country in which it is situated. One cannot see Athens and look upon its wonderful ruins without thinking of its glorious past. A visit here makes one eager to know more of Greek history, to become acquainted with her famous men such as Lycurgus, the great lawgiver; Pericles, the statesman; Alexander the Great, the famous general; Phidias, the great sculptor; and many others.

Thermopylae is one of the places made famous by Greek history. The Persians, at different times, attempted to conquer Greece and make it a part of their own great empire. You have all heard of the battle at Thermopylae, where in a narrow pass, three hundred Spartans held back the whole Persian army. Thousands of the enemy were slain, and the brave Spartans might have been victorious in keeping them back, had not a traitor shown the Persians a narrow footpath which led over the heights to the other end of the pass in which the Greeks were fighting. Even then, brave Leonidas and his little band of three hundred refused to give up, and fought on until all were killed.

Another famous battle was fought against the Persians on the plains of Marathon, twenty-five miles from Athens. When reading about these events, remember that they took place centuries ago, several hundred years, even, before the birth of Christ.

Speaking of Marathon reminds one of the Marathon races. Perhaps you will be more interested in these and in the other games held in Greece than in anything else connected with the country.

The ancient Greeks were lovers of beauty and did everything in their power to make not only their buildings and statues beautiful but also to develop the human body and make it strong and beautiful. Therefore, they were very athletic and fond of all kinds of sports. Every four years they held what were called the Olympic Games, and men came from all over the country to take part in them. People journeyed even from other lands to see them. The victors were crowned with laurel wreaths and were more famous for a time than the emperor himself. Finally, in the fourth century, one emperor, thinking that these games

© Underwood & Underwood

FIG. 168. THE MODERN STADIUM IN ATHENS IS A WONDERFUL
STRUCTURE

were a relic of the time when Greece was a pagan rather than a Christian nation, put an end to them, and for about fifteen hundred years, no Olympic games were held.

In 1896, a wealthy man offered to rebuild the stadium if the games would be restored. This modern stadium in Athens is a wonderful structure, seating sixty thousand people. The athletes today are not all Greeks but come from many different countries. There are contests in jumping, running, discus-throwing, shot-putting, shooting, swimming, and wrestling. In most of these events, American athletes have been represented, and in many cases, they have carried off the prizes.

Marathon is twenty-five miles from Athens. One of the most eagerly contested events is the foot race between the two places. The winner of the Marathon race is considered a greater hero than all the other victors. He is crowned, carried in processions, and given many gifts and privileges. I wonder if any boy now in school who reads these pages will ever be the winner of the Marathon race.

BULGARIA

One of the lost provinces of Turkey is Bulgaria, a country about as large as Pennsylvania. It is a beautiful region of blue mountains, broad, fertile valleys, little rivers, rich pastures, abundant water power, and deep forests.

Its people are hardworking, capable farmers, who have done much to improve their condition and to educate themselves after the centuries of misrule and oppression which they suffered under the Turk. There are few rich people in the country, and had it not been for the wars which for many years took the men from the industries and caused much suffering, there would be few very poor people. The needs of the Bulgarian peasant are simple ones, and most of them can be supplied from their little farms. Agriculture is the most important occupation. Three-fourths of the people are farmers and till their own land. Much of their work is carried on by very different methods from those which are practiced on farms in the United States.

The plows are made all of wood and are very different from those used by the farmers in our country, the iron points of which dig deeply into the soil and give it a thorough overturning. This clumsy, one-handled, wooden implement which the peasant uses today is the same as his ancestors have always used. The buffalo and ox, or in northeastern Bulgaria, the camel, plod slowly back and forth across the dusty field dragging the plow in its shallow furrow, as buffalo and ox and camel have done in these Eastern lands for many centuries. Some modern farm machinery has been introduced into Bulgaria by the cooperative societies to which many of the farmers belong. These implements are rented to individuals who could not afford to buy such expensive tools for themselves.

As in most countries in Europe, the Bulgarian farmers live in villages and often go several miles to their work in the fields.

The little houses of the village are small and have few comforts according to our way of thinking. The women at work in the fields, the lack of modern tools, and the coarse food, all indicate a backward condition of life. It is much better, however, than it was under Turkish rule. Much progress has been made, and, given a few years of peace, when the men can work on their farms and in the factories of the cities instead of spending their time in fighting, killing, and being killed, we shall see a great difference in conditions in Bulgaria.

Already her farm crops are important. As in Hungary and Yugoslavia, the Bulgarian plains of the Danube valley are famous for their wheat and corn. Barley, oats, and rye are also raised. Rape is raised for its seed and hemp for its fiber, which is made into rope in the large rope factories near Sofia. In a trip through the country, we can see also fields of sugar beets and tobacco, its big leaves completely hiding the ground from sight. In the shade of the oak forests and in the sunny open pastures, the boys and girls tend the flocks of sheep and goats, the pigs, and the cattle. Around the little cottages, we see poultry feeding and bees buzzing about the hives. In parts of the country, there are many mulberry trees, and here we might see trays filled with silkworms feeding on the tender mulberry leaves.

We notice that many of the women and some of the men wear clothes on which there is beautiful embroidery. Wonderful needlework is done by some of the Bulgarian peasant women. So fine and even are the stitches that often it is impossible to tell the right side from the wrong.

There are few manufactures in Bulgaria. Some textile and leather factories, some woodworking and furniture establishments, a little silk weaving, and a few other industries are about all that we should find that are of much importance. Bulgaria doubtless will always be an agricultural country, but with the development of water power and the centralizing of industries in towns and cities, manufacturing will in the future grow in importance.

We are so young among the nations of the world that it is hard for us to understand and appreciate the age of many European cities. Sofia, the handsome capital of Bulgaria, is centuries old. It was used by the Romans when they controlled so much of Europe. It was a prosperous town in the ninth century when it was captured by the Bulgars. A hundred years before Christopher Columbus sailed from Spain across the Atlantic, Sofia was captured by the Turks. Save for a short time, the city and the country remained in their hands for more than four centuries, until 1878, when Bulgaria gained its independence.

Sofia is beautifully situated on a rolling plain nearly two thousand feet high, within sight of lofty mountain ranges. In the old days, when the Turks ruled the land, the city was but a poor place with narrow, crooked, unpaved, undrained streets and mean little houses of wood and plaster. Its streets were unsafe, and no Christian woman dared venture out of doors after dark.

Since Bulgaria has been released from Turkish oppression, the capital has been much improved. Parts of the old Turkish town have been torn down, narrow alleys have been widened

FIG. 169. THERE ARE SUCH QUANTITIES TO BE PICKED
THAT THE WORK GROWS TIRESOME
Courtesy of Antoine Chiris Company, Grasse, France

into streets, and the little hovels have been replaced by modern buildings. A new cathedral, costing one and a quarter million dollars, is the largest and finest structure in the city. You would be interested in visiting this cathedral, so different in its appearance and decorations from the churches in our country. You would be interested also in visiting the public bath, which is said to be the finest building of its kind in the world. It is built over a hot spring, the temperature of which is one hundred seventeen degrees, and which has been famous for its healing virtues ever since the days of the Romans.

There is one occupation carried on in Bulgaria very different from all others, and one which you could find in very few other countries of the world. This is the cultivation of roses to be used in that delicious perfume, attar of roses. To see something of this industry, let us go to the southeastern part of the country. There are no railroads to take us there. The roads are so deep with dust in summer or with mud in winter that few loads can

FIG. 170. NEARLY ALL THE FLOWER PERFUME IN THE
WORLD IS MADE IN SOUTHERN FRANCE
Courtesy of Bruno Court, parfumeur, Grasse, France

be hauled over them. A heavy, lumbering ox-cart is the only team used for the little traffic that is carried on between the scattered villages. In many cases, horses or mules carry the loads as well as the drivers on their backs.

We pass orchards of mulberry trees and fields of wheat and corn until at last we find ourselves in the midst of the rose bushes. There are thousands of acres of them, and they stretch in every direction as far as we can see. Such a sight we have never seen before. Some of the bushes are twelve or fifteen feet high, and all, large and small, are covered with fragrant red roses, the delicate odor from which fills the air for miles around. Everybody in the villages near, young and old, works in the rose gardens, for they furnish the chief occupation in that region. The men find employment in planting and caring for the bushes, and the women and children in gathering the petals.

FIG. 171. THE FRAGRANCE MAKES THE AIR SWEETER
THAN ANYWHERE ELSE IN THE WORLD
Courtesy of Antoine Chiris Company, Grasse, France

It takes two hundred pounds of roses to make one ounce of pure oil, and although one's fingers fly very fast indeed, it takes a long time to gather roses enough to weigh two hundred pounds. As the annual product of attar of roses in Bulgaria is several thousand pounds, you can imagine how many blossoms must be picked each year.

Pure attar of roses, as you may suppose from the immense quantity of blossoms required to make it, is very expensive and is worth several dollars an ounce. It is, however, seldom found pure. All of that which is imported into the United States is more or less adulterated with other oils. The odor is very lasting even when diluted, and when pure, it will last for years.

Bulgaria is not the only place where the rose is cultivated for the oil it will yield. You will find vast gardens in India, where the very finest quality of attar of roses is said to be produced. The rose gardens in the Balkan Peninsula are the largest in the world, but certain towns in southern France produce more

FIG. 172. WE CAN SEE THE PEASANT WOMEN GATHERING DEWY VIOLETS
Courtesy of Bruno Court, parfumeur, Grasse, France

perfumes from a greater variety of flowers than are manufactured anywhere else. Let us leave the mud hovels, the poor roads, and the industrious peasants, and go to the Riviera, a very fashionable resort on the French coast.

Perhaps no two places could be chosen which show a greater contrast than the region we have visited in southern Bulgaria and the gay, beautiful watering-place on the shores of the blue Mediterranean. Wealth and rank can be seen in greater display on the Riviera than anywhere else in the continent of Europe or perhaps anywhere in the world. There are the finest hotels, the most expensive costumes, the smoothest roads, the richest shops, and the most beautiful gardens that one can imagine.

Around Grasse, "the sweetest town in the world," there are terraced gardens of narcissi, jonquils, roses, violets, heliotrope, sweet peas, hyacinths, carnations, tuberoses, and orchards of bitter-orange trees. The beauty of the gardens is indescribable, and the fragrance fills the air all around.

Out in the gardens, if we are fortunate enough to be there in the early morning, we can see beneath the cool shade of the trees the peasant women gathering dewy violets, and the

FIG. 173. "THE DONKEYS LADEN ON EITHER SIDE WITH HUGE
BASKETS FILLED WITH THE FRAGRANT HARVEST"
Courtesy of Mr. Adolph Spiehler, manufacturing perfumer, New York

children in the sunny, terraced gardens picking tuberoses, while in the orange orchards the workers are robbing the trees of their fragrant blossoms. The odor of these flowers is so strong that it makes us faint, and we are told that it sometimes affects even the regular pickers.

Up the steep hill come the wagons piled high with their loads of sweetness, and the donkeys laden on either side with huge baskets filled with the fragrant harvest. We will follow the blossoms into the workrooms of one of the factories, where other members of the peasant families find occupation. In one room, there are rows of women sitting on either side of long tables, whose glass tops are smeared all over with a layer of pure, white fat. Great baskets of freshly picked flowers stand beside each worker, who sticks them one by one, face downward, into the fat, which absorbs the odor and retains the real freshness of the fragrance much better than if it were extracted in any other way.

After a few hours, the flowers are removed — poor, limp, unattractive things, minus their beauty and fragrance. The fat is then worked over with a knife so that a fresh surface may be presented, and a new lot of the same kind of flower is stuck

FIG. 174. "GREAT BASKETS OF FRESHLY PICKED
FLOWERS STAND BESIDE EACH WORKER"
Courtesy of Bruno Court, parfumeur, Grasse, France

upon it. The process is continued until the fat is so full of oil from the flowers that it can hold no more.

If the fragrant fat is to be made into pomade, it is chopped very fine and then beaten in huge churns until it becomes as white and soft as newly fallen snow.

Sometimes, the fat, when saturated with the flower oil, is dissolved in alcohol, after which it is ready for use again. The perfumed oil of the blossoms rises to the top of the alcohol in yellowish-green globules. This is the essential oil, the pure extract, which is diluted or mixed with other oils, according to the quality or strength desired. These pomades and oils are the basis of all perfumes and toilet waters made from flowers, and impart the scent to many of the finer soaps.

More perfumes are made in Paris than anywhere else, though other European cities carry on an important business in these products, and millions of dollars' worth are sent from these centers all over the world.

RUMANIA

Another of the lost provinces of Turkey is Rumania. It is the largest, the most northerly, and the most easterly of the Balkan countries, and has a greater population than any other.

Rumania is one of the richest parts of southeastern Europe. By looking at the map, you can see that the whole country lies in the valley of the Danube and that, while the western part is mountainous, in the eastern and southern parts are the rich rolling plains of the river. Rumania is, in fact, a continuation of the great Russian plain, the "black-earth" region of which you have read in another chapter. In Rumania, as in Russia, enormous crops of wheat, corn, barley, and oats have been grown on these fertile plains. Some of the grain produced in Rumania is ground in the river mills along the Danube, but more is sent up the river to Budapest, which manufactures almost as much flour as our own city of Minneapolis. Other grain raised in the country is shipped down the Danube River or is exported from Constanza and other ports on the Black Sea. The great grain country of the "black-earth" region, with Odessa as its port, lies to the

FIG. 175. A RUMANIAN PEASANT WIFE

east of Rumania, and more wheat is exported from this Black Sea area than from any other part of the world except the United States and the Argentine Republic.

Not only the plains, but the mountainous parts of Rumania, also are of great value. The peasants living on the slopes and in the sheltered valleys of this part of the country raise large numbers of cattle and sheep. Here, too, are large ranches owned by wealthy nobles and worked by peasant tenants.

In the early days of the World War, a part of Rumania fell into the hands of the Central Powers. Much of her livestock was killed for food, and her grains, fruits, and vegetables were of great value to her enemies who sorely needed these supplies. The product which was perhaps of greatest use to her foes was petroleum. Rumania is one of the important petroleum-producing countries of the world, while neither Germany nor Austria-Hungary furnished any great amount of this very useful material.

Bucharest, the capital of Rumania, is, next to Constantinople, the largest city in southeastern Europe. It is nearly the size of Washington, but it is a much more lively city than our beautiful, dignified capital. It has many more cafés, restaurants, and theaters. Its hotels are luxurious, its residences handsome, and its business blocks large and modern. At night, the city is very brilliant, the crowds large, and the life gay. One who sees the city only in the daytime is not acquainted with the real Bucharest. Automobiles fly through its broad, well-lighted streets. Splendid

FIG. 176. A PETROLEUM
PEDDLER IN RUMANIA

carriages, drawn by beautiful coal-black Russian horses with long, flowing manes and tails, can be seen everywhere.

Yet, one need go but a short distance out of the city to see a very different life. Here are villages of small, low houses with piles of firewood nearby. From the farmyards come a cheerful crowing, gobbling, quacking, and bleating, as if the very roosters, turkeys, ducks, and sheep were trying to keep up with the merriment of the great city not far away. The oxen chew their cuds while peacefully resting under the shade of the willows and alders, and the creaking wheels of the clumsy ox-wagon beside them are silent for the moment. In the little houses with their mud floors, the women spin their thread on an old-fashioned distaff, weave it into cloth, and ornament it with the most beautiful embroidery.

ALBANIA

Little Albania, less than one and one-half times the size of Massachusetts, lies along the southeastern shore of the Adriatic Sea. Like other countries of the Balkan Peninsula, it is carved out of the former Turkish Empire.

It is a rugged, mountainous country, inhabited by a brave, warlike people who live and work in a most primitive way. The fact that for six hundred years Albania was a Turkish province is sufficient to explain its lack of development. The ordinary village in central and northern Albania is a collection of huts

FIG. 177. BUCHAREST, RUMANIA

and houses of loose rock and mud. They are separated by narrow, winding, dirty passages which serve as streets. There are no roads in the country regions, and all goods are carried on the back of ponies. Southern Albania is more advanced, as it has had some trade with Greece and, during several years of the World War, was under Italian military occupation. They built roads and telegraph lines, established a postal system and schools, and erected hospitals.

Many Albanian farmers have olive orchards, produce good crops of tobacco, and raise large flocks of sheep. The soil is fertile, and there are rich mineral resources.

TOPICS FOR STUDY

I.

1. Westward migration of the Turks.
2. The Crusades.
3. Former and present area of Turkey.
4. The great city of Constantinople.
5. Effect of the World War on Turkey.

6. Surface and coastline of Greece.
7. Ancient Greece.
8. Occupations in Greece.
9. The Corinthian Canal.
10. Corinth and currants.
11. The city of Athens.
12. Thermopylae and Marathon.
13. The Olympic Games.
14. Farms and farming in Bulgaria.
15. Attar of roses.
16. Sofia, the capital of Bulgaria.
17. The plain of the Danube in Rumania.
18. The oil product of Rumania.
19. The city of Bucharest.
20. The country of Albania.

II.

1. Sketch a map to show the former great size of the Turkish Empire. Show on it its present area.
2. Illustrate on a globe the voyages of Columbus and Vasco da Gama.
3. Find out what you can about the Crusades, and tell the class about them.
4. What are the cities in the United States which are larger than Constantinople?
5. In what part of Greece did the Spartans live? Tell something about the life of a Spartan boy.
6. What Greek myth or hero do you know of?
7. Give the boundaries of Bulgaria.
8. Write a list of the capitals of the countries described in this chapter. Opposite each one, write the name of a city in the United States of about the same size.
9. Name the important petroleum-producing countries of the world.
10. Name the countries through which one would pass in a trip down the Danube from its source to its mouth.
11. Of what country do Serbia and Montenegro now form a part? Bound this country. What is its capital?

12. Before the World War, the countries of the Balkan Peninsula had wars among themselves. Can you find out some of the results of these wars?

III.

Be able to spell and pronounce the following names. Locate each place and tell what was said about it in this and in any previous chapter. Add other facts if possible.

Africa	Palestine	Adriatic Sea
Albania	Persia	Aegean Sea
Arabia	Riviera	Black Sea
Argentina	Russia	Corinthian Canal
Armenia	Serbia	Danube River
Balkan Peninsula	Thermopylae	Euphrates River
Bulgaria		Gulf of Corinth
Central Asia	Athens	Gulf of Aegina
China	Bucharest	Mediterranean Sea
France	Budapest	
Germany	Constantinople	Nile River
Greece	Constanza	Sea of Marmora
Hejaz	Corinth	Strait of
Holy Land	Grasse	Bosporus
Hungary	Jerusalem	Tigris River
India	Minneapolis	Transylvanian
Japan	Odessa	Alps
Yugoslavia	Paris	
Marathon	Patras	
Montenegro	Sofia	

GENERAL REVIEW

1. Write lists of the industries, cities, and rivers of each country of Europe. Sketch a map of each country and locate all the places mentioned.
2. What country do you consider the most important? Give the reasons for your answer.
3. Which country do you think the most interesting? Give the reasons for your opinion.
4. What city would you like best to visit? Why?
5. Compare the canal system of Europe with that of the United States. Make a list of the rivers connected by canals. Trace these waterways on a map.
6. Name the chief commercial city and the chief manufacturing city or cities of each country. Locate them on an outline map. What is the most northerly city of which you have read? The most southerly? The most easterly? The most westerly? For what is each important?
7. Name the five largest cities of Europe and give some reasons for their growth and importance.
8. Explain why the climate of western Europe is warmer than that of corresponding latitudes in America.
9. How has the surface of Europe affected the people and industries?
10. Name the five largest rivers of Europe. Compare them in length, usefulness, products carried, and cities with the largest rivers of North America. Which river do you think is the most useful? Give the reasons for your choice.
11. Make a list of the kinds of animals spoken of in these chapters and write beside each one the name of the country with which it is connected. Make a similar list of grains, fruits, and manufactures.
12. Name the monarchies of Europe; the republics.
13. Send vessels from ten different ports in Europe to ten different cities in other continents. Name and locate the shipping and receiving ports, tell the routes followed, and describe the cargoes carried each way.

14. Compare the working classes of Europe with those of the United States.

15. Discuss the advantages or disadvantages of the position of the United States as contrasted with that of European countries.

16. With what country or countries do you associate the following: fiords, toys, corn, mists, sunflower farms, the midnight sun, canaries, bulbs, Göta Canal, sweet chocolate, coral, amber, glaciers, great plains, sawmills, technical schools, skiing, chemicals, river mills, sardines, Kiel Canal, vineyards, currants, cork, olive oil, dense population, forests, great inventions, beautiful lakes, shipbuilding, early explorers, the Iron Gate, sugar beets, black-and-white cows, gypsies, cream of tartar, robber knights, Black Forest Mountains, tunnels, ruins, peat, mules and bullocks, hemp, potatoes, irrigation, flax retting, iron, potassium salts, colonies, butter, lace and embroidery, "Land of the Three Thousand Lakes," wood carving, salt mines, "Mistress of the Seas," lumber, mineral springs, "Queen of Fibers," rose bushes, raisins, soya beans, sagas, sturgeon, cod-liver oil, cleanliness, eider ducks, patience and perseverance, saeters, dikes, fladbrod, caviar, northern lights, Ludwig Canal.

17. With what city or cities do you associate the following: soda water, jute, fish, dressing of furs and skins, islands, fashion center, financial center, canals, lace, whale oil, attar of roses, cod roe, woolen goods, amber, cutlery, salt, the greatest docks, soap, grapes, butter, Vesuvius, Billingsgate, soldiers, the greatest tea market, emigrants, fine parks, the Blarney Stone, ribbons, the "Chicago of Ireland," silk manufacturing, cathedrals, the Forum, the Golden Horn, canneries, peanuts, coral beads, olive oil, tortoiseshell, the Moors, diamond cutting, cheese, fairs, linen, wine, iron and steel manufactures, cotton manufactures, granite, bazaars, wheat, shipbuilding, watches, a wonderful clock, matches, the Kremlin, macaroni, ovarinas, pâte de foie gras, Columbus.